THE BRAVO OF LONDON

'THE DETECTIVE STORY CLUB is a clearing house for the best detective and mystery stories chosen for you by a select committee of experts. Only the most ingenious crime stories will be published under the THE DETECTIVE STORY CLUB imprint. A special distinguishing stamp appears on the wrapper and title page of every THE DETECTIVE STORY CLUB book—the Man with the Gun. Always look for the Man with the Gun when buying a Crime book.'

Wm. Collins Sons & Co. Ltd., 1929

Now the Man with the Gun is back in this series of COLLINS CRIME CLUB reprints, and with him the chance to experience the classic books that influenced the Golden Age of crime fiction.

THE DETECTIVE STORY CLUB

E. C. BENTLEY • TRENT'S LAST CASE • TRENT INTERVENES
E. C. BENTLEY & H. WARNER ALLEN • TRENT'S OWN CASE
ANTHONY BERKELEY • THE WYCHFORD POISONING CASE • THE SILK
   STOCKING MURDERS
LYNN BROCK • THE DETECTIONS OF COLONEL GORE • NIGHTMARE
BERNARD CAPES • THE MYSTERY OF THE SKELETON KEY
AGATHA CHRISTIE • THE MURDER OF ROGER ACKROYD • THE BIG FOUR
WILKIE COLLINS • THE MOONSTONE
HUGH CONWAY • CALLED BACK • DARK DAYS
EDMUND CRISPIN • THE CASE OF THE GILDED FLY
FREEMAN WILLS CROFTS • THE CASK • THE PONSON CASE • THE PIT-PROP
   SYNDICATE • THE GROOTE PARK MURDER
MAURICE DRAKE • THE MYSTERY OF THE MUD FLATS
FRANCIS DURBRIDGE • BEWARE OF JOHNNY WASHINGTON
J. JEFFERSON FARJEON • THE HOUSE OPPOSITE
RUDOLPH FISHER • THE CONJURE-MAN DIES
J. S. FLETCHER • THE MIDDLE TEMPLE MURDER
FRANK FROËST • THE GRELL MYSTERY
FRANK FROËST & GEORGE DILNOT • THE CRIME CLUB • THE ROGUES'
   SYNDICATE
EMILE GABORIAU • THE BLACKMAILERS
ANNA K. GREEN • THE LEAVENWORTH CASE
DONALD HENDERSON • MR BOWLING BUYS A NEWSPAPER • A VOICE LIKE
   VELVET
FERGUS HUME • THE MILLIONAIRE MYSTERY
GASTON LEROUX • THE MYSTERY OF THE YELLOW ROOM
VERNON LODER • THE MYSTERY AT STOWE • THE SHOP WINDOW
   MURDERS
PHILIP MACDONALD • THE RASP • THE NOOSE • THE RYNOX MYSTERY •
MURDER GONE MAD • THE MAZE
NGAIO MARSH • THE NURSING HOME MURDER
G. ROY McRAE • THE PASSING OF MR QUINN
R. A. V. MORRIS • THE LYTTLETON CASE
ARTHUR B. REEVE • THE ADVENTURESS
JOHN RHODE • THE PADDINGTON MYSTERY
FRANK RICHARDSON • THE MAYFAIR MYSTERY
R. L. STEVENSON • DR JEKYLL AND MR HYDE
J. V. TURNER • BELOW THE CLOCK
EDGAR WALLACE • THE TERROR
CAROLYN WELLS • MURDER IN THE BOOKSHOP
ISRAEL ZANGWILL • THE PERFECT CRIME

THE BRAVO
OF LONDON

A STORY OF
CRIME BY

ERNEST BRAMAH

PLUS 'THE BUNCH OF VIOLETS'

COLLINS CRIME CLUB
An imprint of HarperCollins*Publishers*
1 London Bridge Street
London SE1 9GF
www.harpercollins.co.uk

This Detective Story Club edition 2018

First published in Great Britain by Cassell & Co. 1934
'The Bunch of Violets' published in *The Specimen Case*
by Hodder & Stoughton 1924

1

Introduction © Tony Medawar 2018

A catalogue record for this book is
available from the British Library

ISBN 978-0-00-829743-5

Typeset in Bulmer MT Std by
Palimpsest Book Production Ltd, Falkirk, Stirlingshire
Printed and bound in Great Britain by
CPI Group (UK) Ltd, Croydon CR0 4YY

INTRODUCTION

Ernest Bramah Smith, born in 1868, was brought up in Lancashire, England, where he attended Manchester Grammar School. Smith did badly in his academic studies and, after leaving school in 1884, took up farming. While it was an unsuccessful experience, nearly bankrupting his father, farming gave Smith the material for his first book, *English Farming, and Why I Turned It Up*, which was published as by Ernest Bramah. Inspired by the book's modest success, Smith took up journalism and secured a position working for the author Jerome K. Jerome at *Today Magazine* to which Smith contributed numerous short, largely humorous, pieces. He would remain a writer for the rest of his life, editing one magazine—*The Minister*—and contributing to many others including *Chapman's*, *Macmillan's*, *The Storyteller*, *London Mercury*, *Everybody's* and the *Windsor*, as well as the prestigious title *The Graphic*.

In the late 1890s, not long after marrying his wife Lucy Maisie Barker at Holborn, London, Smith created the character that was to make him famous: Kai Lung, an itinerant storyteller whose tales and proverbs help him to outwit brigands and thieves in ancient China.

'My unbecoming name is Kai, to which has been added that of Lung. By profession I am an incapable relater of imagined tales and to this end I spread my mat wherever my uplifted voice can entice together a company to listen. Should my feeble efforts be deemed worthy of reward, those who stand around may perchance contribute to my scanty store, but sometimes this is judged superfluous.'

While many modern readers would dismiss the slyly comic Kai Lung stories as literary yellowface, they were immensely popular on first publication and for many years later and, although Smith never visited China, his portrayal of the Chinese and their customs was accepted as a guide to a country about which most contemporary readers and reviewers knew very little. However, the character of Kai Lung has dated badly and Smith's purple prose, replicating what he and others considered 'Oriental quaintness' and 'the charm of Oriental courtesy', means that his many stories of Kai Lung and other Chinese 'characters' are little read today.

While continuing to write about Kai Lung, Smith showed himself something of a domestic satirist with, in 1907, *The Secret of the League*, 'the story of a social war' inspired by the success of the then nascent Labour Party in the 1906 General Election. In Smith's novel, a Labour Government is elected and, crushed by 'the dead weight of taxation' and other socialist 'evils', the middle classes rise up and, by undermining the coal industry and coal-dependent businesses, cause the Government to collapse. While it anticipates elements of Chris Mullin's 1982 satire *A Very British Coup* by more than sixty years, Smith's novel may seem offensive and naïve. Nonetheless, his predictions of the kinds of policies that a Labour Government would introduce proved in some instances to be not that far off the mark and, despite the anti-democratic tactics of Smith's 'Unity League', his novel was widely praised at the time by Conservative Party politicians and their supporters at the *Spectator* and elsewhere.

It was in 1913 that Smith created his other great character, Max Carrados the blind detective, who first appeared in a series of stories written specially for *The News of the World*, a British weekly newspaper. Carrados was immediately hailed as something new and the stories about him were read avidly. He was not the first blind detective but he was the first whose other senses *more* than compensated for the loss of his sight, which was the result of a riding accident; Carrados therefore has much in common with Lincoln Rhyme, Jeffrey Deaver's quadriplegic New York detective. And while Carrados and his friend, Louis Carlyle, owe something to Holmes and Watson, the detective's closest fictional contemporary would be the preternaturally omniscient Dr John Thorndyke, the creation of Richard Austin Freeman. There are also many similarities between the characters of Carrados's South London household and their North London equivalents in Freeman's Dr Thorndyke stories, while more than one contemporary critic suggested that Carrados might have been inspired by the career of Edward Emmett, a blind solicitor from Burnley, Lancashire, who achieved some celebrity towards the end of the nineteenth century. If Emmett *was* an inspiration, Smith never acknowledged it, rebutting scepticism in later years about Carrados's abilities 'in the fourth dimension' by pointing to the abilities and achievements of Helen Keller and Sir John Fielding, as well as to those of less well-known figures such as the seventeenth-century mathematician Nicholas Saunderson and the soldier and road-builder John Metcalf, better known as Blind Jack of Knaresborough.

In all, Max Carrados would appear in 26 short stories, including *A Bunch of Violets*, the only story about the blind detective not included in any of the three collections of Carrados short stories published in Smith's lifetime. As well as the detective, Smith's stories about Carrados feature some economically drawn but memorable characters: these include his amanuensis, Parkinson, who has an eidetic but erratic memory; the self-described 'pug-ugly' Miss Frensham, once known as 'The Girl with the Golden Mug'; the brilliant 'lady cryptographer' Clifton Parker; and the detective's school-friend Jim 'Earwigs' Tulloch. Moreover, the Carrados stories often feature contemporary concerns like Irish and Indian nationalist terrorism, the perils of Christian Science and the struggle for universal suffrage. Nonetheless, despite the stories' merits, Carrados's hypersensory brilliance can sometimes appear unconvincing, no more so than in 'The Tilling Shaw Mystery' when he is able to detect, by smell and taste, traces of whitewash on a cigarette-paper after it has been used as wadding and fired from a revolver.

During the First World War, in 1916, Smith enlisted in the Royal Defence Corps. This led to his writing non-fiction pieces for *Punch* and various other magazines on subjects as diverse as censorship and the military use of animals. When the war ended, Smith went back to journalism proper, writing a steady flow of short stories and articles, a book on British copper coinage in the sixteenth to nineteenth centuries and a comic fantasy, the novel *A Little Flutter* concerning a middle-aged city clerk's unusual inheritance and the fate of a Groo-Groo, a giant Patagonian bird. Smith later adapted *A Little Flutter* for the stage, and he also adapted two of the Carrados stories, 'The Tragedy at Brookbend Cottage' and 'The Ingenious Mind of Rigby Lacksome', though there is as yet no evidence that any of these scripts were ever performed. But that is not the case with Smith's only original stage play to feature Max Carrados, *Blind Man's Bluff*, which opened at the Chelsea Palace of Varieties on 8 April 1918. Smith had written the play for the actor Gilbert Heron who, the previous year, had had great success with an adaptation of the Carrados story, 'The Game Played in the Dark'. Heron's play, *In the Dark*, had opened at the London Metropolitan Music Hall in February 1917 as a dramatic interlude in a programme that featured the famous ventriloquist Fred Russell and other variety acts. The play was reviewed positively, not least for its 'great surprise finish' when, as in Smith's short story, the final scene was performed in absolute darkness. *Blind Man's Bluff* also includes a blackout, which Carrados brings about in the thrilling climax of a battle of wits with a cold-blooded spy, and—betraying its origins as a music hall act—his play also ingeniously accommodates an on-stage demonstration of ju-jitsu. Both of the plays continued to be included in variety bills until the early 1920s, while *In the Dark* was broadcast on radio by the fledgling British Broadcasting

Company (later 'Corporation' from 1927) several times including, for the last time, in 1930.

The last of Smith's 26 short stories about Carrados was published in 1927 but Smith revived the character for the novel-length thriller *The Bravo of London*, which was first published in 1934 and later adapted—by Smith—for the stage, though again no performances have yet been traced. Although the novel has something in common with the short story 'The Missing Witness Sensation', first published in *Pearson's Magazine* eight years earlier, Carrados's return, in which he faces the monstrous forger Julian Joolby, was welcomed by readers and critics alike, with one reviewer praising the author for 'a sound sense of the macabre and a grim humour which raises his work above the average level of thrillers'. A year later, Carrados took his last bow in a profile written and narrated by Smith for the radio series *Meet the Detective*, broadcast on the BBC's Empire Service in May 1935. While Carrados was not to appear again, Smith continued to write stories about Kai Lung, with the final collection of stories, *Kai Lung beneath the Mulberry Tree*, appearing in 1940, forty years after the wiliest of philosophers' first appearance in *The Wallet of Kai Lung*.

A very private man throughout his life, Smith died in Weston-super-Mare, Somerset, in 1942.

Tony Medawar
March 2018

Contents

CONTENTS

'Abellino,' said the Doge, 'thou art a fearful, a detestable man.'
—*The Bravo of Venice*, Heinrich Zschokke (1771–1848)

Bravo (1) a daring villain.—*The Oxford English Dictionary*

CHAPTER I

THE ROAD TO TAPSFIELD

'A TOLERABLY hard nut to crack, of course,' said the self-possessed young man with the very agreeable smile—an accomplishment which he did not trouble to exercise on his associate in this case, since they knew one another pretty well and were strictly talking business; 'or you wouldn't be so dead keen about me, Joolby.'

'Oh, I don't know; I don't know, Nickle,' replied the other with equal coolness, 'There are hundreds—thousands—of young demobs like yourself to be had today for the asking. All very nice chaps personally, quite unscrupulous, willing to take any risk, competent within certain limits, and not one of them able to earn an honest living. No; if I were you I shouldn't fancy myself indispensable.'

'Having now disclosed our mutual standpoints and in a manner cleared the ground, let's come down to concrete foundations,' suggested Nickle. 'You're hardly thinking of opening a beauty parlour at this benighted Tapsfield?'

The actual expression of the man addressed as Joolby at this callous thrust did not alter, although it might be that a faint quiver of feeling played across the monstrous distortion that composed his face, much as a red-hot coal shows varying shades of incandescence without any change of colour or surface. For such was Joolby's handicap at birth that any allusion to beauty or to looks made in his presence must of necessity be an outrage.

He was indeed a creature who by externals at all events had more in common with another genus than with that humanity among which fate had cast him, and his familiar nickname of 'The Toad' crudely indicated what that species might be.

1

Beneath a large bloated face, mottled with irregular patches of yellow and brown, his pouch-like throat hung loose and pulsed with a steady visible beat that held the fascinated eyes of the squeamish stranger. Completely bald, he always wore a black skull-cap, not for appearance, one would judge, since it only heightened his ambiguous guise, and his absence of eyebrows was emphasised by the jutting hairless ridges that nature had substituted.

Nor did the unhappy being's unsightliness end with these facial blots, for his shrunken legs were incapable of wholly supporting his bulky frame and whenever he moved about he drew himself slowly and painfully along by the aid of two substantial walking sticks. Only in one noticeable particular did the comparison fail, for while the eye of a toad is bright and gentle Joolby's reflected either dull apathy or a baleful malice. Small wonder that women often turned unaccountably pale on first meeting him face to face and the doughty urchins of the street, although they were ready enough to shrill 'Toady, toady, Joolby!' behind his back, shrieked with real and not affected terror if chance brought them suddenly to close quarters.

'The one thing that makes me question your fitness for the job is an unfortunate vein of flippancy in your equipment, Nickle,' commented Joolby without any display of feeling. 'No doubt it amuses you to score off people whom you despise, but it also gives you away and may put them on their guard about something that really matters. This is just a friendly warning. What sort of business should I be able to do with anyone if I ever let them see my real feelings towards them—yourself, for instance?'

'True, O cadi,' admitted Nickle lightly. 'People aren't worth sticking the manure fork into—present company included—but it's frequently temptatious. Proceed, effendi.'

'The chap who has been at Tapsfield already was a wash-out and I've had to drop him. He'll never come to any good,

Nickle—no imagination. Now that's where you should be able to put something through, and I have confidence in you. You're a very convincing liar.'

'You are extremely kind, Master,' replied Nickle. 'What had your dud friend got to say about it?'

'He came back sneeping that it was impossible even to get in anywhere there because they are so suspicious of strangers.'

'To do with the mill, I suppose?'

'Of course—what else? He couldn't stay a night—not a bed to be had anywhere for love or money unless someone can guarantee you bona fide. The fool fish simply dropped in on them with a bag of golf clubs—and there wasn't a course within five miles. You'll have to think out something brighter, Nickle.'

'Leave that to me. Just exactly what do you want to know, Joolby?'

'Everything that there is to be found out—position, weaknesses, precautions, routine, delivery and despatch: the whole business. And particularly any of the people who are open to be got at with some sort of inducement. But for God's sake—'

'I beg your pardon?'

'No need to, Nickle. I only want to emphasise that whatever you do, not a shadow of suspicion must be risked. We haven't decided yet on what lines the thing will go through and we can't have any channel barred. I can give you a fortnight.'

'Thanks; I shall probably take a month. And it's understood to be five per cent on the clean-up and all exes meanwhile?'

'Reasonable expenses, Nickle. You can't spend much in a backwash like this Tapsfield.'

'My expenses always are reasonable—I mean there is always a reason for them. But I notice that you don't kick at the other item. That doesn't look as if you were exactly optimistic of striking a gold mine, Joolby.'

'In your place I might have thought that, but I shouldn't have said it. Now I know that you will make it up in exes. Well, let me tell you this, Mr Nickle: no, on the whole I won't. But what should you say if I hinted not at hundreds or thousands but millions?'

'I should say much the same as the duchess did—"Oh, Hell, leave my leg alone!"' languidly admitted Mr Nickle.

The road from Stanbury Junction to Tapsfield was agreeably winding—assuming, of course, that you were at the time susceptible to the graces of nature and not hurrying, for instance, to catch a train—pleasantly shady for such a day as this, and attractively provided, from the leisurely wayfarer's point of view, with a variety of interesting features. For one stretch it fell in with the vulgarly babbling little river Vole and for several furlongs they pursued an amicable course together, until the Vole, with a sudden flirt like the misplaced coquetry of a gawky wench, was half way across a meadow and although it made some penitent advances to return, the road declined to make it up again and even turned away so that thereafter they meandered on apart: a portentous warning to the numerous young couples who strolled that way on summer evenings, had they been in the mood to profit by the instance. Its place was soon taken by a lethargic, weed-clogged dyke, a very different stream but profuse of an engaging medley of rank grass and flowers—tall bulrushes and swaying sedge, pale flags, saffron kingcups and incredibly artificial-looking pink and white water-lilies, and the sure resort of countless dragonflies of extraordinary agility and brilliance. This channel at one point gave occasion for a moss-grown bridge whereon the curious might inform themselves by the authority of a weather-beaten sign that while the road powers of the county of Sussex claimed the bridge and all that appertained to it, they expressly disclaimed liability for any sort of accident or ill that might be experienced there, and in fact held you strictly responsible and answerable in amercement.

Everywhere was peaceful shade and a cool green smell and the assurance that anything that was happening somewhere else didn't really matter. A few small, substantial clouds, white and rotund like the puffs of smoke from a cannon's mouth in an old-type print, floated overhead but imposed on no one to the extent of foretelling rain. Actually, it was the phenomenally dry summer of 1921.

The single pedestrian who had come that way when the 3.27 down train steamed on appeared to be amenable to these tranquil influences, for he continually loitered and looked about, but the frequency with which he took out his watch and the alert expectancy of his backward glances would soon have discounted the impression of aimless leisure had there been anyone to observe his movements. And, in truth, nothing could have been further from casualness or lack of purpose than this inaction, for on that day, at that hour and in that place, the first essential move was being made in a design so vast and far-reaching that the whole future course of civilization might well hang on its issue. So might one disclose a tiny rill in the uplands of Thibet—and thousands of miles away the muddy yellow waters of the surging Whang Ho obliterate an inoffensive province.

Presently, following the same route, the distant figure of another pedestrian had come into sight, and swinging along the road at a fine resolute gait (indicative perhaps, since he wore a clerical garb, of robust Christianity) promised very soon to overtake the laggard. It is only reasonable to assume that in his case there was less inducement to examine the surroundings, for while the first could be dismissed at a glance as a stranger to those parts, the second was the Rev. Octavius Galton, vicar of Tapsfield, who, as everyone could tell you, paid a weekly visit on that day to an outlying hamlet with its little tin mission hall, straggling at least a mile beyond the Junction.

With the first appearance of this new character on the scene the behaviour of the loitering man underwent a change—trifling indeed, but not without significance. His progress was still slow, he continued to take interest in the unfolding details of his way, but he studiously refrained from looking round, and his watch had ceased to concern him. It was, if one would hazard a speculative shot, as though something that he had been expecting had happened now and he was prepared to play a part in the next development.

'Good afternoon,' called out the vicar as he went past—he conscientiously greeted every wayfarer encountered on his rounds, tramp or esquire, and few were so churlish as to be unresponsive.

'Glorious weather, isn't it?—though of course rain is really needed.' The after-thought came from over his shoulder, for the Rev. Octavius did not carry universal neighbourliness to the extent of encouraging prolonged wayside conversation.

'Good afternoon,' replied the stranger, quite as genially. 'Yes, isn't it? Splendid.'

He made no attempt to enlarge the occasion and to all appearance the incident was over. But just when it would have been, Mr Galton heard a sharp exclamation—the instinctive note of surprise—and turned to see the other in the act of stooping to pick up some object.

'I don't suppose this is likely to be yours'—he had stopped automatically and the finder had quickened his pace to join him—'but if you live in these parts you might hear who has lost it. Looks more like a woman's purse, I should say.'

'Dear me,' said the vicar, 'how unfortunate for someone! No, it certainly isn't mine. As a matter of fact, I never really use a purse—absurd of me I am often told, but I never have done. Have you seen what is in it?'

Obviously not, since he had only just picked it up and had at once offered it for inspection, but at the suggestion the catch was pressed and the contents turned out for their mutual examination. They were strictly in keeping with the humdrum appearance of the purse itself—no pretty trifle but a substantial thing for everyday shopping—a ten-shilling note, as much in silver and bronze, the stub of a pencil, two safety pins and a newspaper cutting relating to an infallible cough cure.

'Dropped by one of my poorer parishioners doubtless,' commented Mr Galton, as the collection was replaced by the finder; 'but unluckily there is nothing to show which. You will, of course, leave it at the police station?'

'Well,' was the reply, given with thoughtful deliberation, 'if you don't mind I'd rather prefer to leave it with you, sir.'

'Oh!' said the vicar, not unflattered, 'but the usual thing—'

'Yes, so I imagine. But I have an idea that you would be more likely to hear whose it is than anyone else might. Then in these cases I believe that there is some sort of a deduction made if the police have the handling of it—not very much, I daresay, but to quite a poor woman even the matter of a shilling or two—eh?'

'True; true. No doubt it would be a consideration. Well, since you urge it, I will take charge of the find and notify it through the most likely channels. Then if we hear nothing of the loser within say a week I think I shall have to fall back on the local constabulary.'

'Oh, quite so. But I hardly think that in a little place—I take it that this is only a village?'

'Tapsfield? A bare five hundred souls at the last census. Of course, the parish is another matter, but that is really a question of area. You are a stranger, I presume? And, by the way, you had better favour me with your address if you don't mind.'

'I should be delighted,' said the stranger with his charming smile—an accomplishment he did not make the mistake of overdoing—'but just at the moment I haven't got such a thing— not on this side of the world, I should say. My name is Dixson—Anthony Dixson—and I am over from Australia for a few weeks, a little on business but mostly as a holiday.'

'Australia? Really; how very interesting. One of our young men—a member of the choir and our best hand-bell ringer, as a matter of fact—left for Australia only last month: Sydney, to be explicit.'

'My place is Beverley in West Australia,' volunteered the Colonial. 'Quite the other side of the Continent, you know.'

'Still, it is in the same country, is it not?' The vicar put this unimpeachable statement reasonably but with tolerant firmness. 'However: the question of an address. It is only that after a certain time, if no one comes forward, it is customary to return anything to the finder.'

'I don't think that need trouble anyone in this case, sir. I expect that there are several good works going on in the place that won't refuse a few shillings. If no one puts in a claim perhaps you wouldn't mind—?'

'Now that's really very kind and generous of you; very thoughtful indeed, Mr Dixson. Yes, we have a variety of useful organisations in the parish, and most of them, as you tactfully suggest, are not by any means self-supporting. There is the Social Centre Organisation, the Literary, Dramatic and Debating Society, a Blanket and Clothing Fund, Junior Athletic Club, the C.L.B. and the C.E.G.G., and half a dozen other excellent causes, to say nothing of a special effort we are making to provide the church heating apparatus with a new boiler. Still, an outsider can't be interested in our little local efforts, but it's heartening—distinctly heartening—quite apart from the amount and the—er—slightly speculative element of the contribution.'

'Well, perhaps not altogether an outsider, in a way,' suggested Dixson a little cryptically.

'Oh, really? You mean that you have some connection with Tapsfield? I did not gather—'

'Actually, that's what brought me here. My father was never out of Australia in his life, and this is the first time that I have been, but we always understood—I suppose it was passed down from generation to generation—that a good many years ago we had come from a place called Tapsfield somewhere in the south of England.'

'This is the only place of the name that I know of,' said the vicar. 'Possibly the parochial records—'

'One little bit of evidence—if you can call it that—came to light when I went through my father's things after his death last year,' continued Dixson. 'Plainly it had been kept for its personal association, though it's only brass and can't be of any value. I mean, no one called Anthony Dixson would be likely to throw it away and by what I'm told one of us always has been called Anthony, and very few people nowadays spell the name D-i-x-s-o-n.'

'A coin—really?' The vicar put on his reading glasses and took the insignificant object that Dixson had meanwhile extracted from a pouch of his serviceable leather belt. 'I have myself—'

'I don't see that it can be a coin because that should have the king—Charles the Second wouldn't it be?—on it. In fact I don't understand why—'

'Oh, but this is quite all right,' exclaimed Mr Galton with rising enthusiasm, as he carefully deciphered the inscription, 'It is one of an extensive series called the seventeenth-century tokens. I speak as a collector in a modest way, though I personally favour the regal issues—"Antho Dixson, Cordwainer, of Tapsfield in Susex", and on the other side "His half peny 1666", with a device—probably the arms of the cordwainers' company.'

'Yes,' said the namesake of Antho Dixson of 1666 carelessly. 'That's what it seems to read isn't it?'

'But this is most interesting; really most extraordinarily interesting,' insisted the now thoroughly intrigued clergyman. 'In the year when the Great Fire of London was raging and—yes—I suppose Milton would be writing *Paradise Lost* then, your remote ancestor was issuing these halfpennies to provide the necessary shopping change here in Tapsfield. And now, more than two hundred and fifty years later, you turn up from Australia to visit the birthplace of your race. Do you know, I find that a really suggestive line of thought, Mr Dixson; most extraordinarily impressive.'

'I can hardly expect to discover any Dixson here,' commented Anthony, with a speculative note of inquiry, 'and even if there were they would be too remote to have any actual relationship. But possibly there are some of the old houses standing—'

'There are no Dixsons now,' replied Mr Galton with decision. 'I know every family and can speak positively. Even in the more common form we have no one of that surname. As for old houses—well, Tapsfield is scarcely a show-place, one must admit. "Model" perhaps, but not picturesque. The church is practically the only thing remaining of any note: if you can spare the time I should be delighted to take you over the building where your forebears worshipped. We are almost there now. Was there any particular train back that you were thinking of catching?'

'As a matter of fact,' said Dixson readily, 'I came intending to stay a few days and look around here. I've always had a hankering to see the place properly, and in any case I don't find that living in London suits me. So I shall hope to see over the church when it's most convenient to you.'

'Oh, you intend staying? I didn't—I mean, not seeing any luggage, I inferred that you were just here for the afternoon. Of course—er—any time I shall be really delighted.'

'I left my traps up at the station. I must find a room and then I can have them sent over. To tell you the truth, I couldn't stand London any longer. I have hardly slept a wink for the last two nights. Perhaps you could put me in the way of a place where they let apartments?'

It was a very natural request in the circumstances—nothing could have been more so—but for some reason the vicar did not reply at once, nor did his expression seem to indicate that he was considering the most suitable addresses. Actually, one might have guessed that he had become slightly embarrassed.

'Almost any sort of a place would suit me—just simple meals and a bedroom,' prompted Dixson, without apparently noticing his acquaintance's difficulty. 'On the whole I prefer a private house—even a workman's—to an inn, but that is only a harmless fancy.'

'Awkwardly enough, a room is practically unobtainable either at a private house or even at one of the inns,' at length admitted

Mr Galton with slow reluctance. 'It's an unusual state of things, I know, but there are special circumstances and the people here have always been encouraged to refuse chance visitors. The consequence is that nobody sets out to let apartments.'

'"Special circumstances"? Does that mean—?'

'Evidently you have not heard of the Tapsfield paper mill, Mr Dixson. The particular circumstance is that all the paper used in the printing of Bank of England notes is made here in the village.'

'You surprise me. I should have imagined that they would be printed in a strongroom at the Bank itself or something of that sort. Surely—?'

'Printed, yes,' assented the vicar. 'I believe they are. But the peculiar and characteristic paper is all made within a stone's throw of where we are. It is really our only local industry and practically all the people are either employed there or dependent on the business. Of course it is a very important and confidential—I might almost say dangerous—position, and although there is no actual rule, newcomers do not find it practicable to settle here and strangers are not accommodated.'

'Newcomers and strangers, eh?' The visitor laughed with a slightly wry good humour.

'I know, I know,' admitted the vicar ruefully. 'It is *we* who are really the interlopers and newcomers compared with your status. But the difficulty is that owing to the established order of things it is out of these good people's power to make exceptions.'

'But what am I to do about it?' protested Mr Dixson rather blankly. 'You see how I am placed now? . . . I can't go back to London for another wretched night, and it would be too late to get on to some other district . . . I never dreamt of not finding any sort of lodgings. Surely there must be someone with a room to spare, even if they don't make it a business. Then if you wouldn't mind putting in a word—'

'Now let me think; let me think,' mused the good-natured

pastor. 'It would be really deplorable if you of all people should find yourself cold-shouldered out of Tapsfield. As you say, there may be someone—'

Since the moment when chance had brought them into conversation, the two men had been walking together towards the village of which the only evidence so far had been an ancient tower showing above a mass of trees, where a querulous congregation of rooks incessantly put resolutions and urged amendments. Now a final bend of the devious lane laid the main village street open before them, and so near that they were in it before Mr Galton's cogitation had reached any practical expression.

'There surely might be someone—?' he repeated hopefully, for by this time, what with one slight influence and another, the excellent man felt himself almost morally bound to get Dixson out of his dilemma. 'I have it!—at least, there's really quite a good chance there—Mrs Hocking.'

'Splendid,' acquiesced Dixson with an easy assumption that this was as good as settled. 'Mrs Hocking by all means.'

'She is an aunt of the youth I mentioned—the one who has gone to Sydney. He lived there, so that she ought to have a bedroom vacant. And I expect that she would like to hear about Australia, so that might make it easier.'

'Quite providential,' was Dixson's comment, and rather inconsequently he could not refrain from adding: 'How lucky that I didn't come from Canada! I am sure that if you would kindly introduce me and put in a good word on the score of respectability, that—coupled with a willingness to pay in advance—would make it all right with Mrs Hocking.'

'We can but see,' agreed Mr Galton. 'I will use my utmost powers of persuasion. She is really a most hospitable woman—I believe she provides the buns for the Guild Working Party tea regularly every other Wednesday.'

'I happen to be very fond of buns,' said Dixson gravely. 'I am sure that we shall get on together famously.'

'Oh, really? As a matter of fact, I never touch them—flatulence. However, her cottage is only just there over the way. Now, had we better—no, perhaps on the whole if you waited by the gate while I broached the matter—what do you think?'

'I am entirely in your hands,' said Dixson diplomatically. 'It's most tremendously good of you. Is there only a Mrs Hocking?'

'Oh, no. She has a husband and a daughter as well—an extremely worthy family—but as they work at the mill, like nearly everyone else here, she will probably be the only one at home just now.'

'Perhaps I had better wait as you suggest then,'—really a *non sequitur*, thought the vicar—'and, if it's any inducement, I'm doing pretty well at home, you know, so that I shouldn't mind something above the ordinary in the circumstances.'

The gesture that Mr Galton threw back as he turned into the formal little garden of a painfully modern cottage might have implied that it would be or it wouldn't—or indeed any other meaning. Dixson strolled on as far as an intersecting lane. It began with a couple of rows of hygienic cottages on the severe plan of Mrs Hocking's, but in the distance a high wall indicated premises of a different use, and from this direction came the regular but not too discordant beat of machinery at work. Less in keeping with the rural scene than this mild evidence of industry was the presence of a sentry-box before what was apparently the principal gate of the place. Plainly a strict guard was kept, but the picket himself was too far away or not sufficiently in view for the actual force he was drawn from to be determined. It was the first indication that Tapsfield held anything particular to safeguard and Dixson experienced a momentary flicker of excitement.

'So that's that,' he summarised as he turned back without betraying any further symptom of interest. He had not long to wait for his new acquaintance's reappearance.

'Our efforts have been crowned with success,' announced Mr Galton, beaming with satisfaction. 'Mrs Hocking only stipulates for no late cooking.'

'Famous,' replied Dixson, a little more careless of his speech now that he had secured quarters. 'I never tackle a heavy meal after sunset myself—insomnia.'

'The question of terms I have left for your own arrangement. But I do not think that you will find Mrs Hocking too exacting.'

'I'm sure. And you'll remember your promise? I'm dying to see the celebrated twelfth-century canopied sedilia.'

'You have heard of our unique Norman feature? Oh, really!' It would have been impossible to strike a better claim on the vicar's favour. 'Really, Mr Dixson, I had no idea that you took an actual interest in ecclesiastical architecture.'

'Well, naturally, I felt a deep regard for the church where my forefathers worshipped. Way out at home someone happened to be able to lend me a sort of guide to Sussex. I simply lapped it. Now I want to go over every nook and cranny in Tapsfield.'

'So you shall; so you shall,' promised the clergyman. 'I will answer for it. We'll arrange about the church as soon as you are settled.' He had turned to go, but before Dixson was through the gate he heard his name called with a rather confidential import. 'And, by the way, while I think of it. We have a little informal entertainment in the school house once a week—a, er, "penny reading" we call it.'

'A sort of sing-song, I suppose?'

'Precisely; but not in any way—er—boisterous. Well, we find it increasingly difficult sometimes—not that everyone isn't most willing; quite the contrary, indeed, but what handicaps us with our limited material is to provide variety. Now I was wondering if you could be persuaded to give a little talk—it need only be quite short, of course—on "Life and Adventure in the Land of the Wombat", or naturally, any other title that commends itself to you. You—? Well, think it over, won't you?'

'That was a tolerably soft shell,' reflected Dixson, as he discreetly avoided discovering any of the interested eyes that had been following the details of his arrival from behind stealthily arranged curtains. 'Now for Mrs Hocking—and the husband and daughter who work at the paper mill.'

CHAPTER II

JOOLBY DOES A LITTLE BUSINESS

STRANGERS who had occasion to visit Mr Joolby's curio and antique shop—and quite a number of very interesting people went there from time to time—often had some difficulty in finding it at first. For Mr Joolby, in complete antagonism to modern business methods, not only did not advertise but seemed to shun the more obvious forms of commercial advancement. His address had never appeared in that useful compilation, the Post Office London Directory, and as yet—surely a simple enough matter—Mr Joolby had not taken the trouble to have the omission righted. The street in which he had set up, while far from being a slum, was not one of the better-known and easily remembered thoroughfares of the East End, so that collectors who stumbled on his shop (and occasionally discovered some surprising things there) more often than not found themselves quite unable to describe its exact position to others afterwards, unless they had the forethought at the time to jot down the number 169 and the name Padgett Street before they passed on elsewhere. 'A couple of turns out of Commercial Road, somewhere towards the other end' was as good as keeping a secret.

Nor would the inquirer's search be finished once he reached Padgett Street, for with the modesty that marked his activity in sundry other ways, Mr Joolby had neglected to have his name proclaimed about his place of business or else he had allowed it to fade from the public eye under the combined erosion of time and English weather. Of the place of business itself little could be gleaned from outside, for the arrangement of the shop window was more in accord with Oriental reticence than in line with modern ideas of display. Dust and obscurity were the prevailing impressions.

Inside was an astonishing medley of the curious and antique and in this branch of his activities the dictum of an impressed collector did not seem unduly wide of the mark: that Mr Joolby could supply anything on earth, if only he knew where to put his hands upon it. And if the arrangement of the large room one first entered suggested more the massed confusion of an extremely bizarre furniture depository than any other comparison, it had what, to its proprietor's way of thinking, was this supreme advantage: that from a variety of points of view it was possible to see without being seen, not only about the shop itself but even including the street and pavement.

At the moment that we have chosen for this intrusion—a time some weeks later than the arrival of 'Anthony Dixson' in Tapsfield—the place at a casual glance had all the appearance of being empty, for the figure of Won Chou, Mr Joolby's picturesquely exotic shop assistant, both on account of absolute immobility and the protective obscuration of his drab garb, did not invite attention. But if unseen himself Won Chou was far from being unobservant and when a passer-by did not in fact pass by—when after an abstracted saunter up he threw an anxious glance along the street in both directions and then slipped into the doorway—a yellow hand slid out and in some distant part of the house the discreet tintinnabulation of a warning bell gave its understood message.

Inside the shop the visitor—no one could ever have mistaken him for a customer, unless, perhaps, qualified by 'rum'—looked curiously about with the sharp and yet furtive reconnaissance of the habitual pilferer. But even so, he failed at the outset to discover the quiescent figure of Won Chou and he was experiencing a slight mental struggle between deciding whether it would be more profitable to wait until someone came or to pick up the most convenient object and bolt, when the impassive attendant settled the difficulty by detaching himself from the screening background and noiselessly coming forward. So quietly and unexpected indeed that Mr Chilly Fank, whose nerves had never been his strongest asset (the playful appellation 'Chilly' had reference to his condition when any risk appeared), experienced a momentary shock which he endeavoured to cover by the usual expedient of a weakly aggressive swagger.

"Ullo, Chink!' he exclaimed with an offensive heartiness, 'blimey if I didn't take you for a ruddy waxwork. You didn't oughter scare a bloke like that, making out as you wasn't real. Boss in?'

'Yes no,' replied Won Chou with extreme simplicity and a perfect assurance in the adequacy of his answer.

'Yes—no? Whacha mean?' demanded Mr Fank, to whom suspicion of affront was an instinct. 'Which, you graven image?'

'All depend,' explained Won Chou with unmoved composure. 'You got come bottom side chop pidgin? You blong same pidgin?'

'Coo blimey! This isn't a bloomin' restrong, is it, funny? I want none of yer chop nor yer pigeon either. Is old Joolby abart? If yer can't speak decent English nod yer blinkin' 'ed, one wei or the other. Get me, you little Chinese puzzle?'

'My no sawy. Makee go look-see,' decided Won, and he melted out of the shop by the door leading to the domestic quarters.

Left to himself Mr Chilly Fank nodded his head sagely several times to convey his virtuous disgust at this pitiable exhibition.

'Tchk! tchk!' he murmured half aloud. 'Exploitation of cheap Asiatic labour! No wonder we have a surplus industrial population and the nachural result that blokes like me—' but at this point the house door opened again, Won Chou having returned with unforeseen expedition, so that Mr Fank had to turn away rather hastily from the locked show-case which he had been investigating with a critical touch and affect an absorbing interest in something taking place in the street beyond until he suddenly became aware of the other's presence.

'Back again, What-ho? Well, you saffron jeopardy, don't stand like a blinkin' Eros. Wag yer ruddy tongue abart it.'

'My been see,' conceded Won Chou impartially. 'Him belongy say: him you go come.'

'My strikes! if this isn't the nattiest little vade-mecum that ever was!' apostrophised Mr Fank to the ceiling bitterly. 'Look here, Confucius, forget yer chops an yer' pigeon and spit it aht straightforward. The boss—Joolby—is he in or not and did he say me go or him come? Blarst yer, which—er—savvy?'

At this, however, it being apparently rather a subtler idiom than the hearer's limited grasp of an alien vernacular could cope with, Won Chou merely relapsed into an attitude of studious melancholy, extremely trying to Mr Fank's conception of the yellow man's status. He was on the point of commenting on Won Chou's shortcomings with his customary delicacy of feeling when the sound of hobbling sticks approaching settled the point without any further trouble.

As Mr Joolby was—ethnologically at all events—white, a person of obvious means, and in various subterranean ways reputedly powerful, Mr Fank at once assumed what he considered to be a more suitable manner and it was with an ingratiating deference that he turned to meet the dealer.

''Evening, governor,' he remarked briskly, at the same time beginning to disclose the contents of an irregular newspaper parcel—fish and chips, it could have been safely assumed if he had been seen carrying it—that he had brought with him. 'Remember me, of course, don't you?'

'Never seen you before,' replied Mr Joolby, with an equally definite lack of cordiality. 'What is it you want with me?'

To the ordinary business caller this reception might have been unpromising but Mr Fank was not in a position to be put off by it. He understood it indeed as part of the customary routine.

'Fank—"Chilly" Fank,' he prompted. 'Now you get me surely?'

'Never heard the name in my life,' declared Joolby with no increase of friendliness.

'Oh, right you are, governor, if you say so,' accepted Fank, but with the spitefulness of the stinging insect he could not refrain from adding: 'I don't suppose I should have been able to imagine *you* if I hadn't seen it. Doing anything in this way now?'

'This,' freed of its unsavoury covering, was revealed as an uncommonly fine piece of Dresden china. It would have required no particular connoisseurship to recognise that so perfect and delicate a thing might be of almost any value. Joolby, who combined the inspired flair of the natural expert with sundry other anomalous qualities in his distorted composition, did not need to give more than one glance—although that look was professionally frigid.

'Where did it come from?' he asked merely.

'Been in our family for centuries, governor,' replied Fank glibly, at the same time working in a foxy wink of mutual appreciation; 'the elder branch of the Fanks, you understand, the Li-ces-ter-shire de Fankses. Oh, all right, sir, if you feel that way'—for Mr Joolby had abruptly dissolved this proposed partnership in humour by pushing the figure aside and putting a hand to his crutches—'it's from a house in Grosvenor Crescent.'

'Tuesday night's job?'

'Yes,' was the reluctant admission.

'No good to me,' said the dealer with sharp decision.

'It's the real thing, governor,' pleaded Mr Fank with fawning persuasiveness, 'or I wouldn't ask you to make an offer. The late owner thought very highly of it. Had a cabinet all to itself in the drorin'-room there—so I'm told, for of course I had nothing to do with the job personally. Now—'

'You needn't tell me whether it's the real thing or not,' said Mr Joolby. 'That's my look out.'

'Well then, why not back yer knowledge, sir? It's bound to

pay yer in the end. Say a . . . well, what, about a couple of . . .
It's with you, governor.'

'It's no good, I tell you,' reiterated Mr Joolby with seeming
indifference. 'It's mucher too valuable to be worth anything—
unless it can be shown on the counter. Piece like this is known
to every big dealer and every likely collector in the land. Offer
it to any Tom, Dick or Harry and in ten minutes I might have
Scotland Yard nosing about my place like ferrets.'

'And that would never do, would it, Mr Joolby?' leered Fank
pointedly. 'Gawd knows what they wouldn't find here.'

'They would find nothings wrong because I don't buy stuff
like this that the first numskull brings me. What do you expect
me to do with it, fellow? I can't melt it, or reset it, or cut it up,
can I? You might as well bring me the Albert Memorial . . .
Here, take the thing away and drop it in the river.'

'Oh blimey, governor, it isn't as bad as all that. What abart
America? You did pretty well with those cameos wot come out
of that Park Lane flat, I hear.'

'Eh, what's that? You say, rascal—'

'No offence, governor. All I means is you can keep it for a
twelvemonth and then get it quietly off to someone at a distance.
Plenty of quite respectable collectors out there will be willing
to buy it after it's been pinched for a year.'

'Well—you can leave it and I'll see,' conceded Mr Joolby, to
whom Fank's random shot had evidently suggested a possible
opening. 'At your own risk, mind you. I may be able to sell it
for a trifle some day or I may have all my troubles for nothing.'
But just as Chilly Fank was regarding this as satisfactorily settled
and wondering how he could best beat up to the next move,
the unaccountable dealer seemed to think better—or worse—of
it for he pushed the figure from him with every appearance of
a final decision. 'No; I tell you it isn't worth it. Here, wrap it
up again and don't waste my time. I'd mucher rather not.'

'That'll be all right, governor,' hastily got in Fank, though
similar experiences in the past prompted him not to be entirely

impressed by a receiver's methods. 'I'll leave it with you anyhow; I know you'll do the straight thing when it's planted. And, could you—you don't mind a bit on account to go on with, do you? I'm not exactly what you'd call up and in just at the moment.'

'A bit on account, hear him. Come, I like that when I'm having all the troubles and may be out of my pocket in the end. Be off with you, greedy fellow.'

'Oh rot yer!' exclaimed Fank, with a sudden flare of passion that at least carried with it the dignity of a genuine emotion; 'I've had just abart enough of you and your blinkin' game, Toady Joolby. Here, I'd sooner smash the bloody thing, straight, than be such a ruddy mug as to swallow any of your blahsted promises,' and there being no doubt that Mr Fank for once in a way meant approximately what he said, Joolby had no alternative, since he had every intention of keeping the piece, but to retire as gracefully as possible from his inflexible position.

'Well, well; we need not lose our tempers, Mr Fank; that isn't business,' he said smoothly and without betraying a shadow of resentment. 'If you are really stoney up—I'm not always very quick at catching the literal meaning of your picturesque expressions—I don't mind risking—shall we say?—one half a—or no, you shall have a whole Bradbury.'

'Now you're talking English, sir,' declared the mollified Fank (perhaps a little optimistically), 'but couldn't you make it a couple? Yer see—well'—as Mr Joolby's expression gave little indication of rising to this suggestion—'one and a thin 'un anyway.'

'Twenty-five bobs,' conceded Joolby. 'Take me or leave it,' and since there was nothing else to be done, this being in fact quite up to his meagre expectation, Chilly held out his hand and took it, only revenging himself by the impudent satisfaction of ostentatiously holding up the note to the light when it was safely in his possession.

'You need not do that, my young fellow,' remarked Mr Joolby, observing the action. 'I know a dud note when I see it.'

'Oh I don't doubt that you know one all right, Mr Joolby,' replied Fank with gutter insolence. 'It's this bloke I'm thinking of. You've had a lot more experience than me in that way, you see, so I've got to be blinkin' careful,' and as he turned to go a whole series of portentous nods underlined a mysterious suggestion.

'What do you mean, you rascal?' For the first time a possible note of misgiving tinged Mr Joolby's bloated assurance. 'Not that it matters—there's nothing about me to talk of—but have you been—been hearing anything?'

It was Mr Fank's turn to be cocky: if he couldn't wangle that extra fifteen bob out of The Toad he could evidently give him the shivers.

'Hearing, sir?' he replied from the door, with an air of exaggerated guilelessness. 'Oh no, Mr Joolby: whatever should I be hearing? Except that in the City you're very well spoken of to be the next Lord Mayor!' and to leave no doubt that this pleasantry should be fully understood he took care that his parting aside reached Joolby's ear: '*I don't* think!'

'Fank. Chilly Fank,' mused Mr Joolby as he returned to his private lair, carrying the newly acquired purchase with him and progressing even more grotesquely than his wont since he could only use one stick for assistance. 'The last time he came he had an amusing remark to make, something about keeping an aquarium . . .'

Won Chou was still at his observation post when the door opened again an hour later. Again he sped his message—a different intimation from the last, but conveying a sign of doubt for this time the watcher could not immediately 'place' the visitors. These were two, both men—'a belong number one and a belong number two chop men,' sagely decided Won Chou—but there was something about the more important of the two that for the limited time at his disposal baffled the Chinaman's deduction. It was not until they were in the shop and he was attending to them that Won Chou astutely suspected this man perchance to be blind—and sought for a positive indication. Yet he was the one who seemed to take the lead rather than wait to be led and except on an occasional trivial point his movements were entirely free from indecision. Certainly he had paused at the step but that was only the natural hesitation of a stranger to the parts and it was apparently the other who supplied the confirmation.

'This is the right place by the description, sir,' the second man said.

'It is the right place by the smell,' was the reply, as soon as the door was opened. 'Twenty centuries and a hundred nationalities mingle here, Parkinson. And not the least foreign—'

'A native of some description, sir,' tolerantly supplied the literal Parkinson, taking this to apply to the attendant as he came forward.

'Can do what?' politely inquired Won Chou, bowing rather more profoundly than the average shopman would, even to a customer in whom he can recognise potential importance.

'No can do,' replied the chief visitor, readily accepting the medium. 'Bring number one man come this side.'

'How fashion you say what want?' suggested Won Chou hopefully.

'That belong one piece curio house man.'

'He much plenty busy this now,' persisted Won Chou, faithfully carrying out his instructions. 'My makee show carpet, makee show cabinet, chiney, ivoly, picture—makee show one ting, two ting, any ting.'

'Not do,' was the decided reply. 'Go make look-see one time.'

'All same,' protested Won Chou, though he began to obey the stronger determination, 'can do heap wella. Not is?'

A good natured but decided shake of the head was the only answer, and looking extremely sad and slightly hurt Won Chou melted through the doorway—presumably to report beyond that: 'Much heap number one man make plenty bother.'

'Look round, Parkinson,' said his master guardedly. 'Do you see anything here in particular?'

'No, sir; nothing that I should designate noteworthy. The characteristic of the emporium is an air of remarkable untidiness.'

'Yet there *is* something unusual,' insisted the other, lifting his sightless face to the four quarters of the shop in turn as though he would read their secret. 'Something unaccountable, something *wrong*.'

'I have always understood that the East End of London was not conspicuously law-abiding,' assented Parkinson impartially. 'There is nothing of a dangerous nature impending, I hope, sir?'

'Not to us, Parkinson; not as yet. But all around there's something—I can feel it—something *evil*.'

'Yes, sir—these prices are that.' It was impossible to suspect the correct Parkinson of ever intentionally 'being funny' but there were times when he came perilously near incurring the suspicion. 'This small extremely second-hand carpet—five guineas.'

'Everywhere among this junk of centuries there must be things that have played their part in a hundred bloody crimes— can they escape the stigma?' soliloquised the blind man, beginning to wander about the bestrewn shop with a self-confidence that would have shaken Won Chou's conclusions if he had been looking on—especially as Parkinson, knowing by long experience the exact function of his office, made no attempt to guide his master. 'Here is a sword that may have shared in the tragedy of Glencoe, this horn lantern lured some helpless ship to destruction on the Cornish coast, the very cloak perhaps that disguised Wilkes Booth when he crept up to shoot Abraham Lincoln at the play.'

'It's very unpleasant to contemplate, sir,' agreed Parkinson discreetly.

'But there is something more than that. There's an influence—a force—permeating here that's colder and deeper and deadlier than revenge or greed or decent commonplace hatred . . . It's inhuman—unnatural—diabolical. And it's coming nearer, it begins to fill the air—' He broke off almost with a physical shudder and in the silence there came from the passage beyond the irregular thuds of Joolby's sticks approaching. 'It's poison,' he muttered; 'venom.'

'Had we better go before anyone comes, sir?' suggested Parkinson, decorously alarmed. 'As yet the shop is empty.'

'No!' was the reply, as though forced out with an effort. 'No—face it!' He turned as he spoke towards the opening door and on the word the uncouth figure, laboriously negotiating the awkward corners, entered. 'Ah, at last!'

'Well, you see, sir,' explained Mr Joolby, now the respectful if somewhat unconventional shopman in the presence of a likely customer, 'I move slowly so you must excuse being kept waiting. And my boy here—well-meaning fellow but so economical even of words that each one has to do for half a dozen different things—quite different things sometimes.'

'Man come. Say "Can do"; say "No can do". All same; go tell; come see,' protested Won Chou, retiring to some obscure but doubtless ingeniously arranged point of observation, and evidently cherishing a slight sense of unappreciation.

'Exactly. Perfectly explicit.' Mr Joolby included his visitors in his crooked grin of indulgent amusement. 'Now those poisoned weapons you wrote about. I've looked them up and I have a wonderful collection and, what is very unusual, all in their original condition. This,' continued Mr Joolby, busying himself vigorously among a pile of arrows with padded barbs, 'is a very fine example from Guiana—it guarantees death with convulsions and foaming at the mouth within thirty seconds. They're getting very rare now because since the natives have become civilized by the missionaries they've given up their old simple ways of life—they will have our second-hand rifles because they kill much further.'

'Highly interesting,' agreed the customer, 'but in my case—'

'Or this beautiful little thing from the Upper Congo. It doesn't kill outright, but, the slightest scratch—just the merest pin prick—and you turn a bright pea green and gradually swell larger and larger until you finally blow up in a very shocking manner. The slightest scratch—so,' and in his enthusiasm Mr Joolby slid the arrow quickly through his hand towards Parkinson whose face had only too plainly reflected a fascinated horror from the moment of their host's appearance. 'Then the tapioca-poison group from Bolivia—'

'Save yourself the trouble,' interrupted the blind man, who had correctly interpreted his attendant's startled movement. 'I'm not concerned with—the primitive forms of murder.'

'Not—?' Joolby pulled up short on the brink of another panegyric, 'not with poisoned arrows? But aren't you the Mr Brooks who was to call this afternoon to see what I had in the way of—?'

'Some mistake evidently. My name is Carrados and I have made no appointment. Antique coins are my hobby—Greek in particular. I was told that you might probably have something in that way.'

'Coins; Greek coins.' Mr Joolby was still a little put out by the mischance of his hasty assumption. 'I might have; I might have. But coins of that class are rather expensive.'

'So much the better.'

'Eh?' Customers in Padgett Street did not generally, one might infer, express approval on the score of dearness.

'The more expensive they are, the finer and rarer they will be—naturally. I can generally be satisfied with the best of anything.'

'So—so?' vaguely assented the dealer, opening drawer after drawer in the various desks and cabinets around and rooting about with elaborate slowness. 'And you know all about Greek coins then?'

'I hope not,' was the smiling admission.

'Hope not? Eh? Why?'

'Because there would be nothing more to learn then. I should have to stop collecting. But doubtless you do?'

'If I said I did—well, my mother was a Greek so that it should come natural. And my father was a—um, no; there was always a doubt about that man. But one grandfather was a Levantine Jew and the other an Italian cardinal. And one grandmamma was an American negress and the other a Polish revolutionary.'

'That should ensure a tolerably versatile stock, Mr Joolby.'

'And further back there was an authentic satyr came into the family tree—so I'm told,' continued Mr Joolby, addressing himself to his prospective customer but turning to favour the scandalised Parkinson with an implicatory leer. 'You find that amusing, Mr Carrados, I'm sure?'

'Not half so amusing as the satyr found it I expect,' was the retort. 'But come now—' for Mr Joolby had meanwhile discovered what he had sought and was looking over the contents of a box with provoking deliberation.

'To be sure—you came for Greek coins, not for Greek family history, eh? Well, here is something very special indeed—a tetradrachm struck at Amphipolis, in Macedonia, by some Greek ruler of the province but I can't say who. Perhaps Mr Carrados can enlighten me?'

Without committing himself to this the blind man received the coin on his outstretched hand and with subtle fingers delicately touched off the bold relief that still retained its superlative grace of detail. Next he weighed it carefully in a cupped palm, and then after breathing several times on the metal placed it against his lips. Meanwhile Parkinson looked on with the respect that he would have accorded to any high-class entertainment; Joolby merely sceptically indifferent.

'Yes,' announced Carrados at the end of this performance, 'I think I can do that. At all events I know the man who made it.'

'Come, come, use your eyes, my good sir,' scoffed Mr Joolby with a contemptuous chuckle. 'I thought you understood at least something about coins. This isn't—I don't know what you think—a Sunday school medal or a stores ticket. It's a very rare and valuable specimen and it's at least two thousand years old. And you "know the man who made it"!'

'I can't use my eyes because my eyes are useless: I am blind,' replied Carrados with unruffled evenness of temper. 'But I can use my hands, my finger-tips, my tongue, lips, my commonplace nose, and they don't lead me astray as your credulous, self-opinionated eyes seem to have done—if you really take this thing for a genuine antique,' and with uncanny proficiency he tossed the coin back into the box before him.

'You can't see—you say that you are blind—and yet you tell me, an expert, that it's a forgery!'

'It certainly is a forgery, but an exceptionally good one at that—so good that no one but Pietro Stelli, who lives in Padua, could in these degenerate days have made it. Pietro makes such beautiful forgeries that in my less experienced years they have taken even me in. Of course I couldn't have that so I went to Padua to find out how he worked, and Peter, who is, according to his lights, as simple and honest a soul as ever breathed, willingly let me watch him at it.'

'And how,' demanded Mr Joolby, seeming almost to puff out aggression towards this imperturbable braggart; 'how could you see him what you call "at it", if, as you say, you are blind? You are just a little too clever, Mr Carrados.'

'How could I see? Exactly as I can see'—stretching out his hand and manipulating the extraordinarily perceptive fingers meaningly—'any of the ingenious fakes which sharp people offer the blind man; exactly as I could see any of the thousand and one things that you have about your shop. This'—handling it as he seemed to look tranquilly at Mr Joolby—'this imitation Persian prayer-rug with its lattice-work design and pomegranate scroll, for instance; exactly as I could, if it were necessary, see *you*,' and he took a step forward as though to carry out the word, if Mr Joolby hadn't hastily fallen back at the prospect.

The prayer-rug was no news to Mr Joolby—although it was ticketed five guineas—but he had had complete faith in the tetradrachm notwithstanding that he had bought it at the price of silver; and despite the fact that he would still continue to describe it as a matchless gem it was annoying to have it so unequivocally doubted. He picked up the box without offering any more of its contents, and hobbling back to the desk with it slammed the drawer home in swelling mortification.

'Well, if that is your way of judging a valuable antique, Mr Carrados, I don't think that we shall do any business. I have nothing more to show, thank you.'

'It is my way of judging everything—men included—Mr Joolby, and it never, never fails,' replied Carrados, not in the least put out by the dealer's brusqueness. It was a frequent grievance with certain of this rich and influential man's friends that he never appeared to resent a rudeness. 'And why should I,' the blind man would cheerfully reply, 'when I have the excellent excuse that I do not *see* it?'

'Of course I don't mean by touch alone,' he continued, apparently unconscious of the fact that Mr Joolby's indignant back was now pointedly towards him. 'Taste, when it's properly treated, becomes strangely communicative; smell'—there could be no doubt of the significance of this allusion from the direction of the speaker's nose—'the chief trouble is that at times smell becomes too communicative. And hearing—I daren't even tell you what a super-trained ear sometimes learns of the goings-on behind the scenes—but a blind man seldom misses a whisper and he never forgets a voice.'

Apparently Mr Joolby was not interested in the subtleties of perception for he still remained markedly aloof, and yet, had he but known it, an exacting test of the boast so confidently made was even then in process, and one moreover surprisingly mixed up with his own plans. For at that moment, as the visitor turned to go, the inner door was opened a cautious couple of inches and:

'Look here, J.J.,' said the unseen in a certainly distinctive voice, 'I hope you know that I'm waiting to go. If you're likely to be another week—'

'Don't neglect your friend on our account, Mr Joolby,' remarked Carrados very pleasantly—for Won Chou had at once slipped to the unlatched door as if to head off the intruder. 'I quite agree. I don't think that we are likely to do any business either. Good day.'

'*Dog dung!*' softly spat out Mr Joolby as the shop door closed on their departing footsteps.

CHAPTER III

MR BRONSKY HAS MISGIVINGS

As Mr Carrados and Parkinson left the shop they startled a little group of street children who after the habit of their kind were whispering together, giggling, pushing one another about, screaming mysterious taunts, comparing sores and amusing themselves in the unaccountable but perfectly satisfactory manner of street childhood. Reassured by the harmless appearance of the two intruders the impulse of panic at once passed and a couple of the most precocious little girls went even so far as to smile up at the strangers. More remarkable still, although Parkinson felt constrained by his imperviable dignity to look away, Mr Carrados unerringly returned the innocent greeting.

This incident entailed a break in which the appearance of the visitors, their position in life, place of residence, object in coming and the probable amount of money possessed by each were frankly canvassed, but when that source of entertainment failed the band fell back on what had been their stock game at the moment of interruption. This apparently consisted in daring one another to do various things and in backing out of the contest when the challenge was reciprocated. At last, however, one small maiden, spurred to desperation by repeated 'dares', after imploring the others to watch her do it, crept up the step of Mr Joolby's shop, cautiously pushed open the door and standing well inside (the essence of the test as laid down), chanted in the peculiarly irritating sing-song of her tribe:

'*Toady, toady Jewlicks;*
Crawls about on two sticks.
Toady, toady—'

32

'Makee go away,' called out Won Chou from his post, and this not being at once effective he advanced towards the door with a mildly threatening gesture. 'Makee go much quickly, littee cow-child. Shall do if not gone is.'

The young imp had been prepared for immediate flight the instant anyone appeared, but for some reason Won Chou's not very aggressive behest must have conveyed a peculiarly galling insult for its effect was to transform the wary gamin into a bristling little spitfire, who hurled back the accumulated scandal of the quarter.

''Ere, don't you call me a cow-child, you 'eathen swine,' she shrilled, standing her ground pugnaciously. 'Pig-tail!' And as Won Chou, conscious of his disadvantage in such an encounter, advanced: 'Oo made the puppy pie? Oo et Jimmy 'Iggs's white mice? Oo lives on black beetles? Oo pinched the yaller duck and—' but at this intriguing point, being suddenly precipitated further into the shop by a mischievous child behind, and honour being fully satisfied by now, she dodged out again and rejoined the fleeing band which was retiring down the street to a noisy accompaniment of feigned alarm, squiggles of meaningless laughter, and the diminishing chant of:

'Toady, toady Jewlicks;
Goes abaht on two sticks.
Toady, toady—'

Sadly conscious of the inadequacy of his control in a land where for so slight a matter as a clouted child an indignant mother would as soon pull his pig-tail out as look, Won Chou continued his progress in order to close the door. There, however, he came face to face with a stout, consequential gentleman whose presence, opulent complexion, ample beard and slightly alien cut of clothes would have suggested a foreign source even without the ruffled: 'Tevils! tevils! little tevils!' drawn from the portly visitor as the result of his somewhat undignified collision with the flying rabble.

'Plenty childrens,' remarked Won Chou, agreeably conversational. 'Makee go much quickly now is.'

'Little tevils,' repeated the annoyed visitor, still dusting various sections of his resplendent attire to remove the last traces of infantile contamination. 'Comrade Joolby is at home? He would expect me.'

'Make come in,' invited Won Chou. 'Him belong say plaps you is blimby.'

'The little tevils need control. They shall have when—' grumbled the newcomer, brought back to his grievance by the discovery of a glutinous patch marring an immaculate waistcoat. 'However, that is not your fault, Won Chou,' and being now within the shop and away from possibly derisive comment, he kissed the attendant sketchily on each cheek. 'Peace, little oppressed brother!'

Not apparently inordinately gratified by this act of condescension, Won Chou crossed the shop and pushing open the inner door announced the new arrival to anyone beyond in his usual characteristic lingo:

'Comlade Blonsky come this side.'

'Shall I to him go through?' inquired Mr Bronsky, bustling with activity, but having already correctly interpreted the sounds from that direction Won Chou indicated the position by the sufficient remark: 'Him will. You is,' and withdrew into a further period of introspection.

In the sacred cause of universal brotherhood comrade Bronsky knew no boundaries and he hastened forward to meet Mr Joolby with the same fraternal greeting already bestowed on Won Chou, forgetting for the moment what sort of man he was about to encounter. The reminder was sharp and revolting: his outstretched arms dropped to his sides and he turned, affecting to be taken with some object in the shop until he could recompose his agitated faculties. Joolby's slit-like mouth lengthened into the ghost of an enigmatical grin as he recognised the awkwardness of the comrade's position.

Bronsky, for his part, felt that he must say something exceptional to pass off the unfortunate situation and he fell back on a highly coloured account of the derangement he had just suffered through being charged and buffeted by a mob of 'little tevils'—an encounter so upsetting that even yet he scarcely knew which way up he was standing. Any irregularity of his salutation having thus been neatly accounted for he shook Joolby's two hands with accumulated warmness and expressed an inordinate pleasure in the meeting.

'But I am forgetting, comrade,' he broke off from these amiable courtesies when the indiscretion might be deemed sufficiently expiated; 'those sticky little bastads drove everything from my mind until I just remember. I met two men further off and from what I could see at the distance they seemed to have come out from here?'

'There were a couple of men here a few minutes ago,' agreed Mr Joolby. 'What about it, comrade?'

'I appear to recognise the look of one, but for life of me I cannot get him. Do you know them, comrade Joolby?'

'Not from Mahomet. Said his name was Carrados—his nibs. The other was a flunkey.'

'Max Carrados!' exclaimed Mr Bronsky with startled enlightenment. 'What in name of tevil was he doing here in your shop, Joolby?'

'Wasting his time,' was the indifferent reply. 'My time also.'

'Do you not believe it,' retorted Bronsky emphatically. 'He never waste his time, that man. Julian Joolby, do you not realise who has been here with you?'

'Never heard of him in my life before. Never want to again either.'

'Well, it is time for yourself that you should be put wiser. It was Max Carrados who fixed the rope round Serge Laskie's neck. And stopped the Rimsky explosion when everything was going so well; and, oh, did a lot more harm. I tell you he is no good, comrade. He is a bad man.'

'Anyhow, he can't interfere with us in this business, whatever he's done in the past,' replied Joolby, who might be pardoned after his recent experience for feeling that there would be more agreeable subjects of conversation. 'He's blind now.'

'"Blind now"—hear him!' appealed Bronsky with a derisive cackle. 'Tell me this however notwithstanding: did you make anything out of him, eh, Joolby?'

'No,' admitted Joolby, determinedly impervious to Bronsky's agitation; 'we did no business as it happens. He knew more than a customer has any right to know. In fact'—with an uneasy recollection of the Greek coin—'he may have known more than I did.'

'That is always the way. Blind: and he knows more than we who not are. Blind: and he stretch out his cunning wicked fingers and they tell him all that our clever eyes have missed to see.'

'So he said, Bronsky. Indeed, to hear him talk—'

'Yes, but wait to hear,' entreated the comrade, anxious not to be deprived of his narration. 'He sniffs—at a bit of paper, let us haphazard, and lo behold, where it has been, who has touched it, what pocket it has laid in—all are disclose to him. He listen to a breath of wind that no one else would hear and it tell him that—that, well, perhaps that two men are ready round the corner for him with a sand-bag.'

'Oh-ho!' said Joolby, sardonically amused; 'so you've tried it, have you?'

'Tried! You use the right word, comrade Joolby. Listen how. At Cairo he was given some sandwiches to ate on a journey. He did ate three and the fourth he had between his teeth when he change his mind and throw it to a pi-dog. That dog died very hastily.'

'Anyone may recognise a taste or smell. Your people mixed the wrong sort of mustard.'

'Anyone may recognise a taste or smell but yet plenty of people die of poison. Listen more. One night at Marseilles he was walking along a street when absolutely without any warning he turn and hit a poor man who happened to be following him on the head—hit him so hard that our friend had to drop the knife he was holding and to take to heels. And yet he was wearing rubber shoes. It is not right. Julian Joolby; it is not fair when a blind man can do like that. The good comrade who warned me of him say: He can smell a thought and hear a look. And that is not all. I have heard that he has the sixth sense too—'

'Let him have; I tell you, Bronsky, he is nothing to us. He only chanced along here. He wanted Greek coins.'

'Greek coins!' This was reassuring for it agreed with something further about Max Carrados that Bronsky remembered hearing. 'That may be very true after all as it is well known that he is crazy about collecting—thinks nothing of paying five hundred roubles for a single drachma . . . Yes, Julian Joolby, if it should become necessary it might be that a hook baited with a rare coin—'

'Don't worry. Next week we shall have moved to our new quarters and nothing going on here will matter then.'

'Ah; that is arrange? I was getting anxious. Our friends in Moscow are becoming more and more impatient as time goes on. The man who pays the piper calls for a tune, as these fool English say it, and the Committee are insist that as they have allow so much for expenses already they must now see results. I am here with authority to investigate about that, comrade Joolby.'

'They shall see results all right,' promised Joolby, swelling darkly at the suggestion of interference. 'And since you fancy English proverbs, comrade, it is well to remember that Rome was not built in a day, one cannot make bricks without clay, and it is not wise to spoil the ship for the sake of a kopeck's worth of caulking.'

'That is never fear,' said Bronsky with a graciously reassuring wave of his hand; 'nobody mistrusts you of yourself, comrade, and it is only as good friend that I tell you for information what is being thought at headquarters. This is going to be big thing, Joolby.'

'I don't doubt it,' agreed the other, regarding his visitor's comfortable self-satisfaction with his twisted look of private appreciation. 'I shall do my best in that way, comrade.'

'Extraordinary care is being take to make sure for wide and quick distribution in China, Japan and India and everywhere agents signify good prospects. The Committee are confident that this move, successfully engined, will destroy British commercial prestige in the East for at least a generation—and by the end of that time there will not be any British in the East. Meanwhile there must be no weak link in the chain. Now, Julian Joolby, what can I report to the Commissar?'

'You will know that within the next few hours. I've called them for eleven. Larch is working on the plates at a safe place now and as soon as dusk we will fill in the time by going to see what he has done and approve or not according to what you think of them.'

'Good. That sounds as business. But why should we go there? Surely it is more fitly that a workman would come and wait on our convenience at your place of living?'

'It isn't a matter of fitness—it's a matter of ordinary prudence. Have I ever been what is call "in trouble", Bronsky?'

'Not as far as to my knowledge,' admitted the comrade. 'I have always understand that you keep you hand clean however.'

'So. And I have done that by sticking to one rule: never to have anything in my place that isn't capable of a reasonable explanation. Most things can be explained away but not the copper plate of a bank-note found underneath your flooring. That is Larch's look out.'

'You are right. It would never do—especially when I is here. We cannot be too much careful. Now this Larch—was he not in it once before when things did not go rightly?'

Joolby nodded and the visitor noticed that his bulging throat sagged unpleasantly.

'That's the chap. There was a split and Larch didn't get his fingers out quickly enough. Three years he was sentence and he came out less than six weeks ago.'

'He is safe though? He has no bad feeling?'

'Why should he have?' demanded Joolby, looking at Mr Bronsky with challenging directness. 'I had nothing to do with him being put away. It was just a matter of luck that while Larch had the stuff when he was nabbed nothing could have been found on me if they had looked for ever—luck or good management.'

'Good management if you say to me,' propounded Bronsky wisely. 'Notwithstanding.'

'The one who has the plates is bound to get it in the ear if it comes to trouble. Larch knows that all right when he goes in it.'

'But you are able to persuade him to risk it again? Well, that is real cleverness, Joolby.'

'Oh yes; I was able as you say it to persuade him. George is the best copper-plate engraver of his line in England; he came out with a splendid character from the prison Governor—and not an earthly chance of getting a better job than rag-picking. I've had harder propositions than persuading him in the circumstances, if it comes to that, Bronsky.'

'It is to your good notwithstanding,' declared Mr Bronsky urbanely. 'The Committee of course officially know nothing of details and are in position to deny whatever is say or done but they is not unmindful of zeal, as you may rely in it, comrade. That is the occasion of my report. Now as regards this business of eleven?'

'You will meet them all then and hear what is being done in other directions. Nickle will be here by that time and we shall be able to decide about Tapsfield.'

'Tapsfield? That is a new one surely? I have not heard—'

'Place where the mills are that make all the official Bank paper,' explained Joolby. 'Naturally the paper is our chief trouble—always has been: always will be. Larch can make perfect plates, but with what we're aiming at this time nothing but the actual paper the Bank of England itself uses will pass muster. Well, there's plenty of it down at Tapsfield and we're going to lift it somehow.'

'I quite agree that we must have the right paper however. But this person Nickle—he is not unknown to some of us—is he quite—?'

'In what way?'

'Well, there is a feeling that he appear to think more of what he can get out of our holy crusade than of the ultimate benefit of mankind. He has not got the true international spirit, Julian Joolby. I suspect that he has taint of what he would doubtless call "patriotism"—which mean that he has yet to learn that any other country is preferable to his own. To be short, I have found this young man vulgar and it is not beyond that he may also prove restive.'

'Leave that to me,' said Joolby with a note of authority, and his unshapely form gave the impression of increasing in bulk as if to meet the prospect of aggression. 'This is London, not Moscow, Bronsky; I'm in charge here and I have to pick my people and adapt my methods. Nickle will fall into line all right and serve us just so far as suits our purpose. So long as he is doing that he can sing "Rule Britannia" in his spare time for all it matters.'

'But in the cause—'

'In the meantime we cannot be too particular about the exact shape of the tool we use to open closed doors with,' continued Joolby, smothering the interruption with masterful insistence. 'We are going to flood China, India and the East with absolutely perfect Bank of England paper so that in the end it will be sheerly impossible for English trade to go on there, and so pave the way for Soviet rule. But it is not necessary to shout that sacred message into every ear, even if for the time they work hand in hand with us. Let them think that they are out to make easy money. Few men work any the worse for the expectation that they are in the way to get fortunes. Does that not satisfy you, comrade Bronsky?'

'So long as it goes forward,' admitted Mr Bronsky with slightly ungracious acceptance, for he could not blink the suspicion that while he himself was an extremely important figure, this subordinate monstrosity would do precisely as he intended.

'It is going forward—as you shall convince yourself completely. In the meanwhiles—you have not, I hope, made dinner?'

'Well, no,' admitted the visitor, with a flutter of misgiving at the prospect, 'but—'

'That is well—you need have no qualms; I can produce something better than kahetia or vodka, and as to food—Won Chou there is equal to anything you would find at your own place or in Soho. Won Chou—number one topside feed, me him, plenty quick. Not is? Is?'

'Can do. Is,' replied Won Chou with impassive precision.

'There you see,' amplified Joolby, with the pride of a conjurer bringing off a successful trick, 'he can do it all right—take no longer in the end than if you went out somewhere. And,' he added, with an inward appreciation of the effect that he knew the boast would have on his guest's composure, 'all that he will use for a six course spread may be a gas-ring and two or perhaps three old biscuit tins.'

CHAPTER IV

CORA LARCH IS OFFERED A GOOD SITUATION

IT was a continual matter of pained surprise to George Larch whenever he came to think about it—and owing to the nature of his work and its occasional regrettable developments he had plenty of time for meditation—that he should have become a criminal. It was so entirely different from what he had ever intended when he set out in life. All his instincts were law-abiding and moral and the goal of his ambition from the day when he put by his first saved shilling had been a country cottage (as he conceived it), some fancy poultry and a nice square garden. Not a damp, broken-down, honeysuckle-clad, spider-infested, thatched old hovel of the sort that artists loved to depict, but a really sound, trim little new red-brick villa, standing well up and preferably in the immediate suburbs of Brighton or Worthing.

As a baby, a child, a boy, he had given his mother no trouble whatever, and at school he had always earned unexceptional reports, with particular distinction in his two favourite subjects— Handwriting and Scripture History. Indeed, on the occasion of his last Breaking Up the schoolmaster had gone out of his way to contrive a test and as a result had been able to demonstrate to the assembled boys that, set a line of copper-plate, it was literally impossible to decide which was George's work and which the copy. As it happened, 'Honesty is the Best Policy. £ s. d.' (the tag merely to fill up the line) had been the felicitous text of this experiment.

Very often in these periods of voluntary or enforced inaction George cast his thoughts back in a distressed endeavour to put his finger on the precise point at which he could be said to have deviated from the strict path of virtue. Possibly it might be fixed at that day in 1898 when a casual but very emphatic acquaintance gave him in strict confidence the name of an unsuspected dead cert for the approaching Derby. Not without grave doubts, for it was quite contrary to his upbringing, but tempted by the odds, young Larch diffidently inquired how one made a bet and ultimately decided to risk half-a-crown on the chances of Jeddah. Still all might have been well but unfortunately the horse did win and—the bookmaker being not only honest but positively delighted—George found himself at a stroke twelve pounds ten (more than the result of a month's conscientious work) the richer.

Then there was Cora. That had been a wonderful thing, so unexpected, so incredible, so tumultuously sweet, and even now, at forty-three, with all that had flowed from it, he would not have a jot of that line of destiny altered if it would have involved losing that memory. Cora was as true as steel and had stuck to—and up for—him through thick and thin, but it was quite possible that her youthful gaiety, her love of pretty, costly things, and the easier views on life and conduct in which she (naïve child) had been brought up might have imperceptibly shaped the issue. It was simply impossible for him not to follow in her rather hectic round and as for refusing her anything—why, the greatest pleasure he could win had been to anticipate whatever she had set her innocent heart on. It goes without saying that no more shillings were being saved; instead there were frequent occasions when pounds had to be—on whatever terms—somehow borrowed. Meanwhile there had been other dead certs: one in particular so extremely dead that coming at a critical hour George had been hypnotised into the belief that it would be the merest form to make use of a comparatively trifling sum when it could inevitably be replaced before the accounts were looked into the following morning . . . So here he was, sitting in the back upper room of an ostensible rag-and-bone shop, fabricating with unmatchable skill the 'mother plate' of a Bank of England 'tenner' and at this particular moment preparing to unlock the door in response to old Ikey's rapped-out signal that 'safe' visitors were below to see him.

Mr Joolby had spoken of visiting Larch 'at dusk', possibly on general precautionary grounds, but it did not escape the notice of those who knew him best that most of the outdoor activity of the crippled dealer was nocturnal. Padgett Street rarely saw him out at all for the rear premises of his shop gave access to a yard from which it was possible to emerge in more distant thoroughfares by way of a network of slums and alleys. A pleasantry current in Padgett Street was to affect the conviction that he burrowed.

It was sufficiently late when Won Chou's peculiarly appetising meal had been despatched to answer to this requirement. Mr Joolby glanced up at the deepening sky of spilled-ink blue as seen through an uncurtained pane, produced a box of cigars curiously encased in raffia and indicated to his guest that they might as well be going.

'It's a slow affair with me,' he apologised as he laboriously crawled about the room, preparing for the walk, 'so you must expect a tiresome round. Now as we have some little distance to go—'

'But is it quite safe—this place we go to?' asked Bronsky who had drunk too sparingly of either wine or spirits to have his natural feebleness heartened. 'It would not do—'

'Safe as the Kremlin,' was the half contemptuous reply, for by the measure of the visitor Joolby was a man of mettle. 'My own chap is in charge there and so far as that goes the place is run as a proper business. Ah-Chou'—raising his voice, for that singularly versatile attendant was again at his look-out—'we go come one two hour. You catchee make dark all time.'

'Alle light-o,' came cheerfully back and although no footsteps were to be heard Won Chou might be trusted to be carrying out his instructions.

'And makee door plenty fast. No one come look-see while not is,' was the further injunction; then piloting his guest into the lumber-strewn yard Mr Joolby very thoroughly put into practice this process as regards the rear premises before he led the way towards their destination. Leading, for most of the journey, it literally was, for much of their devious route was along mere passages, and even in the streets Mr Joolby's mode of progression monopolised the path while Bronsky's superficial elegance soon prejudiced him against using the gutter. He followed his host at a laboured crawl, relieving his mind from time to time by little bursts of 'psst!' and 'chkk!' at each occasion of annoyance. Joolby, unmoved, plodded stolidly ahead, his unseen features occasionally registering their stealthy broadening grin, although he seldom failed to throw a word of encouragement over his shoulder whenever a more definite phrase indicated that the comrade had come up against an obstruction or trod into something unpleasant.

'Well, here we are at last,' was the welcome assurance as they emerged into a thoroughfare that was at least a little wider and somewhat better lit than most of the others. 'That is the place, next to the greengrocer. When we go back we can take an easier way, since you don't seem to like this one, Bronsky, especially as it will be quite dark then.'

'It will be as good that we should,' assented Mr Bronsky, still justifiably ruffled. 'Seldom have I been through such tamgod—'

'Just a minute,' put in Joolby coolly. 'Better not talk until I've made sure that everything is clear,' and they having now come to the rag-and-bone shop he rapped in a quite ordinary way on the closed door. With no more than the usual delay of coming from an inner room and turning a rusty key it was opened by an elderly Hebrew whose 'atmosphere'—in its most generous sense—was wholly in keeping with his surroundings.

'Good evening, Ikey,' said Mr Joolby, still panting a little now that he had come to rest after an unusual exertion, 'I have brought you perhaps a very good buyer. This gentleman is making up a large purchase for export and if it is worth his while—'

'Come in, sirs, come in if you please,' begged Ikey deferentially; the door was held more fully open and they passed into a store heaped with rags, bones, empty bottles, old metal, stark rabbit skins and all the more sordid refuse of a city's back-kitchens. Joolby did not appear to find anything disturbing in the malodorous air and even the fastidious Bronsky might have been perfectly at home in these surroundings.

'It is quite O.K., Mr Joolby,' said Ikey when the door was closed again, and it could have been noticed that he spoke neither so ceremoniously nor in such very audible tones as those which had passed on the threshold. 'If you want him he's upstairs now and there isn't nothing different going on anywhere.'

Joolby grunted what was doubtless a note of satisfaction and wagged assurance at Mr Bronsky.

'There you see,' he remarked consequentially, 'it's exactly as I told you. This isn't the land of domiciliary visits and if the police *are* coming they will always send you printed form giving twenty-four hours notice.'

'No; is that rule?' asked Mr Bronsky innocently, and repeated: 'Good! good! It is comical,' when he saw that the other two were being silently amused at his literalness. 'Come, come,' he hastened to add, thinking that it was time to reassert some of the authority that seemed to have become temporarily eclipsed by the progress of the unfortunate journey, 'this is no business however, and we are not here for evers.'

'Tell George to come down and bring pulls of his latest plates,' confirmed Joolby. The narrow rickety stairs leading to the floor above—little better than a permanent ladder—were impractical for him and scarcely more inviting to Mr Bronsky. Ikey apparently had some system of conveying this message by jerking an inconspicuous cord for almost at once George Larch appeared at the top of the steps, recognising the two visitors as he descended.

'Peace be with you, persecuted victim. The day dawns!' exclaimed the comrade, bustling forward effusively and kissing Mr Larch on both cheeks—an indignity to which he had to submit or lose his balance among the jam jars.

'That's all right, Mr Bronsky,' protested George who had as much prejudice against 'foreign ways' as most of his country-men. 'But please don't start doing that again—I told you about it once before, you may remember.'

'But—but, are we not as brothers?' stammered Mr Bronsky, uncertain whether or not to be deeply hurt. 'In spirit of all-union greeting—'

'Well, I shouldn't like the wife to catch you at it, that's all, Mr Bronsky. I should never think of carrying on like that with a grown-up brother.'

'*Catch* me "at it",' managed to voice the almost dumbfounded Bronsky. '"Carrying on"! Oh, the pigs Englishmen! You have no—no—' At this emotional stress words really did fail him.

'Come, come, you two—what the hell,' interposed Mr Joolby judicially. 'We're here to see how you've got on, George. May as well go into the room where we can have a decent light. Did you bring pulls of the latest plates down? Bronsky here needs to be satisfied that you can do all I've claimed for you.'

At the back of the evil-smelling vault Mr Ikey had his private lair, a mixture of office and, apparently, a living-room in every function. It was remarkably garnished with such salvage from the cruder stock as had been considered worthy of being held over and, as Joolby had foreseen, it possessed a light vastly superior to the dim glimmer that hung over the cavernous store. Here the three chiefly concerned drew close together, the old man remaining behind to stand on guard, while Larch, with the outward indifference that merged his pride as a craftsman and an ineradicable shame to be so basely employed, submitted an insignificant sheaf of papers. Some of the sheets were apparent Bank of England notes in the finished state, others proofs of incomplete plates and various details; both the visitors produced pocket lenses and Mr Bronsky smoothed out a couple of genuine notes that he extracted from a well-stocked wallet. A complete absorption testified their breathless interest.

'Well?' demanded Joolby when every sheet had been passed under review. 'Say what you like, Bronsky, this is as near the real article as—' and he instanced two things which might be admitted to be essentially the same although the comparison was more forcible than dainty.

'It could certainly deceive me, I confess,' admitted Bronsky, 'and yet in ill-spent youth I have experience as bank official. But see,' he added, as though anxious to expose some flaw, and wetting across one corner of a sheet with a moistened finger he demonstrated that it could easily be severed.

'Ah, but you mustn't judge the result by this paper, Mr Bronsky—of course it's no good,' put in Larch, carefully securing the fragments. 'But if we get some of the genuine stuff, as Mr Joolby will tell you he means to do, not even the Chief Cashier of the Bank of England could be dead certain which was which—except for one thing, of course.'

'And that is what?'

'Why, the numbers to be sure. They can refer to their issue.'

'Not so fast, George,' objected Joolby, 'how is that going to help them? Suppose we duplicate actual numbers that are out in circulation, and perhaps hold over the originals? We can triplicate, quadruple, multiply by a hundred times if it suits our purpose.'

'Well, by hokey that's an idea,' admitted simple George Larch. 'Why, they'd have to pay out on all that come in then or risk repudiating their own paper. It's lucky for the Old Lady of Threadneedle Street that we aren't in the wholesale business.'

'Yes, to be sure,' replied Joolby, favouring the other conspirator with a meaningful sideways look. 'Lucky, isn't it, Bronsky?'

'I should think to smile,' agreed Mr Bronsky, combing his

luxuriant beard for the mere pleasure of verifying that dignified appendage. 'Notwithstanding however.'

'There's one thing I should like to mention, Mr Joolby, while you're here,' said Larch, getting back to practical business. 'Do you really mean me to go on with plates for all the high values up to the thousand pound printing?'

'Why not?' demanded Joolby, turning on his props to regard George with the blank full-faced stare that presented his disconcerting features in their most pronounced aspect. 'What's the difficulty?'

'None at all so far as I'm concerned. Of course I can do them just the same as the others—technically there's nothing whatever against it. Only no one ever heard of soft flims for anything like that—only for fives or tens or at the most a twenty.'

'All the more reason why the big ones will go through then. As a matter of fact, George, our friend here has struck special facilities for putting stuff of that sort about in the East. There'll be no risk to any of us at this end whatever happens.'

'But you don't mean that it's going to be negotiable for anything like at value? Why if—?'

'A profitable use will be found for all of them, never fear,' replied Mr Joolby, evincing no intention of pursuing the subject. 'Yes, we're through now, Ikey. You can come off. Well, what is it then?'

'It was Mrs Larch outside at the door,' bleated Ikey in his ancient falsetto. 'I assure her that the place is all locked up and no one here and she laugh at me through the keyhole. She says she will come inside and see for herself.'

'Then she will,' remarked George, who might be supposed to know. 'So you may as well unlock the door and let her.'

'If she is I had perhaps better as well go back into the room,' suggested Mr Bronsky—they were again in the front shop on their way to leave. 'Your wife, for some reason, cannot endure my presence.'

'Oh, I wouldn't go as far as that, Mr Bronsky,' protested

George guiltily, for he knew well enough that he could go exactly that far. 'There must he some sort of a mistake . . . Still, if you think so, perhaps it would be as well at the moment.'

Mrs Larch came breezily in, paying no more attention to the now obsequious Ikey than if he had been one of his own commercial assets—an emaciated thigh-bone. A woman smartly turned out (as she would herself have complacently said) and— if a little floridly—handsome still, she might bear slight resemblance now to the simple angel of George's early dreams, but it was possible to trace something of that unfortunate pilgrim's progress in her rather defiant front, her meretricious embellishment, and in an eye that was not devoid of material calculation. For the moment it was only the unwieldy form of Mr Joolby that stood out in that place of continual shadow.

'Oh, good evening, Mr Joolby,' she exclaimed, sparkling triumphantly over her success at the doorway. 'Of course I guessed that Mr Ikey was telling fibs but I didn't know that I should find you here. I suppose that George is up in the attic as usual? He might just as well be a member of the Carlton for all that I see of him nowadays.'

'No, my dear, here I am,' proclaimed George, emerging from his particular shadow. 'Only you oughtn't to be, after the place is shut up, you know. It isn't prudent.'

'Well, someone had to do something about it. I did go round to Padgett Street first and Mr Peke there—no, that isn't right, is it? but I know that it's some kind of a fancy dog. Anyhow, he seemed to be telling the truth when he said that you "not is" there, so there was nothing for it but to come on here and chance it.'

'But what's the matter, Cora?' asked Larch. 'Has anything happened?'

'Only the landlord this time, my lad—the gas-man was yesterday and the furniture people—oh, you've been home since then, haven't you, and know all about those beauties.'

'But I thought that I left enough to tide over the most

pressing. We figured it out, if you remember, and it seemed—'

'So I thought, but unfortunately it didn't turn out quite as we figured, boy, and some of the others got more pressing,' said Mrs Larch calmly. 'At all events I left the landlord sitting on the landing.'

'He means it?'

'I'm afraid he most decidedly does. There was that nasty little air of finality about the way he picked his teeth with a bus ticket as he talked—I think he must save them up for it—that, as the Sunday school poem says: "Is a certain forerunner of sorrow". "Come now, Mrs Larch," he said, running his suety eye over everything I'd got on, "you can't be hard up you know and you've had a cart-load of warnings. Doesn't your husband make good money?" "Better than most husbands at his job do, I will say," I replied, "but, you know, it's always the cobbler's wife who has the worst shoes, and just at the moment—"' She finished up with the conventional little laugh and held out a hand towards him.

'Come, George, fork out. I'm sorry if you're rocky too but it's an absolute that it's no good going back without it.'

'"Rocky", my God!' said George, echoing her shallow laugh. 'Well—but how much do you need to square it?'

'Oh, a couple might do just to carry on—and of course as many more as you can spare me.'

'A couple, eh, my girl?' he replied, fishing deeply into both his trouser pockets. 'You don't mean tanners by any chance? Well, that's the state of the exchequer.' Two sixpences and a few coppers were the result of his investigation.

'I see. No winners among them today, I suppose, and you'd rather gone it? I might have guessed as much. Well, that being that, Mr Joolby will have to advance you a trifle.'

'What me? Two quids?' exclaimed Mr Joolby aghast. 'You can't be serious. Everyone know that I never advance anything until afterwards and your husband has been paid for a full week and this is only Friday. Oh, I couldn't—'

'All right; only if you don't our place will be sold up and

then where are you going to find George when you want him?'

This was so plainly common sense that there could be only one outcome (to say nothing of the pressure of another development that was duly formulating) but even as he would have capitulated one of the freakish impulses, that occasionally brought out the shifty grin, moved Joolby to change his purpose. Instead of the amount required he slyly picked out another paper and Cora found herself being offered a wholly unexpected five-pound note—in point of fact one of George's most recent productions.

'Oh, Mr Joolby, that *is* kind—' she began gratefully and then flashed to what it was—sensed it in Larch's instinctive frown, in Joolby's half averted face, creased with foolish enjoyment. She bit on to the unpleasant tremor: very well, only Joolby should never again enjoy at her expense that particular satisfaction.

'Well, of all the—' she mock-indignantly declared, and entering into the spirit of the thing crumpled up the note and playfully flung it back at the ogre. 'Nice fix it would be for you, Mr Joolby, if I was nicked for planting a snide 'un. They'd be here after George like one o'clock and then what would become of all the work you've paid him for doing?'

'That's all right, Mrs Larch—it was only our fun,' protested Mr Joolby, leering like his ancestral satyr. 'It isn't likely that we'd risk anything of the sort just now, is it? But I will tell you this: when we get the right stuff you needn't be afraid of walking into the Bank of England with your paper.'

'I daresay. But in the meantime I *am* afraid of the bailiff walking into our flat with his paper. George there knows well enough. I must have something before I can go back and that's all there is about it.'

'Well, so you shall have,' promised Mr Joolby, calling up all the blandishment of his suavest manner. 'And that is not all; I may as well tell you now, though I hadn't intended to until it was quite settled. Very soon we shall have a nice regular job for you with good wages—oh, a splendid position in a beautiful house with very little to do and everything found that you require.'

If Mr Joolby expected the enchanted lady to fall upon his neck (metaphorically, of course, for physical contact was a thing sheerly inconceivable) he was a little out of his reckoning. Cora Larch had experience of considerable slices of life in various aspects. During periods of George's compulsory withdrawal it had been necessary for her to fend for herself, nor, in truth, had she ever found any particular difficulty in so doing. But as a result of the education that had thereby accrued she now approached Mr Joolby's surprising proposal in the spirit that prompts a creature of the wild to walk all round a doubtful morsel before venturing to touch it.

'Oh, and what sort of a job is it, may I ask?' she guardedly inquired. 'And for that matter, what sort of a house where everything is going to be so fairy-like?'

'Well, you see, it's like this,' explained Mr Joolby. 'The time's come when we must have another place—it's getting too risky for all of them to be in and out so often of my shop, to say nothings about coming direct here when at any time one might be followed. Then very soon there will be others—foreign gentlemen—that we may want to put up for a few nights at a time. Oh, I can tell you it won't be altogether money wasted.'

'No, I'm sure it won't if you are doing it, Mr Joolby,' agreed the lady. 'Still, I don't see—'

'Well, as I'm telling you I've taken a private house in a different name—a furnished house right across the other side of London. It must be conducted quietly on highly respectable lines so that it would never occur to anyone outside that it wasn't thoroughly dull and bourgeois. With the milkman and the baker calling every day that oughtn't to be difficult. Nothing impresses the neighbourhood so favourably as two or three bottles of milk taken in regularly every morning and put out again at night. It must be that crooks aren't supposed to drink it. And any account of yourself that you want to put about—we will make that up—you can safely pass on to the baker.'

'Well?' Mr Joolby seemed to think that everything necessary had been said, but Mrs Larch was still expectant.

'Well; don't you understand? You are to be as housekeeper, manage the place and arrange for whoever we send to stay there. All the bills will be paid—only don't be extravagant of course. Deal at the multiple shops and there's a nice street market—and you will have a pound a week for wages.'

'H'm; it sounds promising,' admitted Mrs Larch. The prospect of being able to cap it by giving notice when the insufferable landlord made his next caustic remark was not without an influence. Still, she had not quite completed the cautionary circle. 'But is it part of the—the arrangement that you are going to take up your abode there, Mr Joolby?'

'I?' replied Joolby, with just the flicker of an instinctive glance in the ingenuous George's direction. 'What has that got to do with it? I live at my own place as usual, of course. I may have to come occasionally—'

'Oh, all right. I only wanted to understand—*and have it understood*—from the start. Let me know when I'm to begin and I'll take it on for you.'

'Of course you will. It's a holiday that you're being paid for having, not a job. What do you say, eh, George?'

'I say that if Cora wants to do it she will,' contributed Mr Larch with tempered loyalty. 'It's her affair after all, Mr Joolby.'

'Eh? Oh yes, of course; but that's settled. Well, what about putting this paper out of the way now that Bronsky is satisfied; and you don't leave any of the plates where they can be found at night I hope? We can't be too careful.'

'I'll see to that you may be sure,' undertook Larch and he proceeded to satisfy himself that no dangerous paper had been left about and then climbed up to his quarters. Meanwhile Cora lingered on in the cavernous gloom, waiting for Joolby to redeem his promise—a small detail that seemed to have escaped his memory.

'What sort of a house is it that you're taking, Mr Joolby?' she said at last, finding the man's eyes repeatedly upon her and speaking to break a silence that threatened to become awkward.

'Oh, a very nice house in a first-class neighbourhood and quite the swell side of London. There's a garden all round so we can't be overlooked and a back way out into another street, which is always a convenience. It's costing me a lot of money.'

'Costing your Bolshie friends, I suppose you mean? What size is this house—it sounds rather a handful?'

'Quite a good size. Ten or a dozen rooms, I daresay, and then there are cellars and attics besides. Oh, plenty of room for all that we require.'

'Plenty of work for me more likely. I can't do all that myself you know, Mr Joolby. I must have a maid of some sort if the place is to be kept at all decent.'

'What? A servant to feed and pay wages into the bargain!' cried Mr Joolby in dismay. 'Well, well; you shall have one, Cora. I daresay we can find one of those devoted, hard-working little scrubs who are glad to come for nothing and live on the table leavings. And when there's nothing else for her to do she can always put in some time working in the garden—I have to keep it in order.'

'She shall, Mr Joolby; you can have my word on that. Now what about the rent for me to take back? You said you would, you know—'

'So I did, my dear,' amorously breathed Mr Joolby, coming nearer as he took out his wallet to comply and dropping his voice almost to a whisper, 'and I'm not going back on it or anything else I promise you . . . You think me a bit—careful I dare say, now don't you, Cora? But if only you'll be sensible and meet me half way you'll have no reason to complain that you're short of money. There's the two pounds, and I'll make it five more—well, say three more for a start; that's five altogether—if you're reasonable—' Amid all this tender eloquence, in which Mr Joolby's never very dulcet voice assumed an oddly croaking tone as the combined outcome of the exigencies of caution and his own emotional strain, Mrs Larch realised that her hand was being held and increasingly caressed under the cloak of passing her the money.

'Oh, you beastly old toad!' she impulsively let out, and tore herself away from those fumbling paws, though, characteristically enough, her fingers tightened on the two notes that were already in her possession. 'So it *was* that, after all!'

Whatever had been Joolby's delusion a moment before, that one word Cora had used brought him crashing back to earth as effectually as if it had been a bullet. For a short minute his contorted face and swelling form grew more repellent still, his hands beat the air for help, and swaying then, with his props laid by, it seemed as though he must have fallen. The effect was sufficiently alarming to blur Mrs Larch's disgust, while fearful of lending any physical aid she began to babble, lamely enough, to turn the edge of her incautious outburst.

'Oh, well; of course I didn't mean anything personal, Mr Joolby. You quite understand that I hope, but you ought to be more careful—steadying yourself by clutching hold of one in this dark hole like that. I declare I thought it was a bogie. Now I'd better be getting on I think. You'll let me know when I'm to start housekeeping, won't you?'

'Go; go; get out! Clear off, you harpy. Never show your ugly face again. I've done with you, do you hear?' spat out the stricken creature, hurling the words like missiles. 'Go before I have you thrown out—' Gasping for breath he continued to gesticulate and threaten.

Cora Larch was not particularly long-suffering herself; she had tendered her olive branch and if the beast took it like that he could bloody well go and—A little crude, perhaps, but twenty-five years of her sort of life are apt to take the bloom off even the most peach-like natures.

'Oh, all right, all right,' she threw back, almost as vigorously. 'Keep your hair—well'—with a significant glance at his skull—'keep your skin moist anyway. You know jolly well there's no one else you can trust to put in that house and I'm quite willing to come still *as a housekeeper*, Mr Joolby. Send word by George when you're cool. Ta-ta.' And with an emphatic nod to give point to her self-possession Mrs Larch vanished.

'Cow! Bitch! Camel!' Mr Joolby continued to spit and swell while the distracted Ikey drew near and sheered off again, quaveringly helpless among such violent emotions. 'George—Larch—come here at once—I'll let you know—'

Evidently George was to become the whipping-boy for his wife's transgressions.

Fortunately, perhaps, George was just then too remote to hear, but Mr Bronsky heard and it was that dignified gentleman who, emerging from the den and surveying his friend's condition with grave disfavour, brought him at once to recognise the very unfraternal figure he was cutting.

'What is this, Joolby?' he demanded with authority, planting himself resolutely in front so as to pen his irresponsible associate between the mixed rags and the bottles. 'Are you crazy? Have you become madman? How is this that has possess you? Do you not understand that the row you is kicking up may bring in police? Or have you taken leaves of your senses?'

'You are right—I must have been off my head, but something happened very much to upset me,' admitted Mr Joolby, realising at last how fatuously he must have been behaving. 'No, nothing to do with our affairs, I assure you, Bronsky, but—well, it is of no matter. I must not talk of it—not think of such things—or it may bring on an attack of my old trouble. Now we will go back straight at once and I'll take you in a bus. Or no, I think perhaps it had better even run to a taxi.'

CHAPTER V

THE MEETING AT ELEVEN

WITH the distaste for being subject to promiscuous observation that ordered the routine of his movements, Mr Joolby stopped the taxi-cab before Padgett Street was reached and they arrived at the back yard after a complicated but relatively short process of burrowing. Won Chou was patiently on watch and discharged himself of a faithful account of all that had happened in the interval:

'She-Larch come and do plenty talkee. Say he is? Say not is. Make go.' The subject not calling for any particular elaboration Joolby merely nodded.

He had recovered his equilibrium now and Cora's ungrateful flout, and the jibe that had been its barb, were dismissed into the category of Chilly Fank's reference once to an aquarium and a thousand kindred insults—contributory drops to an ocean of insensate hatred that took little account of individual scores in its unrelenting vendetta against the entire race that was human.

'So far so well,' remarked Mr Bronsky with some complacency when they were again seated in the dealer's private den (though he may have had a still more private one somewhere into which nobody but himself ever penetrated) with cigars and coffee of a very especial flavour before them—waiting, as the comrade vaguely understood, for the arrival of some others. 'The workmanship of itself,' he continued, 'leave no shadow of doubts that Larch will be able to satisfy us. Then Nickle—no, I cannot like that young man—is to say how the paper may be acquired. But the others of that you speak—where do they, as it goes, "come in"?'

'Nickle will tell us all about the mill but after that we shall have to decide on the most suitable lines for getting to work there. There must be no hitch anywhere when once we make a move in that direction, Bronsky.'

'I think so also,' agreed his guest; 'and that is why I ask it.' Mr Bronsky thought intently for a moment, tapping his intellectual brow with a persuasive forefinger until he triumphantly got the happy instance that he was tracking: 'Too many cooks upset an apple cart.'

'Nickle will be able to tell us exactly what we need to know but it will take more than one to put the thing through when it comes to the real business,' replied Joolby, reflecting that as the time had to be passed there was no point in becoming impatient. 'No cause to get anxious on that score, let me tell you, my friend; to all except ourselves this is simply going to be an unusually big and well-arranged plant and their only idea will be to do their share to make it a success so that they can have their pickings. So. But once the paper and the plates are safe with us we can arrange matters according to our own programme.'

'I feel sure you may be right,' assented Bronsky, with his usual pliant acquiescence. 'Now as regards these others who are to come in the swim; it is just as good that I should first be told about them in order to be in a position to judge their ability.'

There were moments when Mr Bronsky's consequential little airs of authority made Joolby realise what a satisfaction it would be to pick up the nearest heavy object and bring it wholeheartedly down on this shallow-witted comrade's lamentable cranium. It was never more than a passing fancy, for he had long since realised that with the barest modicum of tact the formidable deputy was as plastic as a stick of putty, and with such contemptuous success had he kept this end in view that Bronsky firmly believed in Joolby's high regard and dependence on his judgment.

'That's chiefly why they're coming; I want you to meet them here and then tell me frankly what you think of their fitness for whatever we decide on doing. Dodger and Klantz you've seen, but another—Vallett—I don't suppose you've ever heard of. Then of course there will be Nickle himself and George was to be here in case anything comes up that touches what he is doing.'

'Dodger who was call—?' Bronsky's snapping fingers failed to induce the expression. 'It was a word for *skoliskiey*.'

'"Slippery"?—no, "Soapy Solomon", you mean—yes, that is the chap, and Klantz was the man we pulled out of Hamburg when he got into trouble over the Vulkan Works shindy.'

'They should be good men—I would approve them both. But who is this Vallett of what you speak. Is he trustworthy comrade?'

'George Larch picked up with him when he was doing his last stretch, and when Vallett was on his beam ends George sent him round here on the chance that I might find something for him. The fact is, Vallett slipped out of Dartmoor before his time was up and consequently he can't go about much in the day looking for suitable employment.'

'I do not like that very well,' objected Bronsky, feeling that perhaps he had been compliant long enough; 'there is too much of the "Known by the Police" about so many of your people. If there is a description of this fellow put about and he is recognise, they follow him to here and then where is we, to say nothings of our project?'

'Oh, I don't think so, Bronsky,' said Joolby in his most amiable mood; 'I see your point and I'm all for being careful but even if they did nab Vallett here, what about it? I'd be much obliged to the police for opening my eyes about the chap and there would be absolutely nothing to connect him up with us or what we're doing.'

'So far, perhaps—'

'And that's all that concerns us yet—afterwards we may or

may not use him. Besides they won't; Vallett can make up very well indeed—before he got tired of work he was on the stage and if he goes about by day his own mother wouldn't know him.'

'That puts a different complexion on him, I admit'—unfortunately Mr Bronsky did not recognise his own witticism. 'Yes, I begin to think Vallett is all right. What is it that we want him for—what is his way of business?'

'Well, he's tried his hand at several things—from calling to test the gas-meter to posing as a co-respondent. Anything lightly adventurous would suit his book and he has a very gentlemanly manner. That's what I had in mind—we have plenty of heavyweights but we may need to put someone there who can walk plausibly up to the front door. As to his being on the "wanted" list—well, after all, you can't run a knocking-shop with a bevy of virgins.'

This refined adage was entirely to Bronsky's taste and put him in a better humour. 'Good, good!' he exclaimed, showing his splendid teeth; 'I must remember that one. Is it English saying?'

Before Mr Joolby could explain that it was more probably early Egyptian a little bell conveyed its message, and waving aside such trivialities he briefly informed his guest that this indicated the arrival of one of the expected callers.

'I told the boy to send any of them straight through,' he added, 'so he needn't come off the door. Ah—our resourceful friend Nickle! Now this is luck. You are a bit early, Nick, and we can find out where we are before the others cut in.'

It was Nickle safely back indeed, looking extremely brown and fit, but in contrast to the pair who were all interest and affable expectation *his* manner was decidedly offhand and his expression—possibly a defensive pose—one of seasoned boredom. He greeted Joolby with a careless nod and held up—not out—an admonitory hand as Bronsky rose, whatever may have been the comrade's intention.

'I give you fair warning, Bronsky,' he remarked, 'that if you try any of your filthy brotherly love on me I shall stab you. It's much too hot to be embraced. I wonder you haven't gone back to hell, Joolby; you'd find it a damn sight cooler there than it seems to be in Stepney.'

'Kindly put off trying to be funny, Nickle,' said Joolby, beginning to glower. 'Coffee?' Already he guessed that the awaited report was not going to be any too encouraging, while this, if it came to the pinch, was certainly not the way to smooth down the already prejudiced Bronsky. Nickle's failing.

'I prefer any other form of poison, since you are so kind,' was the reply. 'Truth to tell, I'm rather sate of coffee and finger sponge biscuits.'

Not troubling to speak, but with a very ill grace at this further lapse, Joolby produced his bottles. Meanwhile, having sat down again, Mr Bronsky confided a succession of 'psss's' and 'tsss's' into his beard and blew out his cheeks between them.

'Now let's get on to things,' said their host, when amid this rather strained atmosphere Nickle had indicated and received his mixture. 'Our comrade is here specially to hear your report and, since it lies chiefly with us three, there is no particular object at this stage in waiting for the others. You've had all the time you've asked for, Nickle, and with the information you must have got no doubt you've worked out the scheme. Never mind the considerations now—just the bare facts. In a word, how is it to be done?'

'I can tell you that very simply,' replied Nickle, shifting his glass about with trivial deliberation. 'Not in a word perhaps but certainly in five at the outside. It isn't to be done.'

This was worse than Joolby's worst. At the most he had expected a formidable list of the difficulties to be met but he had never doubted that Nickle—of whose nerve and finesse he had proof—would at least have a feasible plan that would be capable of adaption. At this set-back all the familiar symptoms of anger and resentment began to possess the being, but his first words were moderately composed—merely because he refused as yet to credit Nickle's conclusions.

'What do you mean—"It isn't to be done"?' he snarled. 'It must be done. We've got to have that paper.'

'Oh, very well,' said Nickle, very creditably keeping up his pose of nonchalance; 'in that case there's nothing to it but for you to go down there and get it. You take with you my best wishes . . . Look here, Joolby,' he continued, switching on to an entirely different tone, 'I expect you to feel pretty sick, but if you imagine that this means nothing to me either, you are hellishly mistaken. The only difference is that you get it all at once while I've been up against it for a month, slowly finding out at every turn and twist that I couldn't get an inch further. You sent me down to find out the conditions, didn't you? Well, you may take my perishing word that in one way or another I found them. You simply can't get in there by force and there doesn't seem the foggiest chance to frame an act and lift a bunch of the paper. That's my considered judgment. You'd better send someone else to have a look if you won't accept it. Bronsky doesn't seem any too pleased—let him have a go and try it.'

During this harangue Mr Bronsky had been combing his beard vigorously as a practical outlet for his aggrieved feelings, and he now came to his feet and waved his arms excitedly in several directions as an impressive if otherwise ambiguous summing-up of the collapsed situation.

'If this is all,' he proclaimed, 'I may as better go—'

'Sit down, Bronsky,' thundered Joolby, dragging his great body up and coming to himself at last as he realised the crisis, and Mr Bronsky obediently did sit down. 'It isn't all.' His baleful eye surveyed them both with impartial disfavour. 'We need to have that paper for what we are infallibly going to do and whatever stands between we are going to get it. As you both very well know everything has been worked out on the assumption that we shall, and neither Nickle's cold feet nor anyone else's hot air signify a pestilential . . . I've fitted in all the arrangements here to absolute clockwork; Larch is cutting perfect plates that will defy every test that anyone can make, and Bronsky's people are ready with an organisation that would distribute in dead safety . . . And Mr Nickle regretfully informs us'—spitting his concentrated scorn—'"It isn't to be done". . . Now go on and tell us about it, Nickle.'

'Quite so,' agreed Nickle with commendable restraint; 'you've put up the dollars and you're entitled to the change. Well, with a regiment of soldiers forcing your way in would be child's play, wouldn't it? Or if you bought over half a dozen employees there need be no difficulty about lifting half a ton of paper, eh? But we haven't got a regiment as it happens and not a solitary employee is up for sale . . . Continue in your useful line of cross-examination, Mr Joolby; it's all included in the exes.'

'How can you positively say that there is no weak spot you've overlooked or that no one can be got at? How must you *know*? The thing has never even been tried as yet.'

'Oh hell, no.' Nickle shrugged his expressive shoulders at the futility of the inference. 'I know all the ancient history of the place of course and I happen to know that it's simply because they take damn good care that it can never be successful.'

'It has never been attempt at all before?' chimed in Mr Bronsky, gathering new hope. 'Then I am dispose to agree with Joolby that you have missed what you have not seen. It should not be out of the question.'

'Possibly not, Bronsky,' admitted Nickle, behaving his best, 'but unfortunately it is out. The kink in your point of view arises from the fact that whereas neither of you has so much as seen Tapsfield through a telescope, for the last month or so I've been exploring its rural beauties. There isn't an inch of ground that I haven't been over and I don't suppose that there's a man, woman or child working at the mill who won't really miss me. I've had supper at the vicarage, played darts at the Crown and Anchor, deputised for the local scoutmaster, put up a special prize for the best collection of wild flowers at the Tapsfield and District Horticultural—'

'What for?' demanded Joolby crossly.

'To award it to Joyce Jones so that I might call and congratulate her mother who lives at the mill gate lodge. My God, Joolby, I even sang "Dreaming of Thee" at a saturnalia called a "Penny Reading" there, simply because the young lady who whanged the piano had a job of feeding a machine in the drying-room.'

'It was women and young girl you got best on with doubtless?' asked the comrade, screwing up his eyes pleasantly. 'You had agreeable time exploring these local beauties in one way or another, Nickle?'

'Bronsky,' said Nickle gravely, 'you ought to take a fairly strong cathartic immediately before retiring. You have a morbid accumulation of offensive matter somewhere . . . As an actual fact, the person that I most assiduously worked was a young fellow called Tilehurst who is employed in the mill office. He needed someone to improve his tennis a bit and as I was quite equal to that he simply clung to me and wanted me to go round to their place on nearly every other evening. I got all the routine from him; do you think that if there was any way through I shouldn't have spotted it in those circumstances? I'm as keen in the matter of this loot as any of you are, but you may just as well put it out of your minds—it doesn't go this journey.'

'I don't put it out of my mind for the fraction of a second, but I may have to put you out of somewhere, Nickle, if this is the best you can do when you are given a chance of showing. All our work—come in, George' (Mr Larch having that moment made an unobtrusive appearance), 'you may as well know what's going—Bronsky's, mine, and George's—to say nothing of a score of others who are in this thing as well—all this isn't going to be scrapped simply because you, and you alone, have failed in your department.'

'Failed? I like that!' threw back Nickle. 'How have I failed? I went there to find out the conditions. Haven't I?'

'You have failed because you haven't succeeded; that's how. There are no half ways here. You know well enough that you went to find out the best way of getting what we need from there. You say it can't be done. Very well; as we are going to do it we must fall back on our own methods, with just so much or so little as you can help us . . . Now this man Tilehurst you struck—I suppose you know his ways—does he go about alone? Could we hold him up down there if we were fixing it that way?'

'Not the least doubt. He cycles about alone pretty regularly and in those godforsaken winding lanes anything could happen. But—'

'Cut out those "buts" of yours, Nickle. You're only butting up against a brick wall here.'

'And besides, remember, comrade,' put in Mr Bronsky encouragingly, 'that even if it comes to touch and went and it is not well to stay, you would always find asylum with good friend in Moscow.'

'An asylum?' repeated Nickle, with a sufficiently pointed look. 'Yes, I suppose that does about describe Moscow now, but I don't want to go into an asylum just yet . . . And since you dislike the more conventional opening, Joolby—what in hell's name do you suppose is to be got by sticking up young Tilehurst and bringing all the resources of law and order round about our ears?'

'He uses some office keys, one may suppose,' continued Joolby, without paying the slightest attention to this objection. 'Did you happen to make it your business to find out what he actually carries?'

'Naturally. He has the ordinary desk and inner door keys of his own part of the building. None of these are any more service-able than a corkscrew for getting you into the place, while meanwhile the guard would certainly express disapproval of your presence by drilling several holes through you. Finally, if by any chance you did get in, how are you going to get off with all the weight of paper that you seem to have set your mind on lifting?'

'"All the weight of paper!" Mark him, comrades. This is our expert adviser who for the past month has been finding out all about it. Do you know, Nickle—no, of course you don't: you're just from Tapsfield where they make them. Acquaint yourself with the interesting fact that bank-notes for a million pounds can be carried quite comfortably in a single coat pocket.'

'A million pounds? Oh rats—a million rats just as likely! What do you say, George? Why, even Mr Bronsky—'

Joolby swung himself slowly round towards a shelf, creating by his bulk and laboured effort the impression of dumb physical pain that accompanied all his movements. Selecting a moderately small book he drew it out, verified that it was the one he sought, and flung it across the table.

'That inconsiderable book, Nickle, is the approximate surface size of a Bank of England note. How many pages are there in it?'

'Oh, about six hundred,' replied Nickle, his casual manner an ungracious protest against being drawn into this unprofitable discussion.

'"About six hundred"—five hundred and eighty four to be exact, since our friend is not sufficiently interested to be prosaically explicit. That means two hundred and ninety-two bank-note-size sheets of paper. In other words, three little books like that, allowing for the covers and extra pages, represent the bulk of a thousand notes, and a thousand notes, each for a thousand pounds, make a million sterling . . . Put that fact into your trouser-pocket, comrade Nickle, and sit on it!'

'Notes of a thousand pounds!' This time Nickle had been stirred into something like attention. 'My good Joolby, what in the name of sanity—I beg your pardon, Bronsky I—but, seriously, what do you imagine that we are going to do with notes of that fantastic value?'

'A use will be found for them, don't fear. All along, Nickle,

I have tried to make you realise that this stroke was not to be a matter of planting a few soft fivers on racecourse bookies—I used to think that you had imagination. We intend to make notes of all the values and chiefly of the big ones. George there will tell you that one is as easy to do as another and it may further interest you to know—you with your "weight of paper"—that just over two pounds and a half weigh a thousand.'

'All this is very interesting no doubt,' said Nickle, with an air of polite acceptance, 'and might even be useful in appropriate circumstances. But my inherent vein of common sense—flattering as it is to be thought romantic, Joolby—continually brings me back to the bed-rock fact that the first essential is either to get into the place ourselves or to have someone in our pay who will do it for us.'

'So. So,' agreed Joolby smoothly. 'It is one of those that we are going to do—with or without your help, friend Nickle. Now will you take this piece of paper and just sketch for me—quite rough you understand—a plan of the village, showing the mill and the other leading features? We will burn it as soon as I have got it off, never fear.'

'Delighted,' assented Nickle readily enough. 'Only too glad to show you that I know what I'm talking about.'

'Shall I as well not stay?' asked Mr Bronsky, suddenly making up his mind. 'It is more late than I thought, the other ones has not arrive, and, you remember, my hotel is a little unconvenient—' It was only too plain that the comrade's faith in the enterprise had been sadly undermined by the unfortunate turn affairs had taken.

'Just as you like, Bronsky,' replied Joolby, without the least show of ill feeling. 'I ought to have thought of your time but I left it rather open with the others—about eleven,' I believe I said, so they naturally won't hurry. However, I'll send round to you soon and let you know how we're going to fix it.'

'Ah, you still think—?' In the face of the cripple's monumental calm Bronsky's conviction was again veering.

'That this thing is going on? It's as certain as the day after tomorrow. Everything is shaping splendidly now that Nickle has done just as I intended—found out what precautions they usually take and the sort of impression they want to give strangers.'

'You mean that you expected this—that you did not trust of him a way in to discover?'

'Well, scarcely.' Joolby's great face was expressive of the most impeccable assurance. 'Nickle is hardly the kind of chap to help us in that—*you* guessed what he was all along—but he sees what lies on the surface. There's work for the others now and we'll have it all arranged and go straight forward.'

'I begin to think that you may be right. Notwithstanding, my report was to have been off sent—'

'Well, I suppose you can assure them that everything is going very well? In any case, details, even in cypher, could not be put on paper.'

Mr Bronsky's wise nods seemed to imply that this was precisely what he had intended. Nickle was still absorbed in his plan, George Larch away in thought, and there appeared to be no further inducement for the comrade to linger.

'Then I may as well—' he resumed, but his voice was now half apologetic.

'Go by all means and get a good snooze,' was Joolby's cordial advice. 'I'll let you know—a minute, though—here's someone else arriving.'

According to the arrangement he came in unannounced and for a moment stood at the door picking up the scene with a quiet, self-possessed look of well-bred interest. Scarcely the type of man to have earned the nickname 'Soapy Solomon', while the patronymic 'Klantz' would be even less convincing. This, then, must be Mr Joolby's 'gentlemanly mannered' recruit, the ex-convict Vallett. Joolby grunted a careless word, Larch contributed a friendly gesture, but it was Nickle, coming to his feet so impetuously that his chair went spinning back, who startled them all into a confused wonder as to what on earth was happening.

'Tilehurst!' he cried out sharply. 'What in hell's name are you doing here?' Then, as the newcomer continued to stand, amiably discomposed, and the others began to glance away from the two most concerned and to look at one another: 'Why don't you speak? This must be a bloody fine frame-up for you to drop in here. Are all the lot of you in it?' His hand slid to a hip pocket and the blue of steel came level. 'By God, Joolby, if you think that you are going to put me away to suit your game, the same as you did—'

'To blazes with ya next!' roared Joolby, towering above the row as the others began to join in, and killing Nickle's voice before the name was spoken. 'What's ya crazy notion now, ya rotten-hearted rabbit? What'r the hell ya think ya raisin', Nickle?'

'Why have you brought Tilehurst here?—that's what I want to know,' retorted Nickle, still excitedly worked up but beginning to recognise that, as he was hopelessly at sea, he might not have been so seriously betrayed as he had in the first rush of blank surprise passionately concluded. 'There must be some funny double-crossing going on for you to let me talk as I did and never say that he was in it.'

'Nonsense, Mr Nickle, it's you who're being funny,' put in George Larch mildly. 'This chap's name is Vallett—both Mr Joolby and I know him. All this rumpus about Tilehurst is something of your own inventing.'

'He may be Vallett to you and you may both know him,' retorted Nickle. 'But I know him just as well and it's as Tilehurst I've known him.'

'I've been seeing him pretty well every day for the last month, going there to tea and playing tennis with him—is it likely I don't know the fellow when I meet him the day after? If I stood up here just as I am and someone said: "No, this isn't Nickle—his name's Jim Snooks"—would that convince you? Look here,

Tilehurst,'—turning to the stranger—'kindly put the lot of us wise and explain the mystery of this dual existence.'

During all this lively scene Mr Vallett had remained standing near the door. He might, as Mr Joolby had implied, have become too indolent to work but he had the stage aplomb and he waited for the most effective moment to intervene with a natural actor's instinct.

'Thank you all very much indeed for this really fine reception,' he said in a quiet and very distinct tone, at the same time advancing a few steps so as to take up the centre of the picture. 'Now do you mind telling me what it's mostly about as I seem to have missed the caption?'

'Your voice is certainly miles different,' admitted Nickle grudgingly and staring very hard. 'Look here—do you actually mean to say that you aren't Geoffrey Tilehurst?'

'Not to the extent of a solitary brace button so far as I'm aware,' replied Vallett glibly. 'But if there's anything in the nature of a missing heir, or a lonely old millionaire, or even a neglected wife, I'm quite willing to oblige.'

'It's simply incredible. Except for the voice—and, yes, perhaps something in the manner—you would deceive the very devil.'

'Well, you can quite set your mind at rest about it, Nickle,' Larch assured him. 'I've known Vallett for the past two years and most of that time we've both been in—in geological research work for the Government—the granite strata of Dartmoor.'

'Julian Joolby—' purred Bronsky softly.

'I'm listening,' was the reply. Doubtless he was but his deliberate eyes were fixed on Vallett's face and the beat of his throat was distressing.

'If these two peoples are so undissimilar—'

'Crikey!' said Larch, following their thoughts; 'that's certainly an idea.'

Nickle, who ought to have been the first, was the last to catch the suggestion.

'My hat!' he exclaimed, banging the table with his fist, 'if we could put it through, what a dead cinch we should have there!'

'Well, why not?' said Joolby coolly. 'A minute ago you were ready to take your oath that he was Tilehurst. Why should anyone else be so much wiser?'

'But the voice?' objected Nickle. 'I hadn't heard that then. They're no more alike than a sparrow and a cuckoo. If we could get over that—why, dammit, even now when I look, I more than half believe that he must be!' And Vallett's back being turned just then Nickle went a step nearer and called out sharply, as if to take him by surprise:

'Tilehurst!'

But instead of being startled into admission, Vallett merely turned slowly round and politely smiling said: 'Oh, I beg your pardon! What am I supposed to do now?'

'Well, Nickle?' prompted Joolby, with the unspoken insinuation in his tone again, and this time Nickle's vista had responded further to the suggestion.

'Suppose we discount the voice—frankly I haven't a flicker of hope that it could be done, but for the sake of arguing the possibilities . . . Vallett at the most favourable moment appears there . . . He'd be walking on a mine . . . The man's position is technical and detailed; all the coaching that I could give in advance would be general and superficial . . . He must make a false move—he must give himself hopelessly away before we could profit by it. The chances are too grotesque. And the instant the real Tilehurst appeared—when that happens not only the bottom falls out but the sides cave in and the lid comes down on whatever is left of the situation . . .'

'Yes—*when*!' Joolby dropped the word significantly and left it at that to develop the implication.

'You mean—?' Nickle stopped wrinkling his brow and biting his under lip in doubt, to challenge, wide-eyed, this masterful solution.

'Again, why not? "In those godforsaken winding lanes anything may happen".'

'Quite so. But I draw the line at murder.'

'So does anyone but a fool—or a successful hero. Especially when there's no need for it. But gagged men tell no tales and we shall have plenty of nice cellar accommodation . . . Ten minutes ago I told you, Nickle, that we were going to get that paper—not because I had a glimmering how but simply because we must have it. We are still going to get that paper, Nickle—neither more nor less than we were before but perhaps you are not quite so cocksure now that it's going to be impossible to get it?'

'I should like to think we could—and this Vallett stunt is certainly a miracle. At the same time—perhaps because I know the ropes down there pretty well—I don't see how we are possibly to get over—'

'You are not being asked to see how now—from this point on I propose to do all the necessary see-howing. What you are being asked to do is to obey instructions to the letter and not to get the belly-ache whenever you visualise a copper.'

'That's a damned unpleasant thing to say,' retorted Nickle—but not so warmly as he could have wished, for the excitement of the project was taking hold of him and intoxication of any kind may equally either quicken or blunt a Nickle's *amour propre*.

'It's a damned unpleasant thing to have to deal with,' was Joolby's tart reply; 'we must make allowances for one another—Well, comrade, really going?'

It was Mr Bronsky who occasioned this aside—a smooth, complacent, and now wholly reassured Bronsky. Conversation with simple, respectful George Larch and that quite charming fellow Vallett had convinced him that everything was going to turn out finely.

'I may now just as good, since that fool place hotel of mine—' replied Bronsky, vague but unmistakably cordial. 'It goes well, Joolby?'

'It goes even better than we thought, don't you fear, comrade.

You shall hear at the next stage through one of the usual channels. It may be a week—two weeks—even three or four—but it goes; it goes inevitably.'

'I think so too, also, and I shall let headquarter know in like strain,' assented Mr Bronsky. He proceeded towards the shop, waving gracious adieux. 'God be—no! no! *Au revoir*, comrades.'

'Good night, Mr Bronsky,' Larch called after him; Vallett bestowed an engaging smile, and Nickle's casual: 'Oh, go to hell—comrade!' while conversationally given, had been just too late to create unpleasant feeling.

Won Chou, as spiritually detached as a preoccupied cat, was there to 'make unfast' the outer door, and on him the worthy man bestowed a final blessing.

'Hope, class-oppressed little comrade; hope and—!' Mysteriously pressing a finger to his lips Mr Bronsky waited to make his exit.

'Hope some piece silber, alle same, comlade,' prompted Won Chou, displaying an expectant palm, but the comrade suddenly became deeply interested in his watch and passed abstractedly into the unstirring darkness.

'We'll let it go at that, then,' conceded Nickle, reverting to the subject at the point where Bronsky had interrupted. 'You to be solely responsible for the general campaign and the plan of battle. I haven't the slightest objection to the strong, silent man, Joolby, so long as he is silent and doesn't begin to shed sawdust badly towards the finish. Bring it off in whatever way you like provided it shows nuggets, and make no mistake about my being in baldheaded with you. But money I must shortly have or my address will be Young Nick, care of Old Nick, The Shady Corner, Hades. There's one thing though—this coprolite-witted Bronsky.'

'What about him?'

Nickle shrugged his shoulders to indicate the inexpressible ambit of Mr Bronsky's obvious shortcomings.

'What not about him if it comes to that, but, specifically, he isn't in it with us. He's got some wild cat scheme of making everybody happy by making everybody else miserable. It won't wash, you know, Joolby; it isn't economically sound. Now you and I and old George and Vallett and the rest are simply out to snatch the oof, I take it, and that's a rational proposition. But Bronsky with his blasted universal brotherhood is as likely as not to queer the show if he thinks it's to the common disadvantage.'

'Leave that to me, Nickle,' said Joolby, with a reassuring look of mutual understanding. 'We are out to make big money this time and Bronsky will be useful. He can give us facilities for getting the stuff away and for putting it about on a scale that no one else could offer. If he fancies that we are doped by his communistic hog-wash so much the better; he won't work for us any the worse for thinking that we're playing his game, instead of him playing ours.'

'So long as it goes at that—'

'It does go at that, Nickle. As you say, what other end could you and I have in view except to line our pockets? Now I want you to take Vallett in hand and drill him stiff with everything that has to do with Tilehurst and Tapsfield. Of course he'll have to make up quite different and go down there and work Tilehurst for himself before we put it through but he may as well get all he can from you before he goes there.'

'Right you are; I'll put him wise,' undertook Nickle briskly. 'After all, it's entirely your circus. Shall we stay here and—?'

'No, no; take him away now and arrange it yourselves—I'll let you know what the next move is. Go—and take George as well—I want to be alone soon and I have a couple of other chaps due in about five minutes.'

'The hell you have!' said Nickle, glancing at his wrist. 'At twelve? Klantz and Soapy Solomon, I suppose, but didn't I hear you tell Bronsky that you had called them for eleven? And for the matter of that, my friend, you told me it was ten-thirty sharp and then when I was a shade behind the time chipped me for being early.'

'Did I?' conceded Joolby, discreetly vague; 'one forgets these little things when there's so much else needed. I think I must have done about enough for one day, Nickle. I'm feeling tired: very strangely tired.'

It had been a full and exacting day for Mr Joolby, even touching only so much of it as has been told, and now, Klantz and Soapy Solomon conferred with and dismissed, the uncouth bulk of The Toad lay sprawling in collapse within a great arm-chair, nothing but the arresting beat of that pendent throat to say whether he was dead or living. He might have slept indeed, but Padgett Street—itself now settled down into an uneasy drowse on a night when its tarred road bubbled—Padgett Street had long averred that Joolby never slept or even closed his eyes, but this was manifestly wrong since closed they were though his restless distempered brain denied him the relief of oblivion. Flashes of memories, doubts, hopes, hates and plans stabbed broken splinters of bright light across his sanely fanatical mind and if these had been patterned into coherent thought this would have been the thread of expression it followed:

'Help *you* to wealth and the life of easy pleasure that's your ambition, you venal jackal! And help *you* to power and Soviet rule and Universal Brotherhood, you feeble mountebank! . . . Money! Would millions buy me an hour of happiness? Power! Would any but a clown dream that such as I would give my back to be his stepping stone? Soviets, England, China, India, all the nations and the earth itself; capitalists, bourgeoisie and slaves; man and gods, I hate you equally! Universal Brotherhood! to me—to me!

'You dogs, you curs, you fawning, whining, snarling, mongrel, human pack—ah, but I'll use you to my end. Men, women and children—all, all, all alike: nothing to any but a soulless cold-blooded, grotesque toad. No man has ever thought of me with friendship, no woman looked at me without a shudder, no child withheld a stone . . . And I have waited.

'Yes, Bronsky, you shall have your way and play your little part, and after you another, bringing you and your tin-pot state crashing to the ground, and after him another to wreck him, and then another, and another, and another, until chaos meets itself right round the earth and civilization is down at last and no one left to laugh . . .

'And yet that blind man was happy and could smile as though he had lost nothing, while I—have I ever really smiled in all my life? No, I've only pulled a sort of grimace to make them think that I was like themselves. But I'll be even with him yet—that blind man who could be happy—and with Bronsky, the hopeless fool, and with Nickle for his cursed impudence, and with Larch and Vallett and Ikey and Klantz and Solomon and that whore Cora and all the other women who have shuddered and everyone I have ever known. I'll show them . . .

'They've all laughed at me behind my back, mocked and pointed and made signs. I'll see them burn, writhe, and shrivel up. I'll live to see it yet, live to shout out that I—Joolby the Toad—have done it. That will be the best of all—when they look up with their foolish, startled faces and understand at last. Then I can go down among them with a sword in my hand, and stab and slash and spit as I always long to. Oh that the whole world had one single body that I might crush it, that I might tear it with my teeth, that I might smash it into atoms!'

A sudden crash snatched Won Chou straight out of his dream of a flower-junk on the Canton river. The simple child of the East slept in a rug on the boards of the shop, wearing the dress that was his everyday garb. With stealthy glide he approached the door of his master's room, listened, cautiously peeped in, then entered.

Mr Joolby lay on the floor beside his special chair, his face doubly terrible in its rigid set, his body writhing this way and that with spasmodic jerks and contortions. An epileptic, like many exceptional personages of all times, he was only experiencing a visitation of his 'old trouble'. Smashed to a thousand bits—brought down in his fall—the wreck of a rare and delicate Dresden china group lay all about him.

Won Chou took the scene in with a face that betrayed no vestige of emotion. Silently and with neat despatch he pushed the heavy chair out of the way, spread a few draperies about the floor, forced a wad of cloth between Mr Joolby's clenched teeth, turned out the light and left him.

CHAPTER VI

TILEHURST FAILS TO KEEP AN APPOINTMENT

'ANYTHING interesting among your letters, Geoffrey?' asked Miss Tilehurst, concealing a protective curiosity under this sociable wile, since she had already inspected the covers. And to show how purely conversational the inquiry was, she reciprocally added: 'I've had nothing but a long diatribe from Geraldine Churt about her numerous ills. One would really wonder if the foolish woman thinks that her commonplace symptoms are unique or amusing.'

'No, nothing particular, Aunt,' replied Geoffrey, immediately putting the one letter that mattered away in a coat pocket. Then with the unpractised dissembler's inability to let well—or, indeed, any condition—alone, he must needs elaborate it.

'Just a bill and a couple of appeals and a line from Mostyn about the tournament, and—er—so on. None of them exciting. And, egad, is that the time? I shan't half have to do some hoofing.'

'Don't hurry immediately after your breakfast, Geoffrey. You know that clock gains five minutes every day and it's only—' called out Miss Tilehurst, but Geoffrey was technically out of earshot then and the slam of the front door put a full stop to the unfinished monition.

Of course, even if he had not fled, she could not have pursued the subject after his disclaimer—any more than she could have looked into the envelope with the unrecognised handwriting even if he had left it behind with the others now on the table. No—it was as she had guessed—that was the one that he had slipped away. As for the others—there was no harm in just glancing over them since he had said what they were and, for the matter of that, she had known almost as much before he told her. Ellicott's usual bill; Barnardo's Homes and a hospital for the mentally afflicted; a new edition of some encyclopaedia or other; a Dutch bulb grower's list (she had better look through that) and Mr Mostyn's letter. But the one in the unknown script and with a metropolitan post mark—could it be from some London Woman? In spite of having lived in the country all her life and for the most part in remote Devon, Miss Tilehurst had always understood that such beings really existed.

Meanwhile, the subject of her virginal solicitude—perfectly well aware of the clock's chronic lapse—was proceeding on his leisurely way and even finding time to take out the implicated letter again and verify its contents:

Camperdown Hotel, London.
Friday afternoon.

Dear Tilehurst,

I hope you haven't been thinking me an awful oaf for not writing to thank you for so many jolly games after I left Tapsfield? To tell the truth, I've been expecting to get down one afternoon to say 'Good-bye' before I sailed but instead I've been nearly run off my feet every day what with one thing and another. Now to top it all comes a business cable to return at once and I'm going—first part overland—tomorrow.

Now that I am on the point of leaving—with the extreme improbability of ever seeing England again—I seem to recognise how large a share your—may I say, friendship? —has had in making my visit so pleasant.

While looking out my route by that mysterious affair, Bradshaw, I have come across a detail that may enable me to salve my conscience—though it is really putting you to more trouble. The point is that instead of going right through by the connecting train (which stops at Stanbury

Junction) I shall travel by the one before and break the journey there. This will give me fifteen minutes at Stanbury—from 2.29 to 2.44. If it is not asking too much I wonder if you would cycle across and test the dubious resources of the station refreshment room in a final? I seem to remember that you are not generally particularly engaged so early on Saturday afternoon and the whole affair need scarcely take up more than half an hour.

The fact is, I have a small memento of my stay that I would like to hand over to you if you will graciously accept the trifle. I would also ask you to carry a little offering from me to Miss Tilehurst—not to repay her charming hospitality, which would be impossible, but to remind her now and then of my existence. But please don't tell her anything of this until you are back again; I should like it to be a complete surprise. In fact I wish you wouldn't mention about my going through to anyone until after— there are at least a dozen people I ought to see and although I can't help it I feel somehow guilty.

Sorry that you won't be able to let me know in any case but I shall have left the hotel for good before you get this and for the rest of the time I am bung up to the eyes clearing off arrears.

Of course if you have anything important on you must let me down but unless it's really impossible I know you are too good-natured to disappoint me.

Yours ever gratefully,

ANTHONY DIXSON.

The terms and tone of this communication made Tilehurst experience a passing sense of dereliction also.

Had he really done so frightfully much to earn Dixson's gratitude? Oddly enough, he had scarcely thought of him again, once he had passed on and out of Tapsfield, while the chap had apparently meanwhile been regarding him as his especial friend and mentor. Actually, it might be thought quite as much the other way since Dixson had certainly put him up to the knack of improving his back-hand game considerably. And in return? Well, a few hours' play each week, tea or supper if it happened to be about, and an introduction or two so as to give a stranger with plenty of time on his hands somewhere else to go to. Then—yes, he had shown him all over the works, if one could call that entertainment, and certainly these colonial beggars were pretty keen stuff when it came to technical points and wanted to see and know absolutely everything. However, since the fellow looked at it that way, the least that he himself could do would be to push along and meet him. As he said, it would scarcely mean more than half an hour's time, while so early in the afternoon he could hardly expect to encounter Nora Melhuish about if he hung around on the off chance. An opportunity to take Nipper for a good run on a hard road as well—the dog's claws were getting far too long, doing nothing but lying about all day in the garden. Certainly he would meet Dixson.

Nickle had made a wry face over writing the letter but when Joolby told him, dryly enough, to think out a better way, he had to come back to the admission that he could suggest nothing better.

'All the same, it's a dog's trick, getting a man like that,' he commented. 'I don't mind cutting him out—that's got to be done and it's all in the day's work, but a damned hypocritical letter like this—well, it's about the limit.'

'Don't be a fool, Nickle,' replied Joolby, glancing equably over the top of the paper as he considered it. 'You talk like as if you were an old-established country lawyer arranging a mortgage. And let me tell you that there are good dogs and bad dogs if you think that way about it. The good dogs get the bones and pats and the bad ones get into the lethal chamber at Battersea. Now this is a pretty fair letter.'

'Thanks for the pat, kind master,' said Nickle contemptuously.

'All the same, if it was not for the anticipated bones I might relieve my mind a little.'

'If it was not for the bones indeed, Nickle,' was the cool reply, 'what might we not all—However, these interesting side issues are never worth exploring. What is probably affecting your humour at the moment is a sort of half suspicion that the letter may implicate you personally, eh?'

'Since you mention it, whether I was thinking so or not, it certainly does have that appearance. If it comes to a *sauve qui peut* you fellows may get away but this connects me up past explaining.'

'If it comes to a *sauve qui peut*, Nickle, you'll admit that I should be a slow away-getter. For that reason I don't go into this with the idea of it turning out wrong but in the conviction that it's going to be stupendous. You're a poor psychologist, Nickle, but never mind; we'll get the letter back and wind up Anthony Dixson past all tracing.'

While it was reasonably certain that Tilehurst would respond to 'Dixson's' bait, while also the general progress of his doings could be plausibly assumed, there were crucial details on which it was vital to be exact, and arrangements had been made, and were successfully carried out, for following all his movements and for keeping the directing authority informed of each development. These headquarters were represented by a large closed motor car that had taken up a position in the lane which Tilehurst would probably choose if he cycled direct from his house to the station. But since 'Brookcroft' lay half a mile outside the village there were in fact two nearly equal routes and almost the last service of the intelligence section, after their man was seen to be committed to the journey, would be to signal by which approach he was to be expected. Nickle had made a choice of lanes but this at the best was only guesswork and the place had to be selected with an eye to the possibility of slipping round, via the station fork, into the other lane and taking up a position there if need be. In the event, this obligation did not arise. Blissfully unconscious of the fact that every step he took was being shadowed, Tilehurst trundled his bicycle out by the side gate of Brookcroft soon after two o'clock, called the over-joyed Nipper to follow, and after pausing to glance at his watch and light a cigarette, mounted and began to pedal unhurryingly towards the anticipated lane, with the easy thrust of a man who has just made a substantial meal and knows that he has plenty of time and to spare for his appointment. So far nothing could have been better.

But at the moment when everything was going so well, there came one of those unforeseeable chances that reduce even the most circumspectly arranged plots to the significance of a mere toss-up.

That grassy cut-across lane was deserted enough at any time and in the early afternoon of a hot summer day the chances were a good many to one against the risk of interruption. Yet as Tilehurst approached it, from the opposite direction appeared Sprout, the village constable, also a-wheel and bound for the same objective. He touched his hat as he turned into the lane and slackening his pace somewhat looked round to see if the other cyclist was following. With the easy social convention of the countryside (when out of doors) Tilehurst would in the ordinary course have caught him up and they would have progressed companionably wheel by wheel for as far as their way lay together, discussing the simpler aspects of Tapsfield existence. Then in a flash Tilehurst realised that Sprout would quite probably refer to Dixson—possibly to ask if he had been heard from since he had gone, or some equally inconvenient question. The predicament need not have been an embarrassing one, and, given minutes instead of seconds to make up his mind, the Joolby-Nickle plot might have very simply miscarried. But in that ambiguous period, the merest trice, allowed him for decision, Tilehurst only visualised the effect of prevaricating to Sprout about Dixson as they rode along and then—possibly under the policeman's disapproving eyes—being greeted on the platform. In the circumstances he jumped at the easiest thing—he drifted past the lane with an amiable wave of recognition, pedalled slowly along until he had given the other man ample time to have gone well away, then turned and leisurely resumed his interrupted progress in the same direction.

The roomy car now drawn up in the secluded lane had been converted to its purpose by bodily removing the inside seats, but with the blinds drawn against a blistering sun there was nothing in this to detract from its otherwise quite ordinary appearance. The spot it occupied had been picked with every consideration under review and though the available choice of road was not unlimited the place conformed well enough to the necessary conditions. It was in fact a short straight piece of ground with a bend at either end and a comparatively long straight piece of road stretching away from it in both directions. Thus, while screened itself until actually reached, anyone there could command the two approaches by walking the score or so of yards that comprised that section.

In this almost sylvan retreat—a wood behind, in front meadows seen through a grille of hedge—the occupants of the car had decided to halt and picnic, and a real table-cloth spread on the grass by the roadside indicated the thoroughness of the occasion. This development had several effects: it enabled the road to be almost blocked and anyone who passed to be constrained into a desired channel, it explained the presence of as many people lolling about as were required for the venture, and, above all, it allowed the car and its party to remain in that not otherwise very explicable spot for hours if necessary without arousing a scintilla of suspicion.

This was the carefully spread net that Geoffrey Tilehurst approached after he had given P.C. Sprout—his one chance of escape—ample time to get clear of participation. He almost tumbled upon the guileless tableau: the drawn-up car, the two men and the girl talking and laughing around the 'table', the third man—and this reduced his leisured pace still more for it was questionable which side he must pass on—the third man moving about what was left open of the roadway. Then this man appeared suddenly to realise his presence, for instead of standing aside he remained obstructively where he was, interrogation in his poise, and Tilehurst understood that he wanted to stop him.

The motor 'bandit' had not yet arrived and there was no more on the surface of the incident than if you or I had been asked for a match in Piccadilly. The cyclist obligingly pulled up (indeed, by that time he had no option), dropped one foot to the ground and waited for the inquiry.

'I say, I'm awfully sorry to trouble you like this but we haven't the murkiest idea of where we've got to. Do you mind telling me where we really are?'

'Oh, yes,' came a feminine voice from the other side the car. 'Do get to know, Tommy. It's about time we pushed off if we're to do any bathing.'

Tilehurst was one of those amiable creatures who find an altruistic pleasure in performing these small services—telling the time and the way, guiding a blind beggar across the road, recovering a lost ball, making up the penny deficiency in the bus fare for old ladies who have somehow miscalculated their resources. If he gave a thought to the one weakness of the contrivance—for why had they not asked Sprout, that obvious official fount of information?—he at once dismissed it as capable of some very simple explanation.

'Well, it's about a mile and a half to Tapsfield along the lane,' he replied, turning to nod in the required direction. 'The way I'm going will bring you to the cross-road near Stanbury Junction and on to Crowgate or Slowcumber according to which you take. Or, of course, back to Tapsfield if you turn sharp at the Dog and Plover.'

'Ask him—ask him where we *are*,' chimed in the girl's voice again. 'I don't know that we're actually pining to get to any of those earthly paradises he's mentioned.'

The spokesman smiled apologetically. 'You see what it is,' said the look, establishing the male understanding. Then aloud: 'I wish you'd just pick out the place on the map for us; I've got one here quite handy.' Without waiting for the implied assent he opened the near door of the car and disappeared within, reappearing a moment later with a large road map that he spread out, but remaining just inside the car himself so that it became necessary for Tilehurst to go nearer.

One of the other men had meanwhile strolled round and the way was still barred—to use so harsh a term about so fortuitous a happening—against escape in that direction. And now the last man in sight got up from the sward, apparently taking a handkerchief from his pocket to brush stray crumbs away, and casually passing round the car on the unguarded side closed the trap at its final outlet. Still every face had the conventional, agreeable air of those who are being obliged, the girl just across the road began to carol a little popular snatch lightly, and 'Tommy', at the car step, following the line of his own finger was murmuring: 'Now let me see; we are—where?' as he travelled halfway across the county waiting for the obliging stranger to inform him.

Tilehurst knew that he had plenty of time to the good and he did exactly what had been foreseen he would do. In any case the result would have been the same then, although the details might not have dovetailed quite so workmanly. He swung himself wholly out of his bicycle, propped up the machine against the car wheel and turned to the open door to point out the position on the map now held out towards him. The man with the handkerchief was immediately behind, intending seemingly to look on as well. The third man . . . The map was a large limp sheet and Tilehurst was constrained to put out both hands to receive it.

What actually happened he never quite knew himself, for the universe of conscious thought rushed to extinction at one unbearably crowded point and afterwards everything to do with that episode was dim and tangled. But in the other participants' sight it was far from being confused, for every detail had been carefully considered and rehearsed and each one did his part in perfect time and precision. 'Tommy', holding out the map, closed with a rat-trap grip on the wrists of the two hands coming towards him; the saturated cloth was pressed against Tilehurst's nose and mouth; the other man, practising the simple schoolboy stroke, brought their victim to his knees on the running-board, as helpless as a ditched wether among the three men crowding round him. The girl continued to sing about love and undying devotion. In fifteen seconds the anaesthetic had done its work and the inert body was cleanly lifted into the car, to be stripped, reclothed, bound, gagged and left, covered with rugs, unconscious on the floor. It would scarcely be too much to say that people might have gone by without noticing that anything unusual was happening.

Three minutes later an identical Tilehurst emerged from the car; the others paused in their orderly work—they were removing every tell-tale trace and preparing for return—to inspect him critically.

'Oh, boy, but you sure look some!' was drawn from one in frank approval. 'Now that you're in his togs the guy's own mother wouldn't suspish you.'

It was possible indeed, but there was one small faithful friend who was not to be duped by clothes or outward appearance. Nipper, having taken the opportunity of his master's inattention to engage in a private rat hunt along a drain, had voluntarily returned, and after puzzling over the situation unnoticed from several points of view, had abruptly decided that there was dirty work afoot and this spuriosity the villain. Uttering foolishly futile yaps of challenge—his sure undoing—Nipper heroically launched himself against the foe, only to be met by a straight deliberate kick that sent him reeling. Before the little dog could collect himself again Vallett had snatched up the readiest tool—a weighty spanner—and with a single vicious blow had settled all Nipper's doubt and questionings for ever. Four white upraised paws quivered protestingly to heaven, the body shuddered, and a dead dog with a battered skull lay on the reddening herbage. In that moment one seemed to have a glimpse of the cool and desperate convict who had got away from Dartmoor, despite warders' loaded guns, in place of the smiling Vallett.

'Damn you, you brute! Why need you go and do that?' shrilled the girl, suddenly whirled into a flimsy passion. 'I'd have taken the little dog and looked after it myself—I'd have loved to . . . Bloody fine thing being able to out a great big beast like him, I should think . . . bloody well proud of yourself, aren't you?' For quite half a minute she slanged aimlessly on while the others looked at her with no more than grave disapproval. To tell the truth, the unforeseen tragedy of the loyal little terrier had got them all more than anything that had gone before.

'That'll do, kid; shut up your face now, you've shed plenty,' said one of the men with brusque understanding. 'Vallett did quite right; the pup was bound to go and that's all that's to it. Rip off the collar, Pips, and shove the rest under some stuff in the wood there.'

'Yes, but what'n they find it there?' questioned the man who had used the drug, as he carefully handled the body. 'These country birds know all the dogs for miles around so shifting the collar won't help any.'

'What the hell then? It's all of a piece, isn't it? Besides, they most likely won't—get it well away into a thick scrub and it'll likely be there for months before that happens. Now, buddy,'— this to Vallett—'Number two's coming in and he'll go on and give Soapy the nod and then pass it back on you when Soapy's planted. We're through here?'

'Not quite,' said Vallett, who had apparently been dreaming.

'I feel that I ought to carry some marks. The artistic sense demands it. Put me one fairly high—you needn't black an eye or tap the claret—but something that'll show a bruise for the next few days anyhow.'

'You mean it?'

'Didn't I speak?' inquired Vallett politely. The other smiled a dour aside and with a clean crisp right laid the artistic conscience sprawling on the level. He got up with no loss of graciousness, dusting his clothes, but on second thoughts left them as they were, to infer the happening.

'Oh my God!' wailed the girl, looking on with tightly clasped hands. Vallett didn't deign to notice.

'Satisfied?' grinned the big man.

'That will do for that, I expect, but I think I ought to show some scratches.' Going to the hedge he selected and hacked out a bramble switch and brought it back; its curved thorns were as formidable as a wild cat's claws. 'Put that across my face, will you?'

'Don't!' This time the kid rose to a scream of anguish. 'I take it all back about the dog. He had to go, I see. Only don't—'

'You?' cut in Vallett with elegant disdain. 'What in all creation have you got to do with it?'

'I know well enough,' she blubbered. 'You think you're paying me out—'

'Get on with it,' said Vallett curtly. 'Shut your eyes then,' advised the other, taking the switch, and this time he was not grinning. 'I don't want to go and blind you.'

'Keep your own open and then you won't,' was the unconcerned reply. 'I have nothing to shut mine for.'

'Look out then.' The cane slashed across mouth and cheeks and a dozen points of blood followed the thorns' withdrawal. Vallett forbore to wince. The girl ran back to the car making curious noises.

CHAPTER VII

DR OLIVANT ESTABLISHES HIS BONA FIDES

At about the hour when an unobtrusive motor car (its number plate varied for the third time that eventful day) was taking its turn through Reigate, with Mr Geoffrey Tilehurst—now sufficiently recovered to feel extremely sick—a very helpless passenger, and while in Hoggets Lane Mr Vallett was, to use a peculiarly inappropriate metaphor, 'cooling his heels' as he awaited an agreed signal, the sun went off the rose bed in the Brookcroft trim front garden and Miss Tilehurst, armed with leather gloves, sheep shears and a Sussex trug, came out to carry on the unending warfare that exists between man (as represented in the amateur gardener) and relentless nature.

'Yes, of course; just as might have been expected,' she declared after scrutinising the roses. 'Teeming with greenfly— and our rates are seven-and-sixpence in the pound! Ophelia!'

It is, to be sure, impossible to predict what lines of growth a child will take from the evidence of, say, the first seven days, and there have been Ophelias and Ophelias. This one, the offspring of an ill-assorted union between a pig higgler and an idealistic lady's maid, clearly belonged to the second variety. Other mistresses—and the girl had experienced a remarkable succession of these before Miss Tilehurst penetratingly discovered in her certain solid qualities (in the sense of 'dense' to most employers) that covered many shortcomings—other mistresses had invariably called her by what they considered more suitable names, generally Jane or Sarah, without reference to her own feelings. Penelope Tilehurst questioned whether this was 'quite right' and on the other interested party's vague justification that 'some thought one thing and some another', severely retorted that this was not the point and that in any case Ophelia—with appropriate instances—was nothing to be ashamed of.

Ophelia had a way of anticipating wants when she was called. If right, she had discovered that this was regarded as rather clever, but if it happened to be wrong there was no doubt that she was being very stupid. Privately, she thought that a simpler average should be struck, but anyway she was like that, she admitted. She now appeared carrying a filled watering can and, as this happened to be right, she felt that she had established her position sufficiently to remain and sociably discuss botanical prospects.

'That Mrs Buffy I was with was a rare 'un for gardening too,' she remarked as a general opening. 'Only she was all for snapdragers. Funny she shouldn't know their proper name, wasn't it, mum? She always used to call them Auntie Rhinos.'

'Yes, Ophelia, but I shall want several more cans to go on this bed,' replied Miss Tilehurst discouragingly. 'You had better get the other one out as well and keep bringing them.'

'That I will, mum.' Hard work had no terror for the simple girl, especially when, as in the present case, it involved nothing with a tendency to 'just come apart' and contained easy openings for agreeable conversation. 'Oh; what had we better say if they catch us at it?'

'What's that?' demanded Miss Tilehurst sharply. 'What do you mean, Ophelia?'

'It's the notice what that man left—I forgot to give it you,' explained Ophelia, producing a crumpled printed form from the mysterious depths of her apron pocket. 'It says that owing to the draft we shall be incurring a penalty of forty shillings for the first offence and not exceeding fourteen days ever after.'

'Nonsense.' Miss Tilehurst had a sublime faith in the personal equation, which sometimes worked out but occasionally failed to be quite so successful. 'That can't apply to me of course. I pay a water rate and anyone can see that the garden needs watering. Put the notice in the fire and then I shall be able to say truthfully that I haven't seen it.'

'That I will, mum,' undertook Ophelia stoutly.

'And—wait a minute, Ophelia; don't run away, child, when I'm in the middle of speaking. There's someone doing something in the lane out by the side gate—that tinkering has been going on for the past half hour. On your way back just glance out there—you needn't let it appear that you've gone on purpose: you can seem to be looking up the lane as if you expected the baker.'

'He doesn't come till later of a Saturday,' objected Ophelia, entering into the spirit of the strategy perhaps even too precisely.

'That doesn't matter in the least. They are not to know or you may be looking for the butcher. But if there are gipsies or tinmen about we shall have to keep our eyes open after anything they can lay their hands on.'

Of course it was Ophelia's fault; she ought to have come back with a more coherent tale, but when on her return with the second can she breathlessly reported, '. . . the man. Something about water. And—look out, mum, he's coming!' Miss Tilehurst not unnaturally jumped—quite literally, indeed—to the conclusion that this man must be identical with 'that man' and the reference to water was only capable of one construction. In spite of her assurance of personal immunity from the obnoxious order it began to look more serious when this emissary of injustice would seem to have deliberately tracked her down, and it was her rather frantic efforts to conceal her own can among the rose bushes on his approach, and at the same time to induce Ophelia by vigorous gestures to retire in good order with the other, that prevented her from grasping at the outset exactly what it was that the stranger was talking about.

'I wonder if I might trouble you?' was what he really said. 'I see you are busy with it yourself—just a small can of water?' Quite a personable individual he appeared to be—dignified, well-dressed, urbane, and he advanced doffing his distinctive hat with a ceremonialism that could not have failed to impress Miss Tilehurst if she had been composed enough to realise it.

'Oh no, indeed I'm not—I can assure you that I never use a watering can in the garden,' she exclaimed, rather remarkably in the circumstances; meaning, as she afterwards assured herself, that she was not actually using one *then* and that in any case she only watered certain special beds and did not—as so many thoughtless people did—waste precious canfuls drenching the entire garden.

'I—I beg your pardon.' The intruder was, not altogether unnaturally, for the moment nonplussed by the denial he had occasioned, but this did not in the least affect the magnificent composure of his bearing. 'The fact is,' he deigned to explain with gracious allowance for any misunderstanding, 'my chauffeur happens to be away ill and I'm having some bother with my engines and being held up just outside your gate here.'

'Oh. Oh? Oh!' apologised Miss Tilehurst on several notes of emotion. 'Then you are not the—er—the water authority?'

'Madam,' he affably admitted, with the light touch of a playful buffalo, 'I am no authority on water in any form—not even, I regret to find, on the water cooling my own car engines. I'm afraid that my intrusion rather startled you—I ought to have been more explicit. At least permit me to establish my bona fides before I go. My name is Olivant—Dr Olivant of Harley Street. I am merely a stranger, you see, motoring through your charming district and having, so to speak, fallen by the wayside—'

'Oh, Dr Olivant, I *am* so sorry,' protested the lady, deeply mortified at the unfortunate blunder.

'Of course now that I really look at you—' and, without actually being so bold as to put the inference into words, Miss Tilehurst made it abundantly clear that in her opinion no one who really looked at him could by any chance take Dr Olivant for anything resembling a water inspector. 'But seriously, you know, in this water famine the company is driving us half crazy with its absurd prohibitions and regulations. That,' she explained, speaking with extreme clarity and deliberation, 'is what I meant just now when I said that a watering can is never much use in the garden. Of course it needs the hose pipe to be effective.'

'Oh, of course—naturally,' agreed Dr Olivant. 'And they don't permit—'

'Oh my goodness no! It would be a crime of'—the situation had gone a little to her head—'ha! ha! Dr Olivant, a crime of the first water!'

'Ha! ha!' weightily confirmed Dr Olivant. 'Very apt, indeed. "A crime of the first water"! I must tell my colleague, Sir Peter Mullaby, that. He'll appreciate it.'

'And I—ahem!—hear,' added Miss Tilehurst, determined to clear her conscience thoroughly by the white fire of voluntary confession, 'that very soon we *may* not be allowed to use even a watering can.'

'Really?' contributed the doctor, suitably impressed. 'In the circumstances I scarcely like to repeat my request for a small canful.'

'Oh nonsense, Dr Olivant; it hasn't quite come to that yet. Ophelia—give Dr Olivant the can you have. Will that be sufficient for your purpose, Doctor?'

'Oh, quite I think. Thank you; thank you. I won't keep it a minute longer than I can help, I need hardly say.'

'Pray don't hurry. And if you should want any more—Of course'—as he reached the gate—'you unscrew the nozzle for pouring.'

'Oh quite so,' he acquiesced. Really, did the woman take him for a loon or was it that she only wanted to hear the sound of her own silly tongue clacking?

In the circumstances Miss Tilehurst decided to go on gardening there—not watering, which would take Ophelia off her work and could be done equally well later, but just tidying up the beds. Then if Dr Olivant should happen to need—A most distinguished-mannered gentleman—a specialist, of course, being in Harley Street—and how immeasurably different from the usual type of country doctor! Dr Tyser, for instance, was well enough but ineradicably commonplace, while this locum tenens he had just got—well, it was *said* that he had been seen buying fried fish himself at one of those malodorous little places in Mutbury. The idea of Dr Olivant going into—

'Coo-ee!' said a voice in playful claim of recognition.

'Well, well; I wondered if you would run round this afternoon, Nora. How long have you been there? I never heard you coming.'

Nora Melhuish was, it may be recalled, the speculative element in the timetable of Tilehurst's arrangements, and now that we have been permitted to see her the only possible slur on his taste is that he should have taken even the most infinitesimal risk of missing so delectable an encounter. For the rest, she was nineteen, rather small, rather brown, and rather mysterious in her impressions. On this occasion she wore neither hat nor gloves but carried a moderate basket, and as she had come into the garden by the front, or road, gate and along the further path she had evidently failed to encounter the prepossessing specialist.

'Oh, not long,' replied Nora as they went through the ritual of kissing. 'Only I heard you talking to someone so I slunk. Who is he?'

'A Dr Olivant—a Harley Street specialist, or at least I suppose he must be. At any rate his car has broken down just outside there and he wanted some water.'

'That's what everyone seems to be wanting just now—I feel I'm getting it on the brain myself. Mrs Hattock says that the vicar is doubtful if he ought to go on praying for rain any longer—it seems to be making a fool of him when nothing happens.'

'Oh, my dear! Isn't that rather—I mean for a clergyman?'

'Well, perhaps it is but they certainly seem to be getting

much more snappy. Are you watering the roses? Haven't they cut off your supply yet?'

'Good gracious no. Are they going to?'

'They say so—all except an hour or two night and morning. And someone goes round listening at those little trap-door affairs in the road to catch you wasting any. And then fine you.'

'Can they tell that? My dear! what next? And here that tiresome Ophelia is bringing out another canful! Take that back again at once, Ophelia, and don't draw any more.'

'All right,' acquiesced the impassive Ophelia. 'Good afternoon, miss. Just stepped across to see if we were all alive still? Shall I put this lot on the beans, mum?'

'No, we haven't got to waste any. Pour it down the sink quickly.'

'That I will, mum.' A rather constrained silence marked the time until Ophelia was out of hearing. 'Of course I'm glad to find you alive but I really ran across with a few pears if you care to have them,' remarked Nora, displaying the contents of her basket. 'Jargonelles. We've got heaps and heaps and I know that yours are all the late kinds.'

'Thank you, dear. They look delicious. You must let me reciprocate towards Christmas. But how did you know that ours are only keepers?'

'Oh I don't know. Oh yes I do. Geoffrey must have told me.'

'I see. "You plant pears; For your heirs." Well, whoever planted ours must have credited his posterity with remarkably good teeth. And speaking of that young man, you didn't happen to see anything of Geoffrey as you came along, did you?'

'No; isn't he here?' said Nora. 'I expected to find—At least I thought—What I mean is, if we happen to meet and neither of us is doing anything—'

'That's all right, my dear,' said Geoffrey's adopted mother, '—at least I hope that it's going to be. And I'm glad it's you, Nora. It will make me very happy.'

'Oh, Miss Tilehurst, do you really mean that you've noticed anything? I thought that we were both being extraordinarily discreet, and for that matter, he—Geoffrey—hasn't actually said anything.'

'No; I noticed that you were both rather tongue-tied of late,' commented Miss Tilehurst dryly. 'Well, my dear, if I am to lose my only nephew—and of course I know that in a place like this a young man's fancy must turn sooner or later to thoughts of either love or golf—I prefer it to be you.'

'Oh, you are a dear!' exclaimed Nora, who has been placed at a considerable disadvantage by being introduced just at this stage of her florescence. 'It would have been too awful if you hadn't—'

'It's so very handy you living just over the way,' continued Miss Tilehurst, pursuing her own line of speculation. 'At least I shall always know where to find him.'

'Well,' laughed Nora, 'that's one way of looking at it. But I hope that isn't the only reason.'

'No,' admitted Miss Tilehurst circumstantially. 'Still, it's a great convenience all the same.'

'And please, please, don't let Geoffrey know that we have been talking—'

'My dear! I'm not an absolute beginner. I can't think where he can have got to.'

'Why; where did he go?'

'That's just what I don't know. He must have gone off somewhere immediately after lunch without saying anything about it. He may have ridden across to Cobbet Corner to see about some repairs to a few cottages I have there, or he may have gone to arrange some details of the Gymkhana Tournament with Mr Mostyn who'd written to him this morning. But's it's so unlike him not to mention what time to expect him back or where he was going—especially on a day when you might drop in and miss him.'

'But of course he wouldn't have the faintest idea that I should be here, Miss Tilehurst,' protested Nora. 'Why, I had no idea of it myself until I happened to think—'

'Well,' dubiously agreed Miss Tilehurst, 'perhaps he wouldn't. All the same I had a strong presentiment that way myself and there is no reason why the state of his emotions should make him less intelligent.'

'Perhaps Ophelia saw which way he went,' suggested Nora. 'She's just gone across to the coal house.'

'It's quite as likely she asked him where he was going if she did,' declared Miss Tilehurst grimly.

'At any rate it won't be difficult to find out. I'll warrant she only wanted coal on the chance of a little small talk. Oh, Ophelia; Mr Geoffrey doesn't happen to have come in at the back while we've been here, does he?'

'No, mum, or I should have seen him . . . He got his bicycle out after lunch and went off with Nipper . . . He didn't say where he was going . . . When I just said: "Going out for a ride on your bicycle, Mr Geoffrey?" he said: "No, Ophelia, I'm going for a three-legged race only I like to wear this on my watch chain." I thought it sounded funny.'

Presumably Nora thought so too for she found it necessary to turn aside and bury her face in a crimson rambler. Miss Tilehurst found it less amusing.

'Thank you, Ophelia; that will do. Tell him we are out here if he does return that way.'

'Yes, mum.' Ophelia appeared to weigh the conditions with conscientious detail. 'You mean if he returns in a three-legged race?'

'No, no. If he returns without our seeing him—if he comes in the back way.'

'Oh yes. That I will, mum.'

Ophelia retired in the full assurance that this must be one of her good days as she was acquitting herself so successfully and at intervals snatches of her voice could be heard, subdued by the occasional clatter or bang of domestic zeal, as she confided all that was going on to the cat—sole confidant of her deeper feelings.

'Isn't she too dreadful?' lamented Miss Tilehurst, as Ophelia disappeared towards the house. 'But she's really such a good, well-meaning girl that I can't find it in my heart to be strict with her.'

'No, indeed; it would spoil a gem—think of all the priceless things you'd miss hearing. But, you know, if Geoffrey is trundling a pushbike on a day like this, that might easily account for him not getting back as soon as he had intended.'

'True; I expect that's what it is. And speaking of bicycles, Nora, who was the young lady I saw dashing about the road on a motor cycle when I looked out at five o'clock this morning?'

'Well, what's the use of your brother having a motor bike if you can't practise on it when he's away? It's about the only chance I do get.'

'Oh? This is the first I've heard of you taking it up at all. I'm not an authority, I suppose, for I've always been accustomed to regard even a foot tricycle as rather an advanced form of propulsion for a woman but you struck me as being remarkably capable for a learner.'

'I am,' admitted Nora, with what could only be described as a knowing grin; '—but please don't let on to anyone about it. I mean to surprise them one of these days.'

'Them?'

'Yes, all at home—oh, my word! my poor wits must indeed be wool-gathering! Do you know what I came across for?'

'Well,' replied Miss Tilehurst, with a spice of affectionate malice, 'feminine intuition might be equal to the problem. Put into cold words I should say that you came—not to see Geoffrey, of course, but to afford him the unutterable pleasure of contemplating Miss Melhuish.'

'Not at all—that may have been why I came perhaps, but it wasn't what I came for. In spite of that truly feline stroke, dear Miss Tilehurst, I came to do you a kindness. Well, you know all about Uncle Max of course—you've always said how you wished to meet him.'

'What—Mr Carrados?'

'Yes, Uncle Max Carrados. Well, he turned up all unexpected this morning in his usual eccentric way. Shall I bring him across for an hour now? I would have done straight off but I thought you'd like to know he was coming.'

'Yes indeed,' agreed Miss Tilehurst, rather fluttered at the prospect. 'I should certainly be glad of a few minutes to make myself a little more presentable. But do you think that he would really care—?' and with almost tragic eloquence the disparaging hands indicated the circumscribed garden in which they stood, the unpretentious little villa.

'But whatever do you mean? Why shouldn't he?'

'Well, I should be overjoyed by the honour of course but I mean—wouldn't it be rather dull for him? I feel that there ought to be something rather special going on to bring him here for—only there never is for that matter.'

'Oh nonsense, dear. Isn't he with us now, and what's the difference? He doesn't spend every day of his life tracking murderers down and bearding robbers in their dens. Although he's so jolly well off—and rather clever, I suppose—he's really the simplest old dear in the world.'

'Old?' The word was rather startling to Miss Tilehurst. 'I didn't know that Mr Carrados was at all elderly.'

'Oh yes. He must be quite forty now. That's getting on pretty well in years, I should think.'

'Yes, I suppose it is,' admitted Miss Tilehurst with a backward glance. 'It certainly once seemed so. I'll tell you what we'll do to make it something special, Nora: we'll have tea out in the arbour over there. That will be quite like a picnic, won't it, and Geoffrey is certain to be back in time to join us.'

'Splendid!' agreed Nora, already on her way towards the gate; 'I'll dig out Uncle Max and we'll dash back in no time.'

'But you'll give me just a few minutes to—I'm in the middle

of gardening you know; I feel an awful fright,' pleaded Miss Tilehurst who was rooted in a more ceremonial age when important visitors were not flung upon one 'in no time'.

'Right you are—will twenty minutes do? Oh no; never mind the old basket now—I'll take it later on. Cheerio!'

'Splendid!' endorsed Miss Tilehurst to herself as another gate, fifty yards away, reverberated on its sorely tried hinges. 'But how very strenuous!'

CHAPTER VIII

MAX CARRADOS BECOMES INTERESTED IN TRIFLES

WITH twenty minutes—which probably meant half an hour in the end—up her sleeve so to speak, Miss Tilehurst felt that she had the situation well in hand, and she even stayed to finish off her work of cutting out the faded roses from the central bed before she gathered everything into the Sussex trug and began to think of her own preparations. Otherwise she might have missed Dr Olivant on his second incursion into her domain and although the interest of the afternoon had shifted materially with the arrangement for Mr Carrados's visit, it was not to be denied that the doctor—whom even nineteen would scarcely presume to call old—cut a very personable figure.

'I am returning the watering can with very many thanks,' he said in the ceremonious way which Miss Tilehurst thought so distinguished, 'but I am afraid that you will think me no end of a nuisance. I find now that if I am to do any good I shall have to borrow a hammer.'

'Well, I fancy that the resources of my establishment may be even equal to that,' replied Miss Tilehurst with the sort of smile which so arch a reply demanded. 'At all events, if you will wait here a minute—'

'I feel that I am giving you a great deal of trouble.'

'So far I haven't observed it. And in any case you aren't doing now since my very exceptional maid is evidently hovering about on the chance of being useful. She has the remarkable quality, Dr Olivant,' confided Miss Tilehurst, holding up a beckoning finger in Ophelia's direction, 'of generally being there if she is wanted—or, indeed, if she is not wanted. Ophelia, bring this gentleman a hammer, will you? I expect that you'll find one in the kitchen table drawer.'

'That I will, mum,' replied Ophelia, dashing off like a young mustang.

In the circumstances it did not seem quite nice to Miss Tilehurst to leave one who might be technically regarded as a guest standing there alone. Ophelia could be trusted to be back, as she would herself declare, 'in half a jiffy', and the doctor would be equal to the conversational moment.

'What a lovely old-English kind of garden you have,' he dutifully remarked. 'Flowers are a passion of mine, but of course in Harley Street—' a melancholy shake of the head dismissed that famous but unhorticultural thoroughfare from the landscape.

'At all events you shall have one for your button-hole now, Doctor,' said Miss Tilehurst, sacrificing a promising young Betty Uprichard without the least compunction. 'Yes, it is rather flourishing, but of course this dreadful drought—Still, if you are going for a holiday I don't suppose that you will complain on the score of fine weather.'

'I am hoping to reach Eastbourne tonight. Even a doctor—even a nerve specialist—has to knock off now and then—Mrs—er?'

'Tilehurst, Doctor. *Miss* Tilehurst.'

'Miss Tilehurst? Curious. A very old patient of mine—Sir Bellamy Binge—had a sister who married—'

'Here you are, sir,' interposed Ophelia, breaking upon this momentous reminiscence and thrusting a decidedly infirm-looking tool into the doctor's hand. 'Don't think you've gone and done it if the head flies off when you're hitting. It often does.'

'Oh, Ophelia,' said her mistress in some concern, 'surely we have a better—'

'This will do capitally, my dear Miss Tilehurst, I do assure you,' professed Olivant. 'The strain I shall put upon it is not likely to result in any disaster,' and since Miss Tilehurst was not anxious to detain him if it really would do, he retired again to grapple with the intricacies of his car in the quiet side lane while she took the opportunity of apprising Ophelia of the variation in their usual routine as they went up to the house together.

'We shall be having tea in the summer-house this afternoon, Ophelia. Miss Melhuish is bringing a gentleman here and I want to have things a little different.'

'Tea in the summer-house, mum! That will be nice, won't it?' Ophelia was intrigued, visibly impressed, but also inconveniently reminded. 'Did you ever have tea in a hay-field, mum? I did once and you wouldn't believe—'

'No—yes, but never mind that just now, Ophelia. This gentleman who is coming is blind and so I want you to be very careful.'

'That I will, mum. Does he have a toby dog, I wonder?'

'Dog?' repeated Miss Tilehurst vaguely.

'Yes, to lead him about the street. Most of them do. Mother had an Uncle Billy—'

'You must tell me about your mother's uncle—er—William another time—I want you to get on with your work now. Mr Carrados has an attendant, not a dog, but I do not imagine that he will bring him here. Now change as quickly as you can and then put out the things in the kitchen ready.'

'Were you meaning to use the company tea set out there—the little old cups with blue and gold things on them?'

'Yes, the Crown Derby service—and please *do* be careful with them, Ophelia. Then you had better cut both white and brown bread-and-butter, some very thin anchovy paste and cucumber sandwiches, and we will have quince jelly and strawberry jam and for cake cherry and almond.'

'I say!' murmured Ophelia.

'Anything else I will see to myself and I will look in at the kitchen between now and then to make sure that you have all the things ready. And, by the way, Ophelia, you may as well put out cups and so on for five—one never knows; someone else may drop in.'

'You know that I am bringing Uncle Max, don't you, Miss Tilehurst dear? And you know that you are coming to Miss Tilehurst's, don't you, Uncle Max dear? So surely that's enough? I think formal introductions are frightfully stuffy.'

Miss Tilehurst, with everything going well, had been out in the front garden again when her visitors appeared. Visualising Mr Carrados's arrival she had rather dreaded the ceremony of getting the blind man into a chair in her crowded little drawing-room and almost immediately getting him out again. On a day like that nothing seemed more natural than to be sauntering about the lawn, and then they could stroll round the garden until tea appeared. After all, what was the good of taking a man who could not see into a drawing-room?

Both laughed as they shook hands but Miss Tilehurst felt that she had been defrauded of something that she had looked forward to by Nora's offhand manner, and she was glad that Mr Carrados took the occasion to rebuke his niece—though of course it was done in the nicest possible manner.

'I am afraid that the rising generation thinks a great deal that we used to set considerable store by "frightfully stuffy",' he remarked mildly. 'I say "we" hoping that Miss Tilehurst sides with me.'

'So it was, Uncle Max,' retorted Nora. 'Ghastly stodgy. Family pride and great fat dinners and social tradition. All that hank and bunk and tosh and spludge. Sickening.'

'Well, my dear, I hope that I am not too old to learn even yet. I must begin with the New Vocabulary.'

'It is not we who are too old to learn, Mr Carrados; it's they who are too young to understand,' put in Miss Tilehurst a shade tartly. 'Now would you care to walk round the garden and see—oh, forgive me! I—I—'

'You pay me a great compliment, Miss Tilehurst,' said

Carrados reassuringly. 'Already you treat me as an ordinary human being, you see, not as a helpless log. That is what I want people simply to do—flatter me that I'm not a nuisance. Certainly I should like to go round your garden and perhaps I shall not miss much. Here, for instance, at the very start there is something that I haven't come across for years'—he turned to the rose bed near which they had been standing and indicated a particular bush—'you can only find this in an old-established garden nowadays. I hear that it's quite gone out of fashion.'

'Why, is there anything special about it?' demanded Nora. 'It looks a very ordinary sort of flower as far as that goes.'

'Nothing but its extreme rarity: it would almost seem as though modern conditions kill it. Miss Tilehurst knows what it is, I'll be bound. Don't you see: she's laughing?'

'Oh go on, have your little joke, my dears,' said Nora benignly. 'What is the great scream anyway? I know you're dying to tell me.'

'It's only an old-fashioned cabbage-rose, Nora, and it's called The Maiden's Blush. The curious thing is that it has become almost extinct for some reason.'

'Ha! ha!' Nora affected a mechanical laugh such as is current in the school-room to express non-amusement. 'But there are still red cabbages about. They are the sort that get into pickles.'

'Both sorts have their points no doubt. There was a bush of this against the porch of our old home when I was a boy—'

'Now, now, Uncle; if you are going to wax sentimental over a cabbage—well, a cabbage-rose or a rose-cabbage, I don't mind—whatever will you be like when we get to the horse-radishes? Come along, old dear,' she prompted, taking his arm affectionately; 'I think Miss Tilehurst wants to speak to someone for a minute.'

It was, as might be guessed, the punctilious Olivant come to return the tool, for surely it would be extravagant to suggest that he could have any interest in looking into the circumstance of these fresh arrivals in Miss Tilehurst's garden. Nor is it to be assumed that the lady herself had any wish to neglect him, for instead of pleading her guests to get off with a perfunctory 'Oh, thank you', she sent them on ahead, saying: 'Excuse me just a moment, please. Take Mr Carrados along, won't you, Nora?' and waited for the doctor.

'May I thank you and return the hammer?' he said, with his usual air of raising even the slightest act into a courtly ceremony. 'You will be relieved to hear that there was no untoward mishap.'

Uncle and niece had sauntered on but at the first words of that distinctive voice Nora found herself gently detained as Mr Carrados paused to 'look at' a fine dahlia.

'Who is our friend over there?' he asked, dropping his voice to a discreet whisper.

'Oh, he isn't anybody—I mean he doesn't live about here,' she replied, with the same precaution. 'Some London doctor or other. Elephant? No, Olivant, a Harley Street specialist she said. That's his car come to grief in the side lane.'

'Ah.' There must have been some incautious quality in his tone for Nora fastened on the simple interjection.

'Why "Ah" fraught with all that portent, old dear? You don't happen to know him, do you?'

'I don't know any Dr Olivant, Nora.'

'Well then, you don't know him. Why won't you say so in a plain straightforward manner, Uncle Max? I'm afraid you're getting to be rather too fond of being mysterious when there's nothing at all to make a mystery out of.'

'Yes, possibly it is becoming a habit with me, my dear,' he admitted. 'I must reform or I shall become the very worst sort of back number.'

'*Dear* Uncle Max!' murmured Nora happily. Life was all such an enchanting game, wasn't it?

Meanwhile, Miss Tilehurst, having received the hammer with due relief, was furthering the little idea that had occurred to her in the kitchen.

'If you don't actually need to drive off immediately, Dr Olivant, perhaps you would take a cup of tea with us before you go on? We shall be having it out here very simply on the lawn presently.'

'You are really extremely kind, Miss Tilehurst. I should certainly enjoy a cup of tea after my exertions.'

'We are only waiting for my nephew to get back—and if he is much longer we must perforce begin without him. Would about ten minutes—?'

'Admirably for me. I think I've located the trouble but I haven't quite put it right yet.'

'Then that is settled,' she confirmed. 'I will let you know when tea is ready.'

'Isn't it really too bad of Geoffrey just on this of all afternoons?' lamented Miss Tilehurst after she had consulted her ancient gold watch for the fifth time within ten minutes. 'I can only suppose that he has met someone who has inveigled him in for a few games of tennis.'

'Not likely—if he didn't go out in flannels,' objected Nora. 'Ten to one that he has drifted back to that utterly rancid old office to put some extra work in. On a day like this too!'

'Nora!' exclaimed Miss Tilehurst almost severely—the family woman's inherent reverence for the source of bread-and-butter—'the office is his business. My nephew, Mr Carrados,' she explained, 'is connected with the paper mills here where they make the Bank of England note paper. It is, of course, a highly responsible position.'

'Yes,' agreed Carrados, 'naturally—where they make the Bank of England note paper. And how extraordinarily interesting his work there must be. Has he to do directly with the paper when it's made or is his department purely clerical?'

'That I cannot say—except that I know millions of pounds worth of bank-note paper is at times in some way in his keeping. I'm afraid you'll think me dreadfully ignorant, Mr Carrados, but I understand very little about such things and to tell the truth I have always scrupulously refrained from seeming to pester Geoffrey with questions about business.'

They were gathering raspberries into cabbage leaves then, Miss Tilehurst having asked Carrados if he cared for them with cream and having received an enthusiastic admission. She now proceeded to assemble all their spoil on the largest leaf and was surprised to notice that the blind man's contribution to the stock was rather more than either her own or Nora's. Not for the first time that day she wondered secretly whether it was not all an elaborate piece of bluff, with Mr Carrados able to see just as well as she could. Others beside Miss Tilehurst had in the past experienced a similar misgiving.

'I think we have reached the limit of our patience now; Geoffrey must put up with "husband's tea" when he does come,' she declared as the raspberry business was completed. 'If you will bring Mr Carrados round, Nora, I'll run on with these and see if Ophelia has got everything ready. By the way, I asked Dr Olivant to join us at tea—the poor man must be feeling exhausted.'

With the trifling exception of a mishap to the green dessert dish, Ophelia felt—as she confided now and then to Sultan, the lethargic Persian—that she was doing all that could be humanly expected. The fragments of the dessert dish had been temporarily secreted under some rags in the sink cupboard and for the rest Ophelia put her trust in the frailty of human memory and, when it did come out, the softening hand of time. Unfortunately Miss Tilehurst had this very dish in mind when she came in with the raspberries, so that instead of being able to refer casually to something as having happened in a vague and oblivious past, Ophelia was suddenly faced with the discovery of a fault in which she would be detected red handed as it were, and held doubly blameworthy.

'Green dish, mum?' she replied, becoming goggle-eyed with

conscientious effort. 'I wonder what can have become of that? I don't seem to have noticed it about lately. I think the last time must have been when Nipper was eating something out of it. I wonder if he can have broke it somehow?'

'Nonsense,' retorted Miss Tilehurst briskly; 'I saw it myself quite lately. And once again, Ophelia, you *must not* let the animals have our plates and dishes. Never mind looking now'—for the conscientious girl was exploring the most unlikely places—'this one will do instead. Now go and ask Dr Olivant if he would care to wash his hands—they may be dirty after that kind of work—and if he would, show him up to the bathroom and take a can of hot water and put out a towel.'

Ophelia was free to breathe naturally once more, the matter of the green dish being dismissed to a wholly negligible morrow. She sought Dr Olivant in the lane and delivered her message with scrupulous exactness.

'I was to ask you, please, if you'd like to wash yourself after you've done your dirty work, sir.'

Looking at Ophelia it was impossible to suspect her of elaborate guile and Dr Olivant did look at her: for fully five seconds he bent a level glance on her unsophisticated features. Then he looked at his own hands and with a short laugh detached himself from the consideration of engine troubles.

'Well, yes; it would be as well perhaps, wouldn't it?' he admitted. 'Come now, my dear'—as she stood awkwardly waiting for him to lead the way and he for her—'if we are to get on you must be my cicerone.'

'That I never will, sir,' appallingly retorted Ophelia, bristling up into virtuous indignation. 'The very idea—and a gentleman like you too! I shall leave your water outside the bathroom door now.'

'Don't be silly, girl; that only means that you've got to show me where I am to go,' explained Olivant, his manner at once dropping several degrees in the social register. And as he followed he privately commented beneath his breath on her inopportune want of sense in terms that would have been surprisingly fundamental for Harley Street.

'I find that we shall have to give up the idea of sitting in the arbour,' said their hostess as the sauntering pair appeared. 'The table is all right to serve the tea from, but the rustic seats are definitely not equal to the responsibility of being sat on, and I know of nothing more embarrassing than to find one's chair collapsing when you have a cup of tea in one hand and a plate of something in the other.'

'I think it rather fun,' said Nora. 'After all, it helps out a picnic.'

'Then you shall provide the fun, dear,' declared Miss Tilehurst. 'Dr Olivant can do as he likes when he arrives but I insist on Mr Carrados being less humorous. There is a garden form under the catalpa, Mr Carrados, if you prefer the shade, or a chair here in the open—'

'I am all for the sun while it lasts, if you give me the choice,' said Carrados, putting out his hand unerringly and accepting the chair Miss Tilehurst had indicated. 'We don't get so many summers like this in England that you can afford to throw away a minute of one.'

'Heroic man! And you, Nora—seriously, the bench in there is out of the question?'

'Then perhaps I can be useful?' suggested Nora. 'If not, I'll be one of the shady ones.'

'Useful? Well, Ophelia can take the tea but perhaps you wouldn't mind—when Dr Olivant appears—if you would bring him across—he mayn't quite like—'

'That I will, mum!' undertook Nora playfully.

'Sugar and cream, Mr Carrados?' asked Miss Tilehurst, seeing that Ophelia had arrived at the arbour with the tea tray.

'Cream—no sugar, thank you.'

It is as well, since it had some little bearing on the course of events that afternoon, and thereafter perhaps for centuries,

to indicate the rearrangements of positions that had come about
from so trifling a cause as the dilapidation of the summer-house
appointments. The tea, as originally planned, was laid in there,
with Miss Tilehurst pouring out and Ophelia acting as a
connecting link between supply and demand until her services
were dispensed with. Mr Carrados, choosing the sun as we
have seen, sat on an isolated chair some little distance from the
arbour, while on the other side of the grass-plot in the shade
of a catalpa tree, a substantial bench accommodated Dr Olivant
when he came out and Nora and Miss Tilehurst in turn as they
went backwards and forwards refilling cups and offering the
more substantial refreshment. Geoffrey had not yet arrived—but
of course he must any minute now, and in the minds of three
out of the five people there his absence, as the time went on,
was the one thing that engrossed them. Three out of the five:
but which three?

'Your cup of tea, sir,' considerately announced Ophelia,
approaching Mr Carrados and regarding him with fascinated
interest. 'I was to be careful. You're blind, aren't you?'

'Yes, Ophelia. Quite blind,' he replied with a reassuring smile
as he took the cup and saucer neatly from her.

'You don't know of things that go on then?' she elaborated.

'Sometimes kind people tell me of them.' He stirred in the
floating cream deliberatingly. 'If they think it will amuse me.'

'Amuse!' she giggled at the recollection. 'Not half, it wasn't!
You ought to have seen him with his moustache coming off
when he washed his face there. It did look funny, I can tell you.'

'It must have done. Did he know you saw him?'

'Not him! I was looking through the—well, a place where he
couldn't see me.'

'Ophelia! Come, Ophelia,' called out Miss Tilehurst and
with a friendly nod and the consciousness that she had done
her best to 'amuse', Ophelia ambled back to the arbour.

'Bread-and-butter or anchovy sandwiches, Uncle?' inquired
Nora, coming round in turn. 'Charming man that—sort I abhor.

Makes you feel it must lead up to borrowing a fiver every minute. Or raspberries first?'

'Sandwich, thanks.' He dexterously put down the cup on the grass beside him (Nora knew better than to butt in with help) and supplied himself from the plate she offered. 'By the way, don't you want to go out into the road to see if anyone is coming?'

'Not particularly. Why?'

'Oh, I think I should . . . Perhaps because I want you to.'

'Uncle Max, what is to be the hocus-pocus now? You've suddenly gone rather serious.'

'I don't know that there will be any hocus-pocus, Nora. But I think it may have suddenly gone rather serious.'

'Very well. I know that when . . . Tell me what I am to do.'

'Keep your wits about you and don't give anything away. You are going to look down the road to see if Tilehurst isn't coming. Get the number of that car and let me have a description.'

Nora passed on, admirably calm, to the other guest and smiled off on him another anchovy sandwich. Then she returned her stock to the arbour, and securing her own tea and plate began to walk across to the shade of the catalpa.

'Oh, I think I'll just give a look to see if Geoffrey is in sight yet and hurry him up if he is,' she called back. 'He's really naughty.'

'Yes, do, dear,' approved Miss Tilehurst, following her across, 'but don't stay out looking. I'm going to sit with Dr Olivant for a minute now but I feel that we are neglecting our visitors shockingly. It would have been different if we could have all been together in the summer-house. As it is—'

'Have another sandwich, sir, while they're here,' croaked Ophelia confidentially at the blind man's elbow. Being unable, as she argued, to look after himself, she was moved to take him under her special protection. 'I know these picnic parties: once a thing's gone you're never sure if you'll ever see it again. "A bird in the hand" is what I believe in being.'

'I think you are quite right,' he admitted no less confidentially, 'but not yet, thank you. This time I'll risk it.'

Nora came back from the side gate again and for a moment loitered at the bench, claiming her tea and plate with the light flippancies of the occasion.

'No sign of the defaulter yet,' she reported, to Miss Tilehurst chiefly; then nibbling her bread-and-butter she passed on to Carrados to see how he was faring.

'Dark blue Lemartine four-seating tourer; four-wheel brakes; mica screen; disc wheels and carries spare one—cased—left of engine. Sphinx mascot. And the tool box *has a hammer in it*.'

'Good girl,' he commended, taking out a slender note-book and proceeding to make an inconsiderable entry. 'Number?'

'PZ 9741.'

'Just as well to have it, though for a certainty it's bogus.'

'What is bogus for a certainty, you two conspirators?' loudly proclaimed Miss Tilehurst, innocently taking advantage of their absorption and the muting grass to spring this devastating revelation. Carrados felt Nora's sterilised dismay as he smilingly took over the situation.

'My niece thinks she has made a find—one of Wheatley's "Cries of London" in a Mutbury second-hand shop,' he obligingly explained; 'but I tell her that there are a hundred fakes for every genuine copy. Still, it might be worth while—I wonder if Dr Olivant knows anything of prints? Some doctors have uncommonly good things on the walls of their reception rooms. We might ask him.'

'Oh, Doctor, do you know anything about prints?' called out Miss Tilehurst, glad of the opportunity to make the talk more general, and Olivant politely came forward. 'Miss Melhuish thinks that she has discovered a rare engraving in a shop somewhere, only Mr Carrados is afraid that it may be—what is it?—bogus! We wondered if you knew—'

'I fear I must admit my ignorance,' replied Dr Olivant, making the admission sound more weighty than most other people's claim to extensive knowledge. 'It is a subject that—I beg your pardon, Miss Tilehurst?'

'Geoffrey at last!' the interruption had been, her mind off like a bird as the front gate clanged and a man was seen through the laurels. 'Oh, Geoffrey,' she exclaimed in a voice of petulant relief, 'you are a—' and then as he came round the bend, in a voice that was drained of every shade of expression but dismay: '*Geoffrey!*'

CHAPTER IX

IN WHICH THE ASSURANCE OF THE EYE DECEIVES
THE MIND

THE man who had come in by the front gate and who was walking up the path, trundling a buckled and deflated bicycle at his side, looked up at the cry but he made no response nor did he evince any appreciable sign of recognition. His face had a grey strained look, not as of fear or apprehension now but as though some terrible experience had come suddenly and passed and left a benumbed and abiding impression. He took in the five people gathered there with an incurious acceptance that passed them by and it was distressingly obvious that if left to himself he would go straight on by the way he knew and not bestow another glance or a thought about what they were doing. When Miss Tilehurst laid an impulsive hand on his arm he stopped, but it was as an obedient cart-horse stops and without any personal concern in the proceedings.

'Geoffrey, my dear, what is it? Why don't you speak?' implored Miss Tilehurst rather wildly. 'Oh, my goodness, look at his poor face! Have you had an accident, Geoffrey—are you hurt? Do, for God's sake, say something!'

'One moment, my dear lady—you must control yourself,' interposed Dr Olivant, coming forward with the quiet authority of his recognised position. 'Is this—?'

'Yes, my nephew whom we've been expecting. He must have met with an accident—look at his face, look at the machine. But why doesn't he speak? It's so—so alarming, so inconsiderate. He may be badly injured for all we know and trying to keep it from us by not talking. But I can't let him go on like this. We must find out if there's anything worse and what has happened.'

'Yes—yes, of course,' admitted Olivant soothingly. 'You are naturally distressed although it may not be anything like so serious as your first impression leads you to imagine. It is extremely probable that this is only a temporary phase—a matter of hours, or possibly days, and our young friend will be all right again and even laughing at his curious experience.'

'You really think that, Doctor; you aren't just saying it—?'

'My dear Miss Tilehurst, if there were any immediate cause for anxiety I would be the first to warn you. However, at a time like this you naturally don't want a stranger—perhaps I had better go—you will no doubt get along all right. Unless of course,'—a considerate after-thought—'as a doctor who happens to be on the spot you would like me to make a provisional examination? If so—need I say?—I would be only too glad— some slight return—to put my services freely at your disposal.'

'Oh, Doctor, would you? It would be such a blessed relief. I don't mind admitting that I've had a terrible fright and I'm still—perhaps unreasonably after what you've said—very, very anxious.' Almost resentfully: 'If only he would say *something*. Geoffrey, my darling, don't you recognise us here—me— Ophelia—Nora?'

'Geoff, dear,' said Nora, going to his side, 'can't you tell me? Don't I recall anything at all? Humph and Nobbles, you know.' But Geoffrey only looked painfully apart and fixed his eyes on the door for which he had been making.

'Um, yes,' interposed Dr Olivant, capably taking charge with the implication that this was all very well in its amateur way but that it was now time for someone who understood diag-nostics to adopt proper methods. 'This is quite unlooked for, I assume? There has been no previous indication of your nephew being in any way—shall I say strange? Not suffering from any physical or mental shock lately? Not complaining specially of the heat or feeling the sun, for instance?'

'Nothing at all,' declared Miss Tilehurst, searching her mind with conscientious detail. 'Of course we've all grumbled about the weather in an ordinary way, and he may have done too, but it didn't mean anything and he was perfectly happy and normal up to the time I last saw him.'

'And that was—when?'

'At lunch today. Afterwards he seems to have taken his bicycle out and gone off somewhere but I didn't know that he was going or see him go. Ophelia was the last who saw him.'

'Yes, that's right; I saw him go,' confirmed Ophelia, suddenly realising that this trifling circumstance might invest her with a gratifying importance. 'Came through the kitchen with his machine when I was washing up the things after lunch he did. "Going out for a ride on your bicycle, Mr Geoffrey?" I said, and then—'

'Yes, yes; there is no doubt that he did go off,' interrupted Miss Tilehurst, recognising just in time that in the eyes of a very literal man Geoffrey's absurd reply might pass for evidence of an existing state of delirium. 'You may take it for granted that he was perfectly normal when he set out, Doctor.'

'Well, I thought it sounded queer,' stuck out Ophelia, tolerantly resentful of being somehow 'done out' of her scene, but as no one attached any importance whatever to anything that Ophelia might think her testimony faded into the background.

Meanwhile Olivant had taken his patient's unresisting hand and under cover of a flow of smooth commonplace was feeling his pulse, critically looking into his eyes, and inspecting his bruised condition.

'Now, Mr Tilehurst, you've evidently had something of an adventure; can't you tell us a little of what has happened to upset you? Your aunt is naturally concerned to see you behave like this; surely you will make an effort—just a few words—to relieve her anxiety. You—? Yes—? Nothing to say, eh?' For certainly this bland assumption of ability to comply was no more successful than Miss Tilehurst's frenzied appeal or Nora's more recondite suggestion. 'Well, never mind; suppose you simply write down the name of the place where this occurred

or even your signature,' and producing an impressive memo-
randum tablet from his breast pocket Dr Olivant offered it,
together with a pencil, for the purpose.

A sigh of relief went up from at least two throats. Geoffrey
accepted the proffered articles—mechanically, indeed, but at
any rate he understood the purport of what was said—and for
a moment it seemed as though he was engaged in complying
with the requirement. Then he held out the pad again—a few
meaningless scrawls were the only result of the effort.

'Yes, yes; exactly,' commented the doctor, glancing at the
lines and accepting them as if they constituted just what he had
expected. 'Thank you, Mr Tilehurst.'

'Not very much perhaps,' he confided to his audience aside,
'but still, in the circumstances, something.' And to Miss
Tilehurst more especially: 'Oh, he'll be all right again soon; no
need for you to worry.'

'But what am I to do?' she asked, swayed between an intense
relief that this obvious authority should treat the matter so
lightly and a feeling that with Geoffrey like that there must be
something more than Olivant would admit behind it. 'What is
it that has happened?'

'Even without our having anything more than this extraneous
evidence to go on'—a gesture indicated his patient's bruised
and soiled condition and the damage to his machine—'it is
pretty plain what has happened. Your nephew has experienced
a severe shock—mental and physical combined—with the not
unnatural result that for the time certain functions of the brain
have been thrown out of action. Whether he was involved in a
collision with someone else or merely had a spill or—what is
perhaps more probable—received this damage and at the same
time underwent the terrifying experience of what is termed a
"narrow squeak" from something much worse is beside the
question. Something happened and as the result he is now
suffering from what I should confidently predict will be only a
temporary form of motor aphasia.'

'My word, but that sounds bad,' confided Ophelia—in the absence of Sultan—to herself. 'Them motors didn't ought to be allowed—'

'Inability to speak, that is of course,' amplified Dr Olivant with dignified severity. 'And as we see here'—tapping the pad that he still held—'inability to write: agraphia.'

'You don't think that he may be hurt internally somewhere all the time, Doctor, and unable to tell us? It must surely have been a very severe crash—'

'Not at all, not at all. As a matter of fact, physical violence is not necessary to produce the condition of aphasia. Quite recently I was called in to a case where a financier fell into the state as a result of unexpected market reverses. Three days later he suddenly recovered the power of speech completely on seeing his wife breaking some coal with his favourite golf club. Another case I had—a lady saw a ghost apparently coming out of her husband's bedroom. It was really the housemaid, who then admitted that she was a confirmed sleep-walker.'

'You have had other cases? Then you do actually know all about it?' suggested Miss Tilehurst, still more reassured though not perhaps choosing her words quite happily.

'My dear lady, I am a nerve specialist; of my standing as a consultant—that is a matter on which it is more befitting for me to leave others to express an opinion,' replied Dr Olivant with a fine discrimination of manner. 'In Harley Street I deal with analogous cases practically every day. Your own doctor will doubtless confirm my diagnosis if you think it necessary to consult him.'

'I suppose we ought to—he has attended Geoffrey for everything from childhood. But, oh, how very unfortunate! Dr Tyser is away on his holidays and his locum isn't at all—You do think that it would be better for him to be seen by an ordinary doctor as well, don't you?'

'Well, as to that—perhaps you would like me to make a more detailed examination to see definitely if there is any internal trouble and say what I think then? If so—I'm entirely at your service.'

'Oh, I should; I should. But it is so very, so *very* good of you, Dr Olivant.'

'Not at all. Your own man is away and in cases of emergency professional etiquette is mercifully elastic. The circumstances naturally encourage me to take a personal interest in our young friend here. Besides, I am scientifically concerned in observing the curious and varied effects of these sensory disturbances. Then we will go inside for a few minutes if you will kindly indicate where it will be convenient.'

'Yes, yes, certainly, Doctor. You had better be at hand, Ophelia. Dr Olivant may require something bringing.'

'That I will, mum,' promised Ophelia, one might even say with an anticipatory gloating.

'Now, Mr Tilehurst, we are going into the house,' said the doctor; 'suppose you show me the way,' and obedient to the suggestion Mr Tilehurst did lead the way towards the front door almost naturally. Dr Olivant turned to throw a weighty nod of approval towards Miss Tilehurst at this achievement.

'I'm so, *so* terribly sorry that our afternoon has turned out like this, Mr Carrados,' apologised Miss Tilehurst, stopping for a moment beside her visitors before she hurried on to catch up with the others on the door steps. 'You won't mind my running away I know but I do hope that you will stay and finish your interrupted tea—you will look after him, won't you, Nora? I'll let you hear what Dr Olivant says the minute I can, dear. I know that you are quite as anxious as I am. It's all so sudden and alarming—but wasn't it lucky that just the one man in a thousand should be here?'

'Yes; wasn't it!' agreed Mr Carrados, but as his hostess was well on her way towards the house, and, further, his remark had more significance than polite assent, it was not surprising that Nora was disinclined to let it pass unchallenged.

'What do you mean by that, Uncle Max?' she flatly demanded.

'Some people don't believe in luck, you know, Nora—I imagine they prefer to regard it as an intelligent anticipation of contributory circumstances. Perhaps Dr Olivant is one of them,' he temporised.

'Look here, Uncle, I don't want a fencing lesson just now, thank you. I want to understand things.'

'That's what most people really want, Nora. It's what I've been wanting all my life. It's what I go on for. Generally I have to wait someone else's good time for it.'

'Well, won't you help me to understand here—or even let me help you? It's all simple and straightforward to Miss Tilehurst; I mean she accepts it just as it appears on the surface. I can't do that because I know that you don't do curious things without some motive behind and now you've started my suspicions and I . . . It's very strange that Geoffrey shouldn't know even me.'

'Are you quite sure that even you know this Geoffrey of yours?'

'That I know Geoffrey—?'

'Well, very often a girl thinks that she knows a man through and through, only to find out that she doesn't . . . It's even been known to happen with a husband and wife who've lived all their life together.'

'No, it wasn't that,' declared Nora, shaking her head rather sadly. 'You didn't mean that—only you don't quite trust me . . . Uncle Max, you are going on with this, aren't you? You're thinking and planning and finding clues and putting this and that together. Aren't you?'

'A little time ago I came up against a locked door, and something baffling, perhaps even villainous, was going on the other side of it,' vouchsafed the provoking Carrados. 'This afternoon I have picked up a key; it fits the lock but it doesn't work the levers—not just yet.'

'And I don't even know how to begin to set about looking; but I feel as though a shadow, mysterious and sinister, is creeping up. Something has happened to this bright summer afternoon and to this peaceful garden and—I think—to me. It's that sort of feeling . . . And you sit there like a heathen idol, turning everything over in your wonderful mind and not letting me share a particle. Uncle Max'—taking hold of his shoulders and all but shaking him in a transport of exasperation—'don't you understand? I must do something; I can't just sit down and wait. I can't have Geoffrey change—I can't lose him like this. Yes, lose, Uncle Max; we were all but engaged lovers. Of course I know it's the doctor's job about treatment and all that, but isn't one of the first things towards putting him right to find out what it was that put him wrong? Suppose it was done by someone deliberately?'

'Yes, there may be something in that—perhaps more than one might think,' admitted Mr Carrados.

'Let me help you to do it then. You mayn't find me such an utter little rabbit as you might think after all. There are damned few things that I feel I'm afraid of, let me tell you, Uncle Max, and I'm quite ready to take the risks if it comes to that sort of business.'

'My dear,' protested the blind man with his incurable air of insouciance, 'you seem determined to plunge us both into the thick of battle.'

'Well, even you can't be in two places at once and sometimes you have had to make use of other people's eyes to see by. I think I'm up to the intellectual standard of your Parkinson and at any rate you certainly wouldn't miss me half as much as you would him if anything went wrong . . . Dear Uncle Max, if the chance comes along won't you give me a try—can't you use me?'

'That's all very well, my dear, but I don't want to have to fight a duel with Tilehurst when he comes round if I've led you into any scrape meanwhile,' he protested lightly. 'Thank you all the same child, but seriously you know if there should be any real unpleasantness ahead it would hardly be the sort of work to bring a young lady into.'

'Young lady!' Nora achieved almost a shriek of despair. 'Bad language fails me! I always say you are an old dear, Uncle, but you are—oh, you are—you really are—the most utter—'

'Ssh!' warned Carrados. 'Someone coming.'

'Yes; perhaps I had better "ssh"!' retorted Nora, subsiding.

CHAPTER X

NIPPER CONTRIBUTES TO THE PROBLEM

'WILL it do in here?' asked Miss Tilehurst.

It was the door of the dining-room she had opened. 'The morning-room is so dreadfully hot at this time of day and the drawing-room rather overcrowded.'

'This will do admirably,' he replied, taking a deliberate look round. 'Now—'

'There is something you need?'

'A little warm water in a bowl, sponge, towel, and the tincture of iodine if you have any.'

This simple list of requirements was passed on to the palpitating Ophelia and in a commendably short time—scarcely more than sufficient, indeed, for Dr Olivant to stroll across to the window and, having ascertained that it was not inconveniently overlooked, commend the prospect—a tray containing them appeared. The doctor turned to Miss Tilehurst with his nicely discriminative lady-side manner.

'Now I shall ask you to withdraw for a few minutes, Miss Tilehurst. After I have attended to these superficial trifles I shall put our man through a pretty thorough examination.'

'I quite understand,' replied Miss Tilehurst delicately, though, of course, she was yearning to be of some use. 'There is the bell by the mantelpiece. You will not hesitate to ring if there is the slightest—?'

'Now my dear sir,' directed Olivant, as they were in the process of becoming alone, 'I think if you sit down there'—'there' being a severe mahogany chair whose suitability consisted in its position, well out of the line of vision from the door—'it will do nicely. Yes, we will have your coat off for a start. Capital.'

The door being now closed and the window reasonably safe—especially as Olivant, with his back that way, stood between it and his patient—the process of sponging away the traces of injury began and this naturally brought the two heads close together.

'O.K.?' dropped from the elder man's lips, but so circumspectly that one might have been in the room and still not heard the whisper or seen any facial movement.

'O.K. And you?'

'Lapped it. But how the hell have you got yourself in this state? You weren't to have any bumps—it was to be all mental. Had a spill actually?'

'Nothing like. I simply thought it better . . . And then that little s— Mae—oh well, well can all that backwash. I'm here, aren't I?'

'I see. Temperamental. Still, let me tell you, my young friend, it might easily have queered my bit of business. However . . . want anything doing?'

'Nit. But how about the two extras? They're outside calculations.'

'Dropped ins. Man called Carrados; blind. Girl, Nora Melhuish. They'll drift back after a while. They don't matter.'

'Not so sure. She looks like being a snag. Side line I hadn't thought to handle.'

'Oh-ha?'

'T. was damned close about her, I must say. Neither Nickle nor I had an inkling. We're evidently some distance on, but where? As soon as I pick up I shall be expected to do something.'

'Well, that oughtn't to be difficult for you.'

'It wouldn't if I knew where to leave off but it's so infernally easy for me to overact the part in a case like that. Anyway, I shouldn't be sorry if Nora vanished. She's safe to be the sharp one—the old geezer wouldn't have tumbled to it if I'd turned up cross-eyed.'

'I'll tell J., but we can hardly yank the girl out as well. It would raise fire and brimstone.'

'I'm not asking you to. But that's how it stands. You can vamoose now—no question of having to get me out. We've arranged for messages.'

'Right-o. Closing down now ... Yes, I think we'll be satisfied with that'—this resumption of Dr Olivant's hearty self-confident voice coincided with the completion of the use of sponge and towel and the application of iodine to his patient's scratches. 'Now suppose we move across to this couch for the next part of our job. I shall want a little more removed to get on with that. Then you can lie down quite comfortable and it won't take long ... You do understand? Oh capital! Capital!'

'He is with Geoffrey in the dining-room now and they don't expect to be very long. It will be such a relief for me to know that there is no internal complication to fear. I do hope that Nora has been attending to you, Mr Carrados?'

'Steadily, Miss Tilehurst. And I have been capably responding. One of the great advantages of eating is that it enables you to disguise emotion. To the cynical observation that speech is given us to conceal our thoughts it might be added that eating and drinking enable us to hide our feelings. I think that is why food is an institution almost whenever human beings have anything to say to one another. A man has sufficient time to pull himself together under the excuse of even so simple an action as drinking from a cup of coffee.'

'If he didn't there'd be a spill,' said Nora. 'In fact there always is when it happens on the stage. The startled man blowing out his drink is one of the surest laugh-getters of the modern drama ... Don't think me unfeeling, Miss Tilehurst dear—it's only my way of keeping it up. I must be doing something or saying something very fast and Mr Carrados is considerately giving me a lead.'

'Mr Carrados ... lead ... dog,' automatically responded

some obscure process in Miss Tilehurst's sorely tried brain. 'Nora! Nipper!'

'Nipper? I haven't seen him at all since I came. Why, where is Nipper?'

'No; that's it. He went with Geoffrey this afternoon. But he didn't come back with him.'

'Your little terrier, eh?' remarked Mr Carrados. 'Yes, Nipper may have involved a certain difficulty, mayn't he?'

'He would never have left Geoffrey of his own free will, whatever it was that took place. He always recognised his foot-step long before we even heard it and ran out of the house to meet him. What can have happened to him?'

'I think I can tell you that,' volunteered Mr Carrados quietly. 'You must be prepared for another shock, Miss Tilehurst, although, of course, it doesn't compare with the other. Nipper is no more.'

'You mean—dead?'

'Yes, dead, I am sorry to have to tell you. He was found less than an hour ago in Birling Wood and though his collar had seen removed the man who found him recognised the dog as yours.'

'But—an hour ago! You were here then, Mr Carrados. How could you possibly know of such a thing happening?'

For an answer the blind man raised his hand in the direction of the house and nodded. Miss Tilehurst turned to see Ophelia coming along the path towards them. She carried something white in her bent arms and the simple girl was crying.

'Oh, mum—it's poor Nipper! Mr Batts, the keeper, has just brought him to the back door. He says he found him, not a hour ago, under a clump in Birling Wood, because his own dog knew there was something there and as good as said so. I thought it sounded queer too, mum, but Mr Batts did say that his dog stood and pointed at the bush and there when he looked was Nipper. At least he guessed it was yours through seeing it about with Mr Geoffrey although the collar was gone, so he brought it round as he thought you'd better know what had happened.'

'Dead, killed; run over, I suppose, and then thrown aside to save any unpleasantness.'

'Yes, mum, Mr Batts said he reckoned it was one of them hemmed stink kettles on wheels and if he had his way they'd pave the roads with broken bottles 'stead of tarring them. And if you please, mum . . .'

'Yes, Ophelia?' said Miss Tilehurst, gently stroking dead Nipper and smiling sadly. 'What is it?'

'If you please, mum,' wailed Ophelia, bringing her resolution to the boiling point so that a rush of words welled over, 'it wasn't true what I said just now about that there green dish and Nipper. It was me that broke it—not 'im. There'—with obvious relief—'I hope he's heard me say it!'

'Oh, Ophelia!'

'Yes, mum,' acquiesced Ophelia to the pained tone of reproach, in penitent agreement.

'Well, leave it here now and go back. There's nothing to be done by talking and Dr Olivant may be wanting something more. And, oh, Ophelia, ask Mr Batts if he will kindly wait for a few minutes longer as I would like to see him. Isn't it unfortunate?' she continued, to the others. 'It would be bad enough at any time but coming just at this moment—'

'Poor doggie,' said Nora, surrendering the form to Carrados who had stretched out his hands for it. 'I never thought about it but I suppose we must all have been fond of old Nipper.'

'Yes, I'm sure you were,' agreed Miss Tilehurst, 'but I was thinking more of Geoffrey at the moment. He isn't one to make a fuss of his affections but I know that, without becoming maudlin as so many doggy people unfortunately do, he thought a great deal of his faithful little companion. He's sure to ask for him as soon as he begins to speak again and I dread to think how it may upset him. Would it be better to tell him now so as to get it over—or not yet? What do you think?'

'On the whole I should say that it would perhaps be unnecessary to tell him,' replied Mr Carrados.

'You mean until he asks?'

'Exactly—until he asks. When he does of course that will be another matter.'

'I expect you are quite right. Then perhaps we ought to bury the little body now—it would be dreadful if he should happen to come upon it without knowing. But I can't just now—'

'We could hide it for the time—somewhere in the tool-shed,' suggested Nora, seeing that the usually decisive Miss Tilehurst was becoming painfully uncertain. 'Then Draycott could dig a grave when he next comes gardening, couldn't he?'

'Yes, but Draycott only comes two days a week you know, and he won't be here again until Wednesday. I don't know—in this weather—'

'Then why shouldn't Uncle and I get it done while we are only waiting? I can't go until I know what the doctor says—oh, but if he is—I mean if he isn't—' Nora began to flounder.

'We cannot possibly go until we hear, no matter how long the doctor may be, Nora,' reproved Mr Carrados gravely.

'No, of course we can't,' accepted Nora. 'And it will be such a relief to be doing something vigorous like digging. We shall find a spade all right. Mayn't we as well, Miss Tilehurst?'

'But your clothes, your shoes, my dear,' protested the more experienced gardener. 'It would simply ruin those flimsy leathers.'

'I will do the actual digging, Miss Tilehurst,' undertook Carrados, and rather wanly, since only one thing in the world seemed to matter then, Miss Tilehurst stroked Nipper's chalk-white back for the last time and said it would be a weight off her mind if they really would undertake the disposal while Geoffrey was safely out of the way.

'In the rough grass beyond the espalier would be the most suitable place I think,' she added. 'Shall I run down and show you?'

'I know where you mean quite well,' replied Nora, 'and I'm sure you're only worrying if you are away from here for a minute. We'll get on all right, never fear.'

Miss Tilehurst had not long to wait; in fact she met Dr Olivant coming down the steps as she was making for the hall, to take up a useless vigil outside the dining-room door, after she had stood for a moment absently following Nipper's last progress down the garden. On his side there was no inducement for Olivant to linger once he had played his part. He had now to cope his carefully built-up fabric and when that was done the sooner he made himself scarce the better.

'Ah, Miss Tilehurst,' he exclaimed, with a jauntiness appropriate to the character of the report he brought, 'I think now that I can set your mind at rest completely.'

'Oh, Doctor—completely,' she said quickly. 'Does that mean that he is really all right again—that he can speak and answer?'

Dr Olivant made a deprecatory gesture and looked quizzically reproachful.

'Well, no, perhaps not quite all that just yet,' he admitted, 'but what I meant was that you need have no fear—absolutely no apprehension whatever—as regards the future. I have gone thoroughly over our young friend in there—by the way he seems quite content to sit quietly alone and so you'd better let him— and he is definitely uninjured. With the exception of the trifling facial bruises that you have seen he has not been touched; his condition is purely the result of mental disturbance—he has received a shock to put it simply.'

'We have just found out that our little dog that went with him has been killed and the body thrown aside—a man who knew the dog has kindly brought it here. Do you think—?'

'Very likely; very likely indeed. Nothing more probable,' replied the doctor, looking extremely sagacious. 'These reckless drivers! Full speed along a narrow winding lane—no warning. Your nephew sees the inevitable a yard ahead. He hears the despairing death cry of his unfortunate dog and barely escapes by the merest chance himself—the luck of being flung into the hedge and clear of the rushing moloch instead of into the road and beneath it. Yes, there we have the case in a nutshell I think, Miss Tilehurst. Is it any wonder that he emerges from that hedge with his mind temporarily seared?'

'Temporarily, Doctor? You still think that he will get over it before very long then?'

'I don't think, my dear lady; I know. Such cases are—to use rather a vulgar boast—my speciality, and I can absolutely guarantee it. You will find that gradually the normal faculties will come back. Probably he will begin to write—very shakily and unrecognisable at first—when he wants to communicate with you. As we saw just now he is more disposed to write than to speak when the occasion requires.'

'I see. And when he does speak will it be the same as with the writing—not coming back suddenly restored?'

'All experience points that way! Semi-coherent speech at first—stammering and broken you understand—but sufficient to make himself understood and to indicate his requirements. You mustn't be disconcerted if the voice sounds rather strange to your ears at the start—it's only a matter of time, like the writing.'

'I won't mind I can assure you. And in about how long—?'

'Ah, that's more difficult to say. These cases vary. But I should expect that you will notice a material improvement within a few days and in somewhere about a week you may have quite a surprising transformation—quite surprising.'

'That will not seem so very long. And is there absolutely nothing for me to do to help? No matter what, if it only contributes to his recovery ever so little.'

'Nothing beyond what I have already indicated. Nothing active that is to say but a great deal passive. Let him have entirely his own way in what he wants to do. Don't seem to notice him; don't watch him—in fact look at him as little as possible. It's all a reminder that something is wrong, and reminding him of what has happened is the one thing that must be avoided. He'll make absurd mistakes at first no doubt—not know his way about even in places where he is quite familiar; pick up things that don't concern him and, of course, fail to recognise his friends—though as to that I shouldn't make a point of having people in to meet him.'

'Oh, certainly not. I should dislike it myself. And his business, Doctor? We must apply, I suppose, for leave of absence now?'

'Ah, his business to be sure. In these charming rural surroundings one forgets that there is such a thing as business. I shouldn't wonder—What does he do, by the way?'

'He is in the office of the paper mills here. You may have noticed them as you drove by. It is where they make the Bank of England note paper.'

It appeared, however, that Dr Olivant had not noticed them as he drove in; indeed—and this was the single flaw in the impression left by that delightful man—he did not seem to be aware that special paper was required for the issue of Bank of England notes, ever to have even heard of the celebrated Tapsfield mills, or to have the least interest in the subject of the firm's importance. One point only caught his attention and that was when Miss Tilehurst spoke of the responsibility of Geoffrey's position.

'Just so—responsibility,' he commented. 'That impression may persist; it is a curious fact, Miss Tilehurst, that a man's vocational claims are often the predominant subconscious impulse. It is quite on the cards that your nephew will set off on Monday morning in the usual way and turn up at the office. Let me see—are you on pretty good terms with the important people down there?'

'Oh yes. I meet them all occasionally. They'd do anything to help us I am sure.'

'Very well. As this happens to be Saturday it gives you a day's grace. I should go round and see the chiefs tomorrow. Tell them all about it and what I have said. If your nephew should go to the works the very best thing would be to give him free rein to potter about and try to recall his routine. Of course he can't do anything there at first but the association of the place will be helpful.'

'I see. Yes; I quite appreciate that and I am sure that there will be no difficulty in arranging it. They are most considerate and of course they value Geoffrey's services very highly.'

'Oh, quite so—naturally. Well, Miss Tilehurst, I think that is about all—'

'But, Doctor, aren't we to do anything to discover the culprits? A harmless dog is killed, an inoffensive man's reason, if not his life, endangered. Surely someone ought to be called to account—?'

'Yes, yes; not unnaturally I thought of that and then there arises just this difficulty: do we put our patient's recovery or our own feelings first? I say our own feelings, for whatever may have happened (and we cannot exclude, my dear lady, the possibility of contributory negligence) the last thing in your nephew's interest is to recall that disastrous occurrence. Once bring in the police and what is inevitably bound to follow? There will be calls and interrogations and cross-questionings as one wiseacre after another gets what he considers "a clue" until the excellent chance that our patient has of making a quick recovery is blown to atoms. But of course it's for you to say—'

'No,' replied Miss Tilehurst very decidedly. 'Oh no; I could not allow that for a moment. We might make discreet inquiry for ourselves but Geoffrey shall not be worried.'

'Then I can confidently leave his future in your hands: and now I must see about my own interrupted progress, A trying afternoon for you, Miss Tilehurst, but he'll go on all right; he'll steadily improve, never fear.'

'If I don't fear, Dr Olivant, it is entirely due to you. I think you must have been sent direct from heaven.'

'Oh, I shouldn't exactly call it that,' protested Olivant modestly. 'At all events I have no idea of getting back there tonight. Then good-bye, Miss Tilehurst—or possibly *au revoir*. It occurs to me that I may be passing this way back in about a week's time.'

'Oh, would you? I should be so very glad—only next time you must really let me accept it as a professional visit. That quite relieves my mind about not saying anything to that dreadful locum meanwhile. No, Doctor—I am coming into the lane to see you off . . . Oh, the others—my visitors, you know—do you care to see them before you go, or—?'

'I hardly think it is necessary—we scarcely spoke. My apologies, if you don't mind, when you rejoin them.'

'Certainly I will. By the way, Mr Carrados is particularly interested in crime and obscure cases. He has quite a unique reputation for a blind man, I understand. If he should happen to speak to me of what took place—'

'An amateur sleuth—as I believe they are called—eh?' Dr Olivant relaxed to the extent of a grimace of good-humoured if contemptuous amusement. 'Wonderful fellows, provided everything happens their way, if we are to believe the magazine story writers. Well, the less stir and talk there is in any quarter, the better for our patient, but I quite see, Miss Tilehurst, that it may be difficult for you—'

They passed, by the little side gate, into the lane, still talking.

The soil beyond the espalier fortunately was light and easily dug but, even so, Mr Carrados, divested of his coat and with cuffs turned back, more than once bewailed his pliant good nature in taking on the energetic office.

'Alas, poor Nipper; a dog of infinite zest and understanding. A hundred times hath he buried the bones of others here and now we bury his—pest on it,' he declaimed between his efforts. 'This grave-digger business is ill suited to the day, Nora. Why didn't you suggest the dogs' cemetery in Hyde Park where he could have been put away in style and to our material comfort?'

'Probably because I didn't know of it. Is there such a place really?'

'Certainly there is, and a very singular institution though I dare say it's full up now. Remind me when I am next showing you the sights of London and I'll take you . . . Will this about do, quotha?'

'Oh yes, I'm sure it's deep enough now. As you've had all the work so far I'll do my share by filling it up again. Poor old Nipper. And that's the end of him . . . Uncle Max, was Nipper run over by a motor car and Geoffrey nearly run over and frightened out of his senses? I am sure that's what she thinks and it does look like that, doesn't it?'

'Not altogether, Nora. The dog was killed by the single blow of a heavy blunt weapon. The man . . . the man is more complicated.'

'Oh! You mean that someone killed the poor little thing deliberately? But why should anyone? Why, Uncle?'

'A great deal may turn on that. He might have attacked in defence. But there is an immeasurably subtler line of implication that is dangerously attractive.'

'Yes, yes?'

'He could always recognise Geoffrey's step, you know; and, like me, he had a nose that was fatal to deception.'

'Oh, but that's no good since Geoffrey would still be the same to Nipper. I mean it brings us no nearer to what really happened, does it?'

'Perhaps a little. Geoffrey was first chloroformed, I think. The hand that picked Nipper up to dispose of him had certainly touched chloroform just before. Drugged; does that bring us nearer by taking us further away, I wonder?'

This, needless to say, was not very helpful to Nora who was all for other people being explicit.

'That's very profound I dare say, but I simply don't understand anything from it. And I feel that it's all getting rather horrible—like a forest in a nightmare and whichever way I turn

I'm bound to get more and more lost in it. What *is* there to do, my wonderful Uncle?'

'Wait,' he replied, and she was startled by the feeling—almost bitterness—in place of his usual tempered suavity. 'Wait for them to show their hand more plainly. That's a fine thing to have to recommend, isn't it, when just the one clue that may spell all the difference between failure and success is on the point of slipping through our fingers?'

'The one clue?'

'The Harley Street specialist who is so familiarly at home in an East End fence's den—where is he making for when he goes from here?'

'You want to know that, Uncle Max?'

'It might ultimately lead us to the answer. Now it's too late to have a hope of following. If only your brother had been at home I could have put him on to it with a fair chance of shadowing our ingratiating friend to the trysting place with his report of progress.'

'Motor bike! He must make for the Stanbury fork. Dark blue Lemartine. One could overhaul him.'

'Yes, but Tom is somewhere among the Alps just now and there's no one else in this fascinating Sleepy Hollow of yours that we could get in time—even if there is anyone at all who would do it.'

'Oh blow!' exclaimed Nora in sudden irrelevance, 'there's Miss Tilehurst—I suppose she wants me to do the polite by saying good-bye or something silly. Go on filling up, won't you, old dear? Back as soon as I can,' and without offering the necessary opening for the proverbial word that is inserted edgeways, she flew up the garden leaving Mr Carrados still painfully reviewing the circumstances that were leading to the calamity of Olivant's secure retirement.

The engine of the car in the lane gave a few preliminary skirls as the blind man threw back the last spadeful of earth; another minute passed and then the sound grew constant. Nora had not yet returned so presumably she had been pressed into remaining to grace the good fairy Olivant's bouquet-strewn departure. Mr Carrados had no wish to figure in the flourish but, as the measured drone of the unseen Lemartine traced its progress along the lane beyond the wall, he picked up his coat again and sauntered up the path with a passing thought of his usually scrupulous appearance.

'Ah, Ophelia,' he said, recognising her presence as he neared the house, 'you are the very person I'm wanting. Do you think you could bring a clothes brush out and perhaps—? You see the state I've got myself in, burying poor Nipper.'

'Why to be sure I will, sir,' replied Ophelia, surprisingly varying her formula. 'I'll trim you up like one o'clock if you don't mind waiting a couple of jiffies. I'm looking for the mistress now. That Mr Batts doesn't half give me the shivers. He's in the kitchen there with his pocket full of ferrets and they keep getting out and them and the cat does nothing but put their backs up and swear at one another. Says he can't wait no longer.'

'The keeper? Oh, he oughtn't to go until Miss Tilehurst has seen him. I think you'll find her just out in the lane there with Miss Melhuish. If you run across I'll have a word with Mr Batts myself meanwhile and keep him until you come back. He should know a lot about trapping vermin.'

'Right you are,' said Ophelia, with the easy manner which, we are told, is the universal hallmark of good breeding. 'The missis may be there but I don't know about Miss Nora. Not two minutes ago she went through the other gate like a streak of greased lightning and if she isn't at Turnpenny Cross by now she might be.'

'She went out—' considered Mr Carrados. 'Now that's rather odd—' but even as he stood, from the road beyond and then from the lane itself there came a possible, if rather fantastic, answer to his deliberation. It approached as a crescendo hum, gathering into a husky roar as it swept by, and in less than ten seconds the beat was faintly drumming the air in the direction of Stanbury Junction. For just a moment a gauntletted hand had shown above the level of the wall in a gesture that conveyed both hail and farewell.

'Mr Carrados! What on earth can it mean?' Miss Tilehurst was hastening back towards the house from the gate, to meet her only remaining guest who was reversing that process. 'Did you see—bless us, I should say hear? That was Nora, tearing like a wild thing down the lane on her brother's motor cycle. I wouldn't have recognised her she was so got up if she hadn't waved—and do you know I actually believe that she was wearing Tom's leather trousers!'

CHAPTER XI

Mr Carrados's appearance at 'Orchard Close' had been in the nature of a weekend visit and on the Monday following Miss Tilehurst's eventful Saturday afternoon tea-party he returned to his own house in Richmond.

So far as he was concerned the circumstances of what might be called the Geoffrey Tilehurst case had progressed little beyond the elementary coincidental. Geoffrey had gone out for a ride and returned suffering from complicated loss of memory. At the same time there had appeared on the scene the soi-disant Dr Olivant. Dr Olivant was either a medical man curiously in touch with Julian Joolby—that bizarre figure of exotic reputation—or else an impostor masquerading as a doctor. It would be easy to establish by the *Medical Directory* whether there was, so far as the current issue went, anyone of that name with an address in Harley Street but the evidence would not be quite finally conclusive. Dr Olivant had, in fact, been faced with the alternative of personating a specialist who could be referred to at any time or of inventing a fictitious one who might be less convincing but who would be more elusive. That he had returned to a sequestered house in an outer London suburb (as Nora had been able to establish) meant little or nothing yet. That house had still to be investigated.

So far it was difficult to suggest what had necessitated Olivant's function in Tapsfield. The result of his framed-up appearance at Brookcroft had only been to put about what any genuine doctor could have established. The measure of disguise suggested that he had been there before or intended to go again or else that there was a chance of encountering someone while on that lay who might recognise him in his fictitious character. Certainly he had gained a first-hand knowledge of the house and grounds; was Mr Carrados rating the incidentals too high and this nothing but the prelude to a commonplace burglary?

A coincidence is the intersection of two lines, neither of which need possess in itself the least significance. When three lines meet at the self-same point of time or space the laws of chance suggest the probability of some conformable agency. 'I suppose this is getting frightfully complicated?' once remarked an interested outsider for whom Mr Carrados was investigating a case, when one baffling circumstance after another was brought to light as the quest proceeded. 'Not at all,' was his reply. 'On the contrary it is becoming transparently simple.' One or two lines might establish nothing but when a dozen or a score could be 'extended' it was inevitable that they must disclose a centre of origin.

The episode of Nipper's despatch was just one of these detached pointers. In itself it went for little but its line of direction might lead to something and in any case it was the *tertium quid* suggesting that the other incidents were unlikely to be fortuitous.

Nipper had been handled by someone who just before had been associated with chloroform. The dog had not been chloroformed itself for, as Carrados had settled, the head was wholly free from any touch of contact. Mr Batts was also eliminated as a possible conveyer when the opportunity offered.

The supposition that Geoffrey had been chloroformed was a reasonable hypothesis at that stage of the disclosure. Had the dog been brought upon the scene five minutes before he was, the point could have been settled very naturally, but by the time that Mr Carrados's nose had made him a present of that piece of information all chance of such a test had been shattered—quite unintentionally as it happened—by Olivant's effectual treatment of his patient's injuries.

If Geoffrey Tilehurst, Dr Olivant and Nipper were all

connected by an impending theft from the Tapsfield mills it should be possible to deduce—if not the actual plan in detail—at least a theory into which all the existing facts would fit and no construction that did not reconcile all that had happened was worth exploring. Tilehurst was naturally the crux, for the parts played by the other two were obviously contingent to his function. Was it possible that this responsible mill employee had been laid out and doped and was now existing in a mentally inert state by which he became an unconscious tool in the hands of those who had the key to his position? The basis was almost good enough to answer to the test but Carrados knew of neither drug nor process that could be relied on to work satisfactorily in practice under such tenuous conditions, and although Joolby might feasibly have access to some useful family hoodoo it was scarcely an assumption on which to conduct a serious investigation.

It would have been a simple enough move to warn the firm, but Max Carrados's interest lay in the phase of crime rather than in forestalling it, and on that score he had little tangible as yet to lay before a directorate of level-headed business men who would as likely as not regard him as an officious meddler. After all, what did it amount to? A dog had been run over through straying on the road. A man had received some sort of nervous shock that had upset his mental balance for the time being, and the good Samaritan who had come to his aid had a voice which the caller thought he recognised as having heard in a second-hand shop some time before and he might not be on the Medical Register. A curious tale with which to convey a serious warning that it all pointed to a sensational robbery!

On the other hand there was Scotland Yard, which would have lent a very attentive ear indeed, but it had always been the blind man's humour to take the official branch into his confidence after he had found out all he wanted rather than in the course of that process. One other detail was not without its influence. On the Sunday afternoon Mr Carrados again went across to Brookcroft and, somewhat to his amused chagrin, found that Miss Tilehurst did not consider it wise that her nephew should be submitted to the possible excitement of a meeting. Olivant had played his delicate part commendably well and although Nora flatly called it desertion of herself, of Geoffrey, and of the case, Uncle Max good-humouredly accepted the taunt but provokingly declined to be either goaded or cajoled into upsetting his arrangements.

'After all, there are two ends to every stick,' he reminded her, 'and it's quite on the cards for mine to be the one that next waggles. You did finely the other day and it's going to be of very great use, but for heaven's sake, my dear, don't get yourself into any scrape following things up—only if you do, remember that I'm the chap you've always got to fall back on.'

'I'm not going to promise anything after the perfectly fetid way you're running off,' she retorted. 'Still, it's pretty obvious that I shall stay here and do what I can for poor Geoffrey in the circumstances.' It occurred to the hearer, who was accustomed to glean much of his knowledge from the infinitesimals of tone, that there was a spice of 'It is my duty and I will' in this praiseworthy resolve which fell short of the ecstatic resolution of the Saturday Nora. It was an unwelcome suggestion but was this frank high-spirited niece of his becoming slightly calculating?

Mr Carrados was justified in his assumption that it was his end of the stick that might register the next movement, but it was Nora who supplied the action. And if the sudden and unannounced arrival of Miss Melhuish at 'The Turrets' contained any element of surprise for him, his habitual imperturbability enabled him to pass it off with disarming lightness.

'This is uncommonly nice of you, Nora,' he said, before she had had the chance to embark on any explanation; 'I was just wondering what to do next. The dogs' cemetery of course as soon as we've had some sort of refreshment. I'm glad you've taken me at my word about it.'

'Don't,' she begged, and immediately his face responded to the need of another sort of mettle. 'Miss Tilehurst isn't here now. I came because I was frightened.'

'That's even nicer of you, my dear,' he replied, and took a seat on the couch close to her. 'I expect the pair of us can down it.'

'Uncle Max,' she said, with a childlike directness that put such courtesies aside. '*Did you know?*'

At this, every instinct in him threw up a guard. There was always the chance of giving something away by taking too much for granted.

'Did I know?' he repeated, conscientiously searching his mind. 'Surely, Nora, that's a little vague. Did I know *what* exactly?'

'If you do know there's no need to ask,' she replied sharply. 'It can refer to nothing else—that he is not Geoffrey.'

Possibly she had looked for an exclamation, either of incredulity or of assent according to his knowledge, but Mr Carrados merely continued to look pleasantly interested.

'I did not know—I could not really know because I had never up to then met him. I could only admit that such a thing might be, although the chances were a million to one against that explanation. So that is it, actually? How did you find out?'

'I think I must have known all along—without knowing that I knew, if that doesn't sound too silly. You see, Uncle, it isn't anything to do with anything, being in love with a person—no matter how soppy it may sound to you in your wisdom. It's just a sort of Itness to do with one another and it won't work under any form of substitution. At first when I missed something that ought to have been there, I thought that it was just a rather contemptible streak of disillusion that Geoffrey should have been so terrified by anything that could have happened as to be scared into that condition, but of course if Geoffrey really had been it would have only made me care for him all the more.'

'And then?' prompted Carrados, for Nora seemed to be in

danger of losing herself in retrospection. 'Something definite happened?'

'I had seen Geoff—*him* once or twice and tried to get him out of that awful apathy but on each occasion he seemed to fight rather shy of me. Then yesterday I met him in the road—he'd been to the mill, I found—and he more or less *had* to walk with me unless he bolted for it.'

'Do you mean that up to then you hadn't been close to him?'

'I don't seem to have been, when I think it over,' she assented. 'You know that on the Saturday I was with you all the time, and since then it's always been in the house where he likes to keep in the shade and that poor dear tries to make everything go on as though nothing unusual had happened, and at the same time gets between him and anyone else who's there, like a troubled old hen with the last survivor of a brood of chickens.'

'Yes, I think Olivant must have been pretty word-perfect with his piece. I must find out where he was educated.'

'Well, as I say, we walked along the road on the way back. He doesn't speak yet—he doesn't try to, but I knew from his aunt that he has written a few words once or twice, just as that man said he would begin by doing. So I thought I'd try that.'

'Yes?' encouraged Mr Carrados.

'I suppose it must sound terribly sloshy to you, Uncle Max,' faltered Nora.

'Never mind that, my dear. I have always understood that under the most sportswomanlike jumper a tender heart might be beating.'

'I just wrote, "Am I still the same to you, dear?" and gave him the piece of paper. He took it and seemed to read it in that dreadfully detached way he has towards everything and then very slowly and shakily—all straight lines and angles you know—he scrawled, "Dear. Dearest," underneath the other.'

'That was fairly satisfactory at all events. It indicated a sufficiently reciprocal superlativeness of feeling.'

'The words didn't matter in the least. I only tell you exactly what took place for you to see that I had a perfect opportunity of noticing . . . On the Friday—the day before everything happened—we had been playing tennis and in some way Geoffrey jagged a finger-nail so that it kept catching in his things whenever he touched it. You know how beastly that feels and it was on the first finger of his right hand, so I took a little pair of nail scissors that I carry in my bag and filed down the corner of the nail for him until the notch was taken out and as smooth as ever. It was hardly anything, unless you looked for it of course, but one corner of the nail was down close and quite unlike the rest . . . and as I watched him write I found that I was looking at that finger-tip and suddenly it flashed on me that the nail I saw was just the same length all round and it couldn't possibly be the one I had altered.'

'Good,' commented the blind man, coming to his feet and beginning to walk about the room and in and out among the furniture; 'that's the sort of thing that takes *my* eye: *It could not possibly be*—and it couldn't! As evidence I don't suppose that it would be worth mentioning to a jury, who would be perfectly satisfied to convict a man who has been "picked out" of a dozen on the strength of a small brown moustache and a conspicuous limp, and yet it puts everything else behind it. Forgive me!'

'For just a moment I found myself groping among the background of my mind, trying to drag out a possibility that it might have been another finger or the other hand although I knew perfectly well that it wasn't. Then I looked up and saw his face and although every line and every feature was the same I realised all at once that he wasn't in the least like Geoffrey.'

'Did he see that you had guessed?'

'I hardly know. I heard your voice saying: "Keep your wits about you and don't give anything away!" and I pulled myself together. It was all over in a second or two and I got away as soon as I could then and that's the last I saw of him. Oh, Uncle Max, why ever didn't you tell me?'

'How could I, child? I didn't know myself. I only took into

consideration that it might be remotely possible. It was no good putting the idea into your head if it was a false scent but I dropped a hint or two that might back you up if you struck that line on your own initiative. It was really too much to hope for. Consider: of all the hundreds of thousands of pairs who have been said to be "as like as two peas" not one in a thousand could really pass for another. And yet how beautifully it rounds everything off as no other theory could—the presence and exact role of our providential medical friend, the behaviour and deficiencies of the fictitious Tilehurst, and the necessary immolation of the unfortunate dog that couldn't have been hoodwinked by mere externals.'

'That's all very well and I have no doubt that it's frightfully intriguing and all that,' said Nora with some impatience, 'but it doesn't happen to be the one thing that seems of any importance to me to be doing.'

'Implying the real Geoffrey Tilehurst?'

'Naturally—what else? Where is Geoffrey now and what are they doing to him?'

'At all events they are scarcely likely to have harmed him. They took the trouble to drug him to bring off the coup with a minimum of violence. Probably he is being held somewhere until the business is through when they will clear off and release him.'

'Or leave him gagged and bound somewhere so that they may get a longer start. The tender mercies of this particular gang are not likely to be very fastidious, I take it?'

'From what I know of the gentleman who is presumably acting as managing-director of the firm I shouldn't describe them as rabid humanitarians,' he admitted. 'The one thing you can rely on is that they won't do anything unnecessary that is palpably to their own disadvantage.'

'That's very consoling,' she retorted; 'isn't it? Well, Uncle Max, here I am. What do you propose to do to rescue Geoffrey before they happen to find it to their advantage to hold him up between themselves and a splash of C.I.D. bullets?'

'I think you exaggerate the risk, my dear,' he protested mildly. 'Geoffrey is as likely as not to be very well treated wherever he is, and I dare wager that he'd be perfectly willing to stick it for a few more days if that will mean our netting the whole gang with evidence that will convict them.'

'Perhaps he would, Uncle Max, but we can't ask him that and in the circumstances I've got to do what I consider the best thing for his interests. Get Geoffrey clear and then asphyxiate the lot and welcome.'

'But, my child, if Geoffrey is to be got out at this immature stage it blows the gaff completely. Half of the crowd will vanish, including all the worst, and we shall have no proof at all of the real depths of the conspiracy.'

'Sorry, Uncle; I know how attractive that part of it is to you, but Geoffrey's safety is more important to me than unearthing a plot to bomb the Houses of Parliament.'

'Of course, of course,' he hastened to assure her; 'so it is to me—er, theoretically. The only point of difference between us is that I see the extreme desirability of doing both. Secure the offenders in the act and Geoffrey's release automatically follows.'

'It might. On the other hand there might be one of those regrettable hitches where the experiment is perfectly successful only they unfortunately fail to revive the subject. As it is, I have a certain amount of leeway to make up for assuming that Geoffrey had been thrown into a blue funk—perhaps I shan't be quite so heroic about my own nerve until I've shown some.'

'Well, you made up a fair share when you got us that house in Maplewood Avenue, I should say,' he reminded her. 'A good deal may depend on what goes on there before we are through with it.'

'I wanted to ask you about that—the house I followed Olivant to. Have you found out anything yet?'

'Nothing at all, for the sufficient reason that so far the action hasn't reached there—the first move must come from Tapsfield. Of course if I had given Scotland Yard the tip they would have picketed the place but I saw no reason to make the Yard a present of the facts until I had a pretty complete case to gloat over them about. So that without letting it go out of my own hands I could only cover your end. I may decide to let Inspector Beedel in sooner than I had intended now—this dual Tilehurst business considerably modifies the outlook. And, apropos egad—that secluded old roomy house—er, yes; it might be as well to.'

'Go on, Uncle Max,' said Nora pleasantly. 'I like to watch your exceptional mind at work. Apropos the disappearance of Geoffrey, and that big old lonely house, you were saying—?'

'Saying, Nora? Only that if one is to do any good there it will be necessary—in due course—to get considerably more assistance.'

'Exactly what I was thinking as you spoke, dear. Both thoughts. I'm glad that there are points of the case where we have the same ideas. Don't think me presumptuous, Uncle, but it enables me to leave that part in your hands with every confidence.'

'My dear,' said Mr Carrados, bringing his involved perambulation to a close in front of her, 'I feel in a way responsible for letting you into this and no doubt that makes me seem fussy—'

'That's quite all right, Uncle,' replied Nora cheerfully. 'Mother would be ever so much obliged to you, I'm sure. If you—at the other end—happen to see her before I do again I know that you'll be able to satisfy her that I'm not likely to get into mischief.'

'I don't doubt that I shall,' he agreed, with a rueful acceptance of the position. 'I only wish I could satisfy myself as well while I'm about it. But you aren't going already?'

'Yes. It is rather a disappointment, isn't it? But I take it that the ordinary social amenities are suspended for the nonce—whatever a nonce may be—and you've given me what may be rather a bright idea.'

'Then in return perhaps you will give me just an ordinary one—as to what it's your intention to be up to now?'

'Well, I don't quite know yet or of course I should value your advice immensely. You see, Uncle Max, I rather take after you in one thing that I've noticed about your work—we both like to keep an open mind and to be decided by the requirements of the moment.'

'And you are determined to tell me nothing—'

'There's nothing really to tell . . . But isn't there a sort of Right by First Discovery? And, well, in a way I was the one to discover that house that he went to, wasn't I?'

'It seems to me, Joolby,' said Mr Nickle, picking his words with the air of elegant disdain which had the double effect of sometimes making the commonplace sound almost impressive and of always making the cripple secretly hate him rather more than before, 'it seems to me definitely to put the final lid on. If you take my advice you'll cut your losses, call everything off, and get Vallett out of the way so as to red herring the trail before they sight you.'

'If I took your advice, Nickle, and chaps like you, I should be pushing a little truck about Limehouse selling firewood,' replied Mr Joolby. 'Your trouble is that you see blue whenever you hear a whistle round the corner. This is going through, whatever happens.'

'Amiable lunatic,' murmured Nickle, turning again to the cypher message.

There were four of them present in Mr Joolby's back office behind the shop in Padgett Street and to judge by their morose looks things were becoming none too rosy for the Tapsfield undertaking. Joolby himself swelled and fumed in a venomous mood against gods, men, and devils; Nickle stretched his 'I-told-you-so' pose to its most offensive power and the other two, mere hirelings of crime on the dealer's long waiting list, bit their lips gloomily and exchanged looks of mutual support and mutual instigation.

'That's all very well, governor—"whatever happens",' said the more assertive of the two at this grandiose challenge, 'but what about we blokes as'll be left in it? You'll take bleed'n' good care to have plenty of time to do a guy when the fuse blows out, but it'll find Snooky and me stuck in a jam all right and no one's going to cut across and drop the signal.'

'And how am I going to "do a guy", you foolish fellow, if it comes to wrong?' demanded Mr Joolby, glowering heavily. 'You talk as if I could hop, skip and jump and leave everything behind me. Aren't I chained to the ground like what none of you aren't? Aren't I so tied to my house and shop here where I have thousands of pounds-worth of stuff—though, mind you, I can't sell it—that I should starve if I left them behind me? Was there ever such monkey chatter!'

'All the same, governor, what he says is right,' put in the other, anxious to back up his friend now that the first step had been taken. 'You're here, aren't you, if it comes to a bunk but we're there, cut off so to speak, and if anything slips, like what that bloke makes out in his letter, we shan't have half an earthly. Any reasonable risk's neither here nor there, governor, but it's no use blinkin' a blinkin' moral.'

'"If it go wrong," "if something slip," "is that a cop?" "Mammy come and give Bertie his dummy,"' bellowed Joolby, wrought almost to frenzy by the renewed thwarting of his cherished plans. 'Suffering Jesus! Am I the only one in the crowd with guts enough to cross a road in the dark or to walk past a police-station in the daylight? Isn't this the chance of a lifetime? Have either of you ever made a couple of quids at once in your puff before—pinching goods from the back of delivery vans and smooching lead off empty houses? And now in less than a week you'll have enough to keep you in beer to the end of your natural. Doesn't that make you brave enough to face even a chained bulldog?'

'That's right enough, governor, and if there wasn't—'

'Oh my God! I'm going out to breathe the pure air of

Shadwell,' exclaimed Mr Nickle, flinging himself from his chair in an access of fastidious irritation. 'It's like being in a gory squirrel cage with you three going round and round and getting nowhere.'

'How is there anywhere to get but here?' demanded Joolby with stubborn insistence. 'It's going on just as ever, don't I tell you, Nickle?'

'Comlade Blonsky want look-see,' announced Won Chou stolidly. As usual he gave the impression of knowing exactly what was going on without being there to see it, and although the ingenuity of his observation posts discounted the latter part of the assumption the former was probably correct enough.

'All right,' replied his master, with a painfully uncouth gesture of resignation, for the deputy was the last person he could have wished to have to deal with then, and he was feeling very tired. 'Make show glad come in.'

'Thank heaven even for Bronsky,' remarked Nickle, pausing in his door-ward progress. 'Time brings strange revenges!'

If Won Chou gave the impression of knowing everything without the least interest in what it was, Mr Bronsky's bearing was plainly that of a man who had been kept too long in the dark and was now determined to receive his proper meed of due attention. The glossy attire might be slightly less resplendent than when he first appeared, but his entrance had lost nothing of its thick-skinned suggestion that he was there to push his way in and to the front whether he was welcome or unwanted. The kiss of fraternal love had no longer any place in his greeting, in fact the greeting itself was reduced to the most perfunctory word and nod in the host's direction. Social distinctions were indicated by entirely ignoring the presence of both Nickle and the other two worthies.

'What is this which I hear of things going not well, Joolby?' he demanded, coming to the point at once. 'I was definitely to have been keep inform of any of the sort happening.'

'Ah, comrade, sorry that I didn't notice you had come in—

forgive the apparent discourtesy,' intervened Nickle in his most offensive vein of politeness. 'Well, I can only imagine that the omission has been through some underling mistaking his instructions—though possibly our not hearing anything detailed ourselves until now may have had something to do with the unfortunate position.'

'Psss! Tsss!' fumed Mr Bronsky, recognising that he was at a disadvantage in this sort of medium. He accordingly took off his hat and put it on again, sat down at the table with his back towards as many of those present as possible and began to drum loudly and persistently with his fingers.

'I beg your pardon?' remarked Nickle, raising his eyebrows; 'I didn't quite catch your remark,' but as Mr Bronsky merely drummed with increased vigour, what is sometimes called 'an awkward pause' was all that resulted from this brief passage.

'You have the letter, Nickle,' said Mr Joolby with conspicuous mildness. He seemed to have exhausted all his fighting spirit. 'Let him hear what Vallett says about it.'

'It is a message in code,' explained Nickle, shelving for the time being the acuter symptoms of resentment. 'Joolby here sees in it a promising augury of success; everyone else thinks it means that if we don't get out now we stand an excellent chance of getting about seven years a little later. However, I'll decode the essential part and then you can decide which view appeals to you the more.'

'How has this message you say is from Vallett come?' demanded Mr Bronsky with all the importance of one propounding something really vital.

'What the hell does that matter—comrade?' replied Nickle. 'Naturally we have our channels and this has come in quite the usual manner. If you think—but perhaps you would raise that valuable point after I have finished. Vallett writes: "I spotted the girl N."—by that he means a Nora Melhuish who lives near—"to be the chief danger from the beginning. She is mixed up with a man called Max Carrados who is evidently taking a hand in the game though I don't know yet exactly in what direction."'

'Ten thousand million tevils!' exclaimed Mr Bronsky, springing to his feet and glaring wildly round at each one in turn. 'What did I tell you, Joolby? Max Carrados again, and you would have it that he came to buy some of your junk rubbish. He was here that day I come and now he appear on the scene there. And you believe that all he wants are foreign stamps or is it dried ferns to stick into an album! Oh goddam, nobody can say I never warn you!'

'Quite so,' commented Nickle. 'Well, to resume the tale: "Today something missed a cog and whatever it was N. is now all but satisfied that G.T. is not the authentic."'

'She smell a rat?' propounded Mr Bronsky.

'We think he must mean that,' assented Nickle, with suspicious gravity. 'Unless you can cut N. off before she spreads, the big noise may happen any minute and even then I shall have to make some quick tricks to get clear. This is a pity because in all other directions it was going good and I was fixing for next Saturday when there will be a full stock and conditions easy. There you have it, Bronsky.'

'You shall do as you likes but I am done with it,' declared the comrade without a shade of hesitation. 'If it is as he says that this girl knows and is about there—why in name of thunder did you not have her taken care of before this happen?'

'Well, you see, Bronsky, for one thing we aren't in Bolivia here—not even in Chicago. People will talk so in the country— especially if it's a young girl—that we might just as well have floodlit the village while we were about it.'

'All the same, Mr Bronsky's in the right,' chimed in one of the others. 'You must either put this here girl away or else call off the whole business.'

'Precisely,' agreed Nickle. 'And as we can't do that it is called off in the general interest.'

'It is not called off,' spat out Joolby, gathering himself together in a last stand for the glorious hazard that in the course of weeks had become his passionate obsession. 'It is not changed one line, one inch, one minute. All this talk about recognising and risk and whatnot else is nothings but funk and fiddle. It is clear the girl did not be sure or she would have said so out and Vallett must have gone then. If she think there is something queer she is only puzzled what it is and days will go while she is making up her mind what has happened. I tell you these big jobs always has their touch and go and it is the side that does not get the jumps that comes away with the parcel.'

'Howsoever, I cannot be in it now it has come to this,' declared Mr Bronsky, siding with the majority with character-istic firmness. 'It would bring ill name with Commission. After all, Joolby, this is only detail—in the one matter of paper. There will yet be other ways—'

'There are no other ways,' retorted the other harshly. 'It was a perfect scheme and everything hung together. It still is and I'll carry it through myself and be damned to your wet trousers! Remember, Nickle, this was to be in my hands and so long as Vallett stays there—'

'Vallett will not stay there after today,' Nickle interrupted coldly. 'It's sheer madness to let him stay and be taken like a rabbit. I got him there and I'll make it my job to get him away tonight. So put that in those dry trousers of yours, Mr Joolby, and sit on it.'

'You are all against me, so? . . . and it would have been the most terrific smash . . .' muttered the cripple, falling back into his chair and seeming to grow less before their eyes as the realisation of failure closed in upon him. 'You may as well go away now. I do not want you.'

'Well, governor, what else could you expect?' genially put in one of the hirelings, good-naturedly hoping to impart a tinge of cheerfulness to the general leave-taking. 'Come to look at it as a reasonable man—blimey, hadn't you better see what the perishing blighter wants before he cracks the ruddy contrivance?'

Joolby turned listlessly towards the telephone on his desk—he did not appear to have noticed the calls up to then—and with his slow elaborate movements got the receiver to his ear.

'*What?*' they heard him say, and above the top of the desk—caught by the intensity of that one word—they saw his face change as he listened and the lethargy drop from it in such a startling fashion that all four stiffened where they stood, frankly waiting for dropped crumbs of enlightenment.

'Yes; yes; yes. Of course she will. Go easy and notice nothing. Here, hold on a minute, though. I want you to repeat what you've just said to Mr Nickle here. Nickle, get this slick and tell them what it means now.'

'My everlasting Lincoln and Bennett!' faltered Nickle, after he had complied, listened for a moment, and then hung up the receiver; 'this—this is really one beyond the limit! George Larch says that Eliza there has suddenly gone sick and sent a cousin in her place to carry on until she gets over it.'

'Go on, go on,' blared Joolby, swelling and gasping in his chair as Nickle paused and looked round to gather their attention for his dramatic climax. 'Tell them what he said then.'

'The "cousin" is Nora Melhuish from Tapsfield—Soapy recognised her for a cert—and now she's walked in of her own free will and all we have to do is to shut the door and keep her.'

'No need to call it off, you see,' croaked Mr Joolby, enjoying his little triumph quite good naturedly. 'It still goes on, eh, Nickle?'

'Why the hell not?' replied Nickle, with a shrug that might mean anything. 'Joolby, I really begin to think that you must be under divine protection—by "divine" in your case of course I refer to the devil.'

CHAPTER XII

THE STAGE IS SET

'GEORGE, dear,' said Mrs Larch, as her husband put his head in at the door of the dining-room to see what was going on there, 'do come in for a minute or two and make it a bit human.'

'Why certainly; what is it, old girl?' he inquired, amiably complying.

'It isn't anything particular,' she confessed. 'Only this place—it's like a bloody prison.'

'Well, for the matter of that it is one,' he replied—still naïvely pained to hear Cora swear, even as it always came to him as a faint shock to see her drink gin and water. 'That young fellow down there—'

'Oh, don't talk about it,' she said with a deprecatory shudder. 'The way one thing's led to another till we're mixed up in raids and kidnappings and Bolshie plots—! Thank goodness we've nothing to do with what goes on down below. Let his Chinks and dagoes do his dirty dungeon work if he wants it done, I say. It's not what we're paid for. Nothing was said to you about keeping anyone shut up in a cellar when you took it on to come here, was it, George?'

'Not a thing. There was to be more room and it would be safer in a new place for a week or two—that was all I ever heard. I don't like it any more than you do, Cora, but there seems nothing for it now we're here but to hang on for the time and chance it.'

'You may well say chance it, lad. From what I see and what I hear it seems to be getting a pretty near thing which side touches down first, but the old geezer's dead set on going through whatever turns up, and God knows that if it comes to a general bunk he's bound to be the hindmost.'

'Except that he'd throw everyone else out to the wolves to make time to do a getaway,' George amended. 'He's always been very lucky at that so far, has Joolby.'

'Lucky! He has nigger's own luck if you ask me about it. This thing was absolutely down on the rim over what natty Nora had spotted up there, and then, lo and behold, if my lady doesn't coolly walk in to rescue her boy, for all the world like Glory le Roy in a Wild West three-reeler. That gives you the laugh, doesn't it? As if she could have put it across the cat that she was Eliza's cousin.'

'Well, she could have put it across me for that matter if Dodger, who'd seen her up there, didn't happen to call round to do with the business,' admitted George simply. 'All these finches seem to get themselves up in the same way nowadays, till I can't tell one sort of tart from another. But I suppose there's something you go by.'

'There's certainly something I can tell Nora Melhuish by from any cousin Eliza Higgs is likely to have, let alone one who'd be willing to come round here to carry on while Eliza was moulting. All the same, it's none too pleasant for me. I'm used to Elizas. I understand their little ways and if they don't understand mine they pretty soon get to. But this Hilda Kelly as she calls herself knows just how things should be properly done and that puts me at a disadvantage. Now would you say that those chairs ought to be left up to the table between meals, George, or pushed back, and should the cruet be kept on the sideboard or put away in the cupboard? I'm blessed if I know.'

'I'm damned if I do either. But what does it matter?'

'It doesn't. That's just the silly part of it—running the place for a crowd of crooks and roughnecks. But *she* would know, and if it's not done *à la* Ritz she'd put it right after me and make me feel a mut. Wouldn't say anything of course—just show me how it should be.'

'Well it can't be for long now,' suggested George soothingly. 'After this we'll—'

'And then there's another thing,' volubly continued Mrs Larch, to whom the relief of possessing George's ear was scarcely less of a luxury than in the rag-and-bone shop days, 'and I like it rather less than all the other. She's not to be out of my sight for so much as a tick, if you please, unless I pass her on to that half-baked Chink, and all the time I'm not so sure that someone else isn't told off to keep an eye on me—and perhaps on you too, George, for that matter.'

'They're welcome,' said George, with the proud conscious-ness of innocence. 'What I say I'll do I do. Joolby knows well enough that I've never double-crossed anyone.'

'At all events we can go in and out and that's more than Hilda Kelly is to be allowed to. Mustn't answer the door, mustn't touch the telephone, mustn't stir out of the house—I ask you now, George, what's likely to be the end of this sort of thing when her people get the wind up? And if the cops begin to take notice what does it look like on a night like this, when everyone else is sitting in their shirt-sleeves with the windows wide open, and all these are shut up as if we expected a siege—well, I ask you?'

At this, George looked dutifully about and with a wise shake of the head admitted that from this point of view it might certainly strike the unprejudiced outsider as 'a bit rummy'. The place was the dining-room of the old-fashioned, well-retired house in Maplewood Avenue, a spacious, heavily furnished apartment, sufficiently well lit by a single cluster electrolier but with its windows—although they were overlooked from nowhere but its own secluded grounds—not only all scrupulously closed on that torrid summer night but with the curtains drawn, and shuttered. It had been a simple enough matter to keep Geoffrey Tilehurst secure without any elaborate precautions; a cellar, closed by a substantial oak door, and a man deprived of everything faintly resembling a tool could be thrust in and safely left to his own devices. But in Nora's case the fiction of liberty was outwardly kept up and though from the moment of her quixotic intrusion she was shadowed at every step and had not the remotest chance of slipping away if she repented of her boldness, she was even yet unable to decide whether her identity had been discovered or whether the spying and restraint were not merely commonplace details of this very queer household.

'One thing,' added George, after the peculiarities of the situation had been sufficiently admitted, 'it's going to be the last time I'm mixed up in what isn't strictly on the level. If we get clear this once with anything like tidy, old girl, it'll be that little cottage with the pigs and poultry for a moral.'

'Oh, my dear lad, that cottage!' exclaimed Mrs Larch, somewhere between laughing and tears. 'I wonder how many times we've paid a pretty price for it already!' and then on a common impulse this curiously simple pair of habitual criminals were in each other's arms and exchanging fond kisses for all the world like honest lovers.

'Hullo, turtle doves,' remarked Nickle, stumbling in upon this idyll and accepting it with saving coolness. 'Seen anything of Toady since dinner?'

'He was in his own sanctuary about five minutes ago with that latest Alsatian Bolshie. Arranging for the end of the world, I suppose. Did you want him?'

'No, it can wait. It's rather amusing, you know. I'll tell you the very latest.'

'If it's one of your funny stories, Mr Nickle,' interposed George rather hastily, 'perhaps we'd better go—'

'No, that's all right,' said Nickle with a comprehensive smile. 'This is something that really happened just now—not what the barmaid said about the bathing suit to the bishop. I was going across the Triangle down there and who should I run into but our interesting invalid, Eliza Higgs, making her way towards the Rialto Picture House, with an equally young lady friend, both very superbly dressed for the occasion.'

'Well I never!' contributed Mrs Larch.

'Oh yes, I assure you. Jewels flashed and silk garments rustled. Well, seeing that further disguise was useless Eliza capitulated and at the inducement of a strawberry ice—supplemented may I perhaps say by the attraction of my society—permitted herself and friend to be lured into Cushing's Comfy Corner Café where under skilful innuendo she broke down at her third sundae and gave away the whole transaction.'

'She would,' was Mrs Larch's tart comment. 'That's Eliza Higgs all over.'

'Oh well; we mustn't be too harsh. The young lady who dropped down on Eliza from the clouds—she'd evidently been watching for the chance—assured her that it was all a joke, in fact that she'd made a bet she could act as a servant for a week in a strange house without anything being spotted. Then she offered Eliza five Bradburys and what she was wearing at the time to co-operate and Eliza, we may imagine, simply leapt at it.'

'It was a mean thing to give it away though,' remarked George severely. 'After taking the money.'

'Possibly Eliza misunderstood some of the facts. From what she dropped, apropos of what I had said, I gathered that she may have assumed that I was in the secret, on Hilda Kelly's side, from the start,' admitted Nickle glibly. 'However, it didn't really matter either way. We knew pretty well how it stood already.'

'Still, I think that Hilda might have hit on something better in the way of a fairy tale than what she did,' speculated Mrs Larch. 'She seems quite a sharp girl in general.'

'Oh, I don't know,' maintained Nickle impartially. 'Of course since it tore one's inclined to say that, but as things stood what likelier tale could she put up at short notice? She might have got away with it, too, if it hadn't been—Oh, all right; I'll take it.'

The interruption was a telephone call and Nickle crossed over to the small table by the door while the other two, the subject of Eliza talked out, waited to hear if there was any new development. Most of the calls that came were dead matter, for in the directory their number still appeared against the name of the former tenant and less than a dozen intimates were in a position to get through to them.

'It's "Soapy", talking from somewhere down there,' rapped out Nickle, covering the mouthpiece as he spoke back into the room. 'Get Joolby if you can, one of you.'

Mrs Larch nodded to George and hurried out. But Joolby's progress was slow even on the level and this entailed a flight of stairs—or possibly the Alsatian Bolshie was difficult to get away from. At all events the conversation was over and the receiver hung up again before the cripple dragged his trailing feet through the doorway.

'What's this?' he said, the quickened beat of his throat betraying the stress of his exertion. 'Is Dodger there speaking?'

'He was,' replied Nickle, 'but he's gone. He seemed to be pressed for time and I gathered that telephoning at all was rather risky.'

'Well, where was he talking from?'

'God knows,' said Nickle with a shrug. 'Some wayside shrine one would imagine. He is scarcely likely to have rung us up from the village pub and in any case there's no idea of calling on him from our end.'

'Well, what was it?'

'He says it's all right for Saturday still. Nora M. doesn't seem to have done any harm so far but he's getting jumpy about that fellow Carrados. He can't make out what's going on in that direction but he wishes you could do something. That's all.'

'Oh, it is, is it? That's quite satisfactory, isn't it, Nickle? And he's getting jumpy about Max Carrados, is he? Strange that I'm the only one who never seems to get jumpy, isn't it? I suppose it has something to do with my physical peculiarities, for even as a boy I don't remember ever to have gone in much for jumping. Well, as regards Mr Carrados I have already arranged, as he suggests, to "do something".'

'The deuce you have!' said Nickle, staring his curiosity. 'How is it to be wangled?'

'All in good time, my friend; you won't be left out of the performance. Now go down and help Won Chou and Jules to get things ready. They know what will be needed. And you bring Hilda up to me here, Mrs Larch. I want to have a little quiet talk with my new maid-servant.' He waited until they had gone and then looked significantly at Mr Larch. 'You understand all right, don't you, George?'

'Oh yes; I understand all right, Mr Joolby,' replied Larch in his transparent way. 'And so long as it doesn't go actually to extremes—'

'It shan't go actually to extremes, George.' Mr Joolby's voice sounded positively sympathetic.

'I know that it may have to be cut rather fine and stretched rather far at a pinch of course, Mr Joolby. That's in the nature of the business we are on. But I rely on you to give me the nod in time to get Cora clear off whatever happens. I can take my own whack as it comes—as I always have done.'

'Of course, George, of course. Women and children first— that's what the Bible says, isn't it? But not extremes on any account, eh? Well, well!'

'You know what I mean well enough, Mr Joolby. I mean bloodshed. I never have—'

'Here is Hilda, sir,' announced Mrs Larch, reappearing at the door. 'You said you wanted to see her.'

'To be sure; to be sure,' assented Joolby, plainly in his most benevolent mood. 'And you two had better stay as well now you are here. One can't be too careful, I understand, in dealing with emotional young females.'

'As you please, sir,' replied Mrs Larch, remaining between Nora and the door, while George, painfully wishing that he could be away at the more congenial occupation of forging bank-notes, dropped discreetly further into the background.

'So you are our new help, Hilda Kelly, eh, girl?'

'Yes, sir,' she answered rather feebly. It was the first time Nora had encountered Joolby face to face, and at the sight of his monstrous swelling infirmities she realised with a tremor of dismay that unless she could fight it down she might suddenly become faint, or sick, or something discreditably weak, if the ordeal went much further.

'And Miss Nora Melhuish, of Orchard Close, Tapsfield, also?' continued her employer. 'Well, well'—as Nora found herself unable to combat this thrust in her agitated plight—'there's no great harm in having two different sets of names, and nearly all of our aristocracy have at least two separate addresses. Some of the most illustrious characters in history have found it convenient to change their identity from time to time. I have myself, and I dare say that Mr Larch there has been described as alias this or alias that on certain state occasions.'

'I don't see what my private affairs have to do with my employment here so long as I do the work,' she managed to retort, hoping to be let off farther questioning on this tacit admission.

'Very reasonably put,' conceded Mr Joolby, still pleasantly tickled by what was going on, 'and that brings me to another matter. Hearing that your cousin Eliza was feeling indisposed you came here to take her place so that we should not be inconvenienced, didn't you? Very thoughtful and considerate indeed; so different from what one usually hears of the domestic servant classes.'

'If you don't mind I should like to get on with my work, sir,' she put in, as unconcernedly as she could. 'All this has nothing to do with my duties.'

'Your work, eh?' replied Joolby, his mood suffering a remarkable transition as he proceeded. 'Why, yes, of course; that's what you're here for, isn't it? But part of your duties, properly considered, consists in taking instructions and answering your employer's questions and so on, eh, doesn't it? Well, Miss Hilda Nora Kelly Melhuish, in the short time that you have been here among us have you discovered anything unusual or irregular in the conduct of this establishment?' Then as she stood irresolutely dumb at this the cripple unexpectedly swung one of his wooden props and brought it down with a terrifying crash on the bare table lying between them. 'Answer me, girl; have you?'

'No, sir,' she protested faintly.

'You haven't, eh? Then let me tell you that your eyesight is very little better than your Uncle Max's, Hilda Nora. You must have made very poor use of your opportunities here, for, you may as well know now, our business consists in imitating the paper currency of certain foreign countries—countries unfriendly to England and more or less actually at war with us if the truth was known. It's a political business but none the less it's technically illegal and so if it got about we should all get into trouble. You follow that?'

'Well, I suppose it's forgery in fact,' she replied.

'Forgery! What do you know about forgery, girl? If I sign my own name on a telegram it may happen to be forgery in point of law. Think of that.'

'But these are bank-notes you say.'

'Well, what does it matter after all?' suggested Mrs Larch on a note of persuasion. 'I mean to say, there's nothing really *wrong* about imitating things like that—it's only that they've made laws about it. It isn't as though you hurt anyone or did them out of something—which I certainly wouldn't hold with. It stands to reason that one bank-note's as good as another so long as people only think so; at least George's are, in fact they're better than the real ones if it comes to that. I often say it's the people who go kicking up a fuss when they find that they've been slipped a soft one who deserve to be put in the cart. Why can't they pass it on quietly to someone else and then no one would be a penny the worse off?'

'Well, it seems rather queer—' protested Nora, beginning to be a little reassured by the trend of the conversation.

'Never mind what it seems; I didn't have you up to listen to what you think but to tell you what to do,' retorted Mr Joolby, taking over the conversation. 'No doubt you thought you were very clever to get in here, didn't you? Well, we thought we were even cleverer to get you, so it wasn't very difficult you see. Now your Uncle Max Carrados has been interesting himself in our affairs much more than is good for him during the last few days. You say that you have noticed nothing going on wrong here. So why not tell him that and persuade him to drop it. Eh? Eh?'

It sounded too good to be true. All she would have to do would be to—

'Why certainly. I'll go at once and tell him that I've seen nothing at all wrong here.'

'You will, eh? Very good. But you won't have the trouble of going. He may be here any minute now.'

'Max Carrados here?' she exclaimed. 'What is he coming here for?'

'It would appear that you wrote and begged him to come at once,' deliberately replied Mr Joolby, and looking at his face—which she had avoided doing to the extent of her power—the girl suddenly knew that the Thing before her was crudely and inhumanly evil. He was without pity, beyond restraint, and impervious to remorse; all the time he had been playing with her fears and enjoying the thought of the worse terrors he yet had in store for her. Oddly, the revelation helped her. 'The message was rather ambiguously worded,' he continued with meaning, 'but it suggested a good excuse for him to call and it was sufficiently—shall I say disturbing—to make sure that he'd be a little anxious. Oh yes, he will come all right. In fact I can assure you that he is on his way now.'

'So you forged my writing also—it's not only bank-notes it seems! And you think that Max Carrados will walk into a trap like that—or that I would do anything but tell him the whole truth the minute I see him?'

'The whole truth, so far as you are concerned, is that you have found nothing wrong going on here,' he reminded her.

'Convince him of that and all will be well for both of you . . . The little matter of our private activities that I mentioned just now was strictly confidential and you had much better dismiss it entirely from your mind.'

'Yes; why should you have mentioned it at all?' she asked suspiciously. 'Why need you?'

'I needn't. But I want you to understand that we really mean serious business, and that having very heavy risks to face we aren't going to stick at anything.'

'You mean that I should league myself with you in trying to deceive Mr Carrados and the authorities? Is it likely?'

'I think it is quite likely when you have considered a little; so likely that you'll strain every nerve and try every artifice in your power to do it. You are very young to—to meet with an accident, Nora Kelly, and it would hardly be a pleasant thought that you had drawn Max Carrados into a trap with you. Ah; I fancy that must signify our myopic friend's arrival.'

'That' had been the resounding clamour of an ancient bell somewhere below, for, side by side with its electric lights and telephone, the venerable mansion still retained the campanological features of its Victorian prime. Mrs Larch exchanged glances with her employer and significantly withdrew. These details were not lost on Nora (as, indeed, they were intended not to be) but surely her sagacious Uncle Max could be trusted not to be taken in by a ruse so transparent?

'It's no good, Mr Joolby,' she challenged. 'You think that you can frighten me with silly talk like that? You seem to forget that we are in London. Why, I have only to scream out to bring half a dozen policemen in. And I am quite sure that Max Carrados won't walk in here without making it certain that if he doesn't soon come out again the C.I.D. will smash down the door if need be to find out what has happened. I know him well enough for that.'

'People don't scream out here, Hilda Nora,' he replied, and his level assurance struck her coldly. 'If they did nobody outside would hear them.'

'It's no good talking like that,' confirmed George Larch. 'He won't be given the opportunity to arrange anything; he won't even know where he is coming. The person who gives him the note will deliver it when he's alone and he must come at once and be guided here if he is to come. No, Miss Melhuish, if Max Carrados does come here nothing but your doing exactly as we tell you will get either of you out again. And that's the best advice you'll have in this house.'

'You hear what he says,' directed Joolby. 'That's the moderate view of the situation. Ah, here's Mrs Larch coming back. Now we shall know just how we stand.'

'A Mr Carrados is below, sir,' reported Mrs Larch, as indifferently as she might have announced the vicar calling. 'He says he would like to speak with the young person employed here if it's convenient.'

'Ask him to wait a few minutes. And be sure to see that he has something to amuse himself with. Now, girl, you haven't much time to make up your mind. Which is it to be?'

'Just whatever I like,' retorted Nora. 'You can't bluff me into anything and I fancy that Max Carrados will be able to take care of himself if he's come here. That's all.'

'All, is it?' snarled Joolby, beginning to display the familiar symptoms of his ire. 'Oh no; not quite all yet, I think, Nora Hilda. Just open that door, George, and let's see if we can't find another argument why she should listen to reason.'

The door thus indicated was the second one in the room—hitherto unused and not yet mentioned. It led into a small ante-chamber and so out again on to a passage and the stairs, this having been in the house's ampler days either a dressing-room or a service pantry as the conditions called for. This was the door George Larch now crossed over to and threw open and in the pause between the action and anything more happening a dreadful fear began to close in round Nora's heart while her knees grew as flimsy as stubble. *What* would emerge from that darkened room to confront her?

'Geoffrey!' was wrung from her lips as a figure, urged on by someone behind, stumbled into the light; 'oh, my dear, how terrible you look. What are they doing to you?'

Geoffrey Tilehurst stood cowering and blinking in the unaccustomed glare but he seemed to make no effort to reply nor did he respond to her instinctive gesture of compassion. Then as he came further into the room—pushed forward by Won Chou—she understood. He was gagged and his hands tied behind him.

'What's this, Won Chou?' demanded Joolby, as though mildly surprised. 'Who ordered like so fashion?'

'Make much noise,' indifferently replied Won Chou. 'Tellee shall do: do do.'

'In that case it would appear to be his own fault,' approved Joolby coolly. 'Guests must conform to the rules of the house. Remove the gag now and let us hear what he has to say for himself—perhaps he has learned to know better.'

'Nora! You are here to save me?' painfully mumbled Geoffrey, when Won Chou—none too gently as evidenced by a bleeding lip—had complied. 'For God's sake don't believe anything they say. Only get me away from this dreadful place where I'm being—' A menacing gesture from another man who had silently appeared cut off the word and Geoffrey shrank back as though he knew only too well that the threat was no empty promise.

'Oh, Geoffrey, what can I do, only tell me,' she begged—'We had no idea that anything like this—we thought that you were just being kept out of the way. Even now I don't understand—'

'Come, that will do,' interrupted Joolby with an impatient growl; 'talk, talk, talk—that's all it ever comes to with your kind of cattle. Do you still think that you are playing at charades, girl? Can't you see the sort of men you have to do with? You "don't understand—!" No, I do not think you do, but we will very soon explain it . . . For the next three days we must be left undisturbed and to make sure of that there is nothing on earth that we are going to stick at. You and this man'—with a sweep of the minatory crutch—'must remain in our hands that long because you know too much. This Carrados has nosed into our affairs and so he must be reassured and headed off. We can't keep him as well—at least we'd rather not—because he's too influential it seems and he's set inquiry afoot, and before our time was up there might be the hell of a disturbance. Now you have it.'

'But what have I—?'

'What you have to do is to convince him that he's been mistaken. If you do that you have nothing to be afraid of. At the end of three days you can both walk out—the best guarantee is that we have nothing to fear from you then and it would be inconvenient to have to leave someone to keep you. If you refuse—well, you see your friend there? A little more strain—a very little perhaps—and I'm afraid—I really am afraid, Miss Kelly—that his rather disturbed mind may be permanently unbalanced . . . As for yourself, I scarcely like to put into words what will probably happen to you before you get away. These crude Eastern races are so primitive in their ideas of the use they make of female captives.'

'Oh, you fiend!' she flung back; 'you unutterable brute! You would never dare—'

'Dare! I dare?' he retorted, dragging himself nearer to her and raising his form to the full on his props almost with a savage grandeur. 'Look at me, brute that I am; look, look, girl, and then think! What is there that men can do to me now that nature hasn't done already!'

'Nora,' besought the unfortunate Tilehurst, pitifully whining in his distress, 'don't drive them to do worse than I've had already. Get me away on any terms for God's sake before I—I—Do anything they ask you.'

'Oh, you poor, poor—' she cried out in her pain, immeasurably shocked at his pathetic deterioration, Then turning to Joolby again: 'If I do as you want—?'

'No harm will come to either of you meanwhile and at the end of three days you will be free.'

'Tell me exactly what I have to do.' At a sign the prisoner was led away again and the door of the ante-room closed on his humiliation. George Larch alone remained to lend Joolby whatever support the developments might entail and the moment was almost reached towards which so much preparation had been directed.

'When Carrados comes up you must receive him naturally and convince him that it's all been an unfortunate misunderstanding about us here,' said the cripple, in reply to Nora's admission of surrender. 'Don't try any half-and-half shilly-shallying. Make no error about it, girl: you've got to succeed and to do it thoroughly.'

'It isn't an easy thing to deceive Max Carrados. No matter what I say he may not—'

'Agggh!' he snarled impatiently, 'it won't be an easy thing to watch your young man being put through a course or to find yourself strapped down, will it? You're clever enough in your way, I'll be bound, and the fellow's blind anyhow. You came to spy on us here, didn't you? You've—let us say—been in every corner of the house and gone through all the papers. Well, it's—what?—"a bloomer". You have found simply an old fellow who has made a little something by years of hard work in his second-hand shop and is now retiring into private life and doesn't want to be troubled. Eh? Eh?'

'I must succeed,' she whispered, more to herself than in assent. 'God help me!'

CHAPTER XIII

NORA TELLS THE TALE AND CARRADOS
SUPPLIES THE MUSIC

'HERE you are, sir,' announced Mrs Larch, piloting Mr Carrados solicitously into the room and then standing off to survey, as it were, her achievement in getting him safely there with some pride, 'No more nasty stairs to climb up. And there is Hilda.'

'Uncle Max!' exclaimed Nora, in her very brightest manner. 'So you really have come then?'

Like many blind men of ingenious mind Mr Carrados prided himself on his ability to get about by himself and to tell the truth he was occasionally a little unceremonious in his rejection of sympathetic assistance.

'Let me find my own way; I'll manage to do it somehow,' he would remark as he put these well-intentioned people aside. 'If I do knock my shins it will teach me to remember the position of something for ever,' and though none of his closest friends could recall the occasion when Mr Carrados had knocked his shins they all might have instanced rather odd little touches of clumsiness or unaccountable lapses in his form which had at the time seemed surprising. Inspector Beedel, whose Yard record was not unaffected by their acquaintanceship in the past, had his own views of these failings.

'When Mr Carrados makes a break,' he had been known to say, 'it's about time for some blighter to hop it.'

On this occasion, however, there was nothing drastic to deplore. Smiling away Mrs Larch's proffered arm the blind man stretched out his hands right and left and—more than anything from a matter of habit one would judge—touched the door and wall here and there as though to learn thereby the points of his location. Certainly he narrowly escaped a minor disaster at the telephone table which lay in his path but with an exclamation of annoyance at the contact—a mere brush—he neatly verified its position and nature. And if this was a wily snare on the visitor's part to surprise a betraying sound from anyone who lurked, it failed signally in its object. Mrs Larch could not restrain a little gasp of dismay when she saw what nearly happened but Mr Joolby and George from their well-retired positions—the former seated, the more active man standing— were both too wide-awake to betray their presence.

'Well, my dear,' admitted Mr Carrados in answer to his niece's greeting, 'I gathered that you might not be altogether sorry to see me. So'—with a reassuring laugh—'here I am.' A mild amusement at the possible humours of the situation characterised his manner.

'Now I'll leave you two quite alone, if you'll excuse me, Mr Carrados,' tactfully remarked Mrs Larch, with an admonitory glance at the two figures in the background. 'Being a gentleman, I can hardly expect you to understand, perhaps, but as it happens I'm rather busy.'

'Oh, but I do understand,' he gallantly assured her. 'I get rather busy myself sometimes. You mustn't judge me merely from an idle visit.'

All very pleasant, no doubt, but every one of the five people in the room had, in the vulgar phrase, 'other fish to fry'. and Mrs Larch's cue was to get out of the way without delay and give them the opportunity to be at it. This she accordingly now did closing the door with perhaps a little unnecessarily elaborate evidence of her departure, and uncle and niece were left 'alone' together.

'What a very agreeable sort of person, Nora,' he blandly observed, discovering for himself a suitably placed chair and occupying it. 'Made me feel that I was giving no trouble at all in calling.'

'Oh yes, she is,' eagerly confirmed Nora. 'And it's all the

more because I feel so dreadfully ashamed of the trick I've played on them here. Uncle Max, you know we really *have* done it!'

'Ah?' he endorsed vaguely. 'I guessed that there had been something of a fiasco from your hasty note, but—I could see that you wrote rather in a flurry—you know you left it all rather ambiguous. Indeed, from one thing or other you said I half thought that you might be in some sort of'—discreetly lowering his voice—'danger!'

'Danger!' she laughed, in great high spirits; 'what a perfectly priceless notion! No, indeed, old dear; the only danger about here was the danger of making a great goose of myself, and so my first thoughts flew to you as the readiest means of getting me out of an awkward situation.'

'Why of course,' he agreed. 'Always fall back on Uncle Max—if you remember I particularly put you up to that whenever you get yourself in any mischief. And in the present case I feel more or less responsible for I have half an idea that it's partly my fault your being here. Now as we are quite alone suppose you tell me exactly how you are situated?'

'Well, Uncle, it's really been a ghastly mistake from the very beginning. Of course I can't pretend to say what may have been going on anywhere else and certainly from one thing and another there seemed to be enough to make you suspicious. But these people at all events are as innocent of crime—it really makes me want to laugh—as district visitors, and I feel that we ought to do—well, to do anything we can to make up for perhaps getting them suspected.'

'Um, yes; perhaps we ought, now that you've settled it,' he admitted, with just a shade of lingering reluctance. 'By the way, who are the people, Nora?'

'Well, there's Mr Joolby, of course. It's his house I believe and he is more or less—an invalid. He has a shop, an antique shop, somewhere else in London, I understand, but I think he's retiring now and that's why things are rather upset and haphazard yet as he isn't really settled. Then there's Mrs Larch, the housekeeper—you've seen her already.'

'The agreeable lady?'

'Ye-es. Oh, but they are all quite pleasant and agreeable people really.'

'All? There are others then?'

'I mean those who happen to call—visitors. They're quite ordinary, respectable people, you know. I think that they mostly have to do with Mr Joolby's business—I mean his shop of course.'

'Not the sort of people who'd commit burglaries or plan elaborate forgeries?'

'The very idea! One or two of them may be rather foreign-looking perhaps but I suppose a good many people are what one would consider eccentric characters who have to do with the antique business.'

'Yes, I imagine so: Bohemian and all that. And the providential gentleman whose name doesn't seem to figure on the medical register—Dr Olivant. He came here if you remember.'

It was unfortunate that Mr Carrados should have recalled this. So far it had been quite plain sailing among airy generalities but Dr Olivant was a specific case and had to be dealt with concretely. For a moment Nora had to think; luckily the inspiration accorded her was on lines that admitted a certain amount of hesitancy when explaining the facts to an old-fashioned uncle.

'Why yes, to be sure he did, didn't he?' she admitted, with careful deliberation. 'Well it's—it's rather mysterious about him until you know the circumstances. He really has been a doctor and a specialist and he is quite qualified to give advice, only Olivant isn't his proper name. He's—been—been struck off the register. He's a little queer they say, and at times forgets about what has happened.'

'Tshk, tshk; sad, sad,' commented Mr Carrados sympathetically. 'And such an imposing presence.'

'Yes, it does seem a pity, doesn't it? Illegal operations, you know. So of course it's rather a delicate subject with him.'

'Naturally; naturally. How little we know after all, Nora, of the tragedy that may be going on about us under the quiet prosaic surface! And as he came here, I suppose that the doctor has turned his hand to the antique business also, has he?'

'Well, he had to do something for a living I imagine. Of course he can't be a doctor any longer, can he? I think he helps Mr Joolby with the shop in some way.'

'Operates on the damaged articles of virtu doubtless. Well, Nora, you seem to have made pretty good use of your time here.'

'Oh I have; I have. Of course no one suspected me of anything and I have watched them and listened at key-holes and looked at everything that I wasn't supposed to see in the most shameless manner. That's why I can be so positive that there's nothing at all wrong going on here.'

'Then the only thing we can do would seem to be to get out of it as gracefully as possible. There's no point in your staying on any longer. After all, as a domestic help I have no doubt that—without being in any way critical of your abilities, my dear—Mr Joolby can replace you without much trouble.'

Mr Carrados smiled a good-humoured tolerance of the imbroglio in which they had both landed, leaned back in his chair and dropped a careless right into his coat pocket.

'Look here, Nora,' he suggested mischievously, 'I have rather a bright idea. We shall cut pretty foolish figures when it comes to explaining, shan't we? What do you say to slipping quietly out and writing our apologies?'

For perhaps a couple of seconds the girl's mind poised, while her slanting eyes took in at a flash the essentials of the situation: the unguarded door, so near, George Larch away across the room and Joolby quite literally and negligibly 'out of the running'. So much had happened emotionally in the past short half-hour that, as the phrase goes, she scarcely knew which way up she was standing and for the time at least she had entirely lost touch with the vital crux of the situation. It remained for a rather uncanny happening to decide her. Apparently of its own accord the door of the ante-room noiselessly fell open and in the now well-lit space beyond her startled eyes took in the tableau of Geoffrey in his attitude of hopeless terror with the two custodians who had charge standing above him. Almost at once the door was closed again but the reminder had been sufficient.

'No, no; I really couldn't do that—not as things are,' she protested rather wildly. 'Don't ask me to, Uncle Max, because—well, I shouldn't like you to think that I can't stay and face it. And you do understand that everything's all right here, don't you?'

'Oh, bless you, yes,' he replied. 'All the same I think we could carry it off. It might be the simplest in the end. I'm almost inclined—'

'No, no!' she insisted. 'I mustn't think of it. Don't, Uncle; please don't. We could never—I mean it wouldn't be *right* in the circumstances; it really wouldn't. Don't you see, I've bribed and persuaded their servant to let me take her place and if I run away like that they'll be left quite in the lurch—it isn't so easy to get anyone at a moment's notice as you may think and they'd perhaps have to go on for days and days servant-less. That's the only reason I have for staying; it really is. They're quite all right here in every way I do assure you.'

'Oh yes; it isn't that. The boot's on the other foot in fact; I should like to think that we'd been clever enough to be on the right tack from the start but you've quite burst that bubble. Only I wish it had gone the other way for it's devilish awkward for me as it happens. Inspector Beedel of Scotland Yard is relying on my inquiries in this quarter and now I shall have to call it off and admit that I was mistaken . . . You seem rather pleased, my dear'—for Nora had given a sigh that unmistakably conveyed relief and satisfaction.

'Well, it is something of an event to find Max Carrados wrong for once,' she retorted, turning it off into an assumption of skittishness. 'You know, Uncle Max, it was dreadful to live up to your terrible omniscience.'

'I'm afraid, young lady, you won't be the only one to enjoy a chuckle when I report to my professional friends,' he confessed. 'That's the worst of a reputation; but it has to be done. We haven't got a leg to stand on.'

'And you will do that,' she insisted, anxious to clinch the advantage; 'you will stop Scotland Yard doing anything about them here for the next three days, won't you? I mean,' she hastened to amend as she recognised the curious significance of a time limit, 'it mightn't seem reasonable to ask anyone not to do anything, no matter what happened, for ever.'

Possibly Mr Carrados was considering it from his own way round for he did not appear to notice anything in her stumble.

'Naturally I will,' he replied. 'I must, or I may land myself in rather serious trouble. You see, I'm not an official in any sense so I can't plead privilege and invoke the powers to back me. In the eyes of a jury I should be merely an interfering amateur—and there's such a thing as defamation. Well, as you won't be persuaded to come now, when may we expect to see you back from this haunt of ancient peace?'

'Oh, by about Saturday I should think.'

'Ah, Saturday?' he considered. 'That will be three days from now, won't it?'

'Will it? I hadn't thought. It will be the end of the week, you see, and Mrs Larch fancied that by then she could find someone to take my place most likely.'

'We must consider that as arranged then.' He 'looked' round the room in his usual deliberate way, turning his sightless eyes (as it might seem odd to say his nose and ears) to every point of the compass. 'At any rate I'm glad to have seen you in an unusual setting, Nora. I hope your cap's becoming.'

Nora had played her part—there could be no doubt of its

success—but now she was uncertain of what next would be required of her. Her instructions had not gone beyond convincing Carrados—was she to let him go at this point on his assurance of putting things right with Scotland Yard or was some further guarantee required? She shot an inquiring glance in the direction of the two silent witnesses of the curious scene and Mr Joolby evidently decided that the moment had arrived for his own intervention. At a sign from him George Larch noisily threw open the door of the smaller room (they never fell into the mistake of making it too hard for the blind man to follow what was supposed to be going on) and to the accompaniment of a great business with his sticks Joolby 'entered'.

'Hilda, I want you to—' he began, failing for the moment to notice the visitor who was merely standing up in the middle of the room, 'Eh, who have we here?'

'Oh, this is my uncle, Mr Carrados, sir,' explained Nora. 'He just called to see me for a few minutes. Now he's going.'

'Ah, good evening, Mr Carrados,' said the master of the house, his manner, so far, distant without being actually hostile. 'I'm glad I happened to come up in time to see you. You doubtless know who I am, since I think you boast that you never forget a voice and we have met once already.'

'What! Mr Joolby, the eminent authority on Greek numismatics? To be sure we've met. Let me see; the more primitive methods of disposing of one's enemies by obscure venoms, wasn't it?'

'Never mind that now,' retorted Mr Joolby. 'This isn't my shop. I am simply a private gentleman here. Let me tell you that I am not pleased with what has been going on, Mr Carrados. It seems that you have been making unfounded charges against my character and reputation. People are talking—I see them look after me and whisper as I go along. I don't know what isn't being said about me—what slanders aren't being spread. My intention in coming here was to give up my business altogether and lead a quiet but useful life. I might have put up for something—the Borough Council or what not—in time. Now that's all done for thanks to you and a lot of money wasted.'

'Mr Carrados sees that he has been mistaken in what he thought,' ventured Nora, anxious to keep this to the front. 'He is willing—'

'Then there's another thing,' went on Mr Joolby, impervious to soothing. 'This young person who was got into my house on false pretences. There's no doubt that you sent her here to spy on me; the connection is quite obvious. That's a serious matter, Mr Carrados. People have had to pay very large compensation for that sort of thing before now. Not that she could do any harm, simply because there is nothing discreditable to find out, but the imputation is there all the same. In fact it's questionable if it doesn't amount legally to a conspiracy to blackmail and the penalty for blackmail doesn't stop at damages.' With one of his terrifying changes of front he turned suddenly on Nora breathing menace: 'Come now, girl, you've had the run of the house, you know; you may as well own up to it. What have you nosed out here that's wrong. Eh? Eh?'

'Oh nothing, nothing, Mr Joolby,' she protested. 'I've assured my uncle that we have been quite mistaken and that everything here is perfectly straightforward.'

'And so it is. Everything O.K. and above the board. Well, well—'

'I'm quite willing to admit that a mistake has been made, Mr Joolby, and to shoulder all the blame,' interposed Carrados. 'I shall notify Scotland Yard through my friend Inspector Beedel that I have unfortunately been on a wrong tack and in consequence misled them. After that you will have no further trouble.'

'You will, eh? Well, it's about the least you can do as things are, isn't it? Especially as I am considering bringing an action for very heavy damages if I don't get satisfaction. And how am I to know that you will do as you say after all? I haven't any guarantee.'

'Well, really, I—I don't quite know what to say to that,' admitted Mr Carrados. 'What do you suggest for instance?'

Mr Joolby appeared to consider deeply.

'Suppose you write a letter now to Scotland Yard, admitting that you've been mistaken, and let me post it. Then there can't be any double shuffling. You say you are going to notify them, don't you? Well, if you are honest about it you may just as well write a letter here and now and tell them.'

'Just as you like, Mr Joolby, if that will set your mind at rest. As you say, it's the same thing in the end. Have you a sheet of paper handy?'

'Ah!' pounced Mr Joolby with an unpleasant spit of laughter, 'I thought as much! So that was to be the way, was it? On strange note-paper and written with my pen and ink—then it would not be a very hard matter to write a little differently and repudiate the whole business if it is more convenient after-wards, eh, eh? No, no, Mr Carrados; the special tablet that you always use and written with pencil if you please the same as usual.'

Apparently not in any way disconcerted Mr Carrados produced one of the small writing-pads that he invariably carried.

'You seem to be a very well-informed, simple, private gentleman,' he remarked good-naturedly as he began to comply with the injunction.

'You have to be, in the antique line,' retorted the dealer.

'Paper is often the difficulty, I understand,' was the dry thrust. 'Well, how will this do, Mr Joolby? "Dear Inspector Beedel, Not too late in the day to admit a mistake, I hope, I am hastening to let you know that I was entirely at fault in my suspicions of the Joolby *ménage*—"'

'No, I don't like that,' objected the gentleman concerned; '"Joolby *ménage*" is too familiar when you are supposed to be doing your best to get out of the pretty mess you're in; it doesn't sound natural. "Mr Joolby's household" or "the establishment of J. Joolby, Esquire" is more what one would expect to be written.'

'True; perhaps I was becoming a little too colloquial. "The establishment of J. Joolby Esquire." May I, by any chance, add "O.B.E.", some little distinction of that sort? No? A pity but gross oversights were common. Well: "From personal observation I am now satisfied that nothing in the nature of what I had suspected had been going on there."'

Absorbed in the composition of this odd document Mr Carrados alternately spoke and wrote while Mr Joolby, offering frequent helpful comment, betrayed the excited state of his mind shuffling here and there about the room to accompaniment of the continual tapping of sticks and the slither of his crippled extremities, indeed to anyone less deeply engaged than the blind man appeared to be it might have occurred that the amount of noise which this performance raised was out of all proportion with the extent of ground covered. The move was not lost on Nora but she felt that it would be madness to intervene with an open warning that must inevitably precipitate a crisis. Even when Nickle and Won Chou casually but very quietly appeared on the scene she clung to a desperate hope that this did not necessarily mean a breach of faith, but as they began gradually to draw in significantly on each side of Mr Carrados it was no longer possible to doubt some crooked intention.

'Uncle—'

In three swift steps Nickle was by Nora's side. His attitude and action were an open challenge.

'Keep your mouth shut or—' they said as plainly as though it had been spoken.

'"Will you therefore please call off any attention—which might prove embarrassing to me—in that quarter,"' continued the writer, still blandly immersed in his task. '"Now that I am leaving London for a few days—"'

'Uncle! don't—' The words half unconsciously sprang from

her lips as she realised in a flash the possibilities that this opened up and the risk—the fatalness indeed—of the admission. There was no chance of more. Nickle's strong hand closed instantly over her mouth while his arms held her in a grip that smothered all resistance. Won Chou had already glided forward to add his weight and from his sleeve there appeared a stoppered bottle and a pad that had doubtless been intended for another. Neatly, expeditiously, and without a sound that would not pass for Mr Joolby's gasps and clatter, the work was done and the unconscious girl carried away through the open door of the ante-room. Joolby's twisted grin lengthened.

'But, my dear, I've already arranged it all,' protested Carrados, at this point becoming aware of his niece's neglected interruption. 'Thanks, nevertheless—it's very flattering to find that you are so appreciated on the spot, isn't it, Mr Joolby? And I wouldn't say that I'm not every bit as fond of her on my side. Between ourselves,' he continued, writing a line that concluded the letter, 'since our little misunderstanding is now satisfactorily cleared up, I don't mind admitting that I really came here with an absurd fancy that the child might be in some sort of danger.' He chuckled quiet appreciation. 'Sounds absurd now, doesn't it? Eh, Nora? Here we are, then'—running a confirming finger along the words he had last written—'"Now that I am leaving London for a few days and shall not see you before I go I thought it better to put the matter straight at once by letter." There, Mr Joolby, just see if that doesn't satisfy all your scruples.'

Nickle had now returned, leaving Won Chou, aided doubtless by Mrs Larch's practical hand, to cope with any emotional outburst when Nora came round again. There remained Carrados to deal with but even if he should be armed, two useful men—Larch and himself; Joolby didn't count—could settle the issue of that without the possibility of mischance. He noiselessly closed and locked the door of the ante-room as he came back to secure the next few minutes from the chance of disturbing interruption.

In all good faith Joolby accepted the sheet and half turned away to get a better light so as to make sure that this shifty fellow Carrados had been playing no tricks with the composition . . . How it happened he never knew and the other two could not quite see as they were close upon the cripple, and behind, but in the second that his attention was directed to the paper something undoubtedly caused Mr Joolby to stumble back and he floundered into the arms—and incidentally upon the toes—of his fellow conspirators. That was the moment chosen for the room to be blacked completely out and Mr Carrados's dry chuckle from the neighbourhood of the door—the general door—made it comparatively obvious to connect him with the phenomenon. He had not attempted to escape; he had simply snapped the light off, locked the second door, and was now apparently enjoying the effect of his manoeuvre. Exactly what that move implied did not at first convey itself to any of the trio.

'What the hell's happened?' shouted Nickle—the first to find his voice because he was the least involved in the gymnastics. 'Do either of you know—'

'Stop him, you fools—don't talk,' rasped out the more discerning Joolby. 'You know I can't get along. After him, can't you?'

'Blast that table!' was Larch's hearty contribution, and the sound of the impact that had immediately preceded the remark indicated his precise condition.

'That will do nicely,' came Mr Carrados's unruffled voice across the darkness. 'Please all remain exactly where you are or two of your heads may get in line and I don't want to shoot more of you than need be.'

'Has he gone mad?' whispered George in genuine bewilderment. 'He seemed all right up to now.'

'He is still all right, thank you, Mr Larch.' There was a smile yet in the voice but the tone was no longer that of the conciliatory Mr Carrados at the table. 'Possibly it was the initial jockeying for position that may have misled you. You will surely recognise that it was necessary for me to finesse Miss Melhuish out of the room before we got on to the shooting?'

'Shoot and be damned, you skug!' exploded Nickle. 'As soon as we can see, by God! you'll squeal for this pretty loudly.'

'Doubtless,' was the smooth reply '—as soon as you can see. But the point of the situation, Mr Nickle, is that you can't see, and as I am a trained dead shot by sound, it would almost seem as though it might be I who could enforce the squealing.'

'He has us there,' admitted George Larch. 'By golly!'

'Has he!' The scraping of a match against its box-side followed.

Two spurts of light whipped into the black; one upwards from the match, the other across from the door. The match at once went out and Nickle only just saved himself from screaming.

'Damnation!' he yelled, spinning round. 'He's shot the box out of my hand!'

'Quite a safe mark—it was such an explicit sound,' said Mr Carrados reassuringly. 'I was rather afraid that you might strike the match on your trouser seat. That would have been unfortunate, wouldn't it?'

It fell to Mr Joolby to break the silence that hung rather heavily over the room after this demonstration.

'Mr Carrados. I don't pretend to understand what grievance you think you have, but if you will kindly turn on the light again we can all discuss it amicably and no doubt afford you complete satisfaction.'

'Mr Joolby,' replied Carrados, determined to be no less civil, 'whatever grievance I may think I have we can discuss equally well in the dark. And all my arguments are capable of being put even more forcibly in those conditions.'

'But there must be some mistake—' pleaded George Larch, still hopeful.

'I think there really must—but it is yours . . . My dear sirs, did you actually imagine that one could not follow every clumsy move you made, with Joolby's low comedy tramp and the other two stealing in like a couple of hired assassins in a penny gaff melodrama?'

'All this is quite unknown to me—' protested the deeply hurt Joolby.

'But not quite to me. Why, our good friend Larch wears an old family watch that has a voice like an alarum clock to my ears. You, Nickle, use something for your hair that would serve a drag-hunt.'

'You son of a bitch! We'll get you yet,' snapped Nickle. Of the three he appeared to feel the reverse the most—to him, under Carrados's caustic tongue, it was a personal humiliation. Larch was ingenuously amazed, while Joolby—to Joolby, wrapped in an imperforable armour of fatalistic certitude, it could be nothing but a passing trial.

'Ah,' replied Mr Carrados with his unquenchable aplomb, 'I have often wondered where I got my nose from.'

'Be quiet, Nickle,' directed his chief. 'What's the use of foolishness like calling a gentleman bad names when he can gun you in the dark and you're no good even at striking matches? But Mr Carrados will no doubt remember that whatever happens here, somewhere else we hold two hostages.'

'Mr Carrados will,' he assented. 'And Mr Joolby will have no chance of forgetting that in this room I hold three.'

'Short of shooting us all in cold blood how's that going to help you, Mr Carrados?' asked Larch, coming down to the commonplace of the situation. 'It looks like stalemate to me and the sensible thing would be to make it a draw and all call off in good order. As things are what do you think you can *do*, sir?'

'To be quite candid, Mr Larch, so far I haven't given it a thought. But to a man of resource there's always something. If you happen to be a theatre-goer yourself no doubt you've seen a number of ingenious tricks brought off in what I believe are called "crook plays"—the trouble is that one can seldom remember a suitable dodge just when it's wanted. Now there's wireless; any amount of plots turn on that, but how on earth am I to use wireless? If only you happened to have a telephone about the room I might manage to call up reinforcements.'

'And do you think that we'd be mugs enough to let you?' contemptuously came from Nickle.

'Oh, I don't know. You might not—or on the other hand you might. You might be interested in hearing what I should send—at any rate I don't mind telling you in advance and you can say what you think about it. Something—let me see—like this: Yes, Exchange, quite right, but—one moment—this is special and urgent. I want to get through to Scotland Yard—Victoria 7000—but I can't wait for the connection, because it's a matter of life and death. Ask Inspector Beedel there to send Flying Squad to Max Carrados in immediate danger at source of this message. Yes, B-E-E-D-E-L and C-A-R-R-A-D-O-S. You've got that quite all right? Thank you.'

'You bloody fools!' shrieked Nickle, stung by a sudden dreadful inspiration, 'we've let him phone. He *has* got through!' In a transport of infuriation his hand went to his hip and the telephone stand crashed to the floor under the impact of his erratic bullet. Another shot and Nickle's automatic followed his matchbox.

'It only needed that sensational touch to convince the young lady at the Exchange that she was in the thick of the Real Thing,' remarked Mr Carrados. 'Thank you, Nickle. I might have overlooked it. Now we can all close our eyes and open our mouths and see what the Yard will send us.'

'Well, that about puts the lid on,' summed up George Larch philosophically. 'It's all U.P. this journey.'

'Not quite I think,' ventured a sad, unconcerned voice and before Carrados could move—the dramatic opening of the door barred all chance of interference indeed—the light blazed on again, and Won Chou was revealed standing apathetically before them. 'I happen to have met Mr Carrados in the past and knowing how clever a gentleman he is I took the precaution of cutting the wires as soon as I guessed that he was likely to be busy. Always best with a gentleman so brainful. He got nothing through to anywhere.'

'The hell! And how the blazes did you get here? He locked the door.'

'Little tool,' explained Won Chou, modestly displaying a delicate implement from his inexhaustible sleeve. 'Turn keys from other side. Always carry. Very useful.'

'This from the downtrodden brother!' bitterly exclaimed Mr Carrados, throwing away his pistol and folding his useless arms. 'Trick and game to you, Mr Joolby!' True he might still have put up a hopeless fight, but it had been a battle of wits throughout and psychologically he was beaten.

'And this to remember *me* by, you swine!' The blind man went down at the blow—a vicious smashing right, delivered with all the pent-up spleen of a practised boxer, and remained down unstirring. Nickle, in one of his uglier moods, considered that he had settled that reckoning.

CHAPTER XIV

A SIGNAL OF DISTRESS INTO THE UNKNOWN

IT was Saturday morning, the morning of the day when, according to sundry remarks, two things were going to happen. Vallett had promised that by that date he would be prepared to bring off their wholesale raid of the Tapsfield bank-note paper and Nora Melhuish had given Mr Carrados to understand that on Saturday she would be ready to quit Mr Joolby's house and service. Of the two contracts the first seemed immeasurably the more likely to be met for while Vallett was freely at large to mature his plans daybreak found—or would have done if it could have penetrated six feet of earth and several courses of brick and mortar—Nora asleep on a long stone slab which was the chief feature of a cellar that was unpleasantly suggestive of a prison cell or even at a pinch a dungeon. Mr Carrados himself was there also only he happened to be awake, the sleeping accommodation not being of the class to entice a man of slightly luxurious tastes to somnolence. Nora slept as a young animal will: without any particular regard to which way up she was or what she lay on.

No matter how much Mr Carrados might 'look' around there was very little to see and he had long since investigated every loophole. Of these there was quite literally one: a grated opening, six inches square, above the door; possibly not without its use to ventilate the cellar but almost negligible as a source of light since it gave upon a scarcely less dark passage. The only real illuminant had been one candle at a time from the pair that they had found burning when they came to themselves and discovered their plight—the last of them carefully hoarded by Nora, she alone being concerned, but this had long since burned down to its last flicker.

The cellar itself was long and narrow, brick built and white-washed, stone flagged, reasonably dry but intolerably fusty. Its smell was that of ancient lees, decaying mushrooms, bad earth, snails and just a dash of drain to spice it. The low stone bench, running all the length, had doubtless in its palmy days stored casks of wines and beer.

For the hundredth time the blind man paced the meagre limits of their cell and for the hundredth time he found that none of his senses brought the faintest ray of inspiration. The solid oak door—he fingered it again—was as though made to resist a ram, the walls built to withstand a siege, and every stone and brick in wall, bench, or floor was as immovable as the face of a rock. They built well in those days of leisure.

The fittings of the door were in keeping with its timber—massive and bolted through and doubly fixed by rust and long disusage. Under his hand a stubborn latch sprung noisily: on the bench Nora turned in her sleep, half rose with a sudden cry and at once began to pour out a wild string of protestation:

'I tell you it's all right! The people here are absolutely straightforward and honest. They are! They are! You mustn't think because the man is like a loathsome creature—Don't you hear, Uncle Max, I swear it's quite all right and Geoffrey isn't here only if you don't—Oh, that filthy dream again. Nightmares are bad enough but when it comes to night-toads—!'

Uncle Max walked unerringly to where she was, sat down and put a firm arm protectively about her.

'There, there,' he said, as simply as though she had been a child of nine, 'I'm here with you, little woman. This place certainly is enough to give anyone dreams about reptiles—not that there are any here as a matter of fact,' he hastened to assure her. 'But you're awake now and all right, my dear.'

'I'm awake,' she said, making some attempt to shake her hair straight, 'but I don't know so much about the all right. Have they brought us any water yet? Gosh, but I know now what it feels like to be marooned in the Great Desert.'

'Not yet,' he replied, trying to make his voice sound cheerful without being too sanguine. 'It must still be pretty early.'

'It may be early for today but it's jolly late for yesterday and they didn't bring us any all day. Nor the night before—or the year before it may have been: I'm losing count of time here. Any food?'

His arm tightened on her shoulder in compassionate pressure. There was no need to say it.

'Oh well, I don't suppose that I could eat any now if there had been. My throat must be like a roll of emery paper.' Suddenly she discovered by the feel that she had been covered with two rugs as she slept and she turned on him with a show of affectionate indignation. 'Look here, Uncle Max, cheating again! It isn't fair spreading your rug over me when I'm asleep and I won't have it. You know you promised.'

'I found that I didn't need one,' protested Carrados. 'I only had to think of that infernal Chink putting it across me and I went beautifully warm all over.'

'You poor old dear! It does annoy you to be had, doesn't it?'

'It does indeed. And when it involves me in letting someone else be had as well, it's positively vexing.'

'Don't worry, darling. It isn't you who've let me in, but me you. If I hadn't been so large-headed with that fantastic slavey idea of mine you wouldn't have been here.'

'I don't know, Nora,' he speculated. 'I should probably have got myself in somehow simply for the fun of seeing if I couldn't get out again.'

'Oh . . . the fun, is it?' she queried. 'Had you been having many quiet chuckles to yourself before I woke up then? I could do with an occasional laugh myself to keep my throat from congealing.'

'So far, I must admit, the humours of the situation haven't been conspicuous. For all practical purposes we are exactly where we were when we found ourselves here on Wednesday night. Except—'

'Except for being "a day's march nearer home", I suppose you mean? A day? Wednesday night? It seems years. What exact day is it as a matter of fact, if you happen to have been counting?'

'Saturday—Saturday morning early. About six o'clock I should reckon. It's easy enough to keep count of the time but I'd give something considerable to know just where we are in the matter of location. You're sure you don't recognise anything about this place? Long narrow cell—that thundering door—the grid over it?'

'They never let me explore, don't you fear. I hadn't an earthly. But why shouldn't it be just a cellar under Joolby's house? I should think that the most likely.'

'It may be—very probably it is. It conforms to the period and the general feel of the place but so might thousands of others. You see, we were both unconscious for quite a time and we may have been carted anywhere. A cellar under the house is the most reasonable assumption but there's just the element of doubt. That's the rub: we can't be certain.'

'Does it matter where we are? We're here right enough.'

'It only matters if we can get a message out. Then, under some circumstances, depending on what form our medium took, it might be vital.'

'Get a message out?' She fastened hopefully on the faint omen of the phrase. 'Any chance of it?'

'Well, frankly, I don't see a glimmer. However much we may dislike this cellar one has to admit that with all its faults it certainly is not jerry-built. It doesn't seem to have the semblance of a weak spot throughout and they haven't left us the faintest substitute for a tool in any shape or form.'

'Did they take even your penknife?'

'Even my penknife! Good heavens, child, they took my braces and sock suspenders. What a pity young ladies don't wear corsets nowadays; I'm sure Mr Larch would have been too delicate to remove them. I suppose you don't happen to have metal parts about any of your fittings, Nora?'

'Nothing at all but artificial silk and elastic, I'm afraid. Not even a hairpin . . . Uncle Max, don't mind telling me now . . . does that mean . . . it's pretty hopeless?'

'Oh, lord bless you, no,' he replied, with a jerk into cheerfulness that was rather too debonair to be convincing. 'It's never hopeless in this life so long as—'

'So long as you keep on hoping?' suggested Nora tartly. 'That's a very bright thought for the day, old dear, but somehow it would appeal to one more from the Wayside Pulpit than dwelt on in this putrid hole. And, oh my God, I am vilely thirsty! I know now what it feels like to be shipwrecked on a raft—two days after the last drop of water has been served out.'

'Have you tried gnawing a bone button? I don't find it much good myself but I have known people who think there's something in it.'

'I did that yesterday. I was wildly hungry then but there isn't much solid nourishment to be found in a bone button, Uncle. Nor illusion of a bubbling fountain. No, paradoxically enough, the button stunt is a wash-out. But I'm ready to sell my immortal soul for two gallons of ditch water at this moment.'

'Child, child—'

'It's only my idea of fun, Uncle. I must do something to keep my spirits up—even to talk about a long drink may be slightly refreshing. It should at least make one's mouth water only I suppose the apparatus is out of order . . . If ever I get out of here I shall go to see the Niagara Falls. They ought to be well worth watching.'

'This won't do,' thought Max Carrados; 'she will wear her resistance out. All this "Water, water, everywhere" business is the very worst—'

It was not easy to find a subject strong enough to distract her from the other and he had to come down to one that was equally painful if less dangerous.

'What you told me about Geoffrey is very puzzling—'

'Puzzling!' The feeling in her tone left no doubt that he had found the subject.

'Appalling as well, of course, but I was only referring to one side of the queer proceedings. If you remember, I said that Geoffrey would no doubt be closely kept but hardly ill-used. There seems no point in systematic terrorism—apart from sheer cruelty, which isn't common, and certainly wouldn't be business.'

'It was pretty effective in getting me to do all they wanted. I can't imagine acting like that if it hadn't been for poor Geoffrey's pitiable begging.'

'It was effective in getting you to do what they wanted,' he considered; 'yes, Nora. But they must have been at Geoffrey for days to reduce him to a state like that and they could scarcely have foreseen what was going to develop until the Wednesday—'

'That knocking—you said you thought it might be him. Have you heard it again lately?'

'No, not since Thursday. It was two or three walls away . . . They may have moved him.'

'Uncle Max . . . you don't think . . . they've killed Geoffrey?'

'I certainly do not, my dear. These people talk blood and thunder if it suits their book but they have no earthly object in killing anyone—intentionally.'

'Intentionally. Intentionally? But—what is it, Uncle Max? You are keeping something back. You know more than you have told me.'

For a few moments Mr Carrados did not reply. Then he ceased the rather aimless pacing of their prison that he had taken up again and sat down on the bench beside her.

'Listen quietly, my dear,' he said, taking her hand, 'and be the brave girl that I've always known you.'

'I don't feel awfully heroic at the moment,' she confessed. 'But I *am* Captain of the Tapsfield Guides, aren't I? I must live up to that. What is it?'

'I said nothing about it yesterday, Nora, because it might

have been premature, but I think the time has come . . . Since Thursday afternoon this place has been deserted. We are alone here.'

'Alone?'

'Except for Tilehurst possibly, though even he has given no sign. But the others who were in the place—wherever it is—and were moving freely about up to Thursday afternoon, have gone. There isn't a step, there isn't a movement, above us.'

'But why should they—what are you driving at?'

'Who can say why? Anything may have happened. With the exception of Joolby himself—and he's playing a desperate game—they are all birds of passage and must be prepared to fly at a moment's notice. Some of them may even have been arrested. But gone they have.'

'He said they must have three days' grace. Today—Saturday— is the third. Can they have—?'

'Secured the stuff and cleared? That is quite possible.'

'Then they would have no further interest in keeping us shut up here?'

'No further interest . . . but . . .'

'But? But what?'

'There may have been some misunderstanding among them. We—safely out of the way—are the least pressing factors in their plans. Someone who was to have released us when the rest were clear may have—oh, well, anything. But the fact remains. For more than a day and two nights no one has come near. We are abandoned; perhaps, among a wild scramble to get away, forgotten.'

'Then if there's no one about they can't stop us trying to get out?'

'My child,' he reminded her pityingly, 'look at that door— those walls. Do you imagine that I haven't thought of escape every moment of the day and night almost? But they haven't left us a scrap of metal—not even a lump of stone. Nothing but our teeth and nails. Not in a year could we break out of here.'

'Then shout, scream—anything to call attention. People must be passing somewhere near. They're bound to hear us in time—'

He shook his head sadly. 'If there had been a footfall within reach of our shouts, Nora, you may be sure that my ears wouldn't have missed it. But we are muffled in the depths of the earth here; perhaps far from a road; not even on an outside wall. Five minutes of shouting and our poor dry throats would crack and madness begin to stare us in the face. No—'

'But what is to become of us?' she entreated wildly. 'What are we to do?'

'Wait,' he replied, trying by his own calmness to stem her rising agitation; 'wait with all the patience we can muster and reserve every ounce of strength—we may need it. That is why I have told you now—to prepare you for the trial. Sooner or later the search must begin. In our absence suspicion will be raised—'

'Why should it? I had left a good excuse at home for being away and in that letter you said that you were going.'

'I know I did. It was the final touch to make Joolby think he was safe, though the countermine misfired. But my secretary will realise that I had made no preparations of the sort—I had appointments fixed for every day—and Parkinson will not be satisfied. They will—'

'But it may be days—or weeks. Uncle, we can't stay here—I won't—we'd starve to death—we'd die of thirst—'

'Nora, Nora,' he coaxed.

'I must have water,' she insisted, growing more frantic as an understanding of the full horror of their situation sapped away her natural courage, '—I can't die here of thirst—it's terrible—it's getting worse and worse—'

'My dear,' he pleaded.

'I don't care if I do go mad—I mayn't know what it's like then—but I'm not going to wait here until I die of thirst—and I can feel that I am doing—my tongue's all thick and choky—and my throat feels closing up.' She broke from him and sprang to her feet. 'If you won't do anything I will! I'll make someone hear me.'

Carrados had not the heart to restrain her by force, and no other form of argument would apparently have any chance of success. At all events, when she had worn herself out there might be some hope for the return of reason. Meanwhile she had flung herself against the impregnable door and was beating on it furiously with her bare hands, in turn commanding, threatening, pleading, until her poor frayed voice was past any further effort:

'Open the door! Open it, do you hear? I won't be smothered here. I won't die like a rat. Mrs Larch, Won Chou, Mr Nickle, Joolby—Joolby, you toad, you beast, you swine, come and let us out or you'll damned well hang for it. I'm going to—yes, I've written an account accusing you of murder and I've hid it where you can't find it but someone else will and they're sure to hang you.'

There was no answer from the echoing space outside. She bent down, tore off a shoe and began to hammer furiously on and about the door with it.

'Damn and blast you all!—hiding round there and laughing at us, aren't you? When we do get out you'll pay for this; we'll kill the lot of you sooner or later, see if we don't, you yellow mongrels . . . No, I don't really mean that. If only you'll come now we'll give you a thousand pounds—two thousand—five thousand pounds—and get you all let off whatever you've done. Oh please, please, Mr Joolby—' The mood ran out, her voice trailed off and she turned away from the door baffled and broken.

'There, I've knocked the heel off my shoe and done no good at all. It's hopeless—I knew it all along—it was that that strung me out. Just hopeless.'

But Max Carrados had risen from the bench as Nora sank down there in utter despair, and was running his hands up and down the wall against the door post, where some of her wild blows had fallen. He fixed on a spot and tried it several times with bare knuckles.

'I thought it sounded curiously,' he speculated. 'Not so hopeless perhaps, my girl, as it happens. Egad, there may have been a divinity that shaped your ends—your pedal end—when you went off in the tantrums. Anyhow you struck the one inch that may—well, it mayn't, after all, so don't think too much about it.'

There was small need to tell her that. Huddled up in a corner on the bench Nora was taking no interest at all in what went on. Reaction, after the hysterical burst that had given her energy to lash out, was exacting the usual payment.

'Oh for a tool—a little bit of a thing of any sort,' he continued desperately, as he again fell to tapping the spot time after time to confirm the blessed suspicion. And then the thought—the flash of inspiration: 'Nora! that heel—they never reckoned on that. It should be like a rasp. Come, my dear, buck up and do your bit. What did you do with it?'

'Somewhere on the floor,' she replied, just stirred enough by the vigour of his mood to understand but without energy to bear any share in whatever it was that was going. 'What's the use of a heel—these walls—'

He found the heel readily enough without her help and, as he had expected, it was bristling with pointed ends of nails—in its way quite a useful file for working on a suitable material. Up the wall, where the door post stood, ran a couple of inches or so of plaster between the brick and wood. It was on this strip that Carrados now worked with patient skill, filing, crumbling, wrenching and tapping it out bit by bit until he had a sufficient space of the fabric underneath exposed to identify it. It was a lath as he had hoped and once he had bared an end it was an easy enough matter to break out a piece and reach what he had been seeking.

'Wake up, Nora my girl,' he called across, trying to keep the exultation out of his voice until the thing was sure. 'I think you've done the trick. It was a pipe you struck.'

'I don't want a pipe,' she muttered supinely. 'I don't even want a cigarette. I'm just done and finished.'

'Oh no, you're not,' he assured her, going over and pulling her up; 'not by several long chalks this journey. Come, you have a say in this. It's a lead pipe and with our little friend here I can be into that pipe within a few jiffies. But—'

'I thought there was a catch somewhere,' she mumbled.

'I don't,' he declared, 'but there is just the possibility that there may be. A lead pipe ought to mean water but in these old places one can never be quite sure. They used all sorts of stuff for anything . . . So it may be the gas. What do you say?'

'Say? How?'

'If there's water in the pipe we get it. If there's gas it gets us.'

'A good job too,' she replied. 'One way or the other.'

'So be it. It's quite a level chance—in fact it's good odds in our favour.' For the next few minutes there was nothing to be heard but the soft, regular abrasion of the metal; then he dropped the heel with an exclamation.

'Our trick this time, Mr Joolby, I think. *Water!* Nora, your hanky!'

That brought her up quickly enough and the next moment she was squeezing the saturated cambric into her mouth and fancying that the tepid, insipid stuff (it must have been in the pipe for days and nights) was the most delicious nectar she had ever tasted.

'More!'

'Nice stuff, water; eh, Nora?' he remarked, complying.

'Why don't you file it away a lot?' she demanded, pointing to the slight incision he had made. 'I want to wallow in it galore.'

'No need for us to drown ourselves out. This is direct from the main and we might have some trouble in stopping whatever we set going. If we make a big hole and the door fits tight you can calculate how soon in a little place like this—'

'Go on; what are you waiting for? I want more and more—gallons! buckets!'

He had been soaking his own handkerchief for the second time—alternating his turn with hers—when all at once he broke off and fell into an attitude of poignant attention. A finger of one hand closed the newly made leak, those of the other rested on the pipe lower down, as delicately-perceptive as the antennae of a butterfly—so significant of alertness that one might have said they were listening.

'Wait; wait,' he cautioned, without relaxing his poise; 'there's something going on here; some movement on the pipe. Somewhere, somebody else is in communication with it. Who? Where?'

'I know,' exclaimed Nora with a sudden light. 'It's because of the water famine. They did it at Tapsfield; they do it all over the shop. Someone goes round listening at those little trap-door affairs in the road to catch you wasting any.' Just about a week before she had used the self-same words to warn Miss Tilehurst of the risk and now in all unconsciousness she repeated herself exactly.

'It is! It cannot be anything else—direct from the main at this hour. My God! Nora, *listening*! Think, child—I can get him; can he get me? Can he understand? Do you see: our message! Hope, hope, just a tiny flickering light—someone somewhere *listening*!'

He was not wasting the precious seconds now. Almost at Nora's first words he had searched for and found the heel and as he spoke he tapped the pipe sharply with the butt of it in a never varying sequence: short, short, short; long, long, long; short, short, short—time after time repeated.

'What is it you do?' she asked in a half-awed whisper. 'What are you sending?'

'S.O.S.; S.O.S.; S.O.S.,' he explained, rather absently under the intense concentration of listening, touching, *feeling* for a movement in reply. 'Can he hear me? Will he understand?' The seconds passed and nothing came: after all, was it likely?

'Has he gone—was it just the last movement that I heard; or was he only adjusting?' ran his thoughts as he never ceased the tapping. At any rate—'Nora, my dear,'—this time aloud—'the next minute will probably settle our business for good or bad. If you ever prayed in your life before, pray for an answer now, child.'

CHAPTER XV

THE MAN AT THE OTHER END

WHENEVER a house in Maplewood Avenue came on the market—a not infrequent occurrence in point of fact—the house agents were wont to dwell on the rural and secluded amenities of the neighbourhood, rather than draw attention to the architectural, domestic or social attractions of the 'property': wisely, no doubt, since the one could be convincingly adduced, whereas a tolerant if not absolutely apologetic course was desirable when skilfully leading a client on past a too detailed examination of the others. Certainly at six o'clock in the morning the Avenue wore as tranquil an air of detachment from a city's bustle as could be found within the ten miles radius. It was yet too early for dust-carts, milkmen, road sweepers and other kindred sleep-disturbers to be about while the intrusions of the official custodians of the law were, if leisurely in point of motion, in all other respects comparable to the proverbial angels' visits.

Such was the appearance Maplewood Avenue presented to the couple who turned into it, in pursuance of their rather mysterious ends, on the morning of the Saturday that was to be the climax of at least two adventurous enterprises. At that moment the only sign of life—other than vegetable—that the Avenue presented was a large Persian cat seated beneath a sycamore and a full-throated bird pouring out its string of melody from the precise apex of the tree, exactly above the spot where the cat was sitting.

'Now there ought to be a trap somewhere just about here,' said the senior of the two intruders, when in due course their progress along the road had brought them to a part somewhere about midway along the thoroughfare. A substantially built, no-longer-young, level-headed-looking workman of the capable if mildly pragmatic type, his status was sartorially proclaimed, for in addition to wearing the chaste blue uniform provided by the Metropolitan Water Board his official cap was embellished with the word INSPECTOR, clearly rather than aesthetically displayed within a neat oval. His underling, a mere youth who just escaped the category of 'hobbledehoy' by virtue of a couple of months' mild discipline, did not appear to let his superior's rank and authority overawe him. On this not unattractive early morning round at least his usual title of respect was 'uncle' or 'dad' with an occasional lapse into an even freer style if the occasion seemed to permit it. The inspector received it all in the best of parts as became a man who was prepared to give and take, with the full assurance that if the need arose he could assert the dignity of his badge in a perfectly conclusive fashion. Both carried an implement of their craft, that of the inspector being a listening-rod—outwardly nothing more than a service-able walking-stick with an overgrown head—while his underling had a sinister-looking tool that combined the unpleasanter qualities of a small harpoon and a native spear. Actually its industrial use was to impale and open trap-doors but it bore little suggestion of this pacific function.

'It *must* be somewhere just about here,' reiterated the inspector argumentatively. 'See anything of it, 'Orace?'

'Not a trace,' replied Horace, alternating his interest between the bird and the cat in a speculation as to which would afford the better cock-shy. 'Reckon they must have tar-sprayed and gritted it over, same as we found that one in Badger Lane. Miaou! Miaou!'

'Well, dash my nob if the cat isn't sitting right atop it!' exclaimed his chief, now that his attention was turned in that direction. 'Puss, puss. Come along, Thomas, we'll trouble you for that spot for a couple of minutes.' Whereupon the Persian, rightly concluding that in the circumstances it was no use waiting any longer for the thrush to fall straight into its mouth, got up and walked away in a decidedly cutting manner.

'Keeping the place warm for us,' grinned Horace.

'Picking it out to be cool for itself more likely. They're funny in their ways, you might perhaps think, but they have their own ideas,' moralised the inspector. 'Now I suppose you never take any particular notice of cats, 'Orace?'

'Can't say as I do. Except now and then to have a whang at one.'

'Sometimes I wonder what you do take any notice of—except the whistle and short skirts,' speculated his superior. 'But no doubt ideas are germinating.'

'I follow Chelsea,' maintained Horace.

'Well, I should say that's harmless. But speaking of cats, there's a good deal to be learned about women from them, 'Orace. Not in a spiteful sense, mind you, but they're very alike in many ways—cats and women.'

'You let some of them hear you say that and they'd scratch your eyes out.'

'That being a case to wit,' pointed out the inspector. 'But it doesn't follow: it all depends—not on the woman as you might think but on the chap and his manner of putting it. Now if you made such an observation, 'Orace, no doubt, as you say, you'd carry away traces of it, but if it was done diplomatic—'

'Same as you would, for instance?'

'Approximately,' admitted the inspector modestly. 'At any rate I've known very few who wouldn't admit, between ourselves, that most others had a fair streak of the feline.'

'I'm sure,' sniggered Horace. 'Regular old Don John you must have been in your time, I reckon, Uncle.'

'It's not that at all,' protested the inspector earnestly. 'Don't go away with an erroneous impression of that sort, 'Orace, or I shall be sorry I allowed you to talk of your own affairs so freely. I regard the subject from a scientific, you might almost say Darwinian, standpoint. Now—there's no particular hurry, lad; it's no one's time between now and seven—now to give you an instance. When I was about your age we had a farm and one Michaelmas we left it and moved away to another, a dozen or fifteen miles off, that the old man had taken. Of course all the stock went by road and the house cat—a jenny it was— was put into a basket and driven in the trap along with one or two particular things and the women. No doubt its feet were buttered as soon as it was let out but the next morning it was gone and sure enough it turned up again—we heard this after- wards from a neighbour who was there—at the old place, pretty nearly dead beat but evidently come back with the intention of staying. Well—this is the point, 'Orace—that cat was seen to look into every room in the house and when it understood that they were all empty and no one living there, dash my nob if it didn't turn round and disappear again and the next day after that it was back at the new place and stayed on there quite content for ever . . . Do you get anything from that, 'Orace?'

'Everyone knows that cats can find their way back when they've never seen the road. An aunt of mine—'

'You've missed the point, my lad, but I didn't expect any better. Pigeons will do as much—for hundreds of miles if it comes to that—but there's nothing to be learnt—nothing that is to say on the human plane—from the behaviour of pigeons. Well, what about getting on with it now? This is the last road of the round and then we may as well drop down into the High Street and get a snack to carry us on till breakfast. I know a place not so far off where they make coffee of coffee and not chicory and ground peas.'

'Suit me all right,' assented Horace. 'As a matter of fact my internals have been complaining out loud for the past half hour. Reckon they thought that me throat must have got cut or some- thing.'

The inspector had taken up a position of ease, leaning against the sycamore from which the thrush had lately sung, while he proceeded to write up his report-book. At this avowal he looked across at his subordinate meditatively.

'It's symptomatic how most young fellows always seem to be thinking about their stomachs nowadays, if you come to notice it, 'Orace,' he remarked confidentially. 'They don't seem to have any what you might call reserve of endurance somehow. Did I ever happen to tell you how me and another signaller were cut off in a tower outside a little place called Binchey for the best part of a week and all the time we only had—?'

'You did and that,' replied the unimpressed Horace. 'You told me at full length the first day I came on this job and you've referred to it now and then since at stated intervals. Don't gloat so much on that there war, Father William, and the deeds that saved the Empire. It's over and done with and we're never going to have another—not so long as it rests with me anyhow.'

For a moment the inspector seemed to be in doubt whether the point had not been reached when it was desirable for him to explain to Horace the precise obligations of their respective positions. He put the temptation aside on the reflection that there is generally more than one way of attaining an objective. With the butt end of an admonitory pencil he indicated the unopened trap.

'Well, for the love of Moses get on with your job, boy,' he directed severely. 'I don't want to be kept messin' about round here all morning.'

That was the chap all over, thought Horace bitterly, as he spiked open the lid and dropping the business end of his harpoon on to the connection inside applied his ear to the handle. Talk about his own blinking affairs for half an hour and then suddenly turn blinking well round and . . . Fat lot of good expecting anything to be worth while in a blinking shop where . . .

'Come, come, 'Orace,' said the inspector, leisurely elastic-banding his book and putting it away, 'you aren't supposed to be fishing down that hole, you know. Is it O.K. there?'

'Nowhere in sight of it, if you ask me,' replied Horace, diffusing an atmosphere of gloomy satisfaction. 'There's something going on somewhere here that's beyond me.'

'H'm,' said the inspector, either with or without a special meaning. 'That's queer.'

'Yes, it's—'ere, what d'ya mean—"queer"?'

'Well'—the inspector was satisfied now that he had restored correct relations and was mildly satirical—'I was only thinking that it must be queer, lad, if it's something past your comprehension. What's this miracle like?'

'Better have a squint yourself,' suggested Horace, withdrawing his implement and resigning the position. 'Listening posts are more in your line by all accounts, inspector.'

Still smiling inwardly, the inspector stepped across and dropping the end of his rod into the cavity bent down and applied an ear to the bowl-shaped amplifier. Presently he twisted his head round a fraction so as to include Horace in his view and by a return to ordinary conversational terms indicated tactfully that so far as he was concerned their little difference might be regarded as settled.

'It's a rummy thing that we should have been speaking of signalling just now,' he remarked tentatively. 'If such a thing was credible I should have said that someone was talking morse along the pipe at this very moment.'

'Oh,' replied Horace, leaning against the tree in turn and languidly rolling a cigarette—doubtless equally prepared to let bygones go by but, as the aggrieved subordinate, inclined to be more guarded. 'And wha' d'z 'e happen to be saying?'

'Nothing that you might call coherent—just the same word all the time: "sos, sos, sos", over and over again if I understand it right. Half a minute though; that "sos" stands for something surely?'

'Yes it does—sossages. And very nice too for breakfast.'

'Tchk! tchk! Can't you never leave off thinking of food even in your sleep, 'Orace? . . . Still going on: "sos, sos, sos". Why,

of course—where are your wits, lad? It isn't 'sos' at all; it's
"S.O.S." Signal of distress a sinking ship sends out. Now whatever—'

'Why, of course,' contributed Horace, refusing to be
impressed. 'The *Clacton Belle* must have drifted in somehow
and now she can't neither reverse nor turn round in the supply
pipe. Why ever didn't you think of that at first, Uncle?'

But the inspector was not to be put off by the cheap witticism
of irreverent youth. He had not lived for fifty years and gone
all through the war without discovering that very queer things
do occasionally turn up in real life. For a moment he thoughtfully balanced a spanner undecidedly in his free hand; then
kneeling on the pavement he struck the metal connection below
half a dozen times in measured succession.

'What's the game—what does that mean?' demanded Horace,
intrigued into drawing nearer and looking on in spite of his
blasé bearing.

'"R.U."—code. "Who are you?"' explained the other,
returning to the listening attitude again. 'Now we shall see where
we're getting.'

'Seems to me this isn't M.W.B. routine at all,' suggested the
flippant observer. 'You must have got through to the picture
house this time, Dad. "Snatched from Death's Jaws" in seven
snatches—' He stopped short at that for the inspector's right
hand had suddenly shot out in a compelling gesture of warning
and repression.

'Get this down, lad,' he said, with a note of sharp authority
that admitted no discussion. 'You have a bit o' paper and a
pencil, haven't you? "C-A-R-R—"'

'Right-o,' was the brisk assent, as the boy discovered a news-
sheet and a stub of pencil in his pocket, and folded the paper to
afford a white space of margin, '"C-a-r-r". Carry on, sergeant.'

'"-a-d-o-s".'

'Carrados! Why, that's the name of the bloke—' He turned
the page in an excited search for a heading. 'There's something

here about a mystery of his movements. You don't mean to say—'

'Shut it, you pup!' snapped the inspector fiercely. 'Can't you attend two minutes? Here—take it: "T-r-a-p-p-e-d p-h-o-n-e n-e-a-r-e-s-t p-o-l-i-c-e r-e-l-e-a-s-e u-r-g-e-n-t l-i-f-e d-e-a-t-h".'

'My Gawd!' murmured Horace, experiencing a mental display of coloured lights. 'That's the stuff to—'

'"A-m e-n-l-a-r-g-i-n-g l-e-a-k y-o-u l-o-c-a-t-e g-u-i-d-e p-o-l-i-c-e l-a-r-g-e r-e-w-a-r-d".'

'Phew!' whistled Horace softly, drawing in his breath with an ecstatic foretaste of this shower of gain and glory. 'Large reward! . . . Is that all, inspector?' he concluded meekly.

'"A-c-k-n-o-w-l-e-d-g-e i-f g-o-t"—you needn't put that last bit in the message. You know how to telephone, don't you, Horace?'

''Course I do. I was in the yard office before I came on here. And you don't need a number for police; you—'

'That's all right, lad. Slip down into the High Street as quick as you can cut and put that through from the nearest kiosk. Here's a couple of pennies—'

'Don't need 'em for police.'

'Take them all the same—you never know and we're running no risks; in fact you'd better have a few more to be on the safe side. Keep your mouth shut no matter who you meet and for the love of Moses don't stop to get your breakfast on the way, there's a good lad. This is going to mean a gold watch and a week's outing at Southend with full pay for both of us or I'm a Dutchman.'

'Garn!' The prospect, added to the certainty of having a tale to tell that would thrill and fascinate young lady friends for many a bright month to come, was reducing Horace to a state of giggling bliss. 'A silver lighter and a day on Hampstead Heath more likely!'

He set smartly off towards the shops while the inspector,

humming a marching air as an emotional outlet to the suspense, proceeded to note the promised development in the volume of waste and to verify the direction. He was still testing the flow at intervals along the road when, some five minutes later, a closed motor car came along and slowing down as it went by turned in at one of the gardens. He did not fail to make a careful mental record of all its details.

The motorists must have been noticing on their side also for very soon—they certainly could not have been right up to the house—two men came out at the gate in question and stood admiring the day, as proprietorial gentlemen will when the rising sun, as seen from their own demesne, seems to be an individual asset produced for their especial service. Both were observable figures; one a personable individual of foreign cut, the other— obviously in spite of his well-wrapped-up form—a pronounced cripple. Presently they happened to notice the waterman trying the road at no great distance away and—what more natural?— strolled down to take a friendly interest in his doings.

'Morning, inspector,' affably remarked the cripple—he had not failed to observe the badge—'rather early for your job, eh? Nothing wrong with our supply up here, I hope, eh?'

'Nothing at all, sir,' said the inspector. 'Just an ordinary routine round. We do them regularly.'

'Ah, to be sure. I thought perhaps you might be calling here and there to see the taps and so on, eh? One likes to know—'

'No need for that, sir, when it's all O.K. We don't want to give any more trouble than we have to. Shouldn't be here myself only I'm waiting for my mate to knock off now for breakfast.'

'Breakfast, eh? I'll see about mine since you remind me. And if I was in your place I don't know that I should be hanging about my job a minute longer than I had to. You get nothing extra for that, inspector, eh?'

With this pleasantry he swung off again and the pair disappeared into the gateway. The inspector slowly proceeded to fill and light his pipe and then, throwing the implement into the hollow of his arm, began to stroll casually up and down the roadway, never very far distant from that house—waiting for his mate. He had a particularly guileless face and mild speculative eyes that seemed to be quietly considering.

CHAPTER XVI

LAST LAUGHTER

WHEN those two excellent, if not exactly good, companions, Messrs Joolby and Bronsky, approached the house after their interlude with the water-inspector they stood for a moment surveying its uncompromisingly reticent front before making up their minds to enter. To do the cripple justice all the reluctance was on his associate's part for, at the sight of a quietude which might equally be either ominous or reassuring, Mr Bronsky displayed a tendency to hang back and comb his impressive beard in characteristic discretion. Meanwhile the chauffeur who had driven them there—a subordinate member of the band—had garaged his car and was loitering about the drive in the expectation of further instructions.

'You are sure it would be quite all right?' questioned Mr Bronsky for the third time since they had left the vehicle. 'I have grave misgivings.'

'It's both quiet and all right.' Joolby's whole frame, balanced on his props, was pulsing and throbbing with suppressed fires as he regarded the other askance. 'Why shouldn't it be all right, eh? eh?'

'I did not like the affairs of yesterday to be plain-speaking between ourselves, Julian Joolby,' recriminated Mr Bronsky. 'There was air of something in the wind that did not mean nothing. You was not where you said you would and the others could not be found, did not know, or would not say anything. In short, it was dubious behaviour.'

'That's soon explained,' said Joolby, becoming comparatively amiable as he saw that there was nothing serious to rebut, 'only I'm sorry that you should have been put out by it, Bronsky. As a matter of fact I had to go off at a moment's notice to arrange our connection at the coast. Fellow owning the bungalow wanted to crawfish. I left a message with Jake and I hear that one of his brats was run over and so he forgot everything.'

'But however the others?'

'Same as with you. They found out that I had gone somewhere, couldn't get in touch, and that put the wind up and they began to imagine everything. The consequence was that you didn't find them either. That's all right, Bronsky; these little hitches are bound to crop up but a couple of hours more will see everything brought in and us well on our way with it.'

'I hopes so. All same I begin to think it would have been more good to have met you at the other end; only I—'

'Only you wanted to see that we were really going your way when we'd got the boodle, didn't you?' supplied Joolby with rough good-humour. 'Now it seems to me that we're the first here and, what's more, I don't mind laying a farthing bun to a penny tart as that slut Cora's skipped it. Well—' he instanced a crude proverb based on the assumption that in certain circumstances a riddance is no loss which, being obscene in the extreme, had the effect of somewhat raising Mr Bronsky's spirits.

Mr Joolby's surmise proved to be right. When they let themselves into the house it soon became evident that not only were they the first there, but everything pointed to the place having been left unattended for an appreciable period. Noticing one thing after another that showed neglect they climbed up to the dining-room on the first floor, where they had last sat, and there on the table were the uncleared remains of Thursday's lunch, plain evidence of someone's dereliction.

'There you are!' panted Joolby, waving a stick towards the table as if it had been a conjurer's wand and would cause everything to disappear by magic. 'What did I tell you, eh? eh? The bitch never came here yesterday at all. Must have cleared off on Thursday soon after me and the others left. Anything might have happened. Fortunately,' he added, with an eye towards the effect of this disclosure on Mr Bronsky's disquieted nerves, 'fortunately it didn't.'

'No, but it could have might,' contended Mr Bronsky. 'A woman can never be trusted to do the right until she understand that whatever she do it will be wrong.'

'Everything pretty well as usual down below, boss,' reported the third man, who had been sent to investigate the cellars meanwhile. 'That's to say the three cullies is there sure 'nuf, but there's a goodish drop o' watt'r coming under the No. 4 door. Blind guy says he thinks a pipe must have burst or su'thing and he's kind of sore that he and the skirt haven't had nothin' since Thursday.'

'Of course they haven't—with no one here how the hell could they? Well, they'll have to go without an hour or two more. But I won't have it any longer with George and his shirty bit—there's no room for a — madonna in the outfit. I don't half like the business of a water-pipe bursting and that inspector fellow nosing about outside. If I hadn't smoothed him over pleasant he might have wanted to come in and go right through the place and how'd we fix that up at a moment's notice? If it wasn't that we've only a few hours to go—'

'Someone coming round, boss,' interrupted the third. 'He gave the taps all right. Shall I go down and see to it?'

'Yes, yes,' replied Joolby; 'we're coming down as well. It's time they were all here. Which is this one? Look over the stairs, Bronsky.'

His progress, as usual, was slow and by the time they were on the landing the arrival had been admitted. The comrade leaned over the banisters and sent down a fraternal greeting.

'It's the little persecuted brother,' he informed Mr Joolby. And to the victim himself: 'God be with—No! no! I mean: To Hell with order, comrade!'

'Whichever you prefer, comrade,' replied Won Chou politely.

'You came along the back street way, didn't you?' asked his master when they were all in the hall together. Won Chou nodded. 'Any signs that side of Larch or Nickle?'

'Not see. By the way, when George does get here you may find that he has got a grunch about you.'

'Oh, has he? Well, for that matter I happen to have a grunch about him to balance it and unless I'm mistaken mine will have bigger teeth than his will. He got a grunch!' The misshapen thing spat venomously.

'I have been hear of your outdoing that evil fellow Max Carrados just then,' observed Mr Bronsky to the little brother as they stood about, waiting, with their various degrees of unconcern or the reverse, for the arrival of the others. 'Freedom shake you with the hand for the occasion.'

'I shake myself with the hand,' was the modest assent, and he quite literally did so. 'I have owed Mr Carrados one for several years.'

'Is that what?' asked Bronsky.

'When I first met him—in Shanghai—I tried to do a small stroke of business between us. I offer to sell him my little sister Hwa for eighty trade dollars.'

'Eh? Well?' Even at that distracting moment Mr Joolby found himself taking a passing interest in so human a theme. 'What happened about it?'

'Knock me down,' admitted Won Chou simply.

Mr Bronsky gave utterance to a 'tsssk!' of disgust. 'He had not the rightness,' he pronounced with decision.

'No; all my people say it was too cheap; in fact I got a hundred and ten later. That was before I had education at the mission college, of course. Afterwards I learned that it was far better not to sell them—outright.'

'Well, anyhow, it was time that Carrados was roped,' summed up Joolby. 'He was passing the ice too free; Bronsky here got the idea that he was a plaster-of-Paris almighty and could do anyone and knew everything . . . Did he talk Chinese to you, Won?'

'No.' And then, without a flicker in his eye: 'Did he talk Sudanese to you, Joolby?'

'Eh? What's that?' demanded Mr Joolby, beginning to glower ominously. Fortunately, perhaps, just then there was the sound of a car outside and the humbler member of the crew, who had small interest in these personal feelings, put his head inside to announce the arrival of 'the others'. These proved to be Nickle and George Larch who very soon appeared, both burdened with several packages which from their laboured movements had every appearance of being weighty.

'Ah, here we are at last,' said Joolby with obvious satisfaction. 'You've brought the lot, I suppose? Carry them through into the yellow room at the back for the time, you two. You had no trouble, Nickle?'

'Easy as toffee. We came Herriot Lane and there wasn't a soul to be seen. I've just run the car in loose. What about it?'

'Leave it there handy. We'll keep it in reserve and have it follow. Go now and see that both are filled up with enough spare juice for a double journey—we don't want to have to take in anywhere and leave our number. And make sure that everything's running smooth: there's got to be no tinkering this excursion.'

'Say a matter of ten minutes.'

'Eight o'clock's plenty of time. You take first car, cruise, and pick up Vallett and his load near the windmill on Keystone Common not later than two. That gives you five hours to slip into Seabridge at dusk. We'll be there for you.'

'All serene,' undertook Nickle, hurrying out again. Joolby followed the stuff into the yellow room behind and waited for Larch to bring in the last package.

'Now look here, George, this won't do,' he said roughly, when he was satisfied that all he had expected was there. 'Orders are orders and what I say goes or you or any other man will find dam' quick that he's up against it. Your wife was to be here in charge all yesterday, seeing to those three below. Well, what happened?'

'I know all about that, Mr Joolby,' replied George in his usual temperate, respectful way, 'and I'm taking the responsibility for what did happen. You'll remember how I always told you that

Cora must have the first chance to get away if anything went wrong—?'

'Well, well,' interrupted Joolby impatiently, 'what's that got to do with your precious wife being kept on ice? Nothing went wrong anywhere.'

'No, but you thought it would,' said George, keeping his temper with admirable restraint. 'I don't pretend to know what it was but something came through and on Thursday night you fancied anything might happen. When the rest of us were going about our jobs you and one or two others had quietly put on your roller skates and were lying doggo near the coast, waiting to get the tip and ready to do a bunk for safety.'

'Does it sound likely?' The usual symptoms of resentment at being crossed began to suffuse the monstrous swelling body. 'Haven't I got my shop and goods to consider—all I possess? How could I—as you say—skate off and leave everything I have behind? That's the way you talk, you foolish fellow.'

'You sold your shop and stock a week ago, Mr Joolby,' steadily replied George. 'At least all the heavy stuff and I don't doubt that you have the valuables put away somewhere handy. I tell you it won't do, it isn't the square thing—leaving Cora without a chance, to take the first concussion. If I'd known as much—'

'Oh, to hell with you and Cora!' Joolby exploded passionately. 'You talk as if the piece was a bleeding Aphrodite in a tissue-paper chemise. I've had the sjambok put across the hams of better women than her for a dam' sight less than she's done. If you can't keep your Cora in line, Larch, you'd better clear and make way for men with more guts.'

'Oh, so it's that, is it?' speculated George, regarding his employer gravely. 'I thought you were beating up for a split as soon as I'd finished your job, Mr Joolby. Well, I'm quite ready to go—in fact after what you've just said you couldn't possibly keep me—'

'I've paid you up for all . . .'

'You have—at your price—and I hope it'll be the last money

I shall ever earn in that way.' He started to leave the room quietly enough, but as he reached the door a sudden impulse brought him in a couple of strides to Joolby's side and for a moment his placid eyes blazed as he stood with a fist drawn back and the cripple shrinking before it.

'No, you are quite safe after all,' he said, turning away and dropping his hand. 'Things like you burst if a man treads on you.' Without a word to any there he marched from the house with head erect and—as it happened—left the grounds by the back gate; so that, all unknowingly, he passed out of the lane at the exact moment when a high-speed car, unusually well manned, whirled into it at the other end.

'Julian Joolby,' said a disapproving voice, and sheering round—always an awkward move—Joolby saw that Mr Bronsky had looked in by another door and been a witness of the last stage of the quarrel; 'Julian Joolby, when will you learn to snaffle your violent emotion?'

'Eh? Oh nonsense: that was all bunko,' he replied, developing his malicious grin. 'I put that across to work George up. Now he's clear out of it and a good job too, between us.'

'Yes, yes, but is it safe?'

'Of course it's safe or d'y'a think I'd have done it? He's made the plates, hasn't he? He's done the actual work and if he tried to cross us now we could frame it for him to get the heaviest sentence. George knows that all right; besides he has his perishing Cora to think of. His sort never gets you shopped; and in the end they always go quietly. Now, don't you see, he's out of any shares? All in good time I shall work Nickle and Vallett out too. It's the sensible thing to do when it comes to cutting up big money.'

'You have right, I believe. Yes, it's tamgod smart. I had not thought of that,' admitted Mr Bronsky, shedding warm approval. It did not occur to him to speculate whether ultimately he also might not be involved in his fellow conspirator's squeezing-out process.

'All cars as right as rain,' reported Nickle, discovering the two still in the back room. 'Do I take these along?'—he indicated the stack of parcels. 'By the way, what's the matter with old George? He went out looking as if he'd swallowed some hot thunder.'

'Said he had to go to see a man about a rabbit. I think it was all an excuse to get a cooling drink,' replied Mr Joolby in high good humour. 'No, Nickle, the plates go in the second car. We decided to separate so you will only carry the paper.'

'And Vallett? What about him?'

'He goes on with you and Jim. The two with him make their way back independent—they all know exactly what to do and how to do it. We're going to make use of those three passengers to cover the run if anyone tries to open on us. Carrados goes with you; Jim attends to him in the car and then you'll have Vallett later. Now bring up our distinguished myopic friend for a few minutes' conversation, will you? I'm not going down any more steps than I can help, so if you find the cellar unpleasantly damp you must take the change out of him.'

'You bet I will!' undertook Nickle forcibly. 'My infernal thumb pains yet like the very devil. Come along, Jim; you're detailed to it.'

'But are you sure it is quite prudential, Joolby?' put in Mr Bronsky with an anxious flutter. 'This fellow Carrados—'

'Oh, he's all over and washed out. These conjuring tricks don't come off more than once. It isn't that he's specially clever in the light, only our lot are so damned helpless in the dark. Besides, he hasn't so much as a toothpick on him now.'

'But this taking him along when he could be lock up here—? No, I cannot relish the idea of that, Joolby.'

'It's safer, take my word,' said Joolby, lowering his voice. 'The fact is, I like that water burst less and less and I've put things on an hour as it is so as to get away from here as soon as possible. It was just as it happened, of course, but for all we know it may mean someone being sent up along during the day, and that might be considerably sooner than we're timed for. This way we keep them under our eyes anyhow and I've got an idea for using them at the end that cuts the trail finely.'

'Well, it may be as you think,' admitted the dubious Bronsky, 'but all the nevertheless I'd sooner rather—'

The return of Nickle and Jim cut short this interesting proposition. Mr Carrados seemed rather damp and his usually spruce attire certainly conveyed the impression of having been roughly used, but he did not appear to be inordinately depressed himself—not even when Nickle, to give point to his facetious 'Here's the goods!' propelled him unceremoniously forward.

'Ah, our principal guest,' remarked Mr Joolby agreeably. 'I trust you found the poor accommodation adequate, Mr Carrados? Owing to your unfortunate visual defect we knew that you'd forgive the meagre lighting provision of our best spare room. In other matters—well, as I daresay you've learned by now, we are rather rough and ready.'

'Yes,' supplemented Nickle threateningly, 'infernally rough and ready for anything.'

'Scarcely less ready than my companion and myself are—for breakfast,' ventured Carrados. 'Ideas of hospitality may vary, Mr Joolby, but I can't call to mind any civilized tribe where guests—since you call us that—are denied food and drink for forty hours.'

'That's been a mistake—I apologise, I apologise,' professed Mr Joolby, with the air of making amends very handsomely. 'It was entirely without my knowledge—for say what you will when you are free again, Mr Carrados, none of you have been handled any rougher or used any worse than you brought on yourself or the necessity of keeping you safe required.'

'Indeed? I wonder if you expect Geoffrey Tilehurst to subscribe to that?' he challenged.

'Tilehurst!' Eyes glanced from him to meet each other and a knowing smile went round. The blind man intercepted the atmosphere and it gave him a moment's pause but he was too alertly concerned in other signs just then to turn aside for what mattered very little.

'You ask him how he liked it when you next meet, and see,' continued Mr Joolby dryly. 'Now listen for we haven't much time to waste—least of all on passengers. I've said I'm sorry about the grub but we can't wait for that now. We'll take just what we find—most of us haven't had our own breakfasts yet— and you will get your share of what there is and can eat it as you travel.'

'Travel?' interrogated Mr Carrados with some concern. 'You surely can't think of taking me? Consider how a blind man would be in the way on a journey.'

'Leave that to us,' was the curt reply; 'we're going to take you for a ride and—'

'Take me for a ride!' The victim seemed to grow even more apprehensive. 'Not in the transatlantic—I might say the Chicago—sense surely, I hope, Mr Joolby?'

Mr Joolby snapped a raw laugh. 'That depends on how you act,' he replied, not sorry to have the opportunity to introduce the menace. 'Do exactly as you're told and you'll come through all right; lack, and—' He did not resort to melodramatic signs but the hiatus was sufficiently expressive.

'You certainly hold all the cards this hand,' admitted the blind man. 'It's only for me to make the best terms I can as things have turned out.'

This brought in Nickle who had been enduring his chief's derisive courtesy with rising impatience.

'Make terms, you hear!' he cried scornfully. 'I like the beggar's cheek. Do you think it's a case of what you agree to or what you don't, damn your eyes, Max Carrados!'

'You can't do that, Nickle,' replied Carrados with deadly quietness, 'they are blasted already . . . Doesn't that inspire you with—I won't say pity or compunction in your case—but with a sort of vague misgiving? Superstition, if you like, but there has always been an uneasy dread of incurring the just resentment of the sightless. A blind man's curse—'

'Won't wash,' interrupted Nickle. 'Cut him short, for the

Almighty's sake, Joolby. Can't you see he's only playing for time with all this day-of-judgment stuff patter?'

'Rather an ominous phrase in your position, Nickle—"Playing for time". Suppose I get it for you?'

'This "time"—I do not grasp quite what it imply,' put in Mr Bronsky intelligently. 'It is—'

'Just an idiom, Mr Bronsky,' explained Carrados, becoming quietly amused in rather an inexplicable way considering his situation. 'I almost think that you look like finding out what it means also.'

'That's enough,' announced Joolby with decision. 'You've put up all the bluff you know, Carrados, and we've got you dog-beaten. Now listen to what you've got to do, and this time if you deviate a single hair or try any of your monkey tricks it's the deep end you'll go off at. We're going to take you in the car—'

'I don't think so now,' broke in the prisoner, with so marked a change of front—so confident an air and smile—that they were paralysed into holding themselves up and letting him run on from sheer amazement. 'You have waited too long; I've got to like it here. It's peaceful and almost rural. In the early morning— now for instance—one can scent the copse outside (another homonymous word, Mr Bronsky; it means woodland—among other things)—you can hear the song of birds: the early birds out to get their foolish worms. Really, they whistle more than they sing . . . surely you can hear them now?' and, account for it as they might, a series of low sharp whistles at various distances did reach their ears, as though a preconcerted signal was announcing, for instance, that a circle of men had taken up position.

'To hell!' suddenly exclaimed Nickle, making a dash. 'The cops *are* here. They'll be on us next.' An unnerving peal of the ancient bell and an insistent crash of the heavy door knocker gave point to this expression. Without waiting to think twice Nickle flung up a window and dropped down. A shout, a shot, and the sound of hard wood striking something slightly less solid followed in quick succession.

'Nickle will never make a reliable shot,' confided Mr Carrados to the little band of paralysed listeners. 'He always takes sight too low—fault of British army musketry training. Now, about the door? My friends are evidently waiting.'

Won Chou slid his almond eyes to his master's face and getting no guidance from that rigid mask went off docilely on his own account to obey the summons. At this critical moment Mr Bronsky, who from the first suggestion of alarm had been hovering between the expedience of following Nickle's lead, walking out by the front door in a dignified way, hiding under the table, or fainting, decided to be straightforward and honest. Although the detestable myrmidons of the law were not yet on the scene the good Mr Carrados would no doubt bear satisfactory witness.

'There would appear to be somethings going on but I do not gather what ensues,' accordingly remarked Mr Bronsky with convincing detachment. 'I understand that this was a peaceful place where a Mr Joolby merchandises antique wares. I have arrived here soon so as to make early bargains. Mr Joolby,' he continued, raising his voice as steps approached, and cramming his silk hat more firmly on so as to demonstrate the casualness of his presence there, 'if you have any particular articles of choice rarity I would address myself to your negotiations. I am in the desire for buying—'

'Number one man makee say must look-see and come-go every side,' announced Won Chou, a little superfluously it might appear since the official referred to was following him in. There are occasions when members of the force do not trouble to stand on ceremony. But Mr Carrados, at all events, found it amusing.

'No, no, Mr Won,' he protested, laughing appreciation; 'I'm afraid it's really too late to get back to talkee talkee chop now. Not after giving us a taste of your college style, if you remember.'

'Mr Joolby,' insisted the honest customer, rising to a passionate intensity as he realised that Detective-Inspector Beedel was at the door and taking in the situation, 'Mr Joolby, I am wholly a stranger to you, never having seen you formerly to this morning; but I am of the inclination to acquire works of ancient if you have of such for disposition at reasonable costages—'

Having surveyed the room and its inmates the inspector turned to speak over his shoulder.

'Come in, West,' he said to a uniformed policeman behind. 'You other two stay out there in the hall. See that no one passes on any pretext in either direction. Well, Mr Carrados, I'm glad to find that you're all right, sir. I made a dash for it when the district office passed your news on. You got us a bit anxious.'

'No need, inspector,' replied Mr Carrados—he had greeted Beedel's salute with a smile and a nod when he first appeared. 'Children, drunkards, and the blind, you know—we have a special indulgence with providence.'

'Providence—why yes,' admitted his friend. 'But this lot represent the other place, sir! Now let's have a look at them. I suppose,' he spoke back as he strolled across to Won Chou, 'I suppose we may take it that all are concerned, sir?'

'We can assume that much responsibility I think. I have been assaulted and forcibly detained and can identify all as actively or passively involved. Two others—Miss Melhuish and Mr Tilehurst—are still confined in the cellars. And then, of course, there is the original business.'

'If they're in no immediate danger we'll go through the house when we've ticked off this lot, sir. Well, my lad, I think I've seen your face before. "Snow", wasn't it?'

'Very much no savvy,' courteously replied Won Chou, evidently anxious to afford any information he could but unfortunately only imperfectly acquainted with the language.

'You wouldn't. Put them on and pass him out to wait in the hall, West,' said the inspector. 'Ah, Mr Joolby, I believe? I've often thought that I should like the opportunity of going through your little place. You should have some very interesting old stuff there—one sort and another.'

'I am only a poor man,' touchingly protested Mr Joolby, 'but what little I have has been made by hard work and honest dealing. Still, there may be something you want—no matter how careful one is in buying, unscrupulous persons occasionally impose on one with stolen property. At any rate let us go there and you shall pick out whatever you consider doubtful.' In his anxiety to attract the police away from that spot Mr Joolby seemed to have forgotten that he was no longer the proprietor of the East End business.

'All in good time, Mr Joolby,' undertook the inspector. 'But that doesn't come into the charge—so far.'

'What is this charge?' inquired Mr Joolby faintly.

'Well, suppose we have a look at these now'—Inspector Beedel did not appear to have been taking any particular notice of the surroundings so far but doubtless he used his eyes and had his methods, for at the word he turned abruptly, penknife in hand, and a string was cut, the brown paper ripped, and the contents of one of the parcels exposed before Mr Joolby could do anything but give an involuntary cry of shattered hopes, and take a single feebly threatening step forward, or Mr Bronsky get off more than a faint 'psssh' and 'tsssh' of indignation.

'Books, eh?' observed the inspector picking up the topmost. '*Rise and Fall of the Dutch Republic* feels a trifle heavy for *my* taste.' He shook it loosely open and a metal plate fell out and rang upon the floor—a copper sheet engraved, among other details of words and figures, with the name of the Bank of England. 'Ah, I thought as much,' commented Beedel as he recovered the plate and satisfied himself about its purpose. 'George's work, I suppose? He's lucky—for the moment. Well, pass him out too, West.'

'What about—?' The constable indicated Joolby's wrists. 'He can't get along without using his hands, inspector.'

'Search him and take everything away. Then let him keep his sticks,' decided Beedel. 'Be particular you miss nothing he may have got about him and tell them out there.' He turned to give his attention to Mr Bronsky.

'I suppose we must call that the rubber, Mr Joolby,' moralised Max Carrados, as the cripple was being put through this process. 'It's been a very interesting game throughout with its surprising changes of fortune, but the break-up of a party is always a little sad though, isn't it? I'm afraid that it's no good to say that you can claim your revenge when we next meet on equal terms; we shall both be too aged to care about it.'

For a second it looked as if the bankrupt plotter was attempting some reply; the muscles of his uncouth mouth were stirred and twisted, but if the impulse had carried to effect, not to retort by words but to spit venomously at his adversary's face would have been Julian Joolby's final gesture. As it happened, Constable West caught something of the baleful look and with even this meagre satisfaction just too late the prisoner was hustled away beyond the range of his recrimination.

'It is amusing if it should not be laughable,' suddenly exclaimed Mr Bronsky, compelled to realise at last that his person was being regarded as no more sacrosanct than those of all the others. 'Otherwise the injustice shall put back the day of freedom for a hundred year!'

'Oh, I don't think you'll get that long, Mr Bronsky,' the inspector reassured him. 'But it certainly looks like putting back the day of your freedom for about eighteen months or three years. Well, now that the lot's mopped up I'll go down and look into the matter of those two you spoke of, sir. Will you be all right here?'

'Perfectly,' replied Mr Carrados, with a private smile at the ineradicable foible of even those who should know best to regard him as intrinsically helpless. 'But if you happen to be too long I wouldn't say that you won't find me in the larder. By the way, we are not forgetting Tapsfield and that end of it though? Forgive my mentioning it but I take a kind of proprietary interest in that delightfully restful village.'

'Quite all right, sir—just as well to speak. As a matter of fact I've sent a word. Of course after what you'd told me before, your S.O.S. from here put two and two together. I've no doubt that at this moment the place looks just as peaceful as usual and it mayn't be hard to get into the works, but when it comes to getting out and away with it they'll find that they've trod on the live rail.'

Actually Mr Carrados was neither in the larder nor in the room when the inspector was recalled, for as he was examining Mr Larch's consummate work with appreciative touch, a hasty call from the hall beyond brought everyone within hearing scurrying there to lend assistance at this new development. As it happened none was required—at least not what they had thought. Joolby—

'He must be in a sort of fit,' the constable kneeling at his side explained. 'Sitting quietly there and then without a word or sign he rolled clean off the chair and lay here. I can't make it out—you'd think he'd kick or twitch or make some sort of movement, wouldn't you?'

Carrados bent over his fallen antagonist, by the policeman's side, and brought his own face close to the upturned one which now made no motion to retort with venom. ('A damned sight closer than I'd ha' cared mine to go,' was the frank pronouncement of the constable afterwards. 'But then of course he couldn't see what I did—luckily.')

'Not now—he's given his last kick at this hated world,' he said, rising from the contemplation. 'I suppose you'll have to get in a doctor or call up your own man, but it makes no difference really.'

'You mean that he's—gone?' Inspector Beedel was staring hard and inclined to be a shade incredulous in view of the suddenness of the unfortunate proceeding.

'Yes, inspector; he's managed to slip through your hands after all. Poison.'

'He had no poison about him just now—that I will swear,' warmly protested P.C. West, conscious of Beedel's rigorous eyes fixed accusingly on him. 'I don't mind saying that I had that in mind and I went through the lining and every seam for the least screw of paper.'

'Besides, he never made a move to reach anything while he was in here,' loyally confirmed one of the other policemen. 'Just sat with his hands resting on the top of one of his sticks and his face buried in them.'

'Of course—his stick,' exclaimed Mr Carrados, enlightened. 'Please give me the one he had. Yes, there it is—that little cavity at the top. A tiny phial sunk in and undetectably covered over. An ideal place, you see, because he must always have it with him. Then as he sat, apparently sunk in thought, he worked out the little tube and crushed it up between his strong teeth and heroically swallowed the lot. You will find that his tongue is cut—just as it might very easily be in a fit, which makes it all quite convincing. Mr Joolby was a connoisseur of the subtler poisons, inspector, and I don't doubt that he had reserved something very choice indeed for his own consumption.'

'Well I'll go to Hanover!' apostrophised Beedel, after exploring the stick. Despite a lifelong association with the conventional forms of crime, not even the contents bill of an evening newspaper were more liable to be 'amazed' by the least variant of a ruse than was the worthy, and, let it be added, extremely capable inspector.

The net had been fully drawn; every member of the gang had been accounted for and now the outposts stationed in the garden were coming in to take over the work of guarding and escorting the haul of prisoners. Tapsfield was being spoken with over the wire; an antique shop in the East End would be inconspicuously watched by a perhaps rather too noticeably leisured stranger, and George Larch was in the process of being described (and surely we may hope unsuccessfully in his case this once) as 'wanted'. Mr Carrados, his work for the time being done, was following his usual rule of not getting in anyone's way and in conforming to this excellent precept had withdrawn to the deserted dining-room where in his rather famished state he found sufficient material to interest him. Beedel could be trusted to keep his word in the other directions.

'Uncle Max! Oh, my old darling, I *am* glad to find you here safe but please do leave me a spot of marmalade.' Nora, of course, and the inspector had kept his word in that direction at least. 'A policeman let me out but they sort of shuffed me through the hall. What's happening now?'

'Nothing, I imagine. It's all happened I should say. You've had your adventure, my dear, and no power below will ever induce me to put you in the way of another.'

'But Geoffrey?' she interposed, paying no heed to that. 'I thought I might find him up here before me. I wanted to look round down there but the policeman sent me on. Oh, Uncle Max, do you think—?'

'No, I don't,' anticipated Uncle Max cuttingly; 'and I have more than half a doubt whether Geoffrey Tilehurst has ever been in any sort of—?'

'I suppose I may come in since I think I heard my name,' and Tilehurst himself appeared, looking of all three there considerably the most presentable.

'Geoffrey!' exclaimed Nora, running over with joy, and she had started across the room when—account for it how you will—she stopped, repressed by the sight of his remarkably sleek trim and a realisation of her own draggle-tailed appearance.

'I say—Nora, you, really you?' he cried, transported in turn, and to do him justice he did not seem to notice anything aversive in her disorder—or, indeed, to notice anything but her excited young face. 'How on earth do you come to turn up here? I'm rather out of touch with what's been going on but it's like a twist of magic.'

'But surely you could guess that I might still be here,' she said; 'after what happened—in this very room—on Wednesday?'

'Wednesday—in this room?' he repeated darkly. 'But I haven't the ghost of an idea what did happen here. I've been shut up in a beast of a cellar for the past week.'

'You didn't come up and see me here in this room?' she faltered. 'You didn't beg me—to—to save you?'

'Not unless I was talking in my sleep,' he declared, looking still more puzzled. 'Or am now,' he added.

'Geoffrey: let me introduce you to my uncle, Max Carrados. This is Geoffrey Tilehurst, Uncle Max. Now please go on and tell me all about it—I've given it up.' She sat down, helped herself liberally to more bread and marmalade and her eyes ranged incessantly from one to the other in turn as she gorged steadily through the simple banquet.

'I don't imagine that we shall find that too hard,' undertook Mr Carrados. 'By the way, won't you join our modest picnic, Mr Tilehurst? I'm afraid that there's very little marmalade left by now but the cheese is there and the inner part of this loaf is reasonably edible. As you see, we aren't standing on ceremony.'

'Thanks very much, but I'm not particularly hungry,' he replied. 'Of course I haven't had any breakfast yet but it must be pretty early still, I should say. If you don't mind I think I'll wait for something more—er, regular.'

'*You aren't particularly hungry!*' For a moment Nora actually laid down her slice of bread and marmalade. 'Geoffrey: when did you last have anything—er, regular?'

'Why, yesterday,' he replied. 'Though, as a matter of fact, it was a bit out of the routine. Something went different it seems, but old Chou looked in and foraged me a supply from somewhere. Very decent sort, that Chink; he often came down to bring me things and pass the time in one way or another. And that reminds me, by the by. I wonder if either of you would mind lending me a couple of pounds to settle with him until I get back home? You see, I taught him poker yesterday and somehow or other—'

'Uncle Max! You hear that? Why didn't we have—er, something regular?'

Mr Carrados looked slightly apologetic.

'I begin to suspect that Won Chou can't quite like me,' he suggested. 'You naturally come in too on the Chinese family principle.'

'And he was here and about yesterday,' she went on unsparingly, 'and you can hear the slightest footfall! Oh, Uncle Max, after all I've been led to believe—'

'Human, my dear,' he sought to plead, 'human footsteps. That logically excludes panthers, Chinamen and fairies as they are constitutionally inaudible. Against that you may put how I have always maintained that Tilehurst would not be badly used—'

'Yes, you did,' she admitted; 'but now what about the dreadful state he was in on Wednesday?'

'That brings us to the point. Mr Tilehurst, one question please—hypothetical let us say. If a woman—Nora, we will suppose—could save you from a course of torture by submitting herself in your place, how would you decide if it rested with you?'

'Surely you can scarcely ask me that, sir? How could I—or any decent fellow for that matter—accept such a sacrifice from a woman? Especially, as you put it, from one whom he—'

Geoffrey broke off looking ingenuously embarrassed, finding it too emotional to explain the added restriction.

'You see, Nora,' demonstrated Mr Carrados, 'it wouldn't have worked. Our friend here would have hurled back the—er, dastardly proposal.'

'Of course,' added Geoffrey, anxious not to take too much credit for this heroic pose, 'it's difficult to say what mightn't happen under harsh conditions. You have no idea what it feels like merely to be shut up in a mouldy cellar for days—'

'No, perhaps not,' conceded Max Carrados tolerantly, 'but I daresay we can faintly imagine the sensation.'

'But Geoffrey,' insisted Nora, not to be sidetracked from the main issue, 'either you or I are certainly a bit dotty. On Wednesday night they brought you up here—'

'One moment, Nora,' struck in Carrados with his suavest tone; 'forgive me—but before you impugn the sanity of either. You say you saw *Geoffrey* here.' He smiled significantly across at her as he underlined the point. '*Did you notice his finger-nails then?*'

'Did I notice—?' Revelation came with a crash. 'Oh, my gosh! Again! Do you mean he was—? But why—? How—?'

'Why not? It was essential to the plan that you should adopt a certain course and, as we have heard, Mr Tilehurst here was useless for persuasion. Tapsfield is not too far away. The double was free to come and go, and playing the part he could make just the points that would weigh with you.'

'Look here,'—Geoffrey Tilehurst claimed his turn to speak and addressed himself solely to Mr Carrados's attention. 'Most of this is pretty nearly Greek to me but there seems to be one thing that's really important. Did she—that is, was Nora—I mean to say, has your niece come to this infernal house because I—in order to be—well, with some intention of helping me if you understand what I'm driving at?'

'I think I may have a rough idea,' was the genial admission. 'But as to that, Mr Tilehurst, who can say what a young woman does anything for nowadays, if, indeed, most of them have any reason? I can only tell you this—it may help you. When I guessed something of the mad project my niece was embarking on, I said—for of course I felt it my duty to warn her—"You are risking your head inside a lion's mouth." What was her reply? "Uncle Max," she said without turning a hair, "what do I care about that? Isn't Geoffrey's there already?"'

'And if that doesn't do it,' thought Mr Carrados, as he averted his face with the appearance of being moved, 'all I can say is—curse you!'

'Uncle Max!' shrieked Nora at this romantic disclosure, 'I

am sure I never did—' but the time for such maidenly affectations was past. Geoffrey had taken the bit of irresolution firmly between his wisdom teeth and was bolting.

'Oh, you darling darling, did you really care so much?' he demanded hoarsely. 'Why, my precious treasure, I'd gladly go through a dozen lions' mouths to hear that!'

'Why, naturally I cared, Geoffrey dear,' she replied, with infinitely more composure. 'I thought we'd settled all that long ago—but of course it's just as well to ask me.'

'Isn't it simply wonderful, sweetheart'—by this time he has taken possession of her and was demonstrating his affection regardless of the bread and marmalade involved in the process—'isn't it simply wonderful that of all the people in the world just we two should be here—?'

'Yes, dearest,' she tactfully hastened to agree, 'it is. Still you really must remember that there's Uncle Max over there as well and—'

'I beg your pardon, sir,' apologised Geoffrey, 'but you see—'

'No,' amended Carrados sympathetically, 'on this occasion I don't. Never mind us, children,' he added benignly, 'we are both, rest assured, quite blind.'

'Both!' exclaimed two rather startled voices.

'Who—?'

'I mean the somewhat underdressed little fellow over there with the bow and arrows,' he explained, nodding vaguely. 'I think he must have crept in after you two . . . My dears, try to keep him with you always.'

THE END

THE BUNCH OF VIOLETS

AN EPISODE IN THE WAR-TIME ACTIVITIES
OF MAX CARRADOS

WHEN Mr J. Beringer Hulse, in the course of one of his periodical calls at the War Office, had been introduced to Max Carrados he attached no particular significance to the meeting. His own business there lay with Mr Flinders, one of the quite inconspicuous departmental powers so lavishly produced by a few years of intensive warfare: business that was more confidential than exacting at that stage and hitherto carried on *à deux*. The presence on this occasion of a third, this quiet, suave, personable stranger, was not out of line with Mr Hulse's open-minded generalities on British methods: 'A little singular, perhaps, but not remarkable,' would have been the extent of his private comment. He favoured Max with a hard, entirely friendly, American stare, said, 'Vurry pleased to make your acquaintance, Mr Carrados,' as they shook hands, and went on with his own affair.

Of course Hulse was not to know that Carrados had been brought in especially to genialise with him. Most of the blind man's activities during that period came within the 'Q-class' order. No one ever heard of them, very often they would have seemed quite meaningless under description, and generally they were things that he alone could do—or do as effectively at all events. In the obsolete phraseology of the day, they were his 'bit'.

'There's this man Hulse,' Flinders had proceeded, when it came to the business on which Carrados had been asked to call at Whitehall. 'Needless to say, he's no fool or Jonathan wouldn't have sent him on the ticket he carries. If anything, he's too keen—wants to see everything, do anything and go everywhere.

In the meanwhile he's kicking up his heels here in London with endless time on his hands and the Lord only knows who mayn't have a go at him.'

'You mean for information—or does he carry papers?' asked Carrados.

'Well, at present, information chiefly. He necessarily knows a lot of things that would be priceless to the Huns, and a clever man or woman might find it profitable to nurse him.'

'Still, he must be on his guard if, as you say, he is. No one imagines that London in 1917 is a snakeless Eden or expects that German agents today are elderly professors who say, "How vos you?" and "Ja, ja!"'

'My dear fellow,' said Flinders sapiently, 'every American who came to London before the war was on his guard against a pleasant-spoken gentleman who would accost him with, "Say, stranger, does this happen to be your wallet lying around here on the sidewalk?" and yet an unending procession of astute, long-headed citizens met him, exactly as described, year after year, and handed over their five hundred or five thousand pounds on a tale that would have made a common or Michaelmas goose blush to be caught listening to.'

'It's a curious fact,' admitted Carrados thoughtfully. 'And this Hulse?'

'Oh, he's quite an agreeable chap, you'll find. He may know a trifle more than you and be a little wider awake and see further through a brick wall and so on, but he won't hurt your feelings about it. Well, will you do it for us?'

'Certainly,' replied Carrados. 'What is it, by the way?'

Flinders laughed his apologies and explained more precisely.

'Hulse has been over here a month now, and it may be another month before the details come through which he will take on to Paris. Then he will certainly have documents of very special importance that he must carry about with him. Well, in the meanwhile, of course, he is entertained and may pal up with anyone or get himself into Lord knows what. We can't keep him here under lock and key or expect him to make a report of every fellow he has a drink with or every girl he meets.'

'Quite so,' nodded the blind man.

'Actually, we have been asked to take precautions. It isn't quite a case for the C.I.D.—not at this stage, that is to say. So if I introduce him to you and you fix up an evening for him or something of the sort and find out where his tastes lie, and—and, in fact, keep a general shepherding eye upon him—He broke off abruptly, and Carrados divined that he had reddened furiously and was kicking himself in spirit. The blind man raised a deprecating hand.

'Why should you think that so neat a compliment would pain me, Flinders?' he asked quietly. 'Now if you had questioned the genuineness of some of my favourite tetradrachms I might have had reason to be annoyed. As it is, yes, I will gladly keep a general shepherding ear on J. Beringer as long as may be needful.'

'That's curious,' said Flinders, looking up quickly. 'I didn't think that I had mentioned his front name.'

'I don't think that you have,' agreed Carrados.

'Then how—? Had you heard of him before?'

'You don't give an amateur conjurer much chance,' replied the other whimsically. 'When you brought me to this chair I found a table by me, and happening to rest a hand on it my fingers had "read" a line of writing before I realised it—just as your glance might as unconsciously do,' and he held up an envelope addressed to Hulse.

'That is about the limit,' exclaimed Flinders with some emphasis. 'Do you know, Carrados, if I hadn't always led a very blameless life I should be afraid to have you around the place.'

Thus it came about that the introduction was made and in due course the two callers left together.

'You'll see Mr Carrados down, won't you?' Flinders had asked, and, slightly puzzled but not disposed to question English ways, Hulse had assented. In the passage Carrados laid a light hand on his companion's arm. Through some subtle perception he read Hulse's mild surprise.

'By the way, I don't think that Flinders mentioned my infirmity,' he remarked. 'This part of the building is new to me and I happen to be quite blind.'

'You astonish me,' declared Hulse, and he had to be assured that the statement was literally exact. 'You don't seem to miss much by it, Mr Carrados. Ever happen to hear of Laura Bridgman?'

'Oh, yes,' replied Carrados. 'She was one of your star cases. But Laura Bridgman's attainments really were wonderful. She was also deaf and dumb, if you remember.'

'That is so,' assented Hulse. 'My people come from New Hampshire not far from Laura's home, and my mother had some of her needlework framed as though it was a picture. That's how I come to know of her, I reckon.'

They had reached the street meanwhile and Carrados heard the door of his waiting car opened to receive him.

'I'm going on to my club now to lunch,' he remarked with his hand still on his companion's arm. 'Of course we only have a wartime menu, but if you would keep me company you would be acting the Good Samaritan,' and Beringer Hulse, who was out to see as much as possible of England, France and Berlin within the time—perhaps, also, not uninfluenced by the appearance of the rather sumptuous vehicle—did not refuse.

'Vurry kind of you to put it in that way, Mr Carrados,' he said, in his slightly business-like, easy style. 'Why, certainly I will.'

During the following weeks Carrados continued to make himself very useful to the visitor, and Hulse did not find his stay in London any less agreeably varied thereby. He had a few other friends—acquaintances rather—he had occasion now and then to mention, but they, one might infer, were either not quite so expansive in their range of hospitality or so pressing for his company. The only one for whom he had ever to excuse himself was a Mr Darragh, who appeared to have a house in Densham Gardens (he was a little shrewdly curious as to what might be inferred of the status of a man who lived in Densham Gardens), and, well, yes, there was Darragh's sister, Violet. Carrados began to take a private interest in the Darragh household, but there was little to be learned beyond the fact that the house was let furnished to the occupant from month to month. Even during the complexities of war that fact alone could not be regarded as particularly incriminating.

There came an evening when Hulse, having an appointment to dine with Carrados and to escort him to a theatre afterwards, presented himself in a mixed state of elation and remorse. His number had come through at last, he explained, and he was to leave for Paris in the morning. Carrados had been most awfully, most frightfully—Hulse became quite touchingly incoherent in his anxiety to impress upon the blind man the fullness of the gratitude he felt, but, all the same, he had come to ask whether he might cry off for the evening. There was no need to inquire the cause. Carrados raised an accusing finger and pointed to the little bunch of violets with which the impressionable young man had adorned his button-hole.

'Why, yes, to some extent,' admitted Hulse, with a facile return to his ingenuous, easy way. 'I happened to see Miss Darragh down town this afternoon. There's a man they know whom I've been crazy to meet for weeks, a Jap who has the whole ju-jitsu business at his finger-ends. Best ju-jitsuist out of Japan, Darragh says. Mighty useful thing, ju-jitsu, nowadays, Carrados.'

'At any time, indeed,' conceded Carrados. 'And he will be there tonight?'

'Certain. They've tried to fix it up for me half-a-dozen times before, but this Kuromi could never fit it in. Of course this will be the only chance.'

'True,' agreed the blind man, rather absent-mindedly. 'Your last night here.'

'I don't say that in any case I should not have liked to see Violet—Miss Darragh—again before I went, but I wouldn't have gone back on an arranged thing for that,' continued Hulse virtuously. 'Now this ju-jitsu I look on more in the light of business.'

'Rather a rough-and-tumble business one would think,' suggested Carrados. 'Nothing likely to drop out of your pockets in the process and get lost?'

Hulse's face displayed a rather more superior smile than he would have permitted himself had his friend been liable to see it and be snubbed thereby.

'I know what you mean, of course,' he replied, getting up and going to the blind man's chair, 'but don't you worry about me, Father William. Just put your hand to my breast pocket.'

'Sewn up,' commented Carrados, touching the indicated spot on his guest's jacket.

'Sewn up: that's it; and since I've had any important papers on me it always has been sewn up, no matter how often I change. No fear of anything dropping out now—or being lifted out, eh? No, sir; if what I carry there chanced to vanish, I guess no excuses would be taken and J.B.H. would automatically drop down to the very bottom of the class. As it is, if it's missing I shall be missing too, so that won't trouble me.'

'What time do you want to get there?'

'Darragh's? Well, I left that open. Of course I couldn't promise until I had seen you. Anyway, not until after dinner, I said.'

'That makes it quite simple, then,' declared Carrados. 'Stay and have dinner here, and afterwards we will go on to Darragh's together instead of going to the theatre.'

'That's most terribly kind of you,' replied Hulse. 'But won't it be rather a pity—the tickets, I mean, and so forth?'

'There are no tickets as it happens,' said Carrados. 'I left that over until tonight. And I have always wanted to meet a ju-jitsu champion. Quite providential, isn't it?'

*

It was nearly nine o'clock, and seated in the drawing-room of his furnished house in Densham Gardens, affecting to read an evening paper, Mr Darragh was plainly ill at ease. The strokes of the hour, sounded by the little gilt clock on the mantelpiece, seemed to mark the limit of his patience. A muttered word escaped him and he looked up with a frown.

'It was nine that Hulse was to be here by, wasn't it, Violet?' he asked.

Miss Darragh, who had been regarding him for some time in furtive anxiety, almost jumped at the simple question.

'Oh, yes, Hugh—about nine, that is. Of course he had to—'

'Yes, yes,' interrupted Darragh irritably; 'we've heard all that. And Sims,' he continued, more for the satisfaction of voicing his annoyance than to engage in conversation, 'swore by everything that we should have that coat by eight at the very latest. My God! what rotten tools one has to depend on!'

'Perhaps—' began Violet timidly, and stopped at his deepening scowl.

'Yes?' said Darragh, with a deadly smoothness in his voice. 'Yes, Violet; pray continue. You were about to say—'

'It was really nothing, Hugh,' she pleaded. 'Nothing at all.'

'Oh, yes, Violet, I am sure that you have some helpful little suggestion to make,' he went on in the same silky, deliberate way. Even when he was silent his unspoken thoughts seemed to be lashing her with bitterness, and she turned painfully away to pick up the paper he had flung aside. 'The situation, Kato,' resumed Darragh, addressing himself to the third occupant of the room, 'is bluntly this: If Sims isn't here with that coat before young Hulse arrives, all our carefully-thought-out plan, a month's patient work, and about the last both of our cash and credit, simply go to the devil! . . . and Violet wants to say that perhaps Mr Sims forgot to wind his watch last night or poor Mrs Sims's cough is worse . . . Proceed, Violet; don't be diffident.'

The man addressed as 'Kato' knocked a piece off the chessboard he was studying and stooped to pick it up again before he replied. Then he looked from one to the other with a face singularly devoid of expression.

'Perhaps. Who says?' he replied in his quaintly-ordered phrases. 'If it is to be, my friend, it will be.'

'Besides, Hugh,' put in Violet, with a faint dash of spirit, 'it isn't really quite so touch-and-go as that. If Sims comes before Hulse has left, Kato can easily slip out and change coats then.'

Darragh was already on his restless way towards the door. Apparently he did not think it worth while to reply to either of the speakers, but his expression, especially when his eyes turned to Violet, was one of active contempt. As the door closed after him, Kato sprang to his feet and his impassive look gave place to one almost of menace. His hands clenched unconsciously and with slow footsteps he seemed to be drawn on in pursuit. A little laugh, mirthless and bitter, from the couch, where Violet had seated herself, recalled him.

'Is it true, Katie,' she asked idly, 'that you are really the greatest ju-jitsuist outside Japan?'

'Polite other people say so,' replied the Japanese, his voice at once gentle and deprecating.

'And yet you cannot keep down even your little temper!'

Kato thought this over for a moment; then he crossed to the couch and stood regarding the girl with his usual impenetrable gravity.

'On contrary, I can keep down my temper very well,' he said seriously. 'I can keep it so admirably that I, whose ancestors were Samurai and very high nobles, have been able to become thief and swindler and'—his moving hand seemed to beat the air for a phrase—'and low-down dog and still to live. What does anything it matter that is connected with me alone? But there are three things that do matter—three that I do not allow myself to be insulted and still to live: my emperor, my country, and—you. And so,' concluded Kato Kuromi, in a somewhat lighter vein, 'now and then, as you say, my temper gets the better of me slightly.'

'Poor Katie,' said Violet, by no means disconcerted at this

delicate avowal. 'I really think that I am sorrier for you than I am for Hugh, or even for myself. But it's no good becoming romantic at this time of day, my dear man.' The lines of her still quite young and attractive face hardened in keeping with her thoughts. 'I suppose I've had my chance. We're all of a pattern and I'm as crooked as any of you now.'

'No, no,' protested Kato loyally; 'not you of yourself. It is we bad fellows round you. Darragh ought never to have brought you into these things, and then to despise you for your troubles—that is why my temper now and then ju-jitsues me. This time it is the worst of all—the young man Hulse, for whose benefit you pass yourself as the sister of your husband. How any mortal man possessing you—'

'Another cigarette, Katie, please,' interrupted Violet, for the monotonous voice had become slightly more penetrating than was prudent. 'That's all in the way of business, my friend. We aren't a firm of family solicitors. Jack Hulse had to be fascinated and I—well, if there is any hitch I don't think that it can be called my fault,' and she demonstrated for his benefit the bewitching smile that had so effectually enslaved the ardent Beringer.

'Fascinated!' retorted Kato, fixing on the word jealously, and refusing to be pacified by the bribery of the smile. 'Yes, so infatuated has become this very susceptible young man that you lead him about like pet lamb at the end of blue ribbon. Business? Perhaps. But *how* have you been able to do this, Violet? And your husband—Darragh—to him simply business, very good business—and he forces you to do this full of shame thing and mocks at you for reward.'

'Kato, Kato—' urged Violet, breaking through his scornful laughter.

'I am what your people call yellow man,' continued Kato relentlessly, 'and you are the one white woman of my dreams— dreams that I would not lift finger to spoil by trying to make real. But if I should have been Darragh, not ten thousand times the ten thousand pounds that Hulse carries would tempt me to lend you to another man's arms.'

'Oh, Katie, how horrid you can be!'

'Horrid for me to say, but "business" for you to do! How have you discovered so much, Violet—what Hulse carries, where he carries it, the size and shape the packet makes, even the way he so securely keeps it? "Business" eh? Your husband cares not so long as we succeed. But I, Kato Kuromi, care.' He went nearer so that his mere attitude was menacing as he stood over her, and his usually smooth voice changed to a tone she had never heard there before. '*How* have you learned all this? How, unless you and Hulse—'

'Sssh!' she exclaimed in sharp dismay as her ear caught a sound beyond.

'—oh yes,' continued Kato easily, his voice instantly as soft and unconcerned as ever, 'it will be there, you mean. The views in the valley of Kedu are considered very fine and the river itself '

It was Darragh whom Violet had heard approaching, and he entered the room in a much better temper than he had left it. At the door he paused a moment to encourage someone forward—a seedy, diffident man of more than middle age, who carried a brown-paper parcel.

'Come on, Sim; hurry up, man!' urged Darragh impatiently, but without the sting of contempt that had poisoned his speech before. 'And, oh, Phillips'—looking back and dropping his voice—'when Mr Hulse arrives show him into the morning-room at first. Not up here, you understand? Now, Sims.'

After a rather helpless look round for something suitable on which to lay his parcel, the woebegone-looking individual was attempting to untie it on an upraised knee.

'Yes, sir,' he replied, endeavouring to impart a modicum of briskness into his manner. 'I'm sorry to be a bit late, sir; I was delayed.'

'Oh, well, never mind that now,' said Darragh magnanimously. 'Thing quite all right?'

'Mrs Sims isn't worse?' asked Violet kindly.

Mr Sims managed to get his back to the group before he ventured to reply.

'No, miss,' he said huskily; 'she's better now. She's dead: died an hour ago. That's why I wasn't quite able to get here by eight.'

From each of his hearers this tragedy drew a characteristic response. Violet gave a little moan of sympathy and turned away. Kato regarded Sims, and continued to regard him, with the tranquil incuriosity of the unpitying East. Darragh—Darragh alone spoke, and his tone was almost genial.

'Devilish lucky that you were able to get here by now in the circumstances, Sims,' he said.

'Well, sir,' replied Sims practically, 'you see, I shall need the money just as much now—though not quite for the same purpose as I had planned.' He took the garment from the paper and shook it out before displaying it for Darragh's approval. 'I think you will find that quite satisfactory, sir.'

'Exactly the same as the one your people made for Mr Hulse a week ago?' asked Darragh, glancing at the jacket and then passing it on to Violet for her verdict.

'To a stitch, sir. A friend of mine up at the shop got the measurements and the cloth is a length from the same piece.'

'But the cut, Sims,' persisted his patron keenly; 'the cut is the most important thing about it. It makes all the difference in the world.'

'Yes, sir,' acquiesced Sims dispassionately; 'you can rely on that. I used to be a first-class cutter myself before I took to drink. I am yet, when I'm steady. And I machined both coats myself.'

'That should do then,' said Darragh complacently. 'Now you were to have—'

'Ten guineas and the cost of the cloth you promised, sir. Of course it's a very big price, and I won't deny that I've been a bit uneasy about it from time to time when I—'

'That's all right.' Darragh had no wish to keep Mr Sims in evidence a minute longer than was necessary.

'I shouldn't like to be doing anything wrong, sir,' persisted the poor creature; 'and when you stipulated that it wasn't to be mentioned—'

'Well, well, man; it's a bet, didn't I tell you? I stand to win a clear hundred if I can fool Hulse over this coat. That's the long and short of it.'

'I'm sure I hope it is, sir. I've never been in trouble for anything yet, and it would break my wife's 'art—' He stopped suddenly and his weak face changed to a recollection of his loss; then without another word he turned and made shakily for the door.

'See him safely away, Katty, and pay him down below,' said Darragh. 'I'll settle with you later,' and the Japanese, with a careless 'All right-o,' followed.

'Now, Violet, slip into it,' continued her husband briskly. 'We don't want to keep Hulse waiting when he comes.' From a drawer in a cabinet near at hand he took a paper packet, prepared in readiness, and passed it to her. 'You have the right cotton?'

'Yes, Hugh,' said Violet, opening a little work-basket. She had already satisfied herself that the coat was a replica of the one the young American would wear, and she now transferred the dummy package to the corresponding pocket and with a few deft stitches secured it in the same way as she had already learned that the real contents were safeguarded. 'And, Hugh—'

'Well, well?' responded Darragh, with a return of his old impatience.

'I don't wish to know all your plans, Hugh,' continued Violet meekly, 'but I do want to warn you. You are running a most tremendous risk with Kato.'

'Oh, Kato!'

'It is really serious, Hugh. You don't believe in patriotism, I know, but Kato happens to. When he learns that it isn't ten thousand pounds at all, but confidential war plans, that this scoop consists of, something terrible may happen.'

'It might, Violet. Therefore I haven't told him, and I am so arranging things that he will never know. Cheer up, my girl, there will be no tragedy. All the same, thanks for the hint. It shows a proper regard for your husband's welfare.'

'Oh, Hugh, Hugh,' murmured Violet, 'if only you were more often—'

Whatever might have been the result—if indeed there was yet hope in an appeal to another and a better nature that he might once have possessed—it came too late. The words were interrupted by the sudden reappearance of Kato, his business with Sims completed. He opened and closed the door quietly but very quickly, and at a glance both the Darraghs saw that something unforeseen had happened.

'Here's pretty go,' reported the Japanese. 'Hulse just come and brought someone with him!'

For a moment all the conspirators stood aghast at the unexpected complication. Hugh Darragh was the first to speak.

'Damnation!' he exclaimed, with a terrible look in his wife's direction; 'that may upset everything. What ghastly muddle have you made now?'

'I—I don't know,' pleaded Violet weakly. 'I never dreamt of such a thing. Are you sure?'

'Slow man,' amplified Kato with a nod. 'Fellow who walk—' He made a few steps with studied deliberation.

'Blind! It's Max Carrados,' exclaimed Violet, in a flash of enlightenment. 'They have been great friends lately and Jack has often spoken of him. He's most awfully clever in his way, but stone blind. Hugh, Kato, don't you see? It's rather unfortunate his being here, but it can't really make any difference.'

'True, if he is quite blind,' admitted Kato.

'I'll look into it,' said Darragh briskly. 'Coat's all ready for you, Kato.'

'I think no, yet,' soliloquised the Japanese, critically examining it. 'Keep door, 'alf-a-mo', Violet, if please.' His own contribution to the coat's appearance was simple but practical—a gentle tension here and there, a general rumple, a dust on the floor and a final shake. 'One week wear,' he announced gravely as he changed into it and hid his own away.

'Take your time, Mr Carrados,' Darragh's voice was heard insisting on the stairs outside, and the next moment he stood just inside the room, and before Hulse had quite guided Carrados into view, drew Violet's attention to the necessity of removing the button-hole that the Americans still wore by a significant movement to the lapel of his own coat. It required no great finesse on the girl's part to effect the transfer of the little bunch of flowers to her own person within five minutes of the guests' arrival.

'A new friend to see you, Violet—Mr Carrados,' announced Darragh most graciously. 'Mr Carrados, my sister.'

'Not to *see* you exactly, Miss Darragh,' qualified Carrados. 'But none the less to know you as well as if I did, I hope.'

'I wanted you to meet Max before I went, Miss Darragh,' explained Hulse; 'so I took the liberty of bringing him round.'

'You really *are* going then?' she asked.

'Yes. There seems no doubt about it this time. Twelve hours from now I hope to be in Paris. I should say,' amended the ingenuous young man, 'I *dread* to be in Paris, for it may mean a long absence. That's where I rely on Carrados to become what is called a "connecting file" between us—to cheer my solitude by letting me know when he has met you, or heard of you, or, well, anything in fact.'

'Take care, Mr Hulse,' she said. 'Gallantry by proxy is a dangerous game.'

'That's just it,' retorted Hulse. 'Max is the only man I shouldn't be jealous of—because he can't see you!'

While these amiable exchanges were being carried on between the two young people, with Max Carrados standing benignly by, Darragh found an opportunity to lower his voice for Kato's benefit.

'It's all right about him,' he declared. 'We carry on.'

'As we arranged?' asked Kato.

'Yes; exactly. Come across now.' He raised his voice as he led Kato towards the other group. 'I don't think that either of you has met Mr Kuromi yet—Mr Hulse, Mr Carrados.'

'I have been pining to meet you for weeks, sir,' responded Hulse with enthusiasm. 'Mr Darragh tells me what a wonderful master of ju-jitsu you are.'

'Oh, well; little knack, you know,' replied Kato modestly. 'You are interested?'

'Yes, indeed. I regard it as a most useful accomplishment at any time and particularly now. I only wish I'd taken it up when I had the leisure.'

'Let me find you an easy-chair, Mr Carrados,' said Violet attentively. 'I am sure that *you* won't be interested in so strenuous a subject as ju-jitsu.'

'Oh, yes, I am, though,' protested the blind man. 'I am interested in everything.'

'But surely—'

'I can't actually see the ju-jitsuing, you would say? Quite true, but do you know, Miss Darragh, that makes a great deal less difference than you might imagine. I have my sense of touch, my sense of taste, my hearing—even my unromantic nose—and you would hardly believe how they have rallied to my assistance since sight went. For instance—'

They had reached the chair to which Miss Darragh had piloted him. To guide him into it she had taken both his hands, but now Carrados had gently disengaged himself and was lightly holding her left hand between both of his.

'For instance, Hulse and I were speaking of you the other day—forgive our impertinence—and he happened to mention that you disliked rings of any sort and had never worn one. His eyes, you see, and perhaps a careless remark on your part. Now I *know* that until quite recently you continually wore a ring upon this finger.'

Silence had fallen upon the other men as they followed Carrados's exposition. Into the moment of embarrassment that succeeded this definite pronouncement Mr Hulse threw a cheerful note.

'Oh ho, Max, you've come a cropper this time,' he exclaimed. 'Miss Darragh has never worn a ring. Have you?'

'N-o,' replied Violet, a little uncertain of her ground, as the blind man continued to smile benevolently upon her.

'A smooth and rather broad one,' he continued persuasively. 'Possibly a wedding ring?'

'Wait a minute, Violet, wait a minute,' interposed Darragh, endeavouring to look judicially wise with head bent to one side. He was doubtful if Violet could carry the point without incurring some suspicion, and he decided to give her a lead out of it. 'Didn't I see you wearing some sort of plain ring a little time ago? You have forgotten, but I really believe Mr Carrados may be right. Think again.'

'Of course!' responded Violet readily; 'how stupid of me! It was my mother's wedding ring. I found it in an old desk and wore it to keep it safe. That was really how I found out that I could not bear the feel of one and I soon gave it up.'

'What did I say?' claimed Darragh genially. 'I thought that we should be right.'

'This is really much interesting,' said Kato. 'I very greatly like your system, Mr Carrados.'

'Oh, it's scarcely a system,' deprecated Max good-naturedly; 'it's almost second nature with me now. I don't have to consider, say, "Where is the window?" if I want it. I know with certainty that the window lies over here.' He had not yet taken the chair provided, and suiting the action to the word he now took a few steps towards the wall where the windows were. 'Am I not right?' And to assure himself he stretched out a hand and encountered the heavy curtains.

'Yes, yes,' admitted Violet hurriedly, 'but, oh, please do be careful, Mr Carrados. They are most awfully particular about the light here since the last raid. We go in fear and trembling lest a glimmer should escape.'

Carrados smiled and nodded and withdrew from the dangerous area. He faced the room again.

'Then there is the electric light—heat at a certain height of course.'

'True,' assented Kato, 'but why *electric* light?'

'Because no other is noiseless and entirely without smell; think—gas, oil, candles, all betray their composition yards away. Then'—indicating the fireplace—'I suppose you can only smell soot in damp weather? The mantelpiece'—touching it—'inlaid marble. The wallpaper'—brushing his hand over its surface—'arrangement of pansies on a criss-cross background'; lifting one finger to his lips—'colour scheme largely green and gold.'

Possibly Mr Hulse thought that his friend had demonstrated his qualities quite enough. Possibly—at any rate he now created a diversion:

'Engraving of Mrs Siddons as the Tragic Muse, suspended two feet seven inches from the ceiling on a brass-headed nail supplied by a one-legged ironmonger whose Aunt Jane—'

All contributed a sufficiently appreciative laugh—Carrados's not the least hearty—except Kato, whose Asiatic dignity was proof against the form of jesting.

'You see what contempt familiarity breeds, Miss Darragh?' remarked the blind man. 'I look to you, Mr Kuromi, to avenge me by putting Hulse in a variety of undignified attitudes on the floor.'

'Oh, I shan't mind that if at the same time you put me up to a trick or two,' said Hulse, turning to the Japanese.

'You wish?'

'Indeed I do. I've seen the use of it. It's good; it's scientific. When I was crossing, one of the passengers held up a bully twice his weight in the neatest way possible. It looked quite simple, something like this, if I may?' Kato nodded his grave assent and submitted himself to Mr Hulse's vigorous grasp. '"Now," said the man I'm speaking of, "struggle and your right arm's broken." But I expect you know the grip?'

'Oh, yes,' replied Kato, veiling his private amusement, 'and therefore foolish to struggle. Expert does not struggle; gives way.' He appeared to do so, to be falling helplessly in fact, but the assailant found himself compelled to follow, and the next moment he was lying on his back with Kato politely extending a hand to assist him up again.

'I must remember that,' said Hulse thoughtfully. 'Let me see, it goes—do you mind putting me wise on that again, Mr Kuromi? The motion picture just one iota slower this time, please.'

For the next ten or twenty minutes the demonstration went on in admirable good humour, and could Max Carrados have seen he would certainly have witnessed his revenge. At the end of the lesson both men were warm and dusty—so dusty that Miss Darragh felt called upon to apologise laughingly for the condition of the rug. But if clothes were dusty, hands were positively dirty—there was no other word for it.

'No, really, the poor mat can't be so awful as that,' declared the girl. 'Wherever have you been, Mr Kuromi? and, oh, Mr Hulse you are just as bad.'

'I do not know,' declared Kato, regarding his grimy fingers seriously. 'Nowhere of myself. Yes, I think it must be your London atmosphere among the rug after all.'

'At all events you can't—Oh, Hugh, take them to the bathroom, will you? And I'll try to entertain Mr Carrados meanwhile—only he will entertain me instead, I know.'

It was well and simply done throughout—nothing forced, and the sequence of development quite natural. Indeed, it was not until Hulse saw Kuromi take off his coat in the bathroom that he even thought of what he carried. 'Well, Carrados,' he afterwards pleaded to his friend, 'now could I wash my hands before those fellows like a guy who isn't used to washing? It isn't natural. It isn't human.' So for those few minutes the two coats hung side by side, and Darragh kindly brushed them. When Hulse put on his own again his hand instinctively felt for the hidden packet; his fingers reassured themselves among the familiar objects of his pockets, and his mind was perfectly at ease.

'You old scoundrel, Max,' he said, when he returned to the drawing-room. 'You told Kuromi to wipe the floor with me and, by crumbs, he did! Have a cigarette all the same.'

Miss Darragh laughed pleasantly and took the opportunity to move away to learn from her accomplices if all had gone well. Carrados was on the point of passing over the proffered olive branch when he changed his mind. He leaned forward and with slow deliberation chose a cigarette from the American's case. Exactly when the first subtle monition of treachery reached him—by what sense it was conveyed—Hulse never learned, for there were experiences among the finer perceptions that the blind man did not willingly discuss. Not by voice or outward manner in that arresting moment did he betray an inkling of his suspicion, yet by some responsive telephony Hulse at once, though scarcely conscious of it then, grew uneasy and alert.

'Thanks; I'll take a light from yours,' remarked Carrados, ignoring the lit match, and he rose to avail himself. His back was towards the others, who still had a word of instruction to exchange. With cool precision he handled the cloth on Hulse's outstretched arm, critically touched the pocket he was already familiar with, and then deliberately drew the lapel to his face.

'You wore some violets?' he said beneath his breath.

'Yes,' replied Hulse, 'but I—Miss Darragh—'

'But there never have been any *here*! By heavens, Hulse, we're in it! You had your coat off just now?'

'Yes, for a minute—'

'Quietly. Keep your cigarette going. You'll have to leave this to me. Back me up—discreetly—whatever I do.'

'Can't we challenge it and insist—'

'Not in this world. They have at least one other man down-stairs—in Cairo, a Turk by the way, before I was blind, of course. Not up to Mr Kuromi, I expect—'

'Cool again?' asked Miss Darragh sociably. It was her approach that had sent Carrados off into irrelevancies. 'Was the experience up to anticipation?'

'Yes, I think I may say it was,' admitted Hulse guardedly. 'There is certainly a lot to learn here. I expect you've seen it all before?'

'Oh, no. It is a great honour to get Mr Kuromi to "show it off", as he quaintly calls it.'

'Yes, I should say so,' replied the disillusioned young man with deadly simplicity. 'I quite feel that.'

'J.B.H. is getting strung up,' thought Carrados. 'He may say something unfortunate presently.' So he deftly insinuated himself into the conversation and for a few minutes the commonplaces of the topic were rigidly maintained.

'Care for a hand at auction?' suggested Darragh, joining the group. He had no desire to keep his guests a minute longer than he need, but at the same time it was his line to behave quite naturally until they left. 'Oh, but I forgot—Mr Carrados—'

'I am well content to sit and listen' Carrados assured him. 'Consider how often I have to do that without the entertainment of a game to listen to! And you are four without me.'

'It really hardly seems—' began Violet.

'I'm sure Max will feel it if he thinks that he is depriving us,' put in Hulse loyally, so with some more polite protestation it was arranged and the game began, Carrados remaining where he was. In the circumstances a very high standard of bridge could not be looked for; the calling was a little wild; the play more than a little loose; the laughter rather shrill or rather flat; the conversation between the hands forced and spasmodic. All were playing for time in their several interpretations of it; the blind man alone was thinking beyond the immediate moment.

Presently there was a more genuine burst of laughter than any hitherto. Kato had revoked, and, confronted with it, had made a naïve excuse. Carrados rose with the intention of going nearer when a distressing thing occurred. Half-way across the room he seemed to slip, plunged forward helplessly, and came to the floor, involved in a light table as he fell. All the players were on their feet in an instant. Darragh assisted his guest to rise; Violet took an arm; Kato looked about the floor curiously, and Hulse—Hulse stared hard at Max and wondered what the thunder this portended.

'Clumsy, clumsy,' murmured Carrados beneath his breath. 'Forgive me, Miss Darragh.'

'Oh, Mr Carrados!' she exclaimed in genuine distress. 'Aren't you really hurt?'

'Not a bit of it,' he declared lightly. 'Or at all events,' he amended, bearing rather more heavily upon her support as he took a step, 'nothing to speak of.'

'Here is pencil,' said Kuromi, picking one up from the polished floor. 'You must have slipped on this.'

'Stepping on a pencil is like that,' contributed Hulse wisely. 'It acts as a kind of roller-skate.'

'Please don't interrupt the game any more,' pleaded the victim. 'At the most, at the very worst, it is only—oh!—a negligible strain.'

'I don't know that any strain, especially of the ankle, is negligible, Mr Carrados,' said Darragh with cunning foresight. 'I think it perhaps ought to be seen to.'

'A compress when I get back will be all that is required,' maintained Carrados. 'I should hate to break up the evening.'

'Don't consider that for a moment,' urged the host hospitably. 'If you really think that it would be wiser in the end—'

'Well, perhaps—' assented the other, weakening in his resolution.

'Shall I 'phone up a taxi?' asked Violet.

'Thank you, if you would be so kind—or, no; perhaps my own car would be rather easier in the circumstances. My man will be about, so that it will take very little longer.'

'I'll get through for you,' volunteered Darragh. 'What's your number?'

The telephone was in a corner of the room. The connection was soon obtained and Darragh turned to his guest for the message.

'I'd better speak,' said Carrados—he had limped across on Hulse's arm—taking over the receiver. 'Excellent fellow, but he'd probably conclude that I'd been killed . . . That you, Parkinson? . . . Yes, at 155 Densham Gardens. I'm held up here by a slight accident . . . No, no, nothing serious, but I might have some difficulty in getting back without assistance. Tell Harris I shall need him after all, as soon as he can get here—the car that's handiest. That's—oh, and, Parkinson, bring along a couple of substantial walking-sticks with you. Any time now. That's all . . . Yes . . . yes.' He put up the receiver with a thrill of satisfaction that he had got his message safely through. 'Held up'—a phrase at once harmless and significant—was the arranged shift-key into code. It was easy for a blind man to receive some hurt that held him up. Once or twice Carrados's investigations had got him into tight places, but in one way or another he had invariably got out again.

'How far is your place away?' someone asked, and out of the reply a time-marking conversation on the subject of getting about London's darkened streets and locomotion in general arose. Under cover of this Kato drew Darragh aside to the deserted card-table.

'Not your pencil, Darragh?' he said quietly, displaying the one he had picked up.

'No; why?'

'I not altogether like this, is why,' replied the Japanese. 'I think it Carrados own pencil. That man have too many ways of doing things, Darragh. It was mistake to let him 'phone.'

'Oh, nonsense; you heard what he said. Don't get jumpy, man. The thing has gone like clockwork.'

'So far, yes. But I think I better go now and come back in one hour or so, safer for all much.'

Darragh, for very good reasons, had the strongest objections to allowing his accomplice an opportunity of examining the spoil alone. 'Look here, Katty,' he said with decision, 'I must have you in case there does come a scrimmage. I'll tell Phillips to fasten the front door well, and then we can see that it's all right before anyone comes in. If it is, there's no need for you to run away; if there's the least doubt we can knock these two out and have plenty of time to clear by the back way we've got.' Without giving Kato any chance of raising further objection he turned to his guests again.

'I think I remember your tastes, Hulse,' he said suavely. 'I hope that you have no objection to Scotch whisky, Mr Carrados? We still have a few bottles left. Or perhaps you prefer champagne?'

Carrados had very little intention of drinking anything in that house, nor did he think that with ordinary procrastination it would be necessary.

'You are very kind,' he replied tentatively. 'Should you permit the invalid either, Miss Darragh?'

'Oh, yes, in moderation,' she smiled. 'I think I hear your car,' she added, and stepping to the window ventured to peep out.

It was true. Mr Darragh had run it a shade too fine for once. For a moment he hesitated which course to take—to see who was arriving or to convey a warning to his henchman down below. He had turned towards the door when Violet's startled voice recalled him to the window.

'Hugh!' she called sharply. 'Here, Hugh;' and as he reached her, in a breathless whisper, 'There are men inside the car—two more at least.'

Darragh had to decide very quickly this time. His choice was not without its element of fineness. 'Go down and see about it, Katty,' he said, looking Kato straight in the eyes. 'And tell Phillips about the whisky.'

'Door locked,' said the Japanese tersely. 'Key other side.'

'The key was on this side,' exclaimed Darragh fiercely. 'Hulse—'

'Hell!' retorted Beringer expressively. 'That jacket doesn't go out of the room without me this journey.'

Darragh had him covered before he had finished speaking.

'Quick,' he rapped out. 'I'll give you up to three, and if the key isn't out then, by God, I'll plug you, Hulse! One, two—'

The little 'ping!' that followed was not the automatic speaking, but the release of the electric light switch as Carrados, unmarked among this climax, pressed it up. In the absolute blackness that followed Darragh spun round to face the direction of this new opponent.

'Shoot by all means, Mr Darragh, if you are used to firing in the dark,' said Carrados's imperturbable voice. 'But in any case remember that I am. As I am a dead shot by sound, perhaps everyone had better remain exactly where he—or she, I regret to have to add, Miss Darragh—now is.'

'You dog!' spat out Darragh.

'I should not even talk,' advised the blind man. 'I am listening for my friends and I might easily mistake your motive among the hum of conversation.'

He had not long to wait. In all innocence Phillips had opened the door to Parkinson, and immeasurably to his surprise two formidable-looking men of official type had followed in from somewhere. By a sort of instinct—or possibly a momentary ray of light had been their guide—they came direct to the locked door.

'Parkinson,' called Carrados.

'Yes, sir,' replied that model attendant.

'We are all in here; Mr Hulse and myself, and three—I am afraid that I can make no exception—three unfriendlies. At the moment the electric light is out of action, the key of the locked door has been mislaid, and firearms are being promiscuously flourished in the dark. That is the position. Now if you have the key, Hulse?'

'I have,' replied Hulse grimly, 'but for a fact I dropped it down my neck out of harm's way and where the plague it's got to—'

As it happened the key was not required. The heavier of the officers outside, believing in the element of surprise, stood upon one foot and shot the other forward with the force and action of an engine piston-rod. The shattered door swung inward and the three men rushed into the room.

Darragh had made up his mind, and as the door crashed he raised his hand to fire into the thick. But at that moment the light flashed on again and almost instantly was gone. Before his dazzled eyes and startled mind could adjust themselves to this he was borne down. When he rose again his hands were manacled.

'So,' he breathed laboriously, bending a vindictive eye, upon his outwitter. 'When next we meet it will be my turn, I think.'

'We shall never meet again,' replied Carrados impassively. 'There is no other turn for you, Darragh.'

'But where the blazes has Kuromi got to?' demanded Hulse with sharp concern. 'He can't have quit?'

One of the policemen walked to a table in the farthest corner of the room, looked down beyond it, and silently raised a beckoning hand. They joined him there.

'Rum way these foreigners have of doing things,' remarked the other disapprovingly. 'Now who the Hanover would ever think of a job like that?'

'I suppose,' mused the blind man, as he waited for the official arrangements to go through, 'that presently I shall have to live up to Hulse's overwhelming bewonderment. And yet if I pointed out to him that the button-hole of the coat he is now wearing still has a stitch in it to keep it in shape and could not by any possibility . . . Well, well, perhaps better not. It is a mistake for the conjurer to explain.

Preston Beach 1917

THE END

Also available

BODIES FROM THE LIBRARY

LOST TALES OF MYSTERY AND SUSPENSE BY AGATHA CHRISTIE
AND OTHER MASTERS OF THE GOLDEN AGE

Selected and introduced by Tony Medawar

This anthology brings together 16 forgotten tales that have either been published only once before—perhaps in a newspaper or rare magazine—or have never before appeared in print. From a previously unpublished 1917 script featuring Ernest Bramah's blind detective Max Carrados, *Blind Man's Bluff*, to early 1950s crime stories written for London's *Evening Standard* by Cyril Hare, Freeman Wills Crofts and A.A. Milne, it spans five decades of writing by masters of the Golden Age.

Most anticipated of all are the contributions by women writers: the first detective story by Georgette Heyer, *Linckes' Great Case*, unseen since 1923; the unpublished *The Rum Punch* by Christianna Brand; and Agatha Christie's *The Wife of the Kenite*, a dark tale of revenge published only in an Australian journal in 1922 during her 'Grand Tour' of the British Empire.

With other stories by Detection Club stalwarts Anthony Berkeley, H.C. Bailey, J.J. Connington, John Rhode and Nicholas Blake, plus Vincent Cornier, Leo Bruce, Roy Vickers and Arthur Upfield, this essential collection harks back to a time before forensic science—when murder was a complex business.